DAUGHTER OF JOY

Kathleen Morgan, winner of the *Literary Times* Award for Literary Excellence in Romantic Fiction, has also won the following:

BookRak Best-Selling Author Award, 1990–91
BookRak Best-Selling Author Award, 1991–92
Romantic Times KISS Award, 1993
Romantic Times Reviewer's Choice Award, 1994

BRIDES OF CULDEE CREEK • BOOK 1

DAUGHTER OF JOY

Kathleen Morgan

Fleming H. Revell
A Division of Baker Book House
Grand Rapids, Michigan 49516

Published by Fleming H. Revell
a division of Baker Book House Company
P.O. Box 6287, Grand Rapids, MI 49516-6287

Printed in the United States of America

ISBN: 0-7394-0811-9

For Beth Anne, bookseller extraordinaire,
and the dearest of friends.
You've always been there,
encouraging and rooting for me,
even in my darkest moments.
And for Sean . . . always, always, for Sean.

A Word from the Author

Daughter of Joy wasn't an easy book to write. The idea for this book was conceived in 1997, about a year after my youngest son died unexpectedly of cancer. It was a time when, not surprisingly, I was contemplating the direction of my life and its purpose.

Though fervent in my Christian faith when a youngster, over the years I became lukewarm at best. My son's death brought me back to God. There are still times, even now, when all I can do is hang on to Him with all my might and be grateful for that. At other times, though, I cannot help but marvel at how far I've come and how blessed I am. Grieving, I think, is a lot like that—a wild, agonizing, bewildering, yet sometimes glorious ride into the deeper, more essential aspects of self and humanity. It is also, I believe, a ride with no end in sight.

So what does this have to do with *Daughter of Joy*? Writing has always been a journey for me. I strive to portray my characters as authentic human beings, using personal insights and resources to draw on the deep, basic core of my own humanity—good and bad. That, I truly believe, lends realism and heart to my writing. My own struggle with issues of grief, loss, and acceptance of God's will, and my renewed search for a deeper, more spiritual and lasting meaning to life were all catalysts for *Daughter of Joy*.

As I wrote I found inspiration from a line in a condolence card I received: "For every joy that passes, something beautiful remains." That poem became a beacon of hope for me, especially in those early weeks and months after my son's death. It beckoned me ever onward in my quest to survive and, finally, to begin to heal.

I knew God's will—and love—for me was somehow tied up in that simple little verse. I clung to it for comfort. I held it close, examining its every facet. Yet as the weeks, months, then years began to pass, I came to realize I would never fully plumb the depths of its meaning—at least not in this life. Its meaning would always lead me forward, though, providing direction for the rest of my days.

Joy . . . It's a journey we all embark upon from the first moment we draw breath. We search so avidly for it. We cannot help it; it's inherent in our nature. Yet no matter how hard we strive, our joy can never truly be complete until we find it in the Lord.

Daughter of Joy is the story of one woman's—and man's—journey back to that true meaning and purpose in life. It is, in many ways, my story as well. Perhaps there are threads of your own story—and journey—woven there, too.

Kathleen Morgan

ABIGAIL
"Source of Joy"

Restore unto me the joy of thy salvation; and uphold me with thy free spirit.

Psalm 51:12

1

The plains east
of Colorado Springs, Colorado,
October 1895

Speak, LORD; for thy servant heareth.

1 Samuel 3:9

"I can't help it! I've held my tongue as long as I dare. Please, Abby. Take a bit more time and reconsider."

With an affectionate smile, Abigail Stanton glanced at the woman sitting beside her. Then, lightly flicking the buggy whip over the horse's back, she urged Elsie, her sister-in-law's Morgan mare, to quicken her lagging pace. As the horse moved out, flurries of dust swirled in the air, muting for a moment the day's crisp, vibrant fall colors.

"I've hidden away long enough, Nelly." Abby sighed. "It's time to set aside my selfish needs and unreasoning fears. Time to venture back into the world, into life, if only with this first, most tentative of steps."

"Well, perhaps so," Nelly agreed grudgingly, folding her hands primly in her lap. "There's no rush, though, is there? No reason to accept the first position offered you? *Especially* not this one." She rolled her eyes, her dark blond lashes fluttering in horror. "Heavens above! The tales I've heard about that man and his family!"

"I haven't 'accepted' anything yet," Abby murmured in gentle correction, flicking the buggy whip once again, as Elsie veered toward a succulent patch of grass growing along the roadside in a protected cranny of rocks. "This is only an interview. We must both first decide if we even suit each other."

"He's a heathen, Abby! He never even sets foot inside church!" Warming to her tale, Nelly clenched her fist and pounded her knee in emphasis. "Why, it's said his wife hated him so much she ran away, leaving behind her young son. Then, no sooner was she out the door, he took in an Indian squaw and had a half-breed daughter. To top it off, just this past spring, the man's son ran away. Seems he couldn't stomach his father either."

"Let's not forgot to add," Abby offered with a wry grin and chuckle, all the while keeping her gaze riveted on the road ahead, "that none of his former housekeepers have ever lasted more than six months. And that Conor MacKay is reputedly the most unpleasant, evil-tempered man in these parts."

"Well, those *are* the rumors about him." Nelly turned in the buggy seat more fully to face her. "Besides, what of all your fine plans? What of Thomas's mission for penniless outcasts? Just because your husband is gone doesn't mean you have to turn your back on all his hopes and dreams. You used to be so certain the mission was God's will for you. Isn't it still?"

Just then the right buggy wheel hit a large rock in the road. The conveyance bounced into the air, then slammed down again, unseating Nelly. With a squawk, she grabbed for the arm rest and shoved her black straw hat—which had slid down to cover her eyes—back firmly on her head.

"Well, *isn't* it?" she stubbornly prodded through gritted teeth, resettling herself more securely on the seat. "You've suffered greatly in the loss of your husband and son, Abby, but surely the Lord hasn't changed His mind or His plans for you."

Abby blinked back a stinging swell of tears. Hasn't He? she thought bitterly, but said nothing. Nelly had her best interests at heart, but she really didn't need to hear this right now.

It was frightening enough, riding out here to meet some man about whom she'd only heard the worst tales. To pile on agonizing memories and haunting, unresolved questions was almost more than Abby could bear. As it was, her whole world had turned topsy-turvy. For a long while now, she had been going through the motions of living. Living . . . only because she must.

But no one wanted to hear that, much less deal with all its unpleasant ramifications. People tried, God bless them, and Nelly most of all. But someone's personal tragedy was too hard for others to face day after day. Abby couldn't blame them. The loss of two loved ones within one year was more than anyone would ever wish to endure.

Nonetheless, Abby reminded herself, lifting her chin and squaring her shoulders, she must get by the best way she knew how. Get by, and deal with the present moment—which currently entailed surviving the next hour or so.

"I don't know much of anything anymore, Nelly," Abby finally replied, at a loss for anything better to say. "I'm not sure what God has in store for me."

The answer seemed to satisfy—or at least temporarily confound—her sister-in-law into silence. As they drove along, heading ever northeast and away from the Rockies and Colorado Springs, the tall log gates topped by a sign proclaiming the main road to Culdee Creek Ranch appeared at the top of the hill. On all sides, thick stands of dried grass swayed in the wind. Hidden somewhere in the grass, meadowlarks sang.

It was a beautiful, Indian summer day. Still, Abby felt as if she viewed it from afar. It was a fear that visited her more and more of late, the fear that she'd never be able to feel or experience life and living fully ever again.

She hesitated, reluctant to belabor a subject that had become a sore point in her and her late husband's relationship. It was time, though, that Nelly begin to understand. "If the truth be told," Abby forced herself to say, "the mission was always Thomas's idea, not mine. I acquiesced to his plans because he was my husband, and it seemed so important to him."

"Then build the mission now as a tribute to him." Nelly's voice went hoarse with emotion. "Do it for my br-brother." She looked away, blinking furiously.

Distressed that she'd been the cause of another's pain, Abby pulled back gently on the reins. Traces jingled and leather creaked as the Morgan mare slowed, then came to a halt. Abby turned to her sister-in-law, and took one of her hands in hers.

"Ah, Nelly, Nelly." She patted her hand. "I didn't mean to hurt you or lead you to believe I don't still love Thomas. Truly, I haven't given up on the idea of his mission. I just need time to sort things out, to heal. Meanwhile, I have to support myself, not to mention save some money to build the mission. Until I do, any talk of fulfilling Thomas's plans is pointless."

Nelly drew an embroidered lace handkerchief from her skirt pocket, dabbed daintily at her eyes, then blew and wiped her nose. "True enough," she admitted huskily, giving Abby's hand a squeeze. "Until then, though, you could move in with us to save costs, and take another, far more appropriate job in the Springs."

Nelly cocked her head. "You've changed in the past year, you know? You've grown more headstrong, more rebellious. What you used to accept so meekly and obediently as God's will, when Thomas lived, you now . . ."

Her voice faded, and she shook her head. "I'm digressing, I suppose. What I mean to say"—Nelly inhaled a deep breath and forged on—"is that this crazy plan of yours seems like an attempt to run away from your commitments and responsibilities to yourself, to others and, even, to God."

Abby went very still, then released Nelly's hand. She turned back to the mare, who had taken the liberty of edging her way once more toward the side of the road and the grass growing there. Clucking at her, Abby signaled the animal forward. With an indignant snort and irritated flick of her ears, Elsie reluctantly resumed a brisk trot.

Abby stared straight ahead as she turned the mare off the main road toward Culdee Creek's gate. Frustration welled in her. Would no one ever allow her the chance to do what *she* wanted, what she needed?

"Well, maybe I am," Abby finally admitted. "But who doesn't have more of a right? There are just too many memories in Colorado Springs. I need time to get away from it all . . . to sort everything out. To find some peace, some acceptance."

And, she silently added, to find something I'm beginning to think I've been too long denied—myself.

"Yes, you of all people have that right," Nelly replied, "save for one thing."

"And that one thing would be?" Abby demanded tautly. Ah, she thought in rising irritation, would Nelly *never* let things be?

15

"Does anyone ever have the right to run away and shirk her duties to God?"

The thinly stretched thread of Abby's patience snapped. "I'm *not* running away from God!" she cried. "I'd never do that. Never! If anything, I'm running *toward* Him."

Nelly turned in her seat and fixed her gaze on the distant horizon. "Are you really, Abby?" she asked softly. "I wonder if you're able to face the truth or even see things clearly."

Abby clenched the reins, the stiff, unyielding leather cutting into her palms. She choked back scathing words, knowing that whatever she said would soon be regretted. Nelly meant well, but she just didn't understand.

Lips tight, faces pale, the two women topped the hill and headed down the other side in an uncomfortable, tension-fraught silence. A vast panorama of rolling, autumn-browned grasslands spread before them while behind them and far to the west, Pikes Peak, its summit lightly dusted with snow, gleamed against its backdrop in the cloudless sky. Situated in a small valley flanked on the north by a hillside studded with Ponderosa pines and on the southeast by a cottonwood-lined creek that flowed down to a large pond was an impressive, two-story wooden ranch house, painted white and trimmed with dark green.

Several outbuildings of various sizes sat a short distance away. Farther off from the main buildings were two tall, wooden, dark green barns built on high rock and mortar foundations. Two corrals, a pigpen, and a storage cellar adjoined the barns. Hereford cattle grazed lazily in the barbed-wire-enclosed pastures stretching as far as the eye could see.

"I'm sorry if my words hurt you, Abby," Nelly finally said, doggedly returning to the subject at hand. "You know I'd never have said it if I didn't love you. But are you certain this"–her gesture took in the land and buildings that lay before them–"is the answer?"

Fleetingly, Abby closed her eyes, then opened them again. "No, Nelly, I'm not," was her simple, heartfelt reply. "But at least it's a start. One way or another, I cannot hope to know God's will until I begin to search . . . and listen."

ç

Conor MacKay saw the buggy pass through the gate, and head down the long hill leading to the house. He twisted free the last potato clinging to the plant he had uprooted, tossed the dirt-encrusted tuber into the full basket, and rose. "Come along, Beth." He glanced down at his nine-year-old daughter. "Mrs. Stanton's here. It wouldn't hurt either of us to clean up a bit."

The girl dusted off her dungarees and wrinkled her nose in distaste. "What does it matter how we look, Papa? She's just another snoopy old lady who won't like us. And, even if she stays on for a while, she won't last long. None of them do."

"Be that as it may"–Conor took his daughter by the arm, and led her through the rows of rapidly fading potato plants and withered squash vines–"you haven't quite mastered the art of cooking, cleaning, or washing clothes yet. So, until you do . . ."

Beth gave a snort. "I don't care if I *ever* learn how to cook, clean, or wash! I'm never getting married. Why should I, Papa?"

His daughter's words sent a sharp stab of pain through Conor's heart. He didn't expect anything more for himself–not anymore–but he'd hoped Beth might someday find a kind man to care for her. Even at thirty-five, with likely a passel of good years still left in him,

Conor knew someday his daughter would have to make it on her own. After all, now that Evan had run out on them, it looked like Culdee Creek would one day belong to her. When that day finally came, she'd need a good man at her side.

Shading his eyes against the early afternoon sun, Conor could just make out the faces of the two women heading toward them. Both were modestly dressed in pinstriped, long-sleeved, shirtwaist blouses and long, dark skirts, their hair covered by equally dark straw hats. Squinting hard, he could see that the one driving the buggy had dark brown hair and the one sitting beside her was blond.

Prim and proper, he thought, their faces and bodies protected from the harsh, unforgiving sun of the high plains and Rocky Mountain foothills. Conor smiled grimly. If this Mrs. Stanton decided to stay on, she'd soon have to discard that feminine ideal of fine white skin and smooth hands. This was a working ranch.

As dire as the need was for a cook and housekeeper, Conor wasn't looking forward to this meeting. He was tired of flighty, undependable women, too. But Beth was too young to run a house, or cook and clean up after him and his ranch hands. If the truth be told, Conor didn't know if his proud, headstrong daughter would ever be ready, or if he'd have the heart to make her do so when the time came. She'd already been through more than any girl her age should ever have to endure.

They reached the steps leading to the main house's long, covered front porch. Conor paused there. "Go inside, Beth"–he motioned toward the front door–"and at least wash your hands and face, and comb your hair."

"What about you, Papa?" Beth cocked her head. "You could stand a good wash-up and shave yourself."

"The horse trough will do for me. Mrs. Stanton might as well get it clear right off that there are no fine gentlemen at Culdee Creek."

Beth reluctantly obeyed and disappeared into the house.

Conor lingered a moment before heading toward the long, hollowed-out pine log to the right of the house. As much as he hated the idea of taking on yet another interfering, prim and proper housekeeper, the truth was he needed one desperately. Indeed, if he'd been a God-fearing man, he'd be lifting a fervent prayer right about now for a good, hard-working, kind-hearted woman. But those sort of women were few and far between. And he was hardly a God-fearing man.

The MacKay house was bigger and better built than Abby expected. Cleaner, no. Luxuriously furnished, no. But certainly more than adequate.

The parlor was large. The well-equipped kitchen had a big, six-hole cast iron cookstove, a kitchen pitcher pump at the sink, two tall cupboards, and a large wooden table set with eight chairs. Next to the kitchen was a spacious dining room. On the other side of the parlor sat a room Abby guessed had once been a less formal living room, but now appeared to serve as a study.

The second floor held three bedrooms. Above them, up a smaller, steeper staircase, lay the attic. There was also a cellar below the kitchen. The back door off the kitchen led to a smaller version of the covered porch at the front of the house. About fifty feet to the right of the smallest and closest of the bunkhouses, which sat behind at a short distance from the main house, lay a good-sized vegetable garden.

"Well, Mrs. Stanton, you've had the grand tour," Conor MacKay's deep voice vibrated behind her. "Does the set-up suit your fancy?"

At the sardonic edge to his words, Abby wheeled around, nearly knocking Nelly off the back porch's top step. She grabbed her sister-in-law's arm. "Well, of course it does, Mr. MacKay," she choked out, mortified he'd all but read her mind. "You've a beautiful spread. You must be very proud."

Culdee Creek's owner arched a dark brow. "Indeed," he drawled. "A place this size takes a lot of hard work. Are you up to hard work, Mrs. Stanton?"

Some of the tales Abby had heard about Conor MacKay had been right. He was cold and condescending. Yet—Abby could feel her cheeks flushing—he was also a most attractive man.

Easily topping six feet in height, the ebony-haired rancher carried himself with the athletic, effortless grace of a cougar. His body was trim, his shoulders wide, his muscles sleek and toned. He dressed simply, in faded blue denims, scuffed black boots, and a long-sleeved, worn, blue chambray shirt rolled up to the elbows. His skin was tanned, his beard-shadowed jaw strong, and his nose straight.

He was nothing more, though, Abby reminded herself sharply, unsettled by the instant attraction she felt for him, than many other men she'd met before. Still, the reluctant admission of his unusual appeal unnerved her. Perhaps it was his eyes, smoky-blue and piercingly assessing. Perhaps it was that skeptical twist to the corner of his mouth. Or perhaps it was just the way he stood there, one hip cocked, a thumb hooked casually in his front pant's pocket.

Was it all just some arrogant facade, she wondered, purposely intended to intimidate? Or did his manner mask something darker and more threatening—as threatening as some of the tales whispered about him? At the consideration, Abby shivered.

"Come, come, Mrs. Stanton." Conor's voice, tinged now with irritation, plucked at Abby's consciousness. "It isn't that difficult to admit, is it? Surely you must realize you'd never suit us if you aren't used to hard work?"

Stung by his patronizing tone, Abby squared her shoulders and lifted her chin. "Of course I realize that. I'd never have wasted either your time, or mine, if I was afraid of a little work."

MacKay gave a snort—whether of scorn or disbelief, Abby couldn't tell—and signaled for them to reenter the house. "Well, we'll just have to see about that, won't we?" he asked. "In the meantime, why don't we retire to the parlor where we can finish discussing the job particulars, and you can meet my daughter. I gathered from your letter that you've had some teaching experience. I must admit I find that particular aspect of your talents most appealing," he said as he led the two women back inside. "My Beth's temperament has never suited a schoolhouse situation, so a great deal of her education of late has been taught by me . . ."

"'Never suited a schoolhouse,' indeed," Nelly hissed in Abby's ear as they went inside. "If her attitude is anything like her father's, I'd wager she was thrown out of school."

Oh, Lord, if Mr. MacKay overhears, Abby thought as she made a hasty motion to silence Nelly.

A quick glance at the tall rancher at first revealed no sign he had noted Nelly's comment. Relieved, Abby felt the tension ease. Then she noticed the sardonic quirk once more tightening the corner of his mouth. Nelly's words had struck home.

There was something about his smile, however, frozen and automatic as it appeared, that plucked at her.

Was there more to this man than the forbidding exterior he presented?

Yet this wasn't some replacement for Thomas's mission for penniless outcasts, Abby reminded herself sternly. This was only a job, a temporary respite and way station before she resumed the true journey of her life. All she wanted was to take care of herself for a change, pull back a bit, and lick her wounds.

But was such a retreat possible? Certainly Nelly didn't think so, and Abby had to admit to her own doubts, as well. Yet where was the harm in trying? Surely no one would be hurt, or even really care, when she finally decided to leave.

Distracted and now troubled, Abby followed Nelly toward an overstuffed, rosewood trimmed, blue-and-green velvet settee. The parlor, she noted, forcing herself to look about her, was, like the rest of the house, adequately decorated and comfortably furnished.

A fine Turkish rug covered most of the hardwood floor. Two dark leather armchairs were nestled around the moss rock and pine fireplace. Over the mantel hung a portrait of a distinguished older Scottish gentleman, dressed in a blue, green, and black tartan kilt, a basket-hilted sword hanging at his side. Heavy, dark blue oriental tapestry curtains swayed languorously at the open windows, and a massive, carved oak combination bookcase and cupboard stood against the far wall. As an added complement to the fine decor, a thick layer of dust coated all the furniture.

While the two women settled themselves, Conor excused himself and went upstairs to fetch Beth. He found her sitting on her bed playing with her doll. A cursory examination revealed that, though she had washed her face and hands and combed her hair, the effort had been quick and half-hearted.

"Am I all right, Papa?" his daughter asked, noting his frown.

"Barely." Conor motioned for her to come with him.

Beth set aside her doll and climbed off the bed. "Well, you don't look much better." She eyed him from head to toe.

"Maybe not." He scowled and rubbed his beard-stubbled jaw. "But I'm still your father, and you're beginning to get a little too uppity for your britches."

For an instant Beth's expression clouded, and Conor feared she might break into tears. Then, with an injured sniff and head held high, she flounced by him. "Well then," she said, "maybe I should just save my uppity britches for our guests."

Misgiving filling him, he watched her stride down the hall to the stairs. "I just bet you will," he muttered under his breath.

An impulse to call her back struck him, but Conor swiftly quashed it. When it came to Beth, Mrs. Stanton might as well know what she was up against from the start. He had already tried to discourage the woman himself with his less-than-friendly attitude. There was no sense in presenting a false front now.

Conor caught up with his daughter just as she reached the parlor door. Laying a hand on her shoulder, he guided her to stand before Abby. "Mrs. Stanton, this is my daughter, Elizabeth."

A chubby, dark-skinned and brown-eyed girl, her face still streaked with dirt, glared at Abby. Ever so briefly, Abby scanned the girl's hair, hair that was little more than a thick, black, unruly mop, chopped off rather clumsily at the shoulders.

Her clothing wasn't much better, certainly not proper attire for a young lady. Instead of a dress, Elizabeth wore a stained, well-worn boy's wool undershirt, dirty blue canvas overalls, and a pair of mud-caked boots.

If she dared take on this position, Abby realized with a sick, sinking feeling, she definitely had her work cut out for her. A temporary respite and way station, indeed!

She extended her hand. "I'm very pleased to meet you, Elizabeth. How are you?"

The girl studied her outstretched hand as if it were a loathsome thing, then met her gaze once more. "How am I?" Her tone was mocking. "Well, let's see. I go by Beth, not Elizabeth, my mother was an Indian who never married my father, and I can't say I'm all that pleased to meet you."

Beside her, Nelly gave a horrified gasp. Conor heaved a sigh and rolled his eyes. Abby's gaze, however, after skittering off that of her host's, returned immediately to the girl. Dear Lord, she thought, the barely contained panic that had threatened all day perilously close to breaking free, how am I supposed to respond to that?

Unbidden, a verse from Isaiah filled her mind. *You are precious in my eyes and glorious* . . . A sudden surge of compassion flooded Abby.

The girl . . . Beth . . . was so used to rejection that she had learned to reject first, rather than risk being rejected. She was using defiance to shield her vulnerability. There was yet more, far more, Abby sensed, smoldering just beneath the pain burning in Beth's eyes. For now, though, it was sufficient to deal with the present.

"In the minds of some misguided people"—Abby withdrew her proffered hand and placed it back in her lap—"you may seem all those things. In the eyes of God, however, you are precious and glorious. And that, I think, is all that truly matters."

Beth's eyes widened in surprise. Then they narrowed. "My last teacher, just before he threw me out of school, said I was incorrigible."

"Did he indeed?" Abby smiled. "Well, in my experience, I've found some of the most interesting and creative people are incorrigible. Sometimes they just need a little extra love and understanding."

At that, Beth turned beet red. Her lips clamped and she went silent. Conor's hand tightened on his daughter's shoulder. For a long moment he, too, was quiet.

What was this woman about? Conor wondered. Anyone else would've sputtered indignantly, then immediately reprimanded Beth for her lack of manners. But all Abigail Stanton did was quote Scripture and turn the other cheek. And, instead of trading insults, the woman had transformed Beth's self-deprecations into positive attributes.

"Girl, I think you owe Mrs. Stanton an apology."

Beth glanced up over her shoulder at him. "Must I, Papa?"

"Yes."

She turned back to Abigail Stanton, scowled, then pursed her lips. "I'm sorry, Mrs. Stanton."

Abigail nodded. "It's all right, Beth. No harm done."

"Get on with you now." Conor gave his daughter a little shove. "We grown ups have more talking to do."

He watched her leave. Then, refusing to apologize for his daughter, he forced himself to resume discussion of the business at hand. He wasn't a man given, after all, to asking for anyone's forgiveness. He'd no intention of starting now.

"There's still the matter of payment for your services." Conor pulled over one of the armchairs and took a seat in front of them. "I can offer room and board, plus thirty-five dollars a month in salary. For that you cook all our meals and two meals a day for the hands, plus clean this house, launder my and Beth's clothes, and tutor her in her lessons. You'll get one day off a month, once you've completed a full month's work."

Abigail Stanton's eyes widened. "That would be quite sufficient, Mr. MacKay. In fact, your offer is most generous." She paused. "The . . . er . . . bedroom arrangements. Where exactly would I be sleeping?"

Conor's mouth twisted. Here it comes, he thought. A melodramatic display of lady-like vapors and soft cries of outrage.

"The generous salary doesn't entail any extra services, such as warming my bed, Mrs. Stanton." When her friend gasped loudly, and she flushed fire red, he managed a taut smile. "Forgive my bluntness—a trait you'll have to learn to live with if you take this position—but I see no point in jeopardizing a strictly business arrangement. Especially," he added dryly, "when there are plenty of women to be had for such needs, if and when the urge strikes me."

"This is intolerable!" Nelly jumped to her feet and grasped Abigail by the arm. "We've heard quite enough. These people—and their job—just won't suit."

"Nelly, sit down, please." Abby turned to look back at Conor. "As blunt-spoken as Mr. MacKay is, it was I, not he, who brought up the subject. Thank you for clarifying the situation, Mr. MacKay. I feel greatly relieved to have dealt with that particular issue at the outset. Now, exactly where *would* I be sleeping?"

He shrugged, a bit miffed with her ready acceptance of his purported lack of interest in her. A fair share of the younger women—married or unmarried—who'd ever applied for this position were, by this point, beginning to eye him with lustful intent. "Since my son no longer lives here, there's an extra bedroom available upstairs. If that's too close for your personal comfort, the small bunkhouse behind the house is available. It hasn't been used in years and is in desperate need of cleaning and paint. But it has a functioning wood stove and would afford you more space, not to mention privacy."

"The bunkhouse sounds best," she said. "That is, if I decide to accept your position." Abigail stood. "I need time to consider all this, Mr. MacKay. How soon do you require my response?"

Conor eyed her closely. She won't take the job, he thought, inexplicably disappointed. She's too fine a lady. Indeed, whatever had possessed her even to come out here on such a patently inappropriate journey? Curiosity? An autumn day's brief adventure? Some unwholesome need for titillation?

At the last consideration, something in Conor hardened. Whatever the reason, she'd wasted his time. And doubly curse her for stirring that tiny spark of hope, however briefly in him, when she'd first met and talked with Beth.

It was past time, Conor resolved, to put an end to this little charade. He hadn't further time to spare on the likes of her. And he certainly had no intention of serving as grist for the local gossip mill!

"I need an answer now," Conor growled, barely containing his rising anger. "You've pretty much seen how it is here. Either you want the job, or you don't."

Nelly shot to her feet again. "Come along, Abby. He has no right to speak to you like this. Let's be on our way."

Abby held up a silencing hand. "Just a moment, Nelly." She met Conor MacKay's challenging glare. "I beg to differ with you, Mr. MacKay. Though I see nothing here that would preclude my acceptance of this position, I never make decisions in haste."

"So, in the meantime," Conor MacKay snarled as he climbed to his feet, "while you consider, I sit here, holding this position open. Well, I don't think so, Mrs. Stanton."

Secretly, shamefully relieved, Abby expelled a deep breath. "Then I guess I have my answer, Mr. MacKay."

"I guess you do."

She turned to Nelly. "It's time we were leaving. We've already taken up entirely too much of Mr. MacKay's day."

27

He stalked to the door and opened it, swinging it wide. The two women walked past him, down the porch steps, and over to the buggy. Abby untied Elsie from the hitching rail and waited for Nelly to take her seat in the buggy, before handing her the reins. Climbing in, Abby shot Conor MacKay one final look, then took back the reins.

All the while Culdee Creek's owner stood on the porch, his expression frigid, his stance unyielding. The anger in his eyes, however, spoke volumes, and it was a diatribe Abby didn't ever want to endure again.

She slapped the reins smartly over Elsie's back and clucked to her. "Let's go, girl. Get on with you."

Immediately, the horse moved out, pulling the buggy back down the road toward Culdee Creek's main gate. This time, however, Abby sensed it was a journey that somehow was not right . . . or good.

Lord, what would You have me do? she cried out silently. This man doesn't want me here. He is only looking for an excuse to turn me down.

Is he, Beloved?

The unexpected query, springing from the depths of her heart, gave Abby only a momentary pause. What else was I supposed to think? she protested, her mouth going dry, her palms damp.

Fear welled in her. She choked it down, afraid, so afraid of the answer to come—an answer, she knew now, she'd fought desperately not to hear. This could never be just a temporary respite, a place wherein to hide and lick her wounds. This could never be a situation free of emotional involvement.

Not with a man as hard, as cold as Conor MacKay. Not with a man so lost and wandering in the desert. And his daughter. Ah, what a sad, tormented little girl!

Do you see now, begin to understand why I am sending you to them? Do you hear, and know My will at last?

28

Her heart thundering in her chest, Abby halted the buggy. Her breath coming in short, painful gasps, she battled with her own plans and desires, her own needs. Battled . . . and lost.

Do it, and do it now, she ordered herself fiercely. Do it now, before you lose the nerve.

"Here"—she shoved the reins at Nelly—"Hold these. I'll be back."

"W-what are you doing?" Nelly sputtered, staring at her as if she had gone mad.

"I've got something more to say to Mr. MacKay."

Abby climbed down from the buggy. Gathering her skirts in shaking hands, she strode resolutely back to the house.

At her approach, Conor MacKay walked down the porch steps. "Forget something, Mrs. Stanton?"

Once more, that now familiar quirk tightened his handsome mouth. Before the last of her courage failed her, Abby dragged in a deep breath and forced herself to utter the words. "Yes, Mr. MacKay, I have," she said. "I forgot to tell you that I've decided to take the job."

2

How shall we sing the LORD'S song in a strange land?
                                                    Psalm 137:4

A chill wind blew down from the mountains, bringing with it the season's first promise of snow. Thick, gray clouds churned overhead, and the sun peeked only fitfully from behind them. A storm was brewing, blowing strong and bitter over the Rockies. There would be no mercy for the high plains this night.

Conor MacKay drew up the collar of his dark brown, blanket-lined canvas coat, pulled his black Stetson more firmly down onto his head, and glanced at Abigail Stanton. Sitting beside him on the buckboard seat, the woman had not spoken ten words since they had loaded up her gear three hours ago and headed out of Colorado Springs. In most cases a reticent woman would have suited him just fine, especially after seeing her reddened eyes and pale face when she had first answered the door. A smart man did not rile a woman already upset about something.

Problem was, Conor had a lot of things that needed saying, and they needed saying before they reached the ranch. In the past week since their first meeting, he had done a little investigating about the sprightly Abigail Stanton. He had learned she was a widow who had also recently lost her only child.

The information had both surprised and unnerved him. Unnerved him so much he had almost informed her right then and there on her cottage doorstep in the Springs that he would just have to find another house-keeper. As it was, the fool deal they'd struck had been on his mind for the past week.

Still, it made no sense—his strange reluctance to bring her back to the ranch. It made no sense even now. There was just something about the sweet-faced young woman with the green eyes and mass of long, dark brown hair that filled Conor with unease.

Even now he sensed something about her. Something different. She wasn't like the other women he had brought to Culdee Creek.

"Are you warm enough, Mrs. Stanton?" he forced him-self to ask, his voice gone raspy and tight. "There's an extra blanket or two behind the seat, if you need one, I mean."

She shook her head. "I'm fine, Mr. MacKay. I grew up in New England, in Massachusetts to be exact, and am quite used to the cold. Thank you for asking, though."

Silence, as heavy and oppressive as the clouds low-ering overhead, settled once more between them. Conor, however, had no intention of riding the rest of the way to Culdee Creek in such strained company. If this was all the conversation he was going to get out of the woman, he could have let one of the hands tend to her and the buckboard, and he could've ridden straight home!

"There are a few matters I wish to talk about, Mrs. Stanton. Matters best settled before we reach the ranch."

For a moment, curiosity brightened her eyes. She cocked her head. "What would those matters be, Mr. MacKay?"

There was no sense skirting the issue, Conor decided. Best to get it all out in the open, and spare the hurt feelings and arguments later. "First, I want to know why you took this job," he said. "A fine lady such as yourself has never applied before. You've been a teacher. Surely you could've taken up such a position again?"

"Yes, I could have, Mr. MacKay," Abigail replied softly. "But I didn't want to, at least not for a time. My son, Joshua, was just about school age when he died. It would be too painful to work with other boys near his age."

Conor's brow furrowed. "How did he die? Your son, I mean."

She looked away then, her mouth tight, her hands clenching suddenly in her lap. An uncharacteristic pang of remorse filled Conor. "You don't have to tell me, you know," he said. "I shouldn't have pried." Or even cared enough about you and your personal business to pry, he added as an afterthought.

"No, I'll tell you." Abigail met his gaze. "But I warn you. There may be tears. Can you abide a woman who weeps, Mr. MacKay?"

"If you're asking if I turn into a pile of mush when a woman cries, no, I don't. I'm not easily manipulated by tears, or much of anything else, Mrs. Stanton."

"And I, Mr. MacKay, don't cry to manipulate." High color flushed her cheeks. "My emotions are honest and heartfelt. I just didn't want to make you uncomfortable."

"Well, they won't," he growled, suddenly angry and unaccountably embarrassed. "Get on with your story."

"As you wish, Mr. MacKay." She closed her eyes. "Joshua died early last summer, when he caught diphtheria. It started with a sore throat, then the glands in his neck swelled and, in a day's time he could barely breathe. He was dead by the morning of the second day."

There was pain in her voice. Conor struggled to shrug off the sympathy and swell of compassion her words stirred. Her grief wasn't any more unique or heart-wrenching than what many others experienced, he told himself. It was life, and life was often brutal, unfair.

"And your husband?" He was determined to know it all and be done with it. "How did he die?"

"A railroad accident two years ago this July. A bridge collapsed. Thomas was killed trying to rescue the engineer's wife and child."

"So, in two year's time you've lost everything."

Not everything, Mr. MacKay, Abby thought. I still have the Lord.

Yet sometimes, God forgive her, she could not help but rage at the Lord for what had happened. Then, other times, Abby couldn't help but feel envy. Thomas and Joshua were safe and happy in heaven, while she had to remain here—alone and bereft. Sometimes, there seemed nothing left her: no joy, no peace, no semblance whatsoever of the life she had once known.

There were even times, in her darkest moments, when she longed most ardently to die and join them. But Abby knew it could never be. It wasn't yet her time.

Sadness and guilt, tinged with a deep sense of despair, rose to overwhelm her. Her defiant bravado on the journey with Nelly to Culdee Creek last week to the contrary, Abby was no longer certain she really did run toward the Lord anymore. When had she wandered from the true path? When Thomas died? After she had lost Joshua?

"Yes, Mr. MacKay," Abby forced herself to reply finally. "In two years' time, I've lost nearly everything." Everything, she silently added, but my faith in God.

Conor gripped the buckboard reins until his knuckles turned white. "I'm sorry for your loss, Mrs. Stanton," he muttered, feeling inane but not knowing what else to say. "But at least your husband died a hero. There must be some comfort in that."

She fell quiet for a long moment. "Thomas followed the Lord the best way he knew how," she finally said.

He shot her a quick, quizzical look. Somehow, that flat, unemotional comment wasn't what he'd expected. He wanted to delve deeper. There was more to her former marital relationship than what first appeared, but to ask was to care, and Conor didn't dare let himself care. In the end, it was enough that she stayed for a time and did the job—and *only* the job—for which she had been hired.

On a sudden impulse, he halted his team of horses. "Your mention of God," Conor growled, turning to face her. "That brings to mind the second matter I want to discuss with you, Mrs. Stanton."

"Yes, Mr. MacKay?"

"I don't go to church. I don't believe in God. And I'll be"—he caught himself before the word escaped—"I won't tolerate any talk of God in my house, much less any attempt by you to convert me or my daughter. Is that clear, Mrs. Stanton?"

She didn't blink an eyelash. "Quite clear, Mr. MacKay."

Confusion, followed swiftly by exasperation, flooded him. "Then why did you tell Beth she was precious in God's eyes?"

"Because I believe it. Because she seemed so vulnerable, so certain of my rejection." Abigail inhaled a deep breath. "I'm sorry if I offended you. But let me assure you it came from the heart. I love Beth because God loves her."

Conor gritted his teeth. Blast her, she was doing it again, and they hadn't even reached the ranch!

"Suit yourself." Slapping the reins over the team's back, he urged them onward. "Just keep your religious beliefs to yourself from here on out. Neither Beth nor I are interested."

"I try never to force my personal beliefs on others, Mr. MacKay. But I cannot pretend to hide their importance in my daily life, either. That much you should know and understand about me."

He drew in a raw, ragged breath. "Fine. Fine. Just as long as we understand each other."

"Oh, I think we do, Mr. MacKay." A tiny smile twitched at the corner of her mouth. "I think, at long last, we certainly do."

The impending snow held off long enough for them to reach Culdee Creek, and transfer Abby's belongings into the bunkhouse. Two ranch hands—one tall, lanky, and in his mid-fifties, who introduced himself as Frank Murphy, and his younger, shorter, and more heavily muscled compatriot named Henry Watson—unloaded the furniture and leather trunks. Two other hands, whose names Abby quickly discovered were Wendell Chapman and Jonah Goldman, worked to reassemble Abby's iron and brass bed—the bed Thomas had given her as a wedding present. The men came and went, carrying in the sewing machine, then dresser, rocking chair, and little side table. With the assistance of Ella MacKay, the wife of Culdee Creek's foreman who was also Conor MacKay's cousin, Abby directed where things were to go.

Conor MacKay had seen to the refurbishing of the small bunkhouse. A fresh coat of paint had recently been applied inside and out—green with white trim on the exterior, and whitewashed walls within. The two small windows had been scrubbed until the glass panes sparkled. The floors had been swept, and all the cobwebs whisked away.

Someone had even started a fire in the small, pot-bellied wood stove. Despite the frequent opening of the door as the men came and went, the little stove heated the one-room building well. Abby glanced about her and smiled. It was a small, snugly built dwelling. With the stove's help, she should keep plenty warm this winter.

"We can string a rope across the back half of the bunkhouse," Ella offered at one point, eyeing the room critically, "and hang some fabric. That way, you can have a private area for your bedroom and a sitting room in front." Ella, a thin, red-haired, freckle-faced woman in her early forties, seemed delighted to have another woman to talk to.

"That sounds wonderful." Abby smiled back.

"Do you have any children?" Abby asked, at a sudden loss for anything else to say in the uncomfortable silence that frequently falls between two strangers.

Ella threw back her head and laughed. "Oh my, yes. I've two youngsters—Devlin Jr., who's four, and Mary, who's one. I lost my first husband—the Lord bless and keep him—to a blizzard when I was thirty. Didn't marry Devlin Sr. until six years later. The children have been such a gift, considering my age." She cocked her head, her expression suddenly solemn. "I heard about how your man died, but not much about your boy, save that the diphtheria took him. How old was he?"

Abby's smile faded. "Five. Joshua was five."

"I hope you don't mind me asking." Ella walked over and put her hand on Abby's arm. "Being a mother and all, I was curious, and trying to get much information out of Conor is like squeezing blood from a turnip."

"No, I don't mind." Abby's mouth quirked wryly. "And I can well imagine getting Mr. MacKay to do anything must be difficult."

Ella grinned. "Oh, he's not so bad. When it comes to people, Conor's just a very cautious man. He doesn't trust most of them, you know."

"I gathered that."

"But when he does get to know you"—Ella pulled a set of bed sheets from an open trunk and shook them out—"there's no more generous, loyal friend to be had. The things he's done for my Devlin and me . . . well, it boggles the mind."

Though Ella's glowing description of Conor MacKay was a bit hard for Abby to believe, it was reassuring nonetheless. Perhaps her new employer wasn't as bad as he made himself out to be.

"Here,"—Abby motioned to the bed sheets—"give me those. You needn't trouble yourself making my bed. I can make it and put everything away later."

Ella clutched the bed sheets to her protectively. "And what's to keep us from finishing up in here?"

Abby looked out the window. Already, the day was slipping rapidly toward dusk. The first big, fat flakes of snow were beginning to fall. "I don't know when Mr. MacKay likes his supper," she murmured, turning back to Ella, "but I'm sure it's past time to start."

"Supper's already cooking. I talked Conor into letting me prepare the meal this evening, to give you a chance to settle in a bit. The bread's finished baking and in the warming oven. It'll be another hour before the stew's ready." She paused. "You do like beef stew and fresh bread with apple pie for dessert, don't you?"

Abby's niggling sense of homesickness began to ease. Though she had wept herself into a near panic over what she was about to undertake just before Conor MacKay had arrived this morning, Ella's continued acts of kindness warmed her heart. She had been here barely two hours and, already, Abby knew she had made her first friend. Thank you, Lord, she thought, lifting a quick, fervent prayer.

Then she grinned. "It sounds heavenly. Thank you so much for your thoughtfulness. I owe you one very big favor."

Ella laughed merrily. "Don't give it another thought. It was the neighborly thing to do. Besides, you're now the only other woman in ten miles, so one thing is certain. We're sure to be trading favors back and forth a lot!"

From his study, Conor heard the kitchen's back door slam. He laid aside his fountain pen and recapped the inkstand. Though he had planned on catching up on the ranch accounts before supper, his heart was not in it. After the long ride to the Springs today, he was tired.

Not that he could fully blame his distractedness on the long day of travel, he admitted ruefully. Try as he might to keep his mind off of her, his thoughts kept creeping back to his new cook and housekeeper.

Conor leaned back in his chair, placed his arms on the armrests, and closed his eyes. His little talk with Abigail Stanton earlier today had revealed many things. He'd verified what he'd suspected. She was a woman of strong convictions who would not be easily swayed or intimidated. She was also surprisingly honest.

Her claim that she had taken the position at Culdee Creek because she could not bear to work with little boys right now seemed forthright enough. But surely there were deeper, more self-serving reasons at work. There always were.

Conor had but to discover them, and discover them he would.

He expelled a deep breath and shook his head in frustration. Why, oh why had he agreed to hire her? Self-disgust welled in him. He was a fool. He'd always be a fool. Hadn't his father hammered that into him over and over when he was a boy?

"Life's nothing but hard work, disappointment, and pain," his father had slurred many a night, drinking himself into another of his black despairs. "You're a fool if you think otherwise," he would howl, pounding his fists into the walls, the furniture, and sometimes even Conor's young, defenseless body. "There's no fairness, no goodness, no love left in the world!"

Yet still Conor had clung to hope. Surely somewhere there was fairness, goodness, and love left in the world. Surely someday, somewhere he'd find a woman to love him as deeply and unconditionally as had his mother. His good, God-fearing, gentle mother . . .

He'd clung to that hope, Conor thought bitterly. Clung to it tenaciously until Sally walked out and Squirrel Woman died. Then he'd clung to hope no more.

Voices, women's voices, rose from the kitchen. The savory smell of beef stew and the rich, yeasty scent of bread wafted by. Conor's mouth began to water. It had been weeks since he had had a good home-cooked meal.

Straightening in his chair, Conor slowly opened his eyes. Time to get on with it, he told himself. He needed to fetch Beth, who'd refused to come downstairs since Mrs. Stanton's arrival.

He couldn't blame her really. It was hard to take another woman into their home. Would she turn on them, too?

39

Conor shoved to his feet. If he had any say about it, no one would ever hurt his daughter again. And no one was going to hurt him, either. After all this time, his heart had finally hardened into a block of stone.

ა

Abby stood at the back door with the kerosene lamp and watched Ella walk toward her own home a hundred yards beyond the bunkhouse. Though she had all but begged Ella to stay and partake of the meal she had so generously cooked, her new friend had refused. Her own family awaited her. She would come, though, she assured Abby, to visit tomorrow.

Her own family . . .

A renewed wave of homesickness and longing washed over Abby. Oh, how she missed her own family, Thomas and little Joshua. If only . . . if only she'd been a better mother, perhaps Joshua wouldn't have died. If only she had been a more biddable, loyal wife . . .

Hot tears stung her eyes. Abby wrenched her thoughts from her guilty self-torment, pulled the door closed, and turned. Conor MacKay and his daughter stood in front of the kitchen table.

"M-Mr. MacKay," Abby stammered, startled. Furiously, she blinked back her tears. "I didn't hear you come in."

His shuttered glance first took in her—and Abby knew he'd noted her tears—then moved to the table, set with glasses, bowls, spoons, the pot of stew, thick slices of bread, and a crock of sweet cream butter. "We were getting hungry, Mrs. Stanton," he said, his words surprisingly gentle and subdued. "I take it supper is served?"

"Why, yes, so it is." Abby placed the kerosene lamp she was holding in the middle of the table, then hurried to one of the two cupboards and picked up the pitcher of milk sitting there. "Please, sit where you usually do." She lifted the pitcher, relieved to have something to do. "Would anyone like a glass of milk?"

Conor looked pointedly at Beth. The girl didn't reply. "Beth likes milk," he finally answered for her. "Sit down, Beth."

His daughter shot him a mutinous glance but took her seat without a word. Abby moved to her side, filled her glass, then another for herself. "What about you, Mr. MacKay? What would you like to drink?"

He wanted to tell her a stiff shot or two of whiskey would be welcome right about now, but decided against scandalizing his new employee the first night out. As it was, she looked as if, at any moment, she was on the verge of breaking into a fit of weeping. "Water will do me fine, Mrs. Stanton."

Abby pumped out some water into his glass and returned to his side.

"Thank you, Mrs. Stanton," he said, glancing up at her. "Please, sit. I can't abide a woman hovering over me."

Abby flushed. "I'm sorry. I just don't know what you expect of me." She took her seat across from Beth.

The pot of stew sat closest to Conor. He dished up for Beth a portion of dark, rich beef stew, thick with tender carrots, potatoes, and peas, then reached for Abby's bowl. Once he had served himself, Abby passed the plate of bread and crock of butter.

She sat there and waited until all had their food, hoping that, as the man of the house, Mr. MacKay would then lead them in the saying of grace. He, however, never lifted his eyes from his bowl.

Abby turned to Beth, watching to see what she would do. The little girl was even quicker than her father to shove the first spoonful of stew into her mouth.

Abby clasped her hands before her and bowed her head, offering a silent prayer of thanks for the meal the Lord had given. Then, after finally unfolding her hands and placing her napkin on her lap, she lifted her gaze.

Two pairs of eyes were riveted on her, and the look in one particular, smoky blue pair made Abby's heart almost skip a beat. Forcing the brightest smile she could manage, she picked up her spoon and began to eat.

3

Let us run with patience the race that is set before us.
                                        Hebrews 12:1

The next morning at 5:00 A.M. sharp, Abby woke to the raucous clanging of her new alarm clock. Groggy and disoriented, she groped blindly for the unfamiliar instrument, finally finding the button that silenced the bell clapper. Tapping it down smartly, she lay there in the darkness, struggling to make sense out of the unfamiliar surroundings.

A strong gust of wind slammed into the bunkhouse, rattling the little wooden structure. In a rush, it all came back. Culdee Creek Ranch . . . her first day of work for the MacKays. Then, following swiftly on the heels of that came the all too familiar, agonizing swell of remembrance.

Remembrance of that hot July day when they'd brought Thomas home, his bloody, mangled, lifeless body lying in the back of a buckboard, covered by a canvas tarp. Vaguely, Abby remembered ignoring the hands outstretched to help her, and crawling awkwardly on her own up into the back of the big wooden wagon. She remembered ripping back the tarp, then staring down at her husband, so shocked and horrified that, at first, she didn't even recognize him.

It had all seemed like some horrible dream, a dream from which she prayed soon to awaken. Then a big horsefly buzzed by, circled Thomas's face, and landed on his nose. For a crazy instant Abby watched, fully expecting her husband to open his eyes and, with an indignant snort, to swat away the fly. When he didn't, the utter, ugly reality of the situation hit her, slamming into her gut, sucking the breath from her lungs. She sank to her knees, buried her face in her hands, and wept.

Now, with a shuddering sob, Abby shoved out of her bed and knelt beside it.

For a long moment, she drowned in a flood tide of tears. Even after all this time—if there could ever be sufficient time to adequately mourn the loss of loved ones—it hurt just as deeply as those first days. It hurt so very, very badly.

Lord, help me through this day, Abby begged, her hands clenched before her, the tears spilling down her cheeks. Come between me and this pain. Grant me strength, and patience, and guide me in Your ways . . .

Yet, though she shut her eyes and clung as hard as she could to thoughts of God, little by little, like a chill, heavy mist, the hated, unwelcome memories seeped back again. She saw Joshua, lying in his little bed, his skin gray, his lips blue, struggling for breath. She saw herself bend down for the hundredth time, brush aside his sweat-darkened blond hair, and wipe his brow with a damp cloth, all the while consumed with a helpless panic and a sick fear that grew with each passing second. Then, at long last, the minutes and hours of that hideous, harrowing vigil were over. Joshua lay there, cold, silent, and still—gone away . . . away from life . . . from her.

Wave after wave of regret and unrequited longing washed over Abby, gradually undermining her pain, sucking away her emotions until she was, once more, blessedly numb. Only then could she pray anew, though the words gave her little comfort. She prayed on, none-

44

theless, her thoughts lifting heavenward by sheer force of will.

In time, though, Abby wiped away her tears, rose, and lit the kerosene lamp on her bedside table. With a sudden shiver—as the early morning chill struck her now with a vengeance—she hurried to the pot-bellied stove and threw a few sticks of kindling into it. After a few good puffs, the glowing embers again flared to life. Soon, the kindling caught on fire. Abby then added a fat, split pine log.

The pot of water she had placed atop the stove last night was lukewarm. She bundled up in a woolen shawl and climbed back into bed. Even with the fire now burning hotly, it would take at least another twenty minutes for the water to heat sufficiently to use for washing up. Time enough, Abby decided, for a short reading from the Scriptures.

Gradually, tendrils of vapor began to waft languidly upward from the pot of water on the wood stove. Abby reluctantly set aside her Bible, climbed back out of bed, and carried her porcelain wash basin to the small worktable. She placed a clean washcloth, bar of lavender soap, and a fresh towel beside the basin, then retrieved the now steaming pot of water.

Fifteen minutes later Abby had washed and dressed. Her long, thick brown hair was pinned neatly into a bun, and her bed was made. She then donned her warm winter coat, wrapped the woolen shawl over her head, and headed outside, the basin of dirty wash water in her hands. After dumping its contents, Abby returned the basin to the table. She lit an old kerosene lantern, then extinguished the oil lamp, and left the bunkhouse.

Snow had begun to fall before sunset yesterday, but thanks to the blustering winds only a light layer now coated the ground. As she made her way to the chicken coop in the fading darkness, the icy crystals crunched beneath her feet. The chill wind plucked at her skirt, then scurried beneath it. Abby shivered again and quickened her pace.

"At least it's relatively warm in here," she muttered when she finally stepped inside the chicken coop. Setting the lantern down on the dirt floor, she began gathering what few eggs there were from beneath the now irately clucking, highly agitated hens. "Well, warm at least in comparison to the outside," Abby added, as the seemingly indefatigable wind managed at last to find the chinks in the little building's walls, and whistled gleefully inside.

Though the coop could hardly be called toasty warm, Abby envisioned the morning yet to come and decided she would still prefer it over the lack of human warmth she suspected she would find in the main house. Her thoughts drifted back to last night's supper. After the tension-fraught meal and stony looks, Abby was not so sure she ever wanted to break bread with Conor and Beth MacKay again.

It was not as if she had defied Culdee Creek's owner by saying grace. She had only, after all, agreed not to force her beliefs on them. But apparently Conor MacKay hadn't thought so. His scowling countenance for the rest of the meal had all but shouted his disapproval.

On the other hand, Beth had chosen to take a far more active approach. First she had "accidentally" knocked over her glass of milk. Then, after Abby had that mess sopped up and a fresh glass of milk poured, the youngster started pouting that her bowl of stew was cold.

After dishing her up a fresh bowl of stew, Abby barely had a chance to dig into her own bowl of lukewarm stew, when Beth sweetly asked for some raspberry preserves to put on her bread. By then Abby's patience was beginning to wear thin. However, before she had a chance to suggest Beth get up and get her own preserves, her father, also apparently weary of his daughter's little game, ordered his daughter to do just that.

The remainder of the meal passed in silence, save for the unmistakably angry visual messages Beth sent Abby. Recalling her looks, Abby could only guess at the encounters to come this day.

No indeed, she admitted wryly. If she had had her druthers, she would have far preferred to wile away the day in this boisterous chicken coop.

But that wasn't to be, Abby reminded herself as she stood and pocketed four eggs. She had hired on for this job and, one way or another, had just about used up all her druthers in the doing. There was nothing to be done but face up to what lay ahead.

Reluctantly, Abby left the chicken coop and turned toward the main house. Down the hill near the barns, several ranch hands, shrugging on dark canvas jackets and thick gloves, were beginning to leave the big bunkhouse. There were horses to be fed, pigs to be slopped, and gear to be readied for the day's work ahead, Abby knew, before they all trudged up to the main house for breakfast. To the east, a faint hint of rose now washed the sky. Overhead, a few fluffy clouds scudded by. It promised to be a sunny, if rather windy day.

Abby only hoped it would pass pleasantly. She knew it would pass quickly and, thankfully, keep her mind off further memories she'd rather not dwell upon. And there was always, after all the work was done, at least the possibility of a visit from Ella MacKay to look forward to.

Conor cursed as he readjusted the main draft regulator door on the big cookstove for what seemed the hundredth time. Though all the other dampers and regulators were wide open, if he didn't get the draft regulator on this particular stove opened to just the right angle, the fire refused to burn hot enough. Problem was, if it didn't burn hot enough, the water in the coffeepot would take a month of Sundays to heat. And if he didn't get at least one cup of coffee before he headed out to milk Ethel . . .

With a frustrated snarl, Conor slammed the regulator door closed and tried once more to open it just so. He really didn't have time for this, he thought. He still had to wash up and finish dressing before he milked. Since he'd forgotten to inform Mrs. Stanton what time they and then the hands expected breakfast, he'd most likely also have to wake her up on the way out. Of course, Conor added sourly as an afterthought, if the woman had been doing her job, she'd have thought to ask him that very thing last night herself.

To give Abigail Stanton her due, he admitted as he tinkered with the regulator, aside from the blatant defiance of saying grace, she had tried to be pleasant and helpful last night. She had even borne Beth's ill-disguised antics with surprising patience.

Yet Conor knew there were bound to be more problems in the making. There always were, when it came to Beth and a new housekeeper.

He smiled in wry remembrance. There was, to name just a few, poor Mrs. Hutchinson, that officious little biddy who'd soon had her wings clipped when Beth sewed all her underdrawer legs shut. And then there was that busybody Frannie Kent, who had been the shocked recipient of a particularly prickly pinecone in her chair, not to mention having her supply of fine perfumes poured out and replaced with a potent vinegar mixture.

God help both Beth and Abigail Stanton, though, Conor thought, if the pair of them started anything today. He'd slept poorly last night and wasn't in the mood.

The back door creaked opened. A blast of frigid air swirled into the kitchen. Conor stood, then swung around, a sharp reprimand on his lips for the ranch hand who had dared walk in at this hour.

Abigail Stanton, a kerosene lantern clutched in her hand, strode into the kitchen. Even in the dim, flickering lantern light, Conor could see the color flare in her cheeks.

Following the direction of her gaze, he recalled that he stood there, bare-chested and bare-footed, dressed only in his blue denims. Though typical apparel for his early morning forays into the kitchen, it was not at all appropriate garb before a well-bred woman not his wife. There wasn't much he could do about it now, though.

"I always start up water for coffee first thing," Conor offered with a vague motion toward the cookstove. "And, since I didn't expect you'd be up quite so early . . ."

She managed a tremulous smile. "I wanted to get an early start. Besides, it's not like I'm unacquainted with half-naked men, after all." Then, as if realizing how that might be construed, she hurriedly added, "I was speaking only of my husband, of course."

Conor held up his hand. "I'm quite aware who you were talking about, Mrs. Stanton."

He paused, waiting for her to say something more. When she didn't, he motioned toward the cookstove. "Well, since you're here, you might as well start learning about this stove's particular quirks. It'll take you some time before you can regulate it well enough to keep from scorching the soups and burning the breads."

Abigail Stanton walked to the kitchen table and put down the lantern. She removed her shawl and coat, hung them on a peg by the back door, then made her way to his side. "A temperamental stove, is it?" she asked, all seriousness and apparent sincerity.

49

"Very." For a fleeting instant as she squatted beside him at the cookstove, MacKay caught a faint scent of lavender soap. The sudden awareness of her as an attractive female struck him with a painful intensity. His bare skin began to tingle, flush with heightened awareness. His gut twisted. Startled by his unexpected and surprisingly forceful response, Conor sucked in an angry breath.

He angled away until he could no longer smell her fresh-washed fragrance. "This main draft regulator . . . see how easy it is to over- or under-compensate?" As he spoke, he pulled the door open bit by bit, then closed it the same way. "It takes practice to develop the right touch.

"Here"–he scooted aside and pointed to the little door below and to the left of the firebox–"why don't you practice with it while I go back upstairs to wash and dress? It can't be that different from the stoves you're used to. If we're lucky, maybe you'll even have the coffee water boiling by the time I get back."

Abigail shot him a dubious look. "I'll give it a try. If I were you, though, I wouldn't set your hopes on a cup of hot coffee any time soon."

Conor gave a hoarse laugh. A fresh cup of coffee wasn't the only thing he had no intention of setting his hopes on. "Oh, I won't, Mrs. Stanton," he muttered half to himself, climbing to his feet. "I won't."

Abby watched him go, then heaved a sigh of relief. Lord have mercy, she thought, but Conor MacKay was even more attractive with his shirt off than with it on, and that was saying a lot. She knew she shouldn't let his presence unnerve her. She was a grown woman after all, not some flighty schoolgirl–a recently widowed, married woman and mother, no less.

Abby pressed a trembling hand to her breast. Why, even her heart was racing, pounding away like some wild, Indian tom-tom!

What was it about this man that sent her thoughts to spinning? she wondered. Despite their marital difficulties, she still missed and mourned her husband. Despite the fact Thomas had been fifteen years older than her and had most times treated her as if she were some child, she had still loved him. The thought of finding someone else to replace him was the furthest thing from her mind. Indeed, if it ever *did* enter her mind, Conor MacKay would be the last man she would ever consider.

Still, like it or not, Mr. Conor MacKay made her very nervous, stirring emotions–yearnings–Abby had never felt before, not even for Thomas. But then, the affection she had had for her husband had been based on respect and duty and a shared love for the Lord. Indeed, that sense of wifely duty had been the sole reason she had ever performed the marital act. No sense of duty, however, beckoned her now toward Conor MacKay, and she knew it.

After a time of fiddling with the cookstove, Abby finally got the wood in the firebox burning nicely. Deciding it best to leave well enough alone, she turned her efforts to gathering the necessary ingredients for breakfast. Beside her stash of four eggs that she placed in a bowl on the kitchen table, Abby added a bag of flour, some baking powder, a bowl of sugar, and a large tin of what looked like a fancy New England maple syrup.

For an instant her gaze lingered on the syrup tin. The scene painted thereon of dark, skeletal maple trees, snowy backdrop, and a little, red-jacketed man sitting in a sleigh sent a renewed pang of homesickness shooting through Abby. Oh, for those happy, carefree days of her girlhood, running with her brothers through the snowy woods that surrounded their house outside Fall River, Massachusetts! It had been such an idyllic time, when life seemed so safe, so simple, and so very good.

Just then Conor MacKay walked back into the kitchen. Cheeks flaming, Abby swung around. This time, in addition to his well-worn blue denims, he had added a gray woolen, long-sleeved shirt and a pair of boots. His tousled black hair was now combed, his face freshly shaved.

Abby managed a smile and pointed to the coffee pot. "Would you like a cup? It'll be ready soon."

With a curt shake of his head, he walked to the back door and donned his jacket and black Stetson. "Save it. I'll be back in about fifteen minutes anyway." He paused at the door to pick up a covered empty milk pail. "If you're needing some milk for making breakfast, I mean."

"Yes, I will," Abby replied. "Are flapjacks and bacon to your liking?"

The corner of Conor's mouth twitched. "After all the mornings of just a cup of coffee and maybe a slice of bread, most anything will be to my liking. That is, if you and Old Bess can manage to cook a meal without burning most of it."

"Old Bess?" Abby's forehead wrinkled in puzzlement. "Who's Old Bess?"

With a jerk of his head, Conor MacKay indicated the big cookstove. Then, without further explanation or a farewell, he turned on his heel, opened the back door, and walked out.

"Old Bess, indeed," Abby muttered, sending the stove a skeptical glance. "I've heard of naming your horse and even your hand gun, but naming a stove . . ."

She grabbed up the lantern, a sharp knife, and long metal pan, and headed to the cellar door across the kitchen. The room was a dark, chilly place, with hastily dusted cobwebs still clinging doggedly to the corners.

The family washtub and bathing tub were stacked against a far wall. Thick slabs of pork and beef, covered with muslin, hung from the rafters in the middle of the long room. It was there Abby went, to the chunks of smoked and salted bacon. With a few, quick slashes of her knife, she hacked off enough bacon for breakfast, then climbed back up the stairs.

Fifteen minutes later, just as he had promised, Conor MacKay strode in with a pail of warm, foaming milk. He immediately poured the milk into a cheesecloth-covered pail sitting on a small table by the back door, then placed the empty pail on the floor beside it. Hanging up his coat and Stetson, Conor joined Abby at the stove.

The mouth-watering aroma of frying bacon mixed tantalizingly with the smell of fresh coffee. He took one look at the fat strips of bacon sizzling in the iron fry pan, and smiled.

Grabbing a dishcloth, Conor used it to pick up the coffeepot. "I need that cup of coffee now. Would you like one, too?"

Abby glanced briefly over her shoulder, then returned her attention to the bacon. "Yes, please. I take mine black."

The coffeepot still clutched in his hand, Conor walked to one of the cupboards. Taking down two thick pottery mugs, he placed them on the table. After quickly pouring out the coffee, Conor added several teaspoons of sugar to his. Still stirring his coffee, he ambled over to Abby.

"How much longer before breakfast?"

"About ten more minutes." Abby lifted crisp strips of bacon from the fry pan and placed them on a plate. "I'm just about ready to start making the flapjacks. Does someone need to go up and wake Beth, or will she know to get up on her own?"

"I'll go wake her." Conor took a long draught of his coffee. He closed his eyes, almost sighing aloud in pleasure. Somehow, the coffee tasted better this morning than it had in a long time. "She expects me."

Abby glanced over her shoulder and smiled. "Well, I can't think of a more pleasant way for a little girl to greet the new day, than by being awakened by her father. It's good to have some special family traditions. Beth will remember and cherish them even when she's grown."

Her reply nonplused him. "I suppose," he growled, not knowing what else to say but inordinately pleased, nonetheless.

"One thing more, Mr. MacKay."

He had just lifted his mug for another swallow but paused, the coffee halfway to his lips. "Yes?"

"After breakfast. What household chores would you like me to tackle first?" As if to soften any implied insult, she added. "Considering your, er, long-standing problems keeping a housekeeper, I assume some chores have piled up more severely than others?"

His brow furrowing in thought, he considered her request for a long moment. "The laundry, for starters. We've a mess of dirty clothes that need a good washing. That should take most of today. Tomorrow will be soon enough to tackle the rest of the house, the sweeping and dusting. And the clean clothes will need ironing, the floors scrubbing–"

Abigail laughed and held up her hand. "I think I get the idea." She paused. "And what about Beth?"

Conor MacKay went still. "What about her? I hired *you* to be cook and housekeeper."

"That's not what I meant." Abby choked back her exasperation. Considering the circumstances, she must, she supposed, make allowances for an overly protective and indulgent father. "I spoke of Beth's lessons. Would you like me to begin those today, too?"

He eyed her closely. "Yes, that'd be nice, if you think you'll have the time, what with all the other work."

Abby smiled. "There are ways, Mr. MacKay."

"Well, then, I suppose it's time to roust out Beth." He set down his mug. "We'll be back shortly."

"Bring a hearty appetite with you," Abigail called after him as he stalked from the kitchen. She finished laying out the fried bacon, then poured most of the grease into a strainer-topped grease keeper. Humming a tune, Abby next measured out the ingredients for flapjacks into a big, chipped, yellow pottery bowl. Behind her, the fry pan rewarmed on the cookstove. The small spoonful's worth of bacon grease she had left in it began to sizzle and pop.

The morning was not turning out half as badly as she had imagined it might, Abby thought contentedly. Conor MacKay had been almost cordial. So far, the breakfast preparations were going well and, from the sunbeams now streaming into the parlor, the day promised to at least be sunny, if cool. Now, if only Beth's mood—

The acrid scent of burning grease wrenched Abby from her pleasant musings. With a gasp, she wheeled around, flinging fat dollops of flapjack batter from the spoon into the air. Smoke billowed from the fry pan.

Abby quickly tossed the spoon onto the table, grabbed a hand towel, and removed the smoldering pan from the stove. "Blast, but you're the cussedest stove I've ever cooked on!" she muttered, carrying the pan to the sink.

After pumping the pan full of cold water, she hurried back to the stove. Once more, Abby squatted and fiddled with the main draft regulator door hoping, at long last, she'd finally gotten the recalcitrant thing adjusted properly.

By the time Conor and Beth entered the kitchen, Abby had four golden brown flapjacks stacked on each of their plates. "Good morning, Beth." She graced the little girl with what she hoped was her sweetest, most welcoming smile. "Did you sleep well?"

Beth, hair askew and dressed in yet another pair of overalls and boy's woolen, long-sleeved undershirt, scowled darkly, mumbled some unintelligible reply, and plopped down at the table. Wasting no time, she grabbed a handful of bacon and stuffed two slices into her mouth. Then, after dousing her flapjacks with a generous amount of maple syrup, she dug in.

Abby sent Conor an inquiring glance. He just shook his head and rolled his eyes. Beth, she realized, was none too happy with either of them this morning. Deciding it the better part of valor to avoid any direct confrontation first thing with the little girl, Abby turned back to the stove.

She finished the remainder of the flapjacks for their breakfast and took her seat at the table. By then, the stack of flapjacks on both Beth and Conor's plates had diminished considerably.

Abby smiled in satisfaction. "I take it the breakfast met with your approval?" She added three flapjacks and several pieces of bacon to her own plate.

Beth, toying now with the puddle of syrup in the middle of her plate, refused to look up. He father, however, rocking back in his chair and savoring his second cup of coffee, did manage a bit more social grace. "It was delicious, Mrs. Stanton. You and Old Bess seem to be getting along surprisingly well."

Abby gave a wry chuckle. "Let's just say we've agreed to a temporary truce. Just before you returned, we had a few tense moments."

He smiled, leaned forward until all four legs of his chair were once more firmly planted on the floor, and set down his mug. "From the sudden smell of burnt grease upstairs, I gathered there'd been some sort of altercation. To your credit, though, it seems you came out the victor."

"This time, perhaps." Abby laughed outright. Why, miracle of miracles! The man actually had a sense of humor! "Though one battle may have been won, I'd wager the war is hardly over."

"You just watch out," Beth muttered, suddenly coming out of the sullen pout she'd managed to maintain for the entire meal.

Two pair of eyes turned to her.

"And why is that, girl?" Conor asked, an edge of warning in his voice.

Beth focused her now wide-eyed, innocent gaze on her father. "You know Old Bess, Papa. One minute she's sweet. The next, she turns on you, burning everything in sight. If I didn't know better, I'd lay odds Old Bess is just biding her time with Mrs. 'Know-it-all.'"

"Would you now?" An enigmatic smile crossed his lips. "Well, you'll have plenty of chances to find out how much Mrs. Stanton knows, won't you?"

Beth's eyes narrowed. "What do you mean, Papa?"

"Why, what else, girl? It's past time you began your lessons, and today's as good a day as any to start." He looked toward Abby. "Wouldn't you say so, Mrs. Stanton?"

Abby inhaled a steadying breath, then forced what she hoped was a bright, obliging smile. "As good a day as any, Mr. MacKay."

4

And now abideth faith, hope, charity, these three; but the greatest of these is charity.

1 Corinthians 13:13

"Abby? It's me, Ella."

The voice from the kitchen's back door caught Abby by surprise. She dropped the bar of lye soap she had been using on Beth's dirty dungarees. It hit the wash water with a resounding plunk, splattering her with dirty droplets.

She swung around, swiped a damp hank of hair from her sweaty forehead, and grinned. There, in the open doorway, stood Ella MacKay, a rosy-cheeked baby in her arms, a young, red-haired boy clinging to her skirts.

"Come in, Ella." Gratefully, Abby stepped back from the steaming washtub. "Come on in and have a seat."

She wiped her wet hands on her cotton apron, walked to a cupboard, and pulled down two mugs. "Would you like something to drink? A cup of tea, perhaps? I can fetch some milk for the children from the springhouse. It'll only take me a few minutes."

"A cup of tea would be nice, but nothing for the children," Ella murmured as she made her way to the table and took a seat. "They just woke up from their morning nap. Mary's been nursed, and Devlin Jr.'s already

58

had some raisin bread and milk." She looked at her son. "Why don't you go find Beth? She's upstairs in her room, isn't she?"–she glanced at Abby for confirmation.

At Abby's affirmative nod, Ella gave her son a gentle shove. "Skedaddle now."

"Beth really dotes on him," she informed Abby after he had left, "and Devlin Jr. adores her. They can spend hours together, telling stories, playing dress up, and all sorts of other imaginary games."

With a sharp pang, Abby had watched the toddler scurry from the kitchen. For a moment the memory of Joshua, laughing merrily and racing through their old house to join his little friend Caleb outside, was almost more than she could bear.

The two boys weren't much different in age–Joshua, five, and Devlin Jr., four. Though Devlin Jr. had a wild carrot-red thatch of hair and a generous smattering of freckles across his face, and Joshua had been dark blond and fair, they were enough alike that Abby knew it would be hard to see the little boy and not be reminded of her own. But then, she glumly reminded herself, so many things reminded her of her son and would, she supposed, for a very long time to come.

Blinking back a swell of tears, Abby squared her shoulders and headed for the stove. Commandeering the simmering teapot, she moved it to a hotter spot beside the pot of leftover stew she was rewarming for lunch. Walking back to the cupboard, she took down a small, red lacquered wooden tray she had discovered just that morning, added the two mugs, a bowl of sugar, a jar of tealeaves, a silver tea strainer, two spoons, and two blue- and white-checkered cloth napkins.

"I'm sorry there's none of your delicious apple pie left," Abby said, as she carried the tray back to the table. "What little we had Beth finished off just a little while ago." She shook her head in amazement. "For such a little girl, she certainly has an enormous appetite."

Ella shifted Mary to the other side of her lap. "I sometimes think she tries to fill that lovesick hole inside her with food." She hesitated before going on. "I saw the look you gave Devlin Jr. just now, Abby. If it's too difficult for you to be around him, I won't bring him anymore."

"No, no." Abby managed a wan smile. "I've got to get over it sooner or later. After all"—she forced a laugh—"I don't want to be known as 'Old Lady Stanton who can't have children visit.'"

Ella laughed. "I don't think you've got much to worry about, Abby. You don't strike me as a woman who runs away from things."

"On the contrary." She set the tray on the table and began laying out the napkins, silverware, and sugar bowl. "That's exactly what I had hoped this position would be. A place to get away from everything, until I could sort out my life."

"And exactly how long did it take you to discard that foolish flight of fancy?" Ella asked with an impish grin. "The first time you talked to Conor or Beth?"

Abby's smile faded. "Actually, I haven't discarded that plan, Ella. It's just getting harder to convince myself that I can manage it. The running away, I mean."

Even as the words left her mouth, Abby wished she could've called them back. If the sudden, heavy silence that settled between them wasn't confirmation enough of her tactless mistake, the shocked expression on Ella's face most certainly was. This time, however, the shrill whistle of steam escaping the teapot provided Abby with a convenient excuse to busy herself. "Excuse me." She hurried to retrieve the teapot.

In silence Abby filled the tea strainer with tealeaves, placed it over Ella's mug, and carefully poured the boiling water over the leaves. Once Ella's mug was full, she repeated the procedure for her own mug. At long last, though, Abby ran out of excuses to avoid her guest's now concerned, if compassionate scrutiny.

"You're the first decent woman Conor has hired," Ella finally said, "and now you're telling me this job means nothing to you? That you intend to waltz in and out of their lives without a by-your-leave?"

Abby flushed. She gripped her mug between both hands, staring down into its amber depths. "It seemed like the best thing for me at the time. When I first considered the position, I mean." She lifted an agonized gaze. "It was mean and selfish, I know, but I just wanted . . ." Tears clogged her throat and, for a long moment, Abby couldn't speak. "I wanted to be left alone, with no emotional demands placed on me.

"I couldn't do that in Colorado Springs. There were too many memories. And my sister-in-law, Nelly Burgess, just won't let me be. She means well, mind you, but . . ."

With a soft sound of sympathy, Ella reached over and took Abby's hand. Crushed now between the table and her mother's bosom, Baby Mary squirmed and grumbled until Ella finally leaned back. "Maybe it's for the best that you are here," she said, never breaking her gaze. "Maybe it's meant to be, that you were sent to Culdee Creek, rather than to a household that doesn't need you as badly as this one does. And maybe it's time that you, too, begin to fill the lovesick hole inside of you."

Abby frowned in puzzlement. Then, as realization dawned as to the possible meaning of Ella's words, her cheeks flamed hot. "If you think I came here in the hopes of snaring a husband—"

"No, that's not what I mean at all, Abby." Ella laughed ruefully and shook her head. "Sometimes people can help each other. And who can better understand pain, loneliness, and confusion than someone who's experienced it themself?"

When Abby didn't respond, Ella sighed. "It was that way for Devlin and me. I met him about six months after I'd been widowed. It was at an Episcopal Church social in Grand View. He was so kind and patient with me, and it didn't hurt a bit"—she grinned—"that he was one of the best looking men around. As I got to know Devlin better, though, I discovered he had his dark side. The bottle."

Ella's admission shocked Abby. She'd met Devlin MacKay yesterday when he'd stopped by briefly, while she was moving in, to introduce himself and welcome her to Culdee Creek. Even at that first meeting, she'd had to agree that he was indeed—after Conor MacKay, of course—one of the best looking men around.

Though nearly as tall as his boss, Culdee Creek's foreman carried a few more pounds of muscled bulk. His face was craggier, his nose had been broken, and his hands were broad, with short fingers. A working man's hands, her father would have said.

Devlin MacKay's eyes were a rich, warm brown, his gaze open and friendly. His dark brown hair was thick and wavy. A long, lush mustache graced his upper lip, dipping well past the corners of his mouth. It lent him, Abby had to admit, a certain look not unlike some desperado. But, as soon as he threw back his head and laughed, the sinister impression was immediately dispelled.

Charming desperado that he might seem, Devlin was a far less intimidating man than Conor MacKay could ever hope to be.

"What did you do? About his drinking, I mean?" Abby prodded, Ella's startling revelation stirring her interest.

"He'd just lost his father, Conor's father's younger brother. I tried to be there for him, to listen and care. I guess, in the end, we helped each other. As we fell in love, we both found the strength to overcome most of our failings. Overcome them for the sake of the other."

"I'm happy for you," Abby muttered, suddenly and unaccountably jealous. If only Thomas had been willing to do that for her–a pat on the hand and chaste kiss on the cheek weren't always what a wife needed most from a husband, especially when times got rough. "It doesn't work that way for all of us, though."

"It doesn't always work for us, either." Ella looked down at her mug and began to swirl its contents. "Devlin and I have our problems. He still drinks sometimes when things between us go sour." She lifted her gaze. "But I know he loves me, and he keeps trying. I have to love him back for that. Love him, and trust that everything will eventually be as it's meant to be."

A deep sadness darkened Ella's brown eyes. Yet intermingled with that was a peace and joy. Her new friend had had her share of pain and suffering, Abby realized, but she hadn't let it defeat her, or send her running. It hadn't shriveled her soul.

Shame flooded Abby. She had lost much, in the death of her son and husband. She'd lost family, a sense of her place and purpose on this earth, and all her hopes and dreams for the future. The very underpinnings of her life had been wrenched from beneath her. But these weren't reasons to give up. These weren't reasons, but still the way back sometimes seemed next to impossible.

Abby took a deep draught of her cooled tea. The brew was strong and aromatic, tasting of lavender and rich black tealeaves. From across the table, little Mary gurgled happily, then smacked her lips.

Once more that sharp, bittersweet pain lanced through her. Unbidden, a scene flashed across her mind–of newly born baby Joshua, so sweet, so soft, so warm and cuddly!

With an effort, Abby looked up. "I'm trying, Ella," she said, her words low but impassioned. "I want to do right by Beth and Mr. MacKay. I want to do right by myself, too. It's just that I don't know which path to take, or how to journey anymore."

"Give it time, Abby, and trust in the Lord."

She managed a sad, tremulous smile. "Ah, yes. The Lord. He's always with me."

"Yes, He is. Trust in Him, and never stop loving. Do that no matter what, even if you can't manage anything else right now."

Once more, Abby's eyes filled with tears. Though Ella spoke the words now to comfort her, she also knew Ella believed them with all her heart. Believed them, and lived them in her own life, through all the times of happiness and sorrow.

The realization comforted Abby, stirred a tiny spark of hope. Surely if Ella could endure, so could she.

Trust . . . and never stop loving.

"I'll try, Ella," Abby whispered. "I'll try."

As directed by her father, later that afternoon Beth came down to begin her lessons. Clutching a tattered, cloth doll, she flung herself into one of the kitchen chairs and glowered at Abby from across the table. "I'm here because Papa told me to come," she poutingly informed her, "but you can't make me learn."

Abby looked up from one of Conor MacKay's shirts she was ironing. So far, the day had been windy but reasonably warm. The first load of laundry she had hung out by mid-morning, though still damp, was now dry enough to iron.

Her gaze snagged on the dirty doll with the formless, ragged sack dress. How much Beth was like that little doll, she thought. Wide-eyed, disheveled, and hungry for love yet so disagreeable in manner and appearance.

"No, Beth, I can't make you do anything," Abby agreed softly. "Your papa, though, wishes for you to do your lessons, and I'm most willing to teach you."

"I don't like you!"

Abby set the iron back on the stove to reheat, then walked around the ironing board and took a seat opposite Beth at the table. Resting her arms on the cloth-covered surface, she met the girl's hostile glare. "Believe me, Beth. I quite understand that."

Abby's heart went out to the child. It must be so hard to accept a stranger into the house, gradually come to accept her, only to have her leave. Surely someone as young as she was could only interpret that, after a time, as a personal rejection.

Thanks to her talk earlier with Ella, Abby saw now how foolish and self-defeating had been her own intent to distance herself. Indeed, how much different would she be than any of the others? After all, she, too, meant to leave the MacKays sooner or later. How would *her* eventual departure affect Beth?

Maybe it was best if Beth never came to like her. Maybe it was kinder not to try and make friends. Yet even the fleeting consideration of hardening her heart was more than Abby could bear.

She sighed. Why couldn't life ever be simple, or easy?

"I'd get mighty tired myself if some woman was always moving in, taking over and telling me what to do, not to mention changing everything I was used to." Abby smiled in gentle sympathy. "And then, to top it off," she added with a teasing grin, "if that woman couldn't even cook very well . . ."

"Your flapjacks were passable," Beth admitted grudgingly. "But you almost burned Cousin Ella's leftover stew for lunch. And if you're not careful, you might burn that bread you're baking."

"Yes, I just might." Abby leaned back and shot a wary glance in the direction of Old Bess. She inhaled deeply of the mouth-watering aroma of baking bread, suddenly, surprisingly content.

This morning's fiasco aside, the big cookstove now appeared to be cooperating nicely. In the meantime, she thought with some relief, she and Beth were managing to have an actual conversation, as guarded and edgy as it might be. That, Abby decided, was a victory for the both of them.

"Hopefully, though," she forged on, seeking some common ground, "you might be willing to help me with Old Bess. I imagine your papa will be very hungry after working all afternoon. I'd hate for him to go hungry just because of my inexperience."

For a long moment Beth eyed her, her gaze inscrutable. Then she looked down and began drawing imaginary pictures on the blue- and white-checkered, cotton tablecloth. "If Papa went hungry, he wouldn't be very pleased with you, would he?"

Abby's fledgling hope that they were beginning to make some headway vanished. "No, he wouldn't be pleased with me," she answered, well aware she could be playing right into any plans the little girl might have to sabotage her. "But I don't want that to happen. It wouldn't be fair to your papa. He has enough on his mind, without coming home to a poorly cooked meal, messy house, and two squabbling females. I know I don't intend to make his day any harder."

Beth nodded, never lifting her gaze from the table. "You would lose your job then, wouldn't you?"

"Yes, Beth, that's certainly a possibility." Abby paused, waiting until the girl's curiosity finally got the better of her. "Can't you at least give me a chance?" she then asked. "Your papa seems willing to do so."

Angry tears sprang to Beth's eyes. "My papa's desperate. I'm not. Besides, your being here isn't going to turn out any better than the others. Nobody wants to be around me for very long!"

It took all Abby could do not to rise, hurry around the table, and take the girl into her arms. Ah, Lord, she thought, the poor child. How could anyone have been so cruel, or treated her so unfeelingly?

Instead, though, sensing that Beth's innate wariness and animosity would prevent any such overtures of comfort from being well received, Abby forced herself to remain where she was. "You can't know that about me, Beth," she cried, not able to contain her frustration. "Why can't you just give me a chance?"

"Because I don't want to, that's why!" Beth's little body began to tremble, and tears rolled down her cheeks. "You can't make me, either!"

Abby inhaled a steadying breath. This wasn't the way, she told herself. No one as wounded as Beth appeared to be was ever won over solely by fine words and good intentions. Not Beth, *or* her father.

Lord, she thought, what have you led me to, in leading me here?

Abby sighed. "Well, I suppose there's no sense belaboring this just now. Only time will prove the truth of my words."

"Hah!" Furiously, Beth swiped away her tears. "You don't know me. You've no reason to care."

"No, I don't yet know you," was Abby's simple reply, "save as the beloved child of God that you are."

With a violence that startled Abby, the girl threw down her doll, flung back her chair, and jumped to her feet. "There you go again, trying to force your know-it-all ways on us." She stomped her foot, her small body now quivering in anger. "Well, I *still* don't like you, and I sure in tarnation don't like your silly God. *Just leave me alone.* Do you hear me? Leave me alone!"

With that, Beth turned and ran sobbing from the room, leaving Abby to sit alone in the kitchen. Finally she gave another great sigh, and buried her face in her hands. "Ah, Lord," she whispered, "what am I to do? You sent me here for a reason. How am I supposed to reach this child? I don't know how to heal such pain, or even where to begin."

Charity suffereth long, and is kind.

From somewhere deep in her heart, St. Paul's beloved words filled Abby's mind. Tears sprang to her eyes.

"Thank you, Lord," she prayed, gratitude flooding her. "Once again you guide me through the dark times, showing me the way."

Abby shoved back her chair and rose. Moving to the stove, she picked up the reheated iron. Then, as she turned, she spied Beth's cloth doll lying in a heap on the table. A smile on her lips, Abby resumed her ironing, planning all the ways she might use to win a little girl's heart.

The stringing of barbed wire in the new, northwest pasture was going well. While he and Devlin worked the southern end, Wendell, Jonah, Henry, and H.C. Chapman were just as busily engaged stretching wire around the rest of the pasture. With any luck, they'd have the job done by tomorrow. Still, Conor wasn't satisfied with their progress. Something told him he was needed at the house. Something told him things weren't going well for Beth and their new housekeeper.

With a ferocity that had marked the whole day of fence stringing, Conor gripped the hammer and pounded a galvanized metal staple to anchor yet another strand of barbed wire into the fence post. Squatting, he swiftly repeated the procedure for the second, lower strand, then straightened.

"You sure seem in an all-fired hurry to get done today." His cousin's deep voice rose from down the line, where he stood beside the tackle block wire stretcher that held the barbed wire taut. "Do you think you could spare a few minutes for me to take a swig of water? Or are you in too big a hurry to get back to that new housekeeper of yours?"

Conor shot him a narrow glance. Devlin might be his best friend and closest blood relative, but he wasn't in any mood today to put up with even the most good-natured of jibes. "I'm sure she's holding up just fine," he retorted stiffly.

He threw aside his hammer and tossed the extra staples back into the leather pouch tied about his waist. Motioning toward the canteen hanging from the saddle of his big bay gelding grazing placidly nearby, Conor walked to a nearby, rotting tree stump and flung himself down. "If you're bound and determined to take a break, grab my canteen, too, will you?"

Devlin was quick to comply. Soon, both men were propped against the tree stump, hats shoved back on their heads, swilling thirstily from their canteens of lukewarm water. A gentle breeze swirled through the tall, still snow-damp grass. Clouds floated across a piercingly blue, autumn sky. The brassy honking of Canadian geese, their tight ranks flying in a flawless V formation, filled the air.

"Turned into a beautiful day, hasn't it?" Devlin asked from beside him. "There's just something special about our Colorado Indian summers, isn't there?"

69

"Suits me." Conor took another swig of his canteen, then tipped his Stetson forward until it shaded most of his face, and leaned his head back against the tree stump. "By this time of year, I'm glad the bulk of heavy outdoor labor is done. I look forward to winter."

"This has been a difficult year, hasn't it, what with you going through three housekeepers, losing Evan, and Beth finally having to leave school."

His cousin's offhand remark about his son sent a sharp pain lancing through Conor. Though seventeen-year-old Evan had run off over six months ago, even the most casual comment about him still filled Conor with a confusing mix of anger and sorrow. It was bad enough the boy had stolen every red cent Conor possessed, savings most carefully hoarded to pay off taxes and live-stock purchases. But the fact his son had turned his back on him, just like Evan's mother had done, rankled even more deeply. Conor didn't like to fail, and it was common opinion that he'd failed with Evan.

"I've been through better times, and that's for sure," he muttered through clenched teeth, then banished further thoughts of his backstabbing, ungrateful son from his mind.

Devlin lifted his canteen in a toast. "Well, here's to your new housekeeper. May she be the answer to all your problems."

Conor cast him a sour look. "And exactly what's that supposed to mean?"

Devlin shrugged. "Ella said she seems right nice, and the eyeful I got of her yesterday . . . well, let's just say she's a mighty pretty lady."

"I hired her to clean my house, cook the meals, and tutor Beth," Conor growled. He recapped his canteen. "I doubt she even realizes how pretty she is. She certainly doesn't know the first thing about how to attract a man."

Devlin frowned. "I thought you said she was a widow woman?"

"She is."

"Then it seems to me that she's attracted at least one man."

For some reason Conor didn't particularly like being reminded of that. He gave a derisive snort. "Tolerated is more like it." He didn't fool Devlin, though. Devlin knew him better than anybody.

"Sounds to me like you've given a bit of thought," his cousin observed with a sly grin, "to how attractive she is."

Conor rolled his eyes in defeat, then grinned. "I'm not blind. And I'm certainly not dead."

"First impressions and all, she seems a much finer lady than the other women you've had work for you." Devlin's smile faded. "Take Maudie for instance. That one sure took the prize for low morals and pure meanness. Even heard talk that, before she moseyed out to these parts, she'd worked the cribs of Cripple Creek."

Conor stared straight ahead. "You never told me that story," he finally ground out. "It explains a lot."

"Soiled dove or not, she sure reeled you in like a big, fat fish."

Conor fought to keep a tight rein on his temper. "She all but threw herself at me."

Devlin laughed. "Could anyone blame her? She wasn't the first woman to set her sights on some prosperous rancher. She was just more practiced and persistent, that's all. She was also smart enough to figure the way to your heart was through your bed."

"Warming my bed was about all she was good for," Conor muttered. "Maudie was a slovenly housekeeper, and she never did get the hang of Old Bess." He shook his head. "I lost count of all the meals she burnt."

71

"When the wind was just right," Devlin laughed, "Ella and I could sure smell those burnt suppers. Whooee . . . what a stench!"

A wry chuckle escaped Conor, before other, more painful memories intruded. "She hurt Beth, you know? That's the reason I finally let her go. It wasn't her loose ways. It was because she used Beth in the hopes of getting to me."

"Poor little kid. I didn't know."

"I'm not in the habit of sniveling about my woes every time I'm disappointed by someone. You know that."

"Yeah, and I also know that you keep too much to yourself, Conor."

"I knew how to deal with Maudie. I didn't need your help."

"No, I guess you didn't." Devlin recapped his canteen and slung it over his shoulder. "Shouldn't we be finishing up that last run of wire? Looks like there's only another hour or so until sunset."

Conor shoved to his feet, his canteen clenched in his hand. "Yeah, let's get back to work. Something tells me I'm going to have a pair of irate females on my hands when I head back to the house."

A dark brow arched in inquiry. "Beth not taking to your new housekeeper?"

"Can you blame her, after what she's been through?"

His cousin met his steely gaze. "Have you ever thought it might be time to find another wife, Conor? A good woman who'd make Culdee Creek a real home for both you and Beth? A woman who'd offer some stability and permanence?"

"And what brought this little sermon on? Ella already putting ideas about me and Abigail Stanton into your head?" He shook his head in disgust. "The woman's only been here a day!"

"She seems a decent sort. You could do a lot worse."

72

Conor shot Devlin a black look. "And how many times have I told you I'll never get married again?"

"A man needs a woman."

"There's only one way I need a woman anymore, and there's plenty of those just outside Grand View. You know that about as well as I, don't you, Devlin?"

Devlin's brown eyes flashed in anger. "You gonna throw that in my face again?"

For an instant, Conor glared back at him, a scathing reply on his lips. Then shame that he'd used something his cousin had shared with him in confidence against him flooded him. Devlin might ride him too hard at times, but he meant well.

"I'm sorry." Conor forced a quick, apologetic smile. "You just got me riled."

"Guess I'll lay off then."

"Guess you'd better," were Conor's parting words before he turned and headed back to the fence posts and rolls of barbed wire.

5

Later that night, Abby finished stitching the last seam in the blue calico doll dress, leaned back, and yawned. She glanced at her bedside alarm clock through the cloth hangings separating her living area from her bedroom. Half past nine. It had been a long day. If she was to be up and cooking breakfast by the time Conor MacKay came down tomorrow morning, she needed to head to bed.

For an instant longer Abby turned back to the little dress, eyeing it critically. She had done a passable job with some of the scrap material she had brought with her. All it needed now to be finished was a quick hand hem of the long skirt, and a few touches of white cambric embroidered edging at the throat and ends of the long sleeves. It was a dress any little girl would be proud of.

She only hoped Beth would see it that way.

Wearily, Abby laid aside the dress, rose, and took up the oil lamp. Just then footsteps sounded outside on the little wooden platform that served as a porch. Someone paused at her door, then rapped smartly on it.

"Who's there?" she called out.

A deep voice rose from the other side of the door. "It's Conor. Conor MacKay. Could I have a few minutes of your time?"

Abby's mouth went dry. Whatever could he want that couldn't wait until tomorrow? Besides, it really wasn't proper–

"You're more than welcome to come back to the main house," he cut her off in mid-thought, apparently guessing the reason for her hesitation, "if you're so all-fired worried about propriety. Personally, I never concern myself with what others think, just as long as I know I'm doing the right thing."

Abby jerked open the door. Of all the smug, egotistical men she had ever had the misfortune of knowing, Conor MacKay certainly stood out above them all! "You, Mr. MacKay, are also a *man*," she said, glaring up at him, "and judged far less harshly for far greater misdeeds. So please, don't set such low expectations upon me, expectations that are impossible for any decent human being to uphold."

He chuckled softly and shook his head. "Are you always so snippy by this time of night? Remind me not to approach you again after dark."

There was something about this man that seemed to bring out the temper in her, a temper she thought long ago mastered. If the Christian principle of charity wasn't enough to cause shame for her fiery outburst just now, the fact that he was her employer was a sufficient reminder to curb her tongue.

"I beg your pardon, Mr. MacKay." Abby lowered her gaze. "That was rude of me. I guess it's going to take me a while to understand your sense of humor."

"No offense taken, Mrs. Stanton. I've long been accused of a mean streak when it comes to picking at sore spots. And it's quite evident what one of yours is."

75

She lifted her head, suddenly tense. "And that sore spot, Mr. MacKay?" Abby asked, poised for battle. "Pray, exactly what would that be?"

The tall rancher grinned and, in the dim lamplight, his features took on a wolfish cast. "The preservation of your precious reputation, of course. A pointless pastime, to my way of thinking, considering my good name was trampled in the mud long ago. You, however, are apparently still clinging for dear life to yours."

"There's nothing wrong with trying to maintain a good name," she said in her defense. "I'm sure there was a time when the name MacKay was one to be proud of, one that stirred respect in the hearts of all. And it could be again, if you'd take a bit more care with people."

Conor's grin faded. His eyes went dark, and his jaw tightened. "What would you know of the MacKay name and whatever it meant to folks in these parts? Have a care, Mrs. Stanton. Don't venture where you've no right to go."

He spoke true, Abby thought ruefully. Nothing was served in poking and prodding at a man like Conor MacKay.

Abby squared her shoulders. "You came here for a reason, and it was hardly one concerning my reputation, Mr. MacKay."

He took a step closer. Abby had a strange sense of being engulfed by a mysterious, dark threat. A shiver coursed through her.

She refused, however, to back away. Fists clenched, she forced herself to gaze steadily up at him, awaiting his reply.

"Can I come in?" he asked. "I'd rather not talk standing outside."

Abby hesitated, then shrugged off her qualms. She was an adult; she'd been a married woman. Surely she could deal with the likes of Conor MacKay. Besides, this bunkhouse was as much his as was any other building on the property.

"I've no intention of ravishing you, Mrs. Stanton. I thought I made that clear the day of your interview."

His blunt words wrenched Abby back from her thoughts. She felt ashamed. For all his intimidating ways and lack of tact, Conor MacKay had never been less than a gentleman.

"So you did, Mr. MacKay. So you did." Abby stepped aside and motioned him in. "Please forgive the mess." She gestured vaguely around the room. "It'll take a while longer to settle in, I'm afraid."

He glanced about him, his sharp gaze taking in the treadle-driven sewing machine, rocking chair, and open trunk still full of skirts, dresses, blouses, and neatly folded piles of white cotton chemises, petticoats, under-drawers, and an assortment of long, black and white cotton stockings. Just beyond the colorful swatches of fabric–that Abby intended eventually to turn into dresses–now hanging across the rope dividing the room, her white muslin nightgown could be seen, laid out across her downturned, brass bed.

Abby's face flooded with heat. She scooted around Conor MacKay and quickly flipped the lid of her trunk closed. Next, she hurried across the room to pull down the fabric turned back to reveal her bedchamber.

"Please, Mr. MacKay." With a curt, embarrassed motion, Abby indicated the table with its single chair. "Please, take a seat."

"No, you take the seat, Mrs. Stanton." His expression was inscrutable. "I'll just pull over the rocking chair, if that's all right with you."

Somehow his presence made the room seem suddenly close and stifling. Abby nodded and took the seat. By the time, though, that Conor MacKay had settled in the rocking chair he'd carried over to place before her, she'd managed to snatch back the scattered remnants of her composure.

"Well, Mr. MacKay," Abby began, compelled by the need to get the visit over and done with, "I don't mean to appear rude, but it is getting rather late. What did you want to talk about?"

He crossed his leg, balancing the ankle of one booted foot on his other knee, and began to rock, slowly and methodically. As the seconds ticked by he studied her until Abby thought she'd scream.

Conor could tell he was making her nervous. He continued to stare, intent on building the tension, unnerving her. It would drive home his point, when he chose to make it.

His gaze slid over her face, noting her sweet mouth, the high color that swept her cheekbones, the tender curve of her neck. Once more he had to admit it. Abigail Stanton was a most attractive woman.

She reminded him, in some ways, of Sally.

Conor's gut twisted. That was all he needed, he thought sourly. Another woman the likes of his wife.

Yet, on closer inspection, he realized his startling revelation had nothing to do with outward characteristics. The likeness ran far deeper, and it had something to do with the reason he'd first fallen in love with Sally.

Angrily, Conor shifted in the rocking chair and forced his thoughts back to the present. "What else is there to talk about?" he growled, shattering at last the brittle silence. "Beth, of course."

Abby's stomach sank with a thud. So, she thought, the little girl had wasted no time complaining to her father about today. "Exactly what about Beth did you wish to discuss?" she forced herself to ask. "I don't suppose it's a complaint that we didn't make much progress on her lessons today, is it?"

Conor scowled. "No. She wouldn't have any complaints about that." He stroked his beard-shadowed jaw, and eyed her speculatively. "It's about you and your preaching."

"Preaching?" For a long moment, Abby stared in puzzlement. "I don't recall any . . ." Gradually, the memory of her words to Beth about God's love filtered into her mind. Dear Lord, she thought in frustration. Can't I even speak of You in their house as justification for my own actions and beliefs?

"Are you referring to my comments to Beth about God loving her?" Abby tried to keep her tone neutral, her voice calm.

"Yes. Was there more said than that?"

"No." Abby leaned toward him, resting her forearms on her thighs. "And did Beth also tell you in what context I said those words?"

Conor graced her with a glacial stare, and Abby was struck with the realization of how mercurial this man could be. A few minutes ago, he had been smiling, nearly joking with her. And now . . . now he had withdrawn behind a stony countenance, a wall that she knew she'd no hope of breaching.

He lives this way to protect himself, she thought with sudden insight. He keeps people off balance and defensive, unsure of themselves around him. It gives him the upper hand.

Yet, in the doing, though he might maintain control, he paid a heavy price. He paid for it in isolation and loneliness. He paid for it by running in terror from life and living. He paid for it in the false sense of power he imagined it gave him—a power that no one save God could ever truly possess.

A soft, sad, knowing smile touched Abby's lips. It was a truth, at the very least, she'd learned when she'd lost Thomas and Joshua. There was no control in life—at least not over what really mattered. She hadn't been able to prevent Thomas's death, or to keep Joshua alive, no matter how hard she'd tried. Her sense of control, of fairness, order, and purpose, had always been nothing more than an illusion.

An illusion . . . yet truth nonetheless. It was a truth in the facing, however, that had shattered her former way of looking at life. She was, in reality, the master of nothing. And that was a truth that still, at times, terrified her.

In their desperate quest for an elusive, false sense of control, Abby realized she and Conor MacKay were probably more alike than she cared to admit.

"Well, Mr. MacKay," Abby prodded. "Did she tell you the whole story?"

He didn't move, just rocked slowly, methodically, watching her all the while. Finally, though, he spoke. "I really don't care in what context you said the words, Mrs. Stanton. You are not to speak about God in my house."

"And why is that, Mr. MacKay?" she demanded, refusing to back down. "What harm could it possibly do? You told me you don't believe in God. Yet, in refusing ever to have God's name mentioned, you act like you fear Him."

Abby cocked her head. "How can you fear someone you think doesn't exist?"

Anger flashed in his eyes. He stopped rocking. "Does it really matter, Mrs. Stanton?" he asked softly. "The rules remain the same."

In a rush of angry frustration, Abby's patience fled. "How am I to live, if you deny me the right to speak freely of the God I love?" she cried. "How am I to win Beth's trust and affection, if you forbid me the one way I know to convince her of my sincerity?"

She fell to her knees before him, and placed her hands over his. "Please, Mr. MacKay. You said I didn't have to hide my personal beliefs or their importance in my daily life. You said, 'suit yourself.'"

Gazing up at him, Abby searched for any sign of his acquiescence. He stared back, hard, unyielding.

Then something imperceptibly changed. Conor Mac-Kay's gaze slowly, languorously slid up Abby's body until it locked with hers. A chill of recognition, of woman's intuition, swamped her.

She leaned back, attempting to pull her hands from his, but he was too quick for her. His long fingers encircled her wrists, imprisoning her where she knelt. Abby's mouth went dry. Her heart began a mad pounding beneath her breast.

"Mr. M-MacKay . . . I . . ." she stammered.

"Exactly what do you want from me, Mrs. Stanton?" He leaned toward her. "I can't imagine you truly wish to bed me, yet maybe I'm wrong. Rarely do I find women on their knees to me, save in the most compromising of circumstances. Yet here you are . . .

"I must admit, though," he continued, "that you confuse me. One minute you're talking about God, and the next"—his lips lifted in a feral smile—"well, you've been married. I'm sure you understand as well as I."

His breath, redolent of fine whiskey, wafted over Abby. Her heart sank. He'd been drinking, she realized, terror surging through her. He'd been drinking and now he was here, in her room, alone, and in total command.

Total command . . .

The two words stirred deep-seated, long-buried emotions. A memory of a crisp, fall, New England day flooded her mind. She saw her and her father walking through the leaf-carpeted forest near their home and heard, once more, his voice, firm but patient, explaining why she wouldn't be going to college.

"Your place is at the side of a good, God-fearing man," he said. "Only there can you serve the Lord as He truly wishes you to serve Him."

Abby had stopped then, her heart pounding, the blood rushing deafeningly in her ears, and clutched her father's arm. "There are other ways besides marriage to serve the Lord, Papa. I can teach. You always said I had a gift for teaching. And it's not as if I never want to marry. I just want to do other things first, like go to college."

"You don't need a college degree to teach in the mission Thomas wishes to set up, once you and he arrive out West." As if explaining this to a child, her father smiled benignly. "You don't need a college degree to teach the children you will have with him. And surely there will be opportunities aplenty to teach your friends and neighbors, wherever you live, college degree or no. All that truly matters, in the end, is serving the Lord."

But it wasn't the way *she* wished to serve Him, Abby had thought that autumn day now over seven years ago. Neither her father nor Thomas, though, had ever considered, much less asked, what she wanted when it came to serving God. Indeed, they hadn't ever seen the need to. They'd always imagined they knew what she needed far better than she.

With a bitter, resolute shake of her head, Abby forced herself back to the present. Her gaze focused on Conor MacKay's handsome face and slammed into the lustful, predatory gleam in his eyes.

Resentment, followed swiftly by rage, swelled, engulfing her earlier fear. Never again, she vowed silently, glaring back at him. Never again would she allow a man to control her, use her, and expect her to deny her own selfhood.

With a strength fueled by her anger, Abby jerked free and struggled to her feet. "I want nothing from you, Mr. MacKay," she cried, hoarse with emotion but wildly defiant. "Nothing except to be treated with respect and allowed the freedom to live as I believe. I'm sorry that you interpret every overture by a woman, however honest, as some pretense to seduce you. But that is your problem, Mr. MacKay, not mine."

"So am I to take this little tirade as a sign then, that you're rejecting my offer?"

Abby gaped at him. She couldn't believe what she was hearing. The sheer arrogance of the man! No wonder he couldn't keep a housekeeper for long.

In a dizzying rush, exhaustion suddenly overwhelmed her. This was too much to deal with, especially tonight. "I think, Mr. MacKay"–Abby gave a weary sigh and shake of her head–"it's best you leave. I'm too tired, and you've been drinking. Neither of us is clearheaded enough to settle this right now."

With a fluid contraction and relaxation of powerful muscles, the big rancher rose. This time, Abby stepped back.

"I may have been drinking," he said, his voice gone low and intense, "but I'm most certainly not drunk. I never get drunk. Just don't imagine for a minute that we're done with this issue of God."

Conor MacKay slipped past her and headed for the door. He halted when he reached it. "We're far from done, Mrs. Stanton," he said, his voice dropping to nearly a whisper, as he glanced over his shoulder at her, "if, after tonight, you've even the stomach left to stay."

Abby spent a restless night, tossing and turning, her thoughts harking back to Conor MacKay's visit. He had issued an incontrovertible challenge when he'd demanded that she not speak of God in his house. That agreement had at first seemed easy to uphold. But now Abby wasn't so certain she could fulfill her part of the bargain. The love of the Lord and His service was her life. Though she thought she could refrain from openly proselytizing in the MacKay household, Abby didn't know how she could keep from ever speaking about God.

Still, if those were Conor MacKay's terms, then those were his terms. She must either abide by them, or leave.

But to leave . . . Abby turned onto her back and stared at the ceiling. What purpose would that serve? There would always be difficulties to overcome, compromises to be made, no matter where she went. Abby realized that this was part and parcel of life.

As difficult as it would be to work for the MacKays, she sensed there was a need, a hunger here, and it was a need and hunger that equaled her own. In their own way, Conor and Beth weren't so very different from her. Perhaps she could, as Ella had said, be of some help to them just because she, too, had been through such terrible pain, confusion, and loneliness. And perhaps, just perhaps, they could also help her.

Abby rolled over, punched her pillow back into shape, then clasped it to her. Conor MacKay had been unsettling enough before this awful visit. Tonight he had also become a threat. Somehow he had turned predator, and she had become his prey.

Thank the Lord he appeared to be a man who could hold his liquor. Though he seemed not to think too highly of women, he still possessed some shred of honor. Otherwise . . . Abby shivered and squeezed her pillow even tighter.

While she didn't want to admit it, something new was beginning to surface in her. Ever so slowly through the night, thoughts of him as a man nudged their way into her consiousness. She was strangely, inexplicably drawn to Conor MacKay. He angered and frustrated her, yet she found herself wanting to reach out, to hold him, to ease the anguish burning deep in his eyes. She wanted to make him laugh, smile. And, bewildering as it was to contemplate, Abby also wanted him to touch her, hold her, kiss her.

When it came to Conor MacKay, she was beginning to realize she was like a moth drawn to a flame.

But a moth could singe its wings by hovering too close to such scorching power. Indeed, the fire that attracted could well destroy . . . separating her from all she held dear.

In the end, that was what she feared most about Conor MacKay—and why she fought so hard against his strictures regarding the Lord. Shoving up in bed, she pressed her pillow to her. Her heart racing with a trip hammer beat, she faced the awful truth.

Conor MacKay was temptation personified. She was drawn so strongly, so forcefully to him that she might well endanger her immortal soul if she followed where he led.

It had never been his demands that she cease speaking of God in his house, Abby realized with a sudden, piercing insight. She could carry the Lord in her heart no matter where she went or with whom she spoke. She could live with Conor MacKay's strictures, however unreasonable she found them to be. He could never separate her from the Lord with but a few rules.

But there *was* the danger of him separating her from her faith, if she permitted this attraction to him to over-shadow her adherence to the Lord's ways. Conor MacKay's sordid past had obviously robbed him of any moral conscience, and a man without a moral conscience might stoop to anything. Wasn't she, by allow-ing this attraction for him to persist, turning her back on her own morals and conscience?

She must have a care, Abby decided. He was a lost soul, a man seemingly bereft of hope or happiness. Whether he intended to or not, he had the power to pull her down with him into that pit of godless despair.

That was the reason she might eventually have to leave, if a reason must someday be given. But it was not a reason to give just yet. The Lord had wished for her to accept this housekeeping position. She must do her very best to carry out those wishes until her work here was done. Besides, if Culdee Creek's owner could agree to maintain a respectful, platonic relationship from here on out, then this temptation might easily be faced and overcome.

She was in no mood, however, to be belittled and treated like a child ever again. But then, the doubts crept anew into her heart. She'd already failed twice before, first in trying to convince her father, then Thomas. Neither had ever seen her as an individual with her own thoughts and goals. To them she'd always been some dear possession who needed to be cared for.

Abby greatly feared that it wouldn't be any easier to convince Conor MacKay to the contrary, than it had been them.

ċ

With a strange mixture of dread and anticipation at seeing Abigail Stanton again, Conor came down the stairs the next morning. After what had transpired between them last night, he'd lain awake for several hours wondering what her reaction to him would be this morning. Most likely, Conor told himself, it would be one of revulsion. Most likely, she'd also promptly tender him her resignation.

It would be a new record for him, having a housekeeper quit after just one day of work. If it had been any of the others, he could have laughed it off, then been the first one to carry her bags to the buckboard. But this resignation would somehow be a loss. He had not been fair, and Conor prided himself, if in nothing else, in being fair.

There was just something about the little brown-haired widow that scared him. She was pretty enough, and nicely rounded in all the right places, but he had seen prettier women. Besides, her prim and proper bearing should have been more than enough to send him running in the opposite direction.

No, Conor decided as he drew up in the hallway outside the kitchen to finish buttoning his shirt cuffs and buckling his belt. Though his attraction to Abigail Stanton lacked logic, it was not the source of his fear. The satisfaction of his physical needs frequently lacked much logic, and he liked it that way. If his head wasn't involved, neither was his heart.

No, this had more to do with her religious obsession. She was a feisty, obstinate woman. If last night was any indication, she apparently wasn't one to give up on something she believed in. That trait, in itself, was admirable. But when it was focused on God . . .

He didn't like God. If the truth were told, Conor hated Him. She'd struck closer to the mark than she realized, when she had mentioned the inconsistency of his unbelief. Conor knew, as well as she, his rabid insistence that no words be spoken of a being he didn't even believe in made little sense.

It especially made little sense, when he *did* believe in God. He couldn't help but believe . . .

Tugged along against his will, Conor's thoughts drifted back to a time now long ago, when he was eight. It had been a warm September day, and he and his mother had decided to take his religious lessons outside, where they'd sat in the shade of a tall cottonwood tree that grew beside their house. Between bites of a freshly picked plum, Conor had endeavored to answer his mother's questions regarding the Ten Commandments.

"Now, Conor, lad," Margaret MacKay had said, "tell me. What is the first commandment?"

After swallowing the last bite of plum, Conor had paused to pitch the pit as far down the hill as he could. "The first commandment," he replied, "is 'I am the Lord thy God which have brought thee out of the land of Egypt, out of the house of bondage. Thou shalt have no other gods before me.'"

"And what is commanded by the first commandment, laddie?"

Conor pursed his lips and furrowed his brow in thought. "I guess, Mama, that it means we must see God as the one, true God and love Him with our whole heart."

Margaret nodded in approval. "And what of our fellow man? He was created to glorify God forever in heaven. Should we not love our fellow man as well?"

"If you say so, Mama."

"If ye say so?" Horror threading his voice, Robbie MacKay stalked over from where he'd been tying up his horse. He came to stand before his son, his hands balled, his shoulders rigid. "There's no guessing or saying so," he snarled. "Ye either know yer catechism, or ye don't. Now which is it?"

A cold chill ran through Conor. His father had been drinking again—he could smell the whiskey on his breath—and had that mean look about him. He didn't like his father much when he'd been drinking.

"Robbie, don't loom over the boy so," Margaret pleaded, her face taking on a thin, pinched expression. "He'll surely forget all that he's learned if you—"

"He either knows it, or he doesn't!" Her husband leaned down and grabbed Conor by the front of his shirt, lifting him to his feet. "Now, which is it, boy?" He gave Conor a shake. "Should we not love our fellow man as well?"

"Y-yes, Pa," Conor whispered. "We should love our fellow man. And that is why we must, out of love for God, love and help our neighbor. And when he has done wrong to us, we must forgive him and not render evil for evil."

His father's eyes bored into him. For a panic-stricken moment, Conor thought he'd spoken wrong. Then, with a grunt, Robbie MacKay released him. Conor fell backward, losing his balance, and plummeted to the ground. Immediately, he picked himself up, but averted his gaze from his father.

"Just see that ye hold that impertinent tongue of yers from here on out," Robbie said, his voice beginning to slur. "And mind yer catechism, and mind it well, or I'll take ye out behind the woodshed and beat it into ye."

"Yes, Pa."

Robbie turned then and staggered away. Margaret rushed over to Conor and began to dust the dirt and bits of grass off his trousers. "He didn't mean aught by it, lad," she crooned. "He just wants you to love the Lord as much as he loves Him."

Conor stared at the back of his retreating father, his emotions roiling in a confusing tumult of pain, anger, and shame. Yet, though he nodded his acknowledgment of his mother's words, he wasn't so sure he believed them. Indeed, he hadn't believed in a long while now that his father loved God, or that God loved him.

From that day forward, though, Conor had memorized his religion lessons until he could spout page and paragraph. He probably still could, he thought with grim irony, and with only the most minimal of promptings. His father had, at the very least, seen to that.

But, though Conor had continued to practice his faith even after his father's death, that doctrinal knowledge had never particularly endeared him to God. After all, what had God ever done for him? Not much, Conor thought sourly, save take away nearly everyone he had ever come to love.

No, admitting to a belief in and need for God gave God power over the believer, he reminded himself as he squared his shoulders and strode into the kitchen. Placing any hope in that belief was also frustrating, humiliating, and disappointing. It was a can of worms best left undisturbed.

He certainly didn't need some big-hearted little busybody stirring up issues long and safely buried, Conor added grimly as Abigail Stanton, dressed in a bright green calico dress that set off her dark hair perfectly, glanced up from the stove. But then he also wasn't so sure, noting the becoming flush that reddened her cheeks as she caught sight of him, that he wanted to run off this particular, big-hearted little busybody. At least not, he quickly amended that thought, any sooner than he had any of the rest.

6

He hath sent me to heal the brokenhearted, to preach deliverance to the captives.

Luke 4:18

Abby had thought she was ready to face Conor MacKay, but one look at him as he walked into the kitchen the next morning was enough to send her carefully rehearsed speech spiraling into the cosmos. Though circles smudged the skin beneath his eyes, and his lips were drawn in a forbidding line, he was freshly shaven and dressed in his usual boots, blue denims, and a red plaid shirt that complemented his ebony hair. He looked, to Abby, strong and self-assured. He also looked like a man intent upon a mission, and determined to achieve it.

She turned back to the pan of bacon she was frying, hoping her employer would mistake the hot blood flooding her cheeks for the cookstove's heat. As potent a temptation as Conor MacKay remained, Abby did not care to pick up where they had left off last night.

He came to stand beside her. Seconds ticked by but he said nothing, did nothing, save stare at her. Abby's pulse quickened. The breath squeezed from her lungs, and the hand holding the fork turning the bacon began to tremble.

Anger at her cowardice filled her. Oh, blast him, she thought. He only does this to unnerve me. Abby shot him a furious glance. He looked back, a solemn, thoughtful light in his eyes.

"Is there something I can do for you, Mr. MacKay?" she demanded, realizing she was even more uncomfortable with him now than she had ever been before.

He opened his mouth as if to speak. Then, suddenly he shook his head. "Is the coffee ready?"

"Yes, it is."

Taking up a dishtowel, Conor grabbed the coffeepot sitting on the back burner and carried it to the table. Abby didn't dare peek over her shoulder. She began forking slices of crisply cooked bacon from the pan, easily envisioning his actions: placing the pot on the table's little sunflower-shaped trivet, then walking away; the clink of pottery mugs banging together as they were being taken down from the cupboard.

"Would you like some coffee, Mrs. Stanton?"

Abby pulled the last slice of bacon from the pan and placed it on the plate. She shook her head. "No, thank you. I'm about ready to begin frying the eggs. I'll wait until I sit down to breakfast to have coffee."

"Why don't you put that plate of bacon in the warming oven instead"–Conor MacKay poured out first one, then another mug of coffee–"and come sit down? Breakfast can wait a few minutes. Beth's just beginning to stir. She won't be down for another ten or fifteen minutes. We've some unfinished business to settle."

"Really, Mr. MacKay,"–she wheeled around to face him–"I don't think this is the proper time or place–"

"It is if I say it is, Mrs. Stanton," he cut her off. "This is still my house, and you are my employee, are you not?"

It was all Abby could do to choke back a tart response about what he could do with his job. As much as she

92

hated to admit it, though, he was right. It was his house, and she had agreed to be his employee.

"Fine. Whatever you say." Abby turned back to the plate of bacon, picked it up and, flinging open the warming oven door, shoved the plate inside. She resisted, however, the urge to slam the oven door shut.

Conor MacKay pulled out her chair and motioned for her to sit. As she did, he walked around to the head of the table and took his own seat.

"First," he finally said, "I want to apologize about my less than gentlemanly conduct last evening. I should've never come to you in such an inebriated state."

Embarrassed, Abby made a motion of dismissal. "It was as much my fault as yours, Mr. MacKay. I should've never gone down on my knees to you or touched you. It won't happen again."

He leaned forward, gripping his mug. "I think, Mrs. Stanton, that your actions were far more innocently intended than mine. It was I who chose to interpret them in the wrong light."

Abby could not bear to meet the intensity of his gaze. "All I ask is that you not make the same mistake again, Mr. MacKay." She found sudden interest in her coffee. "If such an incident occurs again, I'll be compelled immediately to tender my resignation." She forced herself to look up. "I came to do a job, Mr. MacKay, not warm your bed or win you as a husband. If you'll forgive my bluntness, you are hardly the kind of man I'd care ever do either with."

He leaned back, eyed her quizzically, then laughed. "Well, I suppose I've just been set straight. Come, come, Mrs. Stanton, don't hold back now. Tell me your *true* feelings about me."

Abby frowned, confused by his sudden change in mood. "Really, Mr. MacKay, I don't see the humor in this. I told you the truth in an effort to ease the misunderstanding of last night. And those are my true feelings." Or at least all you'll ever know, she silently added. If you were to guess the complete truth . . .

The consideration of what a man like Conor MacKay might do if he realized the extent of her attraction to him was beyond comprehension. It was also a sure road to ruination.

Her nerves more rattled than she cared to admit, Abby took a sip of her coffee. "Since we seem to have that issue settled," she then said, deciding it the wisest course to change the topic, "I just want you to know I won't say another word to you or Beth about God. That is," she hastened to add, "unless you decide to bring up the subject."

He cocked his head and studied her gravely. "That's quite a concession for you, isn't it, Mrs. Stanton?"

"Yes, Mr. MacKay, it is. But I gave you my word, and I'll stick by it. All I ask in return is that you permit me to worship the Lord as I see fit."

"Does that include going to church on Sundays?"

Abby sucked in a breath. Oh, how she longed to keep holy the Sabbath! "I'd dearly love to attend church every Sunday, Mr. MacKay, but I've agreed to your terms of only one day off a month. If you don't mind, though, I'd at least like to make that one day a Sunday."

He took a deep swig from his mug, then set it down. "Has anyone ever told you that you make a fine cup of coffee, Mrs. Stanton?"

"No, but I thank you for the compliment." Abby paused. "Now about that day off, Mr. MacKay . . ."

He shrugged. "Sure. Whatever you like. Take it as a Sunday. It's a better day than during the week anyway. In fact, as long as your work's done, you can have every Sunday morning off, too, in case you want to go to church in Grand View. It's a good half-hour buggy ride there, but I'm sure you can hitch a ride with Ella and Devlin. They attend the Episcopal Church there. Not that," he added with a wry grin, "Devlin's all that taken with church going. He only does it to please Ella and set an example for the children."

Abby stared, flabbergasted. Conor MacKay was giving her extra time off to attend church? She couldn't believe her ears. Even if it wasn't a church like the one she was raised in by her Methodist minister father, she was sure her father would have given his blessing. And there had never been any doubt in Abby's mind that her Father in heaven would understand.

"That's most generous of you, Mr. MacKay," she murmured, too shocked and pleased to be able to say more.

"You were willing to compromise something of great importance to you, in order to give me something equally important to me. Despite what you may have heard to the contrary, I am a fair man."

"I assure you. I've never heard anything to contradict that."

"Haven't you?" Conor gave a disbelieving snort. "Well, it doesn't matter." He shoved back his chair and stood.

"A moment more, Mr. MacKay."

"Yes?" He arched a dark brow, then softened it with a smile.

For a fleeting instant, Abby hesitated. She was loath to threaten the pleasant sense of fellowship that had formed between them in the past few minutes, but the issue of Beth was yet unresolved. The little girl, however, would remain a bone of contention between them, Abby feared, until she was able to develop some sort of positive relationship with her. But to do that, she needed to know exactly what obstacles that relationship was up against.

She lifted her chin and stared Conor MacKay straight in the eyes. "It's about Beth. I need your help."

Conor's smile faded. A wary look shuttered his gaze. "What about her?"

"She's so guarded and suspicious of me. It's going to be difficult to make much headway in her lessons as long as there's such a barrier between us."

"What do you want me to do?"

Amusement filled Abby. Beth wasn't the only one guarded and suspicious of her. Abby knew she must venture slowly and carefully.

"I don't mean to pry," she began with as much tact as she could muster, "but if you could share some reasons for her animosity toward me . . . well, perhaps it might provide some valuable insights."

Cool, gray-blue eyes regarded her dispassionately. "Neither Beth nor I are ones to snivel when life treats us unfairly. And we certainly don't want anyone's pity."

"Pity!" Abby rolled her eyes. "I think you confuse pity with caring and compassion. I'm not asking for you to snivel, just help me understand Beth better so I can help her." She shoved her mug aside and leaned toward him. "She needs a woman's influence in her life, Mr. MacKay. She needs to learn that she's worthwhile, beautiful, and intelligent."

"Are you implying I don't make her feel that way? That I've failed miserably as her father?"

Abby froze. Now I've really done it, she thought. "No, no." She shook her head vehemently. "That's not at *all* what I meant. It's evident that Beth adores you, and you, her. But she needs more than just what one person can give her—even if that person is her father—if she's to heal that wounded little heart of hers."

"So you're offering to help heal, is that it?" Like a storm on the horizon, Conor MacKay's expression darkened ominously. "Have a care, Mrs. Stanton. You risk much in daring to draw too close to my daughter."

"As much as you risk, in daring to trust me to do it, Mr. MacKay?"

96

A hard, angry look flared in his eyes. "Forgive me if I've somehow stumbled off the path of this conversation," he said, "but I thought Beth was the topic."

"She was," Abby tossed back at him, realizing she was now so embroiled in their renewed battle there was little sense in mincing words. "But it always comes back to you, doesn't it?"

"How so, Mrs. Stanton?"

Something in the tone of his voice warned her that only a fool would tread down that road, but Abby no longer cared. Sooner or later, this father needed to recognize the damage his mistrust and repugnance for others had wrought upon his daughter. His anger and purposeful isolation would ultimately embitter and shrivel not only his soul, but Beth's as well.

As it would anyone who turned from life, Abby realized with a sudden insight, whether from fear, or hurt, or disappointment. As it would with her, if she purposely avoided the path the Lord had so long ago set her upon.

"She needs you to set the example of how to deal with life, Mr. MacKay," Abby said, fired now with a conviction that encompassed them both. "It is your example she'll follow the rest of her days, as you most likely followed your parents. Do you truly want your influence to be one of mistrust, of loathing for her fellow man?"

"Who are you, to lecture me about how I raise my daughter?" he demanded furiously, his broad shoulders gone rigid, his fists clenched at his side.

"No one, Mr. MacKay," Abby replied softly. "I'm no one to you, but it seems there's no other person who dares to tell you, or warn you before it's too late."

Abby extended her hand to him across the table, then caught herself. Realizing it was too late to withdraw it, she slowly fisted her hand instead. "I don't say this to judge you, truly I don't. How can I judge you? I can't begin to know what pain and sorrow life has brought to you. I can't even look into your heart, save to catch a glimpse of the love you bear for your daughter."

He stepped back in rejection of her gesture. "No, you can't." Conor MacKay's voice went hoarse with emotion, "and never will. No one ever will again!"

At the vehement intensity of his words, a deep, aching sadness filled Abby. Ah, his pain, his pain. It was almost past bearing. "Don't you mean no *woman*, Mr. MacKay?"

"That's right." He spat out the words as if they were vile to his tongue. "No woman."

Ethel gave a loud bawl, kicked over the half-filled milk pail, then flung her tail around to hit Conor squarely in the face. With a bellow of surprise, the rancher toppled off the milking stool, falling backward into a moldering pile of soiled straw. Unrepentant, the Jersey cow next turned to scrutinize him, a look of mild reproach in her big brown eyes. Then, ever so calmly, she resumed feeding from the hayrack.

"Okay, okay." Conor climbed to his feet, and dusted off as much of the dung and straw that he could reach. "Maybe I was a bit rough milking. But I couldn't expect you to understand, could I? One way or another, you females all back each other."

"Talking to cows now, are you?"

Conor wheeled around. There in the barn's doorway stood his cousin, a quizzical smile on his lips.

"Is there something I can do for you?" he growled, not in the mood for any more conversation after the one he'd just finished with Abigail Stanton. "If not, I've got a half-milked cow to finish."

With the greatest solemnity, Devlin surveyed the overturned bucket and soaked floor. He couldn't quite hide the smile, however, that tugged at one corner of his mustachioed mouth. "Looks to me like you wasted a good bit of the milk already. Was that your or Ethel's doing?"

The absurdity of the situation finally struck Conor. He heaved a great sigh, shoved a hand roughly through his hair, then grinned. "Ethel kicked over the bucket, but I first had to irritate her, what with my less than gentle handling."

"I've never known you to mistreat an animal." His cousin frowned. "What's eating you, Conor?"

"Nothing that a certain housekeeper couldn't set right by learning to keep her mouth shut," he muttered. "And I wasn't mistreating Ethel. I was just a bit too heavy-handed."

He bent and righted the milking stool, then pulled the bucket once more beneath the cow's bulging udder. With a slow, expert motion of both hands, Conor pulled down alternately on a teat, squeezing out a thin stream of milk. Soon he once again had a good rhythm going. The milk, hitting the metal pail, made harsh *fffit-fffit* sounds.

"So, Mrs. Stanton's already causing problems, is she?" Devlin queried gravely.

"She's gotten it into her head to lecture me about how to raise Beth." Conor shot Devlin a furious glance. "Been here all of two days, and already she thinks she has everything figured out."

"That you're not a good father, you mean?"

"Well, she didn't come right out and say that. She just lectured me about setting a good example for Beth. Then she began nosing around about why Beth doesn't cotton much to strangers anymore."

"Why should she care? All she was hired for was to cook and clean, not gather more dirt for the local gossips."

The milk stream from Ethel's teats slackened, and Conor switched to the other two. "That wasn't her intent. She claimed to want to understand Beth better."

His tall cousin moved to stand beside him, then squatted, meeting Conor eye to eye. "Well, where's the harm in that?"

"It's our business—Beth's and mine—and I already told you I don't want her nosing around."

"There's more to it than that, Conor, and you know it. She's starting to get under your skin, isn't she?" Devlin slapped his thigh in glee. "I knew it, I knew it!"

"What you think you know doesn't amount to a hill of beans," Conor snarled. He pulled the milk pail aside, shoved back his stool, and stood. "She just prods and pokes too much. And I don't like it."

Devlin straightened. "Well, women do that. It's their calling in life. They prod and poke until they get us rearranged just the way they want us."

"That's a married man's lot, not mine." Conor picked up the milk bucket. "I won't stand for it."

"It's really not all that bad." Devlin chuckled. "It's a small price to pay most of the time, for all the comforts you get in return."

"I thought you'd sworn off of pestering me about marriage."

His cousin's mouth dropped, then he grinned sheepishly. "I did, didn't I?"

"Yeah, you did."

Devlin shoved his Stetson back on his head. "I still think you're being too hard on Mrs. Stanton. She seems a decent sort."

"You can pass judgment in two days' time?"

The foreman shrugged. "I'm pretty good at first impressions." He paused. "Why'd you hire her in the first place, if you knew she'd be such a passel of trouble?"

The question took Conor by surprise. Why, indeed, had he hired her, when everything about Abigail Stanton set off warning bells? Was it because of her kindness to Beth when they had first met? Had he softened

100

to her long enough to let down his guard? Yet now all he did was block her efforts at every turn, raging at her in the process, for the exact actions that had attracted him to her in the first place.

It made no sense. That angered Conor. He'd always prided himself on his logic and cool-headed decisions. These attributes had served him well when it came to most women.

He had known from the start that Maudie was little more than a whore, and that the other housekeepers were not much better. He hadn't misjudged Beth's mother, Squirrel Woman, either, for the simple, good-hearted squaw that she was. And, even at seventeen when he had wed Sally, he had known she was immature and self-centered.

Perhaps, though, when it came to women, he wasn't as logical and cool-headed as he liked to imagine. Perhaps he really was just a softhearted, addlebrained fool. Or perhaps, just perhaps, he still longed for what he could never have, a woman as good and kind and brave as his mother.

He'd certainly hoped that Sally would eventually become that kind of woman. There was always something about her, Conor mused, his thoughts harking back to that first day he'd met her. She was fourteen, and she'd just moved to Grand View from Missouri. The new butcher's youngest child, the blond-haired, brown-eyed Sally had been an exotic rose in a field of more common wildflowers.

True, she was well aware of her beauty, and played it to her fullest advantage when it came to all the local boys. Yet still, from the first moment her gaze met Conor's, he'd known she was special, that she was for him. Sally must have known it too. She'd tried to please him in every way she could, with every resource in her limited, girlish command. From the first he'd known she'd wanted him as much as he'd wanted her.

His problem, Conor supposed, had always been in his misguided fantasy that he could control Sally or any woman, and eventually mold her to his way of things. Was this what he'd hoped to do with Abigail Stanton? All he'd managed to gain for his efforts was an increase in her stubborn resistance, and to have her threaten to leave.

Perhaps, just perhaps, the truth of the matter was he didn't really want to change much about Abigail Stanton. That admission startled Conor. What exactly was it about the woman anyway?

"Have I stumped you with that question?" Devlin asked, the amusement in his voice dragging Conor from his jumbled reverie.

"No . . . no, you didn't," Conor pretended otherwise. "I was just thinking, that's all."

"Yeah, sure. I'd say, rather, you've met your match in that woman, and you haven't the guts to admit it."

"She's a smart one; I'll give her that." Conor shifted the pail of milk to his other hand. "But I'm far from ready to believe she's as sweet and pure as she pretends to be. A decent woman wouldn't have taken this job, and you know it."

"Why, because of all the talk about you?"

"Why else?"

Devlin scratched his jaw. "I don't know. Maybe she's smart enough to see past all those tall tales to the truth."

"And what truth is that?"

"That you're a decent sort," Devlin said with a grin, "and Beth's just a sweet little girl who's never been given a fair shake."

Conor grimaced. "I hardly think Abigail Stanton could've figured that out, leastwise not after how we've treated her so far."

"Some folks are special, Conor. Some folks are able to see past all the rubbish and cut straight through to the heart of the matter."

"And you're saying that's how it is with her? Is that it?"

"Maybe. Maybe not." His cousin shrugged. "Why not give her a chance, and see what happens?"

Why not? Conor asked himself. But he already knew the answer. For all practical purposes, Abigail Stanton was still a stranger. And strangers couldn't be trusted.

Perhaps he wasn't giving her, as Devlin put it, a "fair shake." If it had only been himself involved, he might have been willing to do so. After all, he was a grown man. He could handle anything Abigail Stanton could dish out.

But Beth . . . Conor's thoughts turned lovingly to his cherished daughter. Beth was so vulnerable, so battle-scarred from the women who had already passed through. And after that incident with that teacher . . .

"No," Conor ground out, settling on his decision, "I don't think so. She got all the chance she's going to get. I've allowed her into my house. The rest is up to her. If she really cares to win Beth over, then she's just going to have to put in the time and effort it'll take to do it. She's going to have to figure it out by herself."

"And the same goes for you?" Devlin swatted a piece of straw from his trousers. "She's just going to have to figure you out all by herself, too?"

Conor fixed his cousin with a glacial stare. "Yeah." His voice dripped with sarcasm. "And hell will freeze over first."

7

Except a man be born again, he cannot see the kingdom of God.

John 3:3

Abby scooped the last bit of hot cinders from the back of the cookstove's ashpit and dumped it in the ash bucket. After covering it with the lid, she carried the bucket to the back door to cool. She planned to dump the contents in the vegetable garden beds later to sweeten the soil for next spring's planting. For now, though, the ashes could sit where they were.

She worked with a sense of urgency. There was so much to do this morning, just to set the kitchen back to rights. Her conversation earlier with Conor MacKay, unfortunately, only added to Abby's sense of frustration and stress.

He had refused to help her with Beth. Indeed, it was almost as if he had dared her to succeed with the little girl. To top it all off his mercurial behavior, as he swung from moments of near cordiality and kindness to a frigid, distrustful demeanor, was even more upsetting than if he'd just been hostile all the time.

Grabbing a handful of old newspapers, she cleaned the stovetop, then wiped the surface with an oiled rag to shine and help protect it from rust. That done, she cleared the table of breakfast dishes and put them in the sink to soak. Once the tablecloth was wiped clean of crumbs, Abby swept the floor. Then, with a bucket of soapy water at her side, she began on hands and knees to scrub it.

When the floor was half-done, Abby paused to carry the bucket of now dirty water outside. She dumped it, then lingered for a few minutes to enjoy the fresh, crisp air and bright sunshine before reentering the house. She found Beth sitting at the kitchen table, stuffing a sugar cookie into her mouth. On the tablecloth before her lay a stack of six more cookies.

At sight of Abby the girl shoved back her chair and jumped to her feet. Grabbing up the remaining cookies, she turned to leave.

"Beth," Abby called as she shut the back door. "Wait. There's no need to run off. It's all right to eat your cookies here. In fact," she added, walking to the cupboard, "why don't you wash them down with a glass of milk? It's nice and fresh. I was just going to pour myself a glass before I took the rest of it to the springhouse."

Beth swallowed the cookie she was chewing, then reluctantly walked back and sat down. "I'm not supposed to have snacks. At least that's what the other housekeepers told me. They said I was too fat."

"Did they now?" Abby brought over two glasses of milk. She set one before Beth, then carried the other around to the opposite side of the table and sat. "What does your papa say about it? Does he think you're too fat?"

Beth took a drink of her milk, wiped away the white mustache it had formed with the back of her hand, then shook her head. "Nope. Papa tells me I'm the most beautiful, perfect young lady he's ever met." She cocked her head. "But you think I'm fat, don't you?"

"I think you have a healthy appetite, and that you eat what you eat because you need to." Abby eyed Beth's pile of cookies. "Are there any left in the cookie jar?"

"Nope." With a smug little smile, Beth took a big bite of another cookie, then another drink of milk.

"Do you think you could spare me one cookie then? To go with my milk, I mean?"

Bright brown eyes studied her. Abby could almost see the wheels turning in the little girl's head.

Finally, Beth nodded. "I suppose you could have one." With quite evident reluctance, she shoved a cookie across the table. "But only because my papa taught me to share, not because I like you or anything like that."

Abby accepted the cookie and took a bite. "Sharing is good," she offered, once she had chewed and swallowed her mouthful of sugar cookie. "Manners are good, too. You never know when they might stand you in good stead."

Beth gave a snort of disgust. "Manners! Some folk in these parts wouldn't recognize a manner if it hit them square between the eyes!"

"No, some folk wouldn't," Abby conceded, carefully not mentioning the fact that neither would Beth. "But good manners are as much to your benefit as to those you give them to. In the end, it's just as important that a lady, or gentleman for that matter, knows in her heart that she did well by others." Abby paused, then laughed. "Do you understand what I mean, Beth? I'm not even sure myself if I said that straight."

"Yeah." The girl mumbled from around another sugar cookie. "It comes down to honor and what's in your heart."

Abby smiled. "That's correct, Beth. You've hit it right on the head." She bit into her cookie.

Beth shoved yet another cookie into her mouth, then washed it down with the rest of her milk. After wiping her mouth clean, she pushed back her chair and stood.

"I need to go see Cousin Ella. I promised her I'd play games with Devlin Jr. this morning."

"That sounds like a fine plan. We really must begin your lessons today, though." Abby eyed her. "How about you be back here in an hour? That'll give us a couple of hours to look over some books I brought along especially for you, before it's time to start the noon meal."

Beth scowled. For an instant, Abby was sure the girl was going to refuse. Then she nodded. "Okay. I haven't much choice anyway. Papa told me last night I had to start my lessons today, or risk a good hide tanning."

Abby's eyes widened. "He threatened to beat you?"

"Nah." Beth laughed. "Papa's more bark than bite, leastwise when it comes to me."

"That's good to hear."

Beth turned and headed toward the back door. When she reached it, she paused and glanced over her shoulder. "By the way," she said, "you can have the rest of my cookies if you want. Four filled me up just fine."

Abby smiled. "Well, thank you, Beth. But I think I'll just put them back, in case you get hungry for a snack later on."

"Suit yourself."

"Beth," Abby said as the girl turned back toward the door.

"Yeah?" Her tone had suddenly turned sullen, her look guarded.

"I have this,"–Abby hurried to the other cupboard and picked up a small, cloth-wrapped package–"for you. I made it last night."

Beth eyed it warily. "What is it?"

"A gift." She held it out to the little girl. "It's nothing expensive or anything, but I thought you might like it."

"I shouldn't be accepting gifts from you," Beth muttered as she took the package. "Papa says we don't need nothing from nobody."

"That's 'anything from anybody,'" Abby automatically corrected, watching Beth begin to unwrap the little parcel.

Beth shot her an irritated look. "Yeah. Isn't that what I said?" She pulled out the doll dress. "What's this for?" she demanded, holding it up.

"For your doll, of course." Abby bit back her rising exasperation. Couldn't the child at least accept a present with some pretense at graciousness? "I don't know very many little girls who don't enjoy a new dress for their doll from time to time. Perhaps you might eventually even enjoy making some doll clothes of your own. I have a whole box of pretty fabric scraps that would make some wonderful—"

"I don't want to learn to sew. That's prissy girl's work, and I'm no prissy girl!" Beth threw the dress on the table. "I don't want this, either. Papa was right. Accepting gifts always puts you in someone else's debt."

"Not necessarily, Beth." Abby placed her hand over the little girl's. "Sometimes a gift is given out of friendship, for the sheer joy of giving. You owe me nothing just because you accept this dress, any more than learning to sew would place you in my debt. Sewing is an extremely useful skill for everyone, not just 'prissy girls.'"

"Well, it doesn't matter." Beth's face darkened with anger. Abby could tell a storm was about to break. "I don't want your dress!"

Whatever hope she had had of making any headway with Beth disintegrated. Abby released Beth's hand and stepped back. "Fine. But if you change your mind, let me know. In the meanwhile, I'll keep it in my bunkhouse."

"You just do that." The girl backed away. "And it can rot there, for all I care!" With that she turned and ran from the kitchen.

Abby finished her cookie and milk. Then she cleaned up and resumed her scrubbing of the floor. On hands and knees she swung the scrub brush to and fro, rhythmically, mindlessly, fighting back her tears of frustration.

"What, L-Lord, am I doing wr-wrong?" Abby asked, her voice wobbly with emotion. "What m-more do you want me to do?"

Her thoughts flitted back over the events of the morning. Everything had started off pleasantly. Yet she had soon antagonized both father and daughter to the point they'd stomped off in anger.

Was it her careless tongue? Or was she just pushing them too fast in her eagerness to help, to heal?

Abby gave a shrill, wry laugh. Who was she to imagine she could help or heal anyone, especially right now? She could barely manage her own life, much less even drag herself from bed some days. Indeed, what was there to drag herself from bed for?

Tears filled her eyes. Though Abby knew they were tears of self-pity—which made her even more angry and upset—she let them flow nonetheless. She cried long, guilty, gulping sobs, the tears falling to mingle and meld with the floor's dirty wash water. Yet, all the while, she scrubbed, fiercely attacking the wooden floor as if her life depended on it.

She knew she shouldn't feel this way. After all, she was a Christian; the Lord was always with her. God would protect and deliver her even from this most terrible time in her life, if only she trusted, and had patience. But, even knowing and believing this with all her heart, Abby still sometimes found it so very, very hard. Indeed, right now, fighting the battle of living from day to day seemed the hardest battle she had ever fought.

"Lord, why can't You help me just a bit more to cope with and overcome the pain of my losses?" she moaned softly. "Why can't You soften the hearts of Conor and Beth MacKay just a little faster? All I want is a little peace without stress and strife," she sobbed. "Is that too much to ask, after what I've been through, to expect things to go easier for a time?"

The Lord spoke so often of walking in love, of the need for patience and perseverance. But sometimes Abby wondered if she had sufficient strength left anymore for the immense task of living God had set for her. Sometimes, especially now in the aftermath of her grief, she feared there wasn't enough of herself left to pull back together.

Like now, Abby thought. How easily my spirit tumbles into despair over a few slights and thoughtless words. I never fell apart so quickly before . . . before Joshua and Thomas died.

Was this, then, the terrible consequence of grief and loss? The destruction of everything that had once so well served you? If so, why did the Lord permit such catastrophes to occur? And what good could possibly come from them?

Even before the questions filtered fully through her mind, Abby had her answer. It had been there all along. The Lord Jesus had given His answer through the Scriptures. They were words, beloved words, inscribed forever in her heart.

Except a man be born again, he cannot see the kingdom of God.

Born again. Abby had once imagined those words spoke of the rebirth inherent with baptism, and the acceptance of God as one's personal Savior. But now, now she was beginning to see a greater, far deeper meaning.

Everything that happened in life—whether for good or bad, joyous or tragic reasons—held the potential to sanctify and bring one closer to the Lord. Even, Abby realized, the personal pain and horror of loss. In life's catastrophic upheavals, in the self-fragmentation, confusion, and spirit-shattering grief, there was always the hope of rebirth to a new and even better life–a life not of this world but of the Spirit.

A surprising peace, a deep joy, filled her. Gradually, Abby saw the frustrating, discouraging events of today through new eyes–the Lord's eyes. Though little progress except that she could attend Sunday services had been made, even this was a major concession for a man such as Conor MacKay. And, though the talk with Beth had ended poorly, Abby sensed she'd begun to span the chasm of mistrust and hostility separating them.

Things were indeed progressing, but in God's own good time, not hers. Patience. Patience, diligence, and unrelenting trust in the Lord were all she needed. She would show Mr. Conor MacKay the stuff a good and faithful Christian was made of. She would win his daughter over with or without his help. And she would win him over, too.

Abby awoke early Sunday morning. For a moment she lay there, mildly confused over her immediate and most forceful sense of eager expectation. Then the joyous realization filled her. Church . . . she was going to church today.

She flung back the covers and leaped out of bed, not noticing, for a change, the ice cold floor and chilly room. In record time, she finished her morning ablutions and was soon scooting out the bunkhouse door. After a quick breakfast, Abby prepared Sunday dinner, placed it in Old Bess's care to begin cooking, then hurried back to the bunkhouse to put on her best Sunday suit.

A good half hour remained before Devlin and Ella would come by in the buckboard to pick her up. Abby decided it was past time to write her first letter to Nelly.

She carried her writing supplies to the worktable, sat, and after pausing a moment to gather her thoughts, put pen to paper.

November 3, 1895

Dearest Nelly,

I know I promised to write often, but the past days have been so hectic that I must confess I'm only now getting out my first letter to you. I'll try my best from here on, though, to be more regular.

Where to begin, with all that's happened so far? Perhaps it's best to start with Beth. For all her complexity and demanding ways, she, at the very least, is far easier to deal with than her father.

Though she frustrates me on a regular basis, Beth is finally beginning to talk with me and, I fervently hope, unburden her heart. She's an extremely bright young lady, grasping almost anything I present to her in record time. She's perhaps half a year behind on her ciphering, but her reading, geographical knowledge, and nature study are advanced, as is her penmanship.

I'm also working on her manners and way of speech, as well as her attire. Her grammar is making the most progress. I've yet to get Beth into anything remotely ladylike. But then, her few dresses are in sad need of repair, and nearly too small for her at any rate. Her manners, I'm sorry to say, are also making very slow headway.

I suppose the same could be said for my progress with her father—very slow headway, I mean. Mr. MacKay, in a totally unexpected display of largesse, recently offered to allow me, in addition to my one full day off a month, to attend church services each Sunday with his cousin and his wife, who also live here at Culdee Creek. You know, Nelly, the longer I'm around Conor MacKay, the more convinced I become that a truly decent man is hiding beneath that rough, gruff exterior of his.

112

Now, please don't be cross with me over what I'm next going to tell you, or immediately accuse me of disloyalty to Thomas's memory, but I must confess that I'm most attracted to Mr. MacKay. Yes, I know he's hardly more than a heathen and not at all the kind of man I could ever consider taking as a husband, but there are times when he says or does something that deeply touches me. Indeed, there are even times when I feel such a kinship with him that I almost believe I can see into his heart and understand him. I'd like to think he's beginning to understand and respect me as well.

Then there are also times when he frightens me like I've never been frightened before. He's so experienced in the ways of women, and I know only what my dear, godly Thomas taught. I fear my unseemly attraction for Mr. MacKay might be my undoing. You know as well as I of his unsavory past. Who am I to imagine it would be any different with me?

Now, don't, I beseech you, order your dear husband to ride out here to fetch me the day after you receive this. My body—and soul—are far from mortal danger. Mr. MacKay, as promised, has continued to mind his manners. I just thought, as a more experienced married woman, you might be able to offer me some words of advice about how to deal with my unsettling attraction. I suppose, as a young widow, I'd have had to eventually deal with such feelings at any rate, so any advice will be welcomed.

Well, it's nearly time to leave for Grand View and services at the Episcopal Churh there. May the dear Lord hold you close, as I know He'll do with me. I'll write again soon.

Fondly,
Abby

"I can't tell you how happy I am that Conor allowed you to come with us to Sunday services," Ella said, as her husband helped her and then Abby into the back seat of the buck-board. "I told you, didn't I, that he was a good man?"

"Yes, you did." Abby smoothed the wrinkles from her good, navy blue woolen suit jacket and skirt, then pulled on a pair of fine kid gloves to protect her hands from the cool morning air. "Still, his offer came as quite a surprise, considering I have only been here a week tomorrow. I didn't think I'd done enough yet to prove my worth."

Ella laughed as she accepted the baby, wrapped warmly in a thick shawl, from her husband. "Conor's a very discerning man, isn't he, Devlin? I'm sure he took the measure of your true worth quite soon after you arrived here."

Climbing into the front seat to sit beside his son, Devlin glanced over his shoulder and grinned. "Oh, quite sure," he agreed amiably. "Quite sure."

There was something, however, in the veiled glance that passed quickly between husband and wife that made Abby uneasy. Had they been talking about her and Conor?

Devlin took up the reins. "Ready?"

"Just a minute." Ella pointed to a neatly folded, scarlet woolen blanket lying beneath the front buggy seat. "Abby, would you mind opening that and spreading it over our laps? I think we might appreciate its warmth once we start moving. There's quite a bite to the air, even for the first week in November."

Abby pulled out the blanket and, unfurling it, settled it over their laps. "Thanksgiving will be here sooner than we think."

"Which brings to mind," Ella said as her husband slapped the reins over the backs of the two horses, "the arrangements for the Thanksgiving meal."

"I can't say I've given it much thought as yet," Abby admitted. "What's usually done at Culdee Creek?"

114

"Well, the tradition has been to have a big meal in the main house and invite all the unmarried hands. In the past I've prepared and served the meal, with more or less help from the current housekeeper."

"How many people usually come?"

Ella wrinkled her brow in thought. "Hmmm, there's us–we've always been included in the past–and Conor and Beth, of course. As far as the hands go, this year the unmarried ones include Frank and Henry, as well as Wendell Chapman, Jonah Goldman, and H.C. Miles." She laughed. "Just to save you from asking, since it embarrasses the spit out of H.C., the initials stand for Hezekiah Calvin."

"Oh, I see." Abby smiled.

"So, including you, that comes to"–Ella paused to make a mental calculation–"eleven people, considering Mary doesn't eat enough yet to count."

Abby nodded slowly. "That's a few more than I'm used to cooking for, but I suppose I can manage it."

"I can do it again, if you don't think you're up to it. Or we can do it together."

"Let's do it together." Abby squeezed Ella's free hand. "It'll be much more fun that way."

Ella smiled. "I think so, too."

Abby released her hand and leaned back. The buggy headed southeast away from the forest's edge, toward the rolling plains. The day was overcast. The sun shone bleakly through a small rent in the clouds. A chill wind blew, reddening their cheeks and making their faces tingle.

Nonetheless, Abby found it all quite invigorating. Nothing could mar the day. She was going to church.

From time to time, Devlin would point out things to his son, who looking so very proud and excited, was perched beside his father on the front seat. A red-tailed hawk passed over on a high current of air, his keening cry both lovely and haunting. A cottontail rabbit poked out his head from some scraggly brush near the road, his pink nose twitching. In the distance, pronghorn antelope grazed, apparently unperturbed by the sound of the approaching buggy.

It was a wild, untamed, pristine land, Abby thought. It took a special kind of man—and woman—to settle it and not only survive, but thrive here. Life could be difficult enough in the relative comfort of Colorado Springs. What with the severity of winter this close to the Rockies, and the frequently arid climate and vagaries of the weather all year around, scrabbling a living this far out in the country could be downright dangerous.

Yet, for all the potential and very real hardships, something drew Abby to this place. Here in these wide open spaces, with the mighty Pikes Peak looming behind her, she felt the majesty and grandeur of the Lord so much more deeply than she ever had at home back East. There was indeed a great and glorious adventure to be had.

"How're things going for you, Abby?" Ella asked, interrupting her thoughts. "I'm so hoping you'll stay. If there's anything I can do to help . . ."

Abby chuckled. "Just having you around has more than helped, Ella. And I'm determined to give this position a good chance."

Ella shot her husband a quick look. Father and son were engrossed in a discussion about pronghorn antelopes. She scooted closer to Abby and said, "I probably shouldn't be telling you this—I want to assure you that I don't gossip or spread tales with every housekeeper Conor hires—but Devlin told me he thinks Conor likes you."

Though a thrill of pleasure shot through Abby, she forced a disbelieving laugh. "Forgive me for saying so, but that's the most absurd thing I've ever heard. I've never met a man more intent on throwing obstacles in my path. Why, it's almost as if—"

"As if he were testing you?" Ella offered.

"Rather, as if he dislikes me," Abby countered firmly. "Besides, why would he test me?"

The red-haired woman shrugged. "Who knows? Maybe he sees something special in you. Unfortunately, Conor cannot trust easily anymore. So maybe he's testing your mettle. One thing I do know. He never did this with the others. I think he knew from the start exactly what he got when he hired them. He's a realistic man in that way, you know?"

"Pessimistic is more like it," Abby muttered.

"On the contrary, I think he suspects you're too good to be true." Ella cocked her head. "Devlin says Conor gets defensive, and is surprisingly quick to anger, when the topic turns to you. Believe me, he never let any of the others bother him like that."

She leaned even nearer. "Do you know what I think?" Her voice barely rose above a whisper. "I think he not only likes you, Abby, but he's attracted to you, too."

Ella eyed her closely. "Tell me true, because I promise I won't breathe a word of this to anyone, even Devlin. Exactly how do *you* feel about Conor?"

8

Not my will, but thine, be done.

Luke 22:42

Abby stared back at Ella. How was she supposed to respond to such a question? She knew Ella meant well, that she had both her and Conor's best interests at heart. Such a question, at the very least, though, was premature. As physically attractive as she may find him, she would never consider marrying Conor MacKay. It was one thing to care about him and wish to ease his pain. It was quite another to wish to bind her life to his.

"How do I feel about Conor MacKay?" she repeated softly. "It's far too early to tell, Ella. He's certainly not as bad as the tales would have him be. There are even moments when he pleasantly surprises me, but . . ."

"You're being very cautious." Ella nodded in approval. "There's nothing wrong with that. But can you honestly tell me that you don't find him attractive? Why, next to my Devlin—"

"Good looks are a gift of God and granted equally to the bad as to the good," Abby stated firmly. "As a Christian, though, it's the heart of the man, his soul, that must ultimately interest me."

"As well it should." Ella leaned back in the buggy seat. "But then, I know Conor's heart, and it's fine and good."

"Well, I don't, Ella."

"Conor's a proud man. Too proud to reveal his pain and disappointment. It takes a long time, and a lot of trust, for him to open himself to anyone." Ella shot her a considering look. "His wife, Sally, left him when their son, Evan, was five. Ran off one day with her music teacher, without a fare-thee-well, or anything. Left Evan all alone in the house. Conor came home after a long day of work to find his son crying in a corner, and no sign of Sally."

"She must have been very unhappy to do such a thing."

"She probably was. Those early years here at Culdee Creek—especially after Conor's father died unexpectedly—were hard ones. They had married very young, you know. Conor was only seventeen, and Sally fifteen. She bore Evan the very next year. In fact, she was just twenty-one when she left."

Perhaps she shouldn't ask, Abby thought, afraid it might border on prying into Conor MacKay's personal business. But if she could just understand the MacKay history better, it might ease her way with them. "You don't have to tell me this," she ventured carefully, "but I'd like to know more about Conor's wife. What kind of a person was she? What eventually happened to her?"

Ella grinned. "Well, considering it's all but common knowledge anyway, I think it's safe to tell you. Sally moved here from Missouri when she was fourteen. She was a pretty little thing, with a mass of golden curls and beautiful brown eyes. The boys swooned over her. She had them all at her beck and call. All, that is, but Conor."

Her brow furrowed in thought. "I think that's what first attracted Sally to him. He was different, aloof and, even at sixteen, very dark and handsome. Sally, the spoiled and vain girl that she was, found Conor a chal-

119

lenge. Eventually they fell in love. Against both sets of parent's objections, they wed."

"Sounds romantic." Abby smiled sadly. "What happened?"

Ella shrugged. "The harsh reality of Colorado ranching, the difficulties of child-rearing. Conor was struggling mightily back then to keep the ranch out of debt. He didn't have enough time and attention to shower on Sally. I think her music teacher, who Conor finally hired to placate her, played to Sally's need for attention."

She sighed and shook her head. "Sally always had a pretty voice. She imagined she was destined for great things in the music world. I suppose her teacher, enamored by her talent and beauty, encouraged those dreams so as to lure her away from Conor."

"So she walked out on her husband and son?" Abby frowned. "What about 'in sickness and in health, til death do us part?'"

"Sally didn't see it quite that way."

"How many years has it been now since she left?"

"Over twelve," Ella replied. "But it doesn't matter anymore. Conor got word that both Sally and the music teacher died in a Denver boardinghouse fire, eighteen months after they had run away."

"How sad." Abby exhaled a deep, pensive breath. "I was hoping she might still return to Culdee Creek and recapture the love they'd once shared. It might be just the thing to free Conor at last from his bitter pain."

Ella shook her head. "I doubt Conor would take her back now, even if she still were alive. He's never forgiven her. He loved her deeply and was grievously hurt by her desertion. He waited for her for nearly a year and a half, hoping against hope she would return." She smiled sadly. "I almost counted the news of her death as a blessing. Her betrayal was tearing Conor apart.

Once he knew she was dead, he was free, and soon able to pick up his life and go on."

"Then he wed Beth's mother."

"No." Ella sighed again. "Conor never married Squirrel Woman. Oh, he loved her, but not as passionately or wholeheartedly as he had loved Sally. She was good for him, though, like a soothing balm to a hideously wounded soul. But he never married her."

Abby choked back her rising horror. "So Beth's words were true. How could Conor do that to a child—*his* child? One sin doesn't justify another. All he's done is perpetuate the cruelties that his first wife began."

She clutched a fist to her mouth. "Poor, poor little Beth!" Abby breathed. "The most innocent, yet the most punished."

Once more Ella leaned close and took her hand. "Do you see now why I hope you'll stay, Abby? Why I pray that you and Conor . . ." She caught herself and blushed. "Both Conor and Beth are in pain, but I fear that Beth's pain will never heal, unless Conor's heals first. You'd be good for him, Abby. You're the kind of woman he needs."

Abby averted her gaze and, lips tight, stubbornly shook her head. "Don't say that, Ella. I've only been here a week. You can't know me, or who I'd suit. Not yet, anyway."

"I know enough, Abby. You're good, kind, and decent. You're a God-fearing and God-honoring woman. You've known great pain and loss, and can understand what it does to a person. You've been a wife and mother. And you're not afraid to face life head on, or"—she added with a wry grin—"as difficult a man as Conor MacKay can sometimes be."

Abby turned to fully face her friend. "On the contrary, I'm frequently not nearly as wonderful a person as you make me out to be. In the end, though, what really matters is that Conor might not care to take me to wife, or

121

I, him. Sometimes two people can be the most wonderful people in the world, yet still not be right for each other. And I'll tell you true, Ella. Conor frightens me."

Ella arched a brow. "Frightens you? How?"

"His pain and anger against life and God are a mighty force. I don't know if I'm strong enough to withstand the power of those emotions."

"But you won't give up, will you, Abby?" Ella squeezed her hand, entreaty in her voice. "You'll stay on and keep trying, won't you? It'll take time and patience. And I'll help you any way I can."

There was something in the tone of Ella's voice, a hint of desperation, that both touched and worried Abby. *She's afraid for them. She fears they'll be lost, if something isn't done soon.*

If the truth be told, Abby feared the same thing. She recognized the signs of lost souls, teetering on the brink of self-destruction. Indeed, she recognized that special empty, aching desperation all too well. She had experienced the same emotions herself many times in the past two years.

Despair, if tasted too often and deeply, could do that to anyone. It was a drug that slowly but surely numbed the heart, and weakened the spirit, until one finally lost all will to go on. If not for her love for the Lord, Abby feared she would have succumbed long ago.

But Conor and Beth didn't even have God to comfort and carry them when life's burdens became too heavy to bear. They had nothing, nothing save each other. Yet both were crippled, their emotions shriveled and weak. Neither could really bolster or comfort the other as each truly and deeply needed.

Ah, Abby thought, *if only they knew and trusted in God's love!* It was all the strength and comfort one could ever need. It was a light to guide one through the darkness. It lent purpose and direction when nothing else seemed to matter.

Was this the real reason the Lord had brought her to this place? In her own seeking journey back to life, was she also meant to lead others to Him?

If so, Abby quailed before the task. It was not a calling she was worthy of. She lacked the strength, the courage, the wisdom. She had lost more than just a family when she'd lost her husband and son—she had lost her self.

But then perhaps she had never known who she truly was. All her life, to the first moment she'd arrived at Culdee Creek, had been dedicated to pleasing others and fulfilling their expectations of her. When had she ever before thought—or dared—to please herself? When had she ever felt worthy to do so, or seen the purpose in it?

Indeed, could there truly be any worthwhile purpose served in seeking out one's own self-fulfillment? And could it be pleasing to or ultimately serve God? Abby didn't know.

Just then the shrill whistle of the Union Pacific, Denver, and Gulf locomotive echoed over the grassy hills and prairie encompassing the town of Grand View. A flurry of smoke belched from the passenger train's soot-blackened smokestack as it neared the town and began to slow. Scantily clad women leaned from the windows of a large, lavender and pink gingerbread-trimmed house at Grand View's outskirts, hooting and waving as the train pulled into the depot.

Cheeks warm with embarrassment, Abby quickly averted her gaze, knowing without being told that the garishly painted house must be a bordello. She riveted her attention, instead, on the people standing on the wooden platform before the train depot, watching as they surged forward in eager anticipation. Two men sitting at buckboards parked nearby jumped down to join them.

Dogs barked from nearby houses, pigs squealed, a burro brayed, and horses neighed. A cold wind, careening briefly but wildly through and around the buildings, howled eerily. As they entered the long row of false-fronted buildings and boardwalks of what looked to be the town's main street, Abby could make out signs for Edgerton's butcher shop, Mrs. Lombardy's rooming house, Nealy's blacksmith and livery, and the feed lot gates that led, on the other side of the street, to what looked to be the livestock loading area of the train depot. Gate's Merchantile sat nearby, butting up against one side of the town hall. On the other side was the Crown Hotel, then the icehouse and, finally, the town scales.

The firm pressure of Ella's hand, squeezing it once again, finally beckoned Abby from her avid perusal of the town. She turned to her friend and smiled, knowing that she still awaited an answer to her heartfelt plea.

"No, I won't give up," she assured her softly. "I'll stay on and keep trying, but not for hope of any earthly reward such as taking Conor MacKay as husband. I'll do it for the Lord, Ella."

"And if He ultimately means for you to wed Conor and be a mother to Beth? What then, Abby?"

The question took Abby aback. Marry a man the likes of Conor MacKay? Could such a thing possibly be in God's plan for her? The Lord would never unequally yoke her with an unbeliever—that Abby knew—though, at this point, that was definitely what Conor MacKay appeared to be. But what if, in God's great, far-seeing wisdom, He knew Conor would someday turn to Him? What then?

"If it's the Lord's will that I wed Conor MacKay," Abby finally replied, her emotions in such a confusing jumble that she didn't dare examine them, "then so be it.

But only if it's the Lord's will," she added. "Not mine, or yours, or anyone else's."

§

Three hours later, after dropping Ella and the children off, Devlin finally halted the buggy before the main house. He jumped down and quickly went around to where Abby sat, helping her down.

"Thank you, Mr. MacKay." She smiled up at him in gratitude. "I appreciate your taking me with you and your family to church."

The tall man grinned down at her, his long, dark mustache lifting to reveal strong, white teeth. "My pleasure, Mrs. Stanton. And please, call me Devlin. I'm not much with formalities."

"Only if you'll call me Abby."

"It's a deal."

He held out his hand, and Abby shook it before gathering up her skirts. "I'd better not tarry. I've a ham baking in the oven, and potatoes simmering on the stove. Though Mr. MacKay agreed to keep an eye on Old Bess while I was at church, I'm sure he'll be expecting his Sunday dinner soon."

Devlin laughed. "I honestly doubt Conor yet knows what to expect from you, Abby. But then, it's good to keep him a bit off balance. Good for his heart, *and* his head."

Abby shot him an uncertain glance, then turned and headed up the porch steps. Devlin MacKay, she decided, was no more above matchmaking than was his wife. Best she ignore both of their attempts as well as she could. There was no sense fanning the flames.

Neither Conor nor Beth was anywhere to be found. She hurried to the kitchen, checked and basted the ham—which was cooking nicely—and added a cup of water to the pot of potatoes. The apple cobbler for dessert was cooling on the table, while the dish of glazed carrots baked alongside the ham.

Dinner would be ready in another half hour. Just enough time, Abby decided, to return to her bunkhouse and freshen up.

As she neared her little dwelling she noticed the door slightly ajar. Frowning in puzzlement, Abby stepped up onto the small porch.

The sound of her footsteps striking the wooden deck must have startled whoever was inside. There was an audible gasp, then a sharp clatter as something hit the floor. Abby shoved open the door.

Beside one of her open trunks stood Beth, her eyes wide, her mouth moving in soundless terror. In one hand, she clutched the doll's dress Abby had made. Her other hand was fisted and pressed to her breast. At her feet lay an overturned silver frame that held Abby's daguerreotype of Joshua as a baby.

For a moment she surveyed the scene, myriad responses darting through her mind. Finally, she settled on the most obvious. "What are you doing in here, Beth?"

The little girl swallowed hard and held up the doll dress. "I-I just came for this. You said it was mine."

"Yes," Abby replied slowly, "that I did. I didn't mean for you to come in here without my permission, though. Just as I respect your privacy, I also expect you to respect mine. What would your father think? How would he feel if he knew you'd come in here?"

Beth paled. Her eyes filled with tears. "You'll tell him, won't you? You'd like nothing better than to get me in trouble." She threw down the little dress. "I should've known better than to trust you or take any presents from you. It was a trap, wasn't it? *Wasn't it?*"

126

Abby closed the door and walked over to her. "A trap? Whatever are you talking about?"

"You want to make me look bad to my papa, so as to make you look good. You don't care about me. All you want is to impress my papa and win him over, just like"–the youngster choked on a sob–"that mean, nasty Maudie !"

"Beth, Beth." Abby removed her jacket and laid it aside. Pulling over a stool, she motioned for Beth to sit on it. The girl sullenly complied, and Abby took her own seat in the nearby rocking chair.

She leaned forward and rested her forearms on her skirt-covered thighs. "I don't care a fig whether I impress your father or not. I do the best I can for the both of you, and hope that it's enough. And I don't want to make you look bad. On the contrary, I want us to be friends. That's why I made the doll dress for you."

Tears trickled down the little girl's cheeks. Angrily, she swiped them away. "Then let me take it and leave."

"You're free to leave." Abby sat back. "But you don't have to. Now that I'm here, why don't you stay and visit a few minutes? Just the next time, ask me if you want to come in here, okay?"

Beth grimaced and rose. "Okay." She squatted, picking up the daguerreotype. "Who's this?" She offered it to Abby. "Your little boy?"

"Yes. His name was Joshua." Tenderly, Abby accepted the daguerreotype and placed it back on the table beside the pictures of Joshua taken on his fifth birthday, and that of Thomas and her on their wedding day. "He was a little over six months old when this was taken."

"Papa said he died of a fever. Did you love him very much, beings as how he was a boy and all?"

Startled, Abby stared in puzzlement. "Don't you like boys?"

127

She shrugged. "Well, my papa's all right, and Cousin Devlin, and most of the hands. But I can't say as how I cared much for any of the boys at school."

"They were mean to you?"

Beth's expression clouded. "Yeah, they were mean." Her lips tightened. "But then, so were most of the girls, too."

"If I'd been your teacher, I wouldn't have let that happen."

The girl lifted her gaze to meet Abby's. "Mr. Sullivan wasn't about to go up against a whole mess of parents just for me. Papa tried his best. Even went to the school board, but everyone backed Mr. Sullivan. So Papa told them what he thought of them, then pulled me out of school."

Beth grinned. "Wish I'd been there to hear it. Cousin Devlin told me there was a mess of shouting, and a whole lot of red faces by the time Papa was done."

Compassion filled Abby. No wonder the little girl thought she wasn't worth anything. Her teacher, classmates, and the entire school board had all but told her so.

But at least her father had defended her. Abby's opinion of Conor MacKay rose a few extra notches.

Abby was tempted to ask Beth what had happened to her at school, then thought better of it. To pry into something so personal at this stage of their relationship might well do even more damage.

She managed a taut smile. "I'm glad your papa was there for you. He loves you very much."

Beth nodded solemnly, her little chin lifting in proud agreement. "Yes, he does."

"Well,"—Abby shoved out of the rocking chair and stood—"I need to get back to the kitchen and our Sunday dinner. Would you like to look around, see my sewing machine, and some of the other books I brought for your lessons before we leave?" She gestured broadly to the room.

128

The little girl climbed to her feet. "What's that?" She walked to the fabrics draped over the rope dividing the room.

"Cloth I bought to make clothes and curtains and other things." Abby joined her. "See"–she fingered one piece of cloth–"this pretty green-flowered fabric is calico, and this is a fine plaid gingham, and this"–she moved down a few feet–"is a lace stripe novelty gingham. I also have a delightful maroon challis." She pointed to a richly printed, tightly woven cotton material. "I was planning to make this into a lady's evening costume."

She sighed. "But that was a few years ago, before my husband died. Now there's little point in such fripperies."

"Why's that?" Beth reached out and stroked the smooth fabric. "Aren't you allowed to go dancing?"

Abby shook her head. "It's not about being allowed or not allowed, Beth. I'm just not interested in dancing anymore."

"My papa can dance, you know? My grandpa, his papa, taught him all sorts of Scottish Highland steps. Our ancestors came from Scotland, you know."

The image of the stoic Conor MacKay, dressed in a tartan like the man in the painting in the parlor, made Abby grin. "Now that would be a sight to behold. Maybe you can talk your papa into doing a Highland dance for Thanksgiving."

"I don't think so. He doesn't dance anymore, either."

Beth's statement, as simply couched as it was, stabbed into Abby's heart. Misfortune and personal choice had pushed Conor MacKay to the very fringes of life. They had thrown up walls to separate him from others. But the man he once was, and the man he was still capable of being, Abby sensed, was still there beneath it all.

It was there in his love and devotion to his daughter, in his friendship with his cousin and his wife, and in

129

the pride and hard work he put into Culdee Creek. She even caught occasional glimpses of it in his interactions with her. Conor MacKay might be hard, angry, and unyielding at times, but he also strove to be fair and rewarded true effort.

Yet, like herself, Conor MacKay didn't dance anymore. Dance again he would, though, Abby vowed. Dance with joy, with wild and holy abandon. It would be her gift to him, if she gave him nothing more. And his dancing would be a gift to her, too.

"Well, Beth,"–Abby began to lead the little girl to the door–"if we can't get him to dance for Thanksgiving, then sometime soon. One way or another, I think it's very important that your papa dance again."

"It went rather well, wouldn't you say?" Ella asked Abby as they cleaned up after the Thanksgiving meal. "The hands ate like there was no tomorrow, Conor actually smiled a time or two, and even Beth was on her best behavior. Yes," she said smugly, half to herself, "I'd say just about everything is finally beginning to go well."

Abby busied herself fixing up a plate for Brody Gerard, the new hand hired just two days ago. He had missed the meal because of an imported, prize Hereford cow about to deliver. "Do say?"

Just then Beth, dressed in a warm coat, knit cap, and mittens sauntered in. Both women paused in their conversation.

"Hi," the little girl offered, never breaking stride.

"And 'hi' to you, too. Going out to work off some of that big turkey dinner, are you?" Ella asked with a smile.

"Nothing better to do." Beth tossed the reply over her shoulder as she paused at the back door. "All the men folk are doing is talking about cattle prices, and it sure is boring."

"Well, have fun outside then."

"I will." Beth walked out the back door.

"Yes, I *do* say." Ella turned back to Abby and immediately picked up the thread of their interrupted conversation. "Why, Conor hardly flinched at all when I insisted we say grace. That's a big improvement for him."

Though Abby couldn't help thinking there'd have been more than a flinch if she'd been the one to suggest such a thing, she didn't voice the opinion. Ella was as puffed up and proud as a hen who had laid her first egg. It would hardly be kind to burst that egg over so tiny and insignificant a detail.

She added a big scoop of mashed potatoes to the plate of stuffing, green beans, and thick slices of turkey, then poured a ladleful of gravy over it all. After covering the food with a pie pan to protect it, she placed it in a big basket already filled with silverware, two buttered rolls wrapped in a cloth napkin, a slice of pumpkin pie, and a mug of cider.

"I'll be back in ten minutes." Abby threw a warm shawl over her shoulders, then carefully slipped the basket onto one arm. "I feel sorry for Mr. Gerard having to sit in a drafty barn with a cow, while the rest of us are snug and warm, stuffing ourselves on a Thanksgiving feast."

Ella scowled. "It can only do him good, cocky young buck that he is. If I'd been Devlin, I'd never have hired him. That Brody Gerard isn't a decent sort. You watch yourself, Abby."

Abby laughed. "Oh, Ella, he can't be *that* bad."

"And how many times have you talked to him? None, I'd bet, or you wouldn't say that. In fact," Ella added, "let me fetch Devlin from the parlor. He hired him. He can take him his supper."

"No." Abby shook her head firmly, and strode to the door. "Let the men relax and savor their full bellies. I'll be back before Devlin could even get up from his chair and stretch out his kinks."

A raw wind, gusting down from churning grey clouds in the north, engulfed her in its frosty grip. Abby tugged the shawl up over her head, hunched her shoulders against the cold, and quickened her pace to the barn.

As she walked, she smiled to herself in amusement. Ella could get so protective at times. She only wondered if that protectiveness truly extended to her, or if Ella also meant to protect what she imagined to be Conor's interests. After all, though Abby had not actually spoken to the man since his arrival, she hadn't failed to notice Brody Gerard's striking good looks as he worked around the ranch. He was sure to have left more than a few broken hearts in his wake.

After the chill, blustery wind, the barn provided a relative warmth. Abby inhaled the pungent odor of animals and the sweet fragrance of cured hay, then closed the small door set to the side of the larger main door. She headed across the barn's great interior to the stall illuminated by a kerosene lantern. The Hereford had delivered. The newborn calf, even then, was struggling to its spindly, unsteady little legs.

Brody Gerard glanced up from where he stood, leaning on the wooden stall rails. His handsome, swarthy countenance brightened. "Come bearing gifts, Mrs. Stanton?" He sniffed the air. "Smells like a turkey dinner. But I can't decide what I like better, the meal, or the perfume of the beautiful woman bearing it."

"Considering I don't go in for such artifices as bottled scents, Mr. Gerard, I'd say it'd better be your supper." She slid the basket off her arm and held it out to him.

He took the basket from her and placed it on the ground beside him. Before Abby could bid him farewell and turn to leave, however, Brody straightened and took a quick step toward her. His hand snaked out toward her, and he grasped her by the wrist.

"Mrs. Stanton," he said, his voice low and seductively deep, "won't you stay and keep me company while I eat? After all, everyone else has had the pleasure of your presence for the past few hours. It's only fair that I be treated in a like manner."

Any other time, out of kindness if nothing else, Abby might have been tempted to acquiesce. There was something in the man's voice, though, and the way his gaze traveled down her body as he spoke, that filled her with unease. There was also something, she decided, about his manner—so self-assured and confident that he'd get what he asked—that set her teeth on edge. She wished she had listened more closely to Ella's warnings.

Abby shook her head. "I'm sorry, Mr. Gerard. Perhaps some other time."

She tugged back on her hand, fully expecting him to release it. His grip, however, only tightened. Her heart rate quickened. "Mr. Gerard," she croaked, suddenly afraid. "Please let me go."

"Well, if you won't stay, at least let me have a kiss. *If* you even want me to let you go, once I'm done kissing you."

With that, he pulled her to him, tugged her shawl from her hair, and grasped the back of her head, imprisoning it. Abby tried to twist free, but he was too strong. She opened her mouth to cry out for help, but it was too late. With a speed and power that shocked her, Brody Gerard slammed his mouth down on hers.

9

I have trodden the winepress alone; and of the people there was none with me.

Isaiah 63:3

For a split second, Abby stood there, frozen in horrified disbelief. Then anger flooded her. How dare he! *How dare he!*

She reared back, breaking his hold, and slapped his face. "Let me go!" she screamed. "Let me go!"

Brody smiled, his lips lifting in a feral grimace that reminded her of a snarling wolf. "I kinda like screamers. Besides, I heard talk of the sort of housekeepers MacKay hires. At least you've got the pick of the litter with me."

With that, Brody Gerard swung Abby up into his arms. Before she could gather her wits about her for a full-throated scream, he shoved her face against his chest and pinned her head there. Frantically, blindly, Abby fought to break free as he carried her to a pile of straw heaped in the furthest corner of the barn.

Panic filled her. Disbelief that this was happening numbed her. She fought and she prayed. Prayed for deliverance, for some hand to rescue her.

When he reached the corner, Brody knelt and threw her down on the straw. Abby shoved up and scrambled as far back from him as she could.

"Don't do this," she pleaded. "I'm not that kind of a woman!"

Hands perched on his hips, he leered down at her. "Yes, you are. I heard you were a widow woman. You know what it's like. You need it."

"No!" Abby screamed as he crept toward her. "No! Help me. Somebody h-help m—"

Gerard smothered her further cries with his mouth. She struck out at him wildly, kicking, clawing. He grabbed her, dragged her beneath him, and covered her with the heavy weight of his body.

Dear God! Abby begged in silent, terror-stricken desperation. *Dear God, help me!*

❧

"Can't say as I'm pleased with the price our beef has gotten these past three years," Conor observed before downing the last of his whiskey. "If the amount of rainfall doesn't improve next summer, and the grass doesn't get a chance to catch up, we're in for another expensive year."

"Yeah," Devlin agreed, glancing outside from his spot across from Conor in the other fireplace chair. "Makes you almost wish for open range grazing again, doesn't it?"

Frank Murphy shifted on the sofa and cleared his throat. All eyes turned to him. "Those were the good old days, the roundups, your meals cooked over a campfire, sleeping under the stars . . . But, as good as it was, those days are gone. It's just lucky for us Culdee Creek's got a lot of its own grazing land, and Conor here's a good manager of his money. Some of the other ranchers haven't been quite so fortunate."

Henry and H.C. nodded in unison. "Yeah," H.C. then spoke up, "like the Rockin' B. I heard it's on the selling block. And there's rumors the Big Sandy ain't doing too well, either."

"Rest assured"—Conor stood and walked over to refill his glass at the side table—"Culdee Creek is holding its own. And a lot of that success is thanks to your—"

"Papa, can I talk to you for a minute?"

Conor turned to find his daughter, cheeks flushed, still dressed in her jacket, woolen cap, and mittens, standing in the hall doorway. "What is it, girl?" he asked.

She lowered her gaze and began to shuffle her feet. "I-I'd rather talk to you in private, Papa." Beth glanced up. "It's . . . it's about Mrs. Stanton."

"Mrs. Stanton?" Conor frowned. He set down his glass. "Guess I'd better see what kind of spat these two have managed to get into this time," he said to the men.

Devlin groaned and rolled his eyes. The other hands just grinned.

Taking Beth by the hand, Conor led her out of earshot of the parlor and of Ella, who was still working in the kitchen. "What's it now, girl?" he demanded, his irritation rising. Obviously, from the men's reactions just now, his housekeeper's and daughter's ongoing battles were becoming common knowledge. "I thought you two were beginning to get along better?"

"It's not me this time, Papa." She sidled close and lowered her voice. "It's Mrs. Stanton. I saw her in the barn just now, kissing Mr. Gerard!"

For a split second, Conor thought he had misunderstood. But the telling color that flooded Beth's face confirmed her words. He squatted and took hold of her by both arms.

136

"You stay here," he rasped, clamping down on his rising anger, and equally intense sense of disappointment. "Do you hear me? *Stay here.*"

She jerked her head up, her eyes now big as saucers. "Y-yes, Papa."

Conor rose, then turned and walked to the parlor doorway. "I've got to step out for a spell, boys. Enjoy the whiskey but save me some. I might be needing it."

Before anyone could reply, he wheeled about, stalking down the hall and through the kitchen.

A startled Ella looked up from the sink of soapsuds and dishes. "Conor, did you need—"

Ignoring her question, he jerked open the back door and kept on going, giving no care to a jacket or the wind blowing now in frigid, bone-numbing gusts. With long, strong strides, Conor covered the distance to the closer barn, knowing that was where Brody Gerard was keeping an eye on the prize heifer. And, as he moved along, Conor battled the confused rage burgeoning inside him.

She said she was a decent, God-fearing woman. Why, she'd even spurned his overtures. Yet now she was in the barn with a hand who'd hardly been here a week, kissing him and doing God knew what else by now?

Well, what did *he* care? he asked himself. So what if Abigail Stanton, for all her fine airs and false protestations, was a woman of loose morals? As long as she did her work, and treated Beth decently, what did it matter if she bedded half the hands at Culdee Creek?

In the end, he'd always known she was no better than the rest.

Yet still, as Conor approached the barn, his pace slowed. He paused in the doorway for a split second, surprised to find his heart pounding, his fists clenched. What in the Sam Hill was the matter with him?

It was almost . . . almost as if he were afraid to know the truth.

Conor forced himself on. He strode across the barn's expanse, passing the lamp-lit stall with the heifer and her new calf, a basket of untouched food sitting nearby, all the while scanning the interior. At last he found them, sprawled in a far corner in a pile of straw, Brody Gerard atop a passionately writhing Abigail Stanton.

Conor slid to a halt, his mind reeling at the sight before him. Just turn and leave, he told himself. Leave them to their sordid activities.

Then Abigail let out a long, low moan. Something in Conor exploded. With a growl of pure, animalistic rage, he closed the distance, reached down, and grabbed Brody Gerard by the waistband of his trousers, jerking him to his feet.

"What the–"

The big hand staggered backward, then gained his footing. Hands clenched, he whirled around. Quickly, Conor assumed a fighting stance, his weight poised on the balls of his feet. His own hands fisted, he waited, ready to fend off any blow.

Then Brody Gerard recognized him. "Mr. MacKay. I didn't know it was you."

Behind him, Abigail Stanton shoved to a sitting position, and fumbled to rebutton the front of her blouse. "Thank the Lord you came when you did, Mr. MacKay." She climbed to her feet. "I don't know what I would've done–"

Brody Gerard chuckled. "Oh, I reckon we all know what you would've done, don't we, honey?" He turned to face Conor. "I'm sorry you caught us like this, Mr. MacKay. She came in here, and one thing led to another. But I never wanted anyone to know. Even ladies like her prefer to keep up appearances."

"Ladies like me?" Abigail Stanton pushed her way past him. Her hair was a tumbled, disheveled mass. Her eyes were unnaturally bright. Beneath her hastily refastened

138

white blouse, her bosom heaved in a most disconcerting way.

With an effort Conor jerked away, hardening himself to his sudden surge of desire. She didn't want him, never had, he fiercely reminded himself. Yet her wanton behavior just now was ample evidence she did want someone!

"He's lying, Mr. MacKay!" Her impassioned cry wrenched him back to reality. "He was the one who forced it all. If you hadn't gotten here when you did—"

"I don't care what you do or with whom, Mrs. Stanton," Conor cut her off. "All I ask is that you use more discretion in the future. My daughter saw you two groping each other in the straw. I'd prefer she not be subjected to such a disgusting display of vulgarity again. Is that clear?"

Struck speechless, she turned ashen. Then, as realization as to the meaning of his words seemed to fill her, her eyes flooded with tears.

"You—you believe him over me?" Abigail Stanton finally ground out hoarsely. "You don't even care to hear my side of it, do you! You've always, *always* held me in such low regard!"

"My regard for you has never been a requirement for employment," Conor snarled. "I thought I made that clear. Just obey the rules from here on out, and we'll get along fine."

"Rules? Rules?" She glared at him, her tears apparently all but forgotten in her growing anger. "Hang your stupid rules! I'm not some child who needs rules, especially not yours. And how dare you dictate to me what you'll tolerate as my moral behavior? Don't you dare. Your standards are far too low ever to satisfy me!"

"Well, I can see I'm not needed here anymore," Brody Gerard interjected with a smirking grin. "I'll just take my Thanksgiving supper and head on back to the bunkhouse."

The now enraged Abigail Stanton rounded on him. "No, Mr. Gerard, that's where you're wrong. You're far more important to Mr. MacKay than I could ever be. You stay here with him, and *I'll* leave."

She turned back to Conor, her eyes flashing, her chin lifted defiantly. "Yes, Mr. MacKay," she cried, "that's exactly what I'll do. I've had all I can take of you and your condescending, cynical attitude. I quit, do you hear me? First thing in the morning, you can just make arrangements for one of your more gentlemanly hands to take me and my belongings back to the Springs!"

ॐ

Long after everyone had returned to their dwellings Conor sat in the parlor, yet another glass of whiskey cradled in his hand, staring into the fire. The room was warm, cozy even. Any other evening after a day's hard work he would, by this time, be fighting off drowsiness.

Beth had gone upstairs a couple of hours ago to play with her dolls. He knew he should head up soon to tuck her in and give her a good-night kiss. For some reason, though, Conor couldn't seem to find the energy needed to impel his limbs from the chair.

Abigail Stanton was leaving on the morrow. Just as he had feared, he had managed to set the record of all records, running her off quicker than all the rest of his former housekeepers. The thought, however, was not at all amusing. In fact, it downright hurt.

He should have known it would come to this. She had always seemed too good to be true.

Conor leaned back in his chair and closed his eyes. Stupid fool, he silently berated himself. You should have known better. Stupid, lonely, vulnerable fool . . .

A soft footfall sounded a few feet away. Conor jerked upright. Beth stood there in her long, white cotton nightdress. She clutched her rag doll to her. Her eyes were red, swollen. She had been crying.

Laying aside his drink, Conor extended his arms to her. "Come here, girl. Come and let Papa hold you."

With a soft cry, Beth ran and threw herself into his arms. She drew up her legs beneath her nightdress, laid her head on his chest, and clasped her doll tightly to her. Conor enclosed his daughter in the cocoon of his body and arms. Bending over her, he kissed her forehead.

"What is it, girl? Tell Papa what made you cry."

"M-Mrs. Stanton and th-that m-man," she sobbed anew. "I-I should've never told you."

"Rather," Conor corrected her gently, "I wish you'd never seen them in the first place. I had hoped she'd set a better example than that for you."

"No, no, I shouldn't have told you what I did," Beth wailed.

"Yes, you should've, and you did. You were right to tell me."

His daughter squirmed against his protective clasp, breaking free at last to rear back and look him in the eyes. Her chubby face was wet with her tears but her gaze, as she met his, was unwavering and direct.

"No, Papa," she said, "I shouldn't have told you what I did because it was a lie. I didn't come on them. I was already there. I wanted to see if the heifer had had her calf, so I climbed up into the loft over the birthing stall."

Conor's gut clenched. There was no way Beth could've only seen a kiss, trapped as she was above them. Blast Abigail Stanton!

Tenderly, he wiped away his daughter's tears. "It's all right, girl. Did you see things . . . things you didn't understand?"

"Oh, Papa!" Beth rolled her eyes. "I didn't lie 'cause I was embarrassed at what they did. I know all about that stuff from watching our horses and dogs and cattle!"

Conor cocked his head, puzzled. "Then what did you lie about, Beth?"

She inhaled a deep breath. "I lied when I said Mrs. Stanton kissed Mr. Brody. She didn't want him to kiss her or touch her. He did it anyway."

Conor went very still. "Go on, girl. Tell me everything."

"She told him to let her go. She even slapped him, but he just laughed and picked her up and carried her into that pile of straw. That's when I climbed down and ran to get you."

If you hadn't gotten here when you did . . .

Abigail Stanton's words pierced clear through him, and into the gaping hole left in its wake surged nausea. God above! Brody Gerard had meant to rape her! And he'd nearly left the man to do it! Her moans had been ones of terror, not of delight. Yet he . . . he had been willing, no, *eager,* to think the worst of her.

Clutching Beth, Conor leaned back in the chair and closed his eyes. "Ah, girl, girl," he groaned, "it doesn't matter. What matters is what I did to hurt Mrs. Stanton. I hurt her so badly she's leaving."

"That's why I lied, Papa," Beth whispered. "Because I thought you wanted her to leave. And if I could make it seem that she was just like Maudie . . ."

Words—words Abigail had spoken to him that morning in the kitchen—pricked at the edges of Conor's memory. *It is your example that she'll follow . . . Do you . . . want that influence to be one of mistrust for her fellow man?*

142

Conor choked back an acrid swell of self-loathing and regret. She had been right all along, Abigail Stanton had. It always came back to him. And he *had* failed once again as a father, if this recent action of Beth's was any example of the influence he had had upon his daughter.

Despair swallowed him. He had failed first with Evan when his harsh, unyielding ways had run him off, and now he was slowly but surely doing the same thing to Beth. Would she too eventually leave him, heartsick and bitter over what he'd become? Conor didn't think he could bear it if he also ended up losing Beth. As much as he tried to deny it, despite what his son had done, Conor missed Evan. Missed him so badly that, at times, it was almost a physical, bone-deep pain.

In the end, he was no better than his father. He was *worse* than his father. His father, mired in the misery of his own unhappy childhood, in thrall to his whiskey bottle, didn't know what he did. But he, Conor MacKay, knew.

He had Abigail Stanton to thank for that precious, if exquisitely painful, revelation. Though he had struggled mightily to discount and deny it, she had been trying to warn him almost from the first time she had met him that his own bitterness corrupted more than just himself.

At the memory of that first day she had come to Culdee Creek, Conor's lips lifted in a bleak parody of a smile. From the start, Abigail had stood up to him. From the start she had dared tell him what few others had either the insight or the courage to say.

But why? Why had she risked herself, even jeopardized her position here? And what had she received from him in return?

You—you believe him over me? he heard her hoarsely demand. *You've always held me in such low regard.*

Shame and bitter regret filled him. Humiliation was all he had ever offered her, in return for her efforts on his and Beth's behalf. And now, now even she had had enough. Abigail was leaving.

"I was very wrong to let you think I wanted Mrs. Stanton to leave," he said, gazing tenderly down at his daughter. "I don't want her to leave. Do you?"

For a long moment Beth eyed him carefully. "Not really, Papa," she admitted finally. "She's been nice to me, even when I haven't been so nice to her. She told me she wants to be friends. But if you don't want me to, I won't, Papa," his daughter hastened to add. "You come first, Papa. You always will."

He smiled, then leaned down to kiss her once more on the forehead. "And you'll always come first with me, girl. I don't think that means you can't be friends with Mrs. Stanton, though. You're growing up mighty fast. I'd lay odds she could teach you a lot about being a young woman. What do you think?"

Beth grinned. "Yes, I think so, too, Papa."

"Well, good then." Conor slid her off his lap and set her on her feet. "It's getting late, and you need to be abed. Let me tuck you in first."

"And then what, Papa?"

"Then," he said, rising and taking her hand, "I need to have a very important talk with our Mrs. Stanton."

10

With little care as to how she was doing it, Abby threw her clothes into the big luggage trunk. She had cried out all her tears hours ago, and grim reality had finally set in. She was leaving on the morrow. When Conor MacKay, or one of his hands who had been delegated to take her back to Colorado Springs, arrived at her door, she would be packed and ready to go.

After tossing in two shirtwaist blouses, four petticoats, and six pair of underdrawers, Abby paused to search out the next items to pack. The room was in a state of chaos, the bed rumpled from her repeated bouts of frustrated weeping, one pillow pounded flat, the other on the floor. The second large trunk sat open, all the sewing fabrics hastily folded and dumped inside. Her school books sat piled precariously on the edge of the small worktable beside her flower-painted white porcelain teapot, her beloved, framed daguerreotypes carefully stacked nearby. Finally, Abby's gaze came to rest on the small, nickleplated box with the combination lock.

Myriad emotions churning within, she walked to the table, picked up the box, and carried it over to the rocking chair where she sat and opened it. Inside were her most precious possessions. She sorted through them, her eyes misting over once more.

Oh, how she missed them: sweet Martin, her youngest brother; impetuous John, the middle one; and shy, studious Edward. Good boys one and all, she thought as she fingered their pictures tenderly.

Her gaze snagged on a scene of her mother, waving gaily beside a massive white lighthouse situated somewhere along the New England coast. Her mother, industrious, virtuous, the ideal minister's wife. Had her father ever truly realized what a crown she was to him?

But then her father, so focused on serving the Lord, failed frequently to notice or appreciate what the Lord had gifted him with. Abby smiled sadly. As well-intentioned as he was, her father viewed his family solely as instruments to be used in his ministry. All were sacrificed in his pursuit of God, with little thought given to the needs and feelings of those closest to him.

It was why she had married Thomas, Abby thought, fingering a daguerreotype of her husband. Her father had decided—without consultation with either her or her mother—that Thomas, a full fifteen years older and recently widowed, was the proper life mate for Abby.

No matter that Abby hadn't loved Thomas. No matter that they hadn't anything in common but their love for the Lord. All that mattered was that her father's will be done.

With a sigh, she set the daguerreotypes aside. It didn't matter anymore, anyway. She was free at last of the two domineering, if well-meaning men in her life. And, on the morrow, she'd also at last be free of an unfair, judgmental, and supremely exasperating one, too.

Her glance fell on the items that remained within the metal box: baby booties, a gold, oval brooch holding a lock of Joshua's hair, her wedding ring, several of her son's childish drawings, and a small, wooden toy train. These were all Abby had left of her former life.

She choked back a freshened swell of tears. All that truly mattered had been relegated to this one small box. Indeed, what else was left her?

Abby had thought she'd turned the corner on her grief when she'd come to Culdee Creek. The events of the past few weeks had seemed to signal a gradual thawing in Conor MacKay's frigid reserve. Beth had at last accepted the doll dress she'd made for her. Things seemed to be getting better.

But now . . . now Abby saw that she had been wrong. She had failed. Failed herself . . . failed the Lord. Abby knew she couldn't stay.

To remain while Brody Gerard continued on at Culdee Creek would be too humiliating. And, if that wasn't shame enough, Abby feared the new hand now would have few qualms about accosting her again.

But this was only part of the reason behind her departure. In her heart of hearts, Abby knew Conor MacKay was the real reason. To stay on now would be to surrender her growing sense of self. She had standards and values. She wanted her walk with the Lord to guide others, too.

Perhaps it was prideful to feel this way. Perhaps she was still blind to the Lord's true will. But one thing she did know. She could no longer serve God here. Conor MacKay stood in the way.

Abby closed the metal box and locked it. With a despairing sigh, she buried her face in her hands.

Ah, Lord, I cry unto Thee, and Thou dost not hear me, Abby lifted her thoughts heavenward as she uttered the prayer of the despondent Job. I stand up, and Thou regardest me not.

"What else do you wish of me, Lord?" she whispered. "Tell me, I beseech you, before–"

A heavy tread sounded on the porch. A firm hand rapped upon the door.

She jumped. Terror rippled through her. What if . . . what if it were Brody Gerard, come to finish what he'd earlier begun?

Frantically, Abby looked around. The cast-iron poker beside the stove caught her eye. She hurried to it and picked it up.

The knocking, more insistent now, came again.

"G-go away." She gripped the poker, never moving from her spot by the stove. "I'm not receiving visitors tonight."

"It's me, Abby. Conor. Conor MacKay."

Confusion filled her. Why, tonight of all nights, would Conor MacKay wish to speak with her?

"Go away, I s-say." Abby's voice quavered.

"No, Abby, I won't go away."

Abby. He'd called her Abby! Why now? Her suspicions rose.

Poker in hand, Abby strode to the door. "I'm not fool enough to let you in," she angrily called to him through the wooden barrier. "Not after today. If you've come to say something, just say it now, through the door."

After a long pause, she heard a chuckle.

"Well, I suppose, after my behavior of late, I deserve that. And, if this must be my penance, standing out here in the cold, talking to you through this door like some miserable supplicant, then so be it."

She bit back a harsh reply. "Just say what you came to say."

"Beth came to me just a while ago, and told me she'd lied about what she'd seen in the barn. She told me you

148

resisted Brody Gerard, not encouraged him. She also told me she doesn't want you to leave."

Conor's voice moved closer. Abby could almost imagine him pressing his forehead against the door. Her throat went dry; her hands turned clammy.

"I don't want you to leave, either, Abby."

The softly spoken words touched her, plucking at Abby's heart. Yet, though they were words she'd longed to hear since she'd first come to Culdee Creek, she was no longer sure they were enough now to keep her here. What did they really mean, anyway, when spoken by a man such as Conor MacKay?

She leaned against the door, and laid her cheek to it. "I'm sorry, Mr. MacKay, but it's too late. What you said to me today was the culmination of what you've thought of me all along. Why else would you have so quickly jumped to the conclusion you did?"

Her question pierced clear through to Conor's heart. He closed his eyes. Why else, indeed? he asked himself bitterly. Though this woman had intrigued him from the start, he had kept his guard up against her, automatically attributing nearly everything she did to self-serving, ulterior motives. After all these years, he knew no other way to protect himself against the inevitable rejection.

But did he dare risk sharing such a personal insight? Did he dare to disarm his heart after all these years, even if just a little? And was keeping Abby here really worth such a gamble?

Somehow, Conor knew it was. He was tired. Tired of fighting alone. Yet he was also so very, very afraid. Afraid to hope, to trust, to let himself depend on someone ever again.

His fear waged a mighty battle against his growing need and, for the first time in a long while, Conor allowed his need to win. This time he had to risk it. He leaned more heavily against the bunkhouse door. If he didn't, he would lose Abigail Stanton and the flicker of hope beginning to burn in his heart.

"You're right," Conor forced himself to say. "I did jump to a false conclusion today, based on my own sorry, sordid expectations. But, blast it, Abby,"–he slammed his fist against the door–"it was never through any fault of yours. The fault was mine. Do you hear me?" he groaned. "Mine."

The latch rattled. The doorknob turned. It was all Conor could do to straighten and leap back before the door swung open. Lamplight flooded the small porch, illuminating Abigail Stanton's pale face and reddened, swollen eyes.

For long seconds they stood there, facing each other, silent and staring. Then she moved slightly. Conor caught sight of a cast-iron poker clutched in her hand.

He grinned. "Planning to beat me to death rather than compromise your honor?"

Her glance skittered momentarily down to the stove tool, then back up to his. "If necessary, yes," she replied, defiance in her eyes and voice. "At first I grabbed it because I thought you might be Brody Gerard. Then, when I discovered it was you, it seemed equally as handy. I couldn't be sure, after what you said today, what your intentions were, either."

"Gerard will be out of here first thing in the morning," Conor growled, now angry. "I won't keep a man on Culdee Creek who abuses a woman. I'm not, and never have been, that kind of a man. All I came to do was talk to you."

"Like last time, Mr. MacKay?"

Her note of challenge reminded Conor of the innuendoes he'd made that night he'd all but invited her into his bed. Heat flooded his face.

"No, not like last time. I came to apologize for my stupidity and my cruel words. I was wrong, plain and simple."

Abby saw the shame burning in his eyes. It was in stark contrast to the defiant tilt of his chin, the tight line of his lips. Yet, he'd called himself stupid. He had admitted his words were cruel. This was, she realized, a hard admission for a man as proud as Conor MacKay.

But it had been hard on her, too. He had humiliated her, cut her to the quick. Could she possibly open the door of her heart to him again?

"I accept your apology, Mr. MacKay," Abby muttered tautly. "But it's still too late." She began to close the door. "Good night."

"No!" He shoved his booted foot between the door and frame. "It's *not* too late. I won't let it be too late. I can't."

Her heart pounding beneath her breast, Abby stared up at him. "Please, Mr. MacKay," she whispered, her throat gone tight and dry. "Don't–"

"Don't what?" he snarled, his blue eyes flashing. He gripped the door so she couldn't close it. "Don't expect forgiveness from you? But I thought that was the *Christian* thing to do?"

She staggered back. The poker clattered to the floor, and she stood there trembling with the power of her emotions. Emotions that were a confusing jumble of fear, anger, and heartrending need.

"I said I accepted your apology," she finally gritted out the words. "What more do you want?"

"I want *forgiveness.* I want you to give me another chance. Me and Beth." He slammed open the door and strode inside. "Is that such a hard thing for a good Christian woman like you to do?"

Forgiveness, Abby thought. Why was it suddenly so hard for her to grant? The Lord had instructed to forgive seventy times seven if need be. Yet to truly forgive this man would mean trusting and trying again. It would mean accepting his request to stay on at Culdee Creek. And it might even mean opening her heart to loving him.

151

The realization terrified her. She'd thought she was safe at last, now that she'd finally made the decision to leave. Every instinct shouted—no *screamed*—for Abby to get away while she still could. She sought desperately for an excuse, any excuse, to flee this place—and this man. But Conor MacKay wouldn't give her that excuse. And neither, it seemed, would the Lord.

Tears filled her eyes. "Yes, Mr. MacKay," Abby said softly, "it is hard to forgive you. But it's not because I'm not a good Christian. It's because I'm weak and afraid."

The tears trickled down her cheeks, but through the tears, Abby saw an answering moisture spring in Conor MacKay's eyes. The realization gladdened her, and eased the pain of her next words. "With the Lord's help, though, I can do all things."

"So you'll forgive me and give us another chance?"

A final, fleeting impulse to turn and run before it was too late swamped Abby. But an equally strong certainty that the Lord had answered her prayers rushed in to sweep away those lingering doubts and fears.

Ah, Lord, I cry unto Thee, and Thou dost *hear me!*

"Yes, Mr. MacKay," she said. "I forgive you, and will give you and Beth another chance."

December 6, 1895

Dearest Nelly,

I must admit I anguished over how I should reply to your last letter. Though I know I may have sounded a trifle naive in my feelings about Conor MacKay, your demand as to how could I, as a good Christian woman, allow myself to be attracted much less tempted by such a worldly, unprincipled man was rather harsh. Things have markedly changed between us, and especially so in the past week. Though I won't go into the details, suffice it to say that he begged my forgiveness for his cynicism and mistrust of me. Begged my forgiveness as a good Christian, Nelly. What else could I do but forgive him?

Though my forgiveness was initially hard to give, I admit now I'm glad I gave it. Since then the change in both Conor and Beth has been downright shocking. Pleasantly shocking, but shocking nonetheless. Beth has become shyly friendly, surprisingly polite, and utterly cooperative. And Conor—he now insists we go on a first name basis—isn't at all the same man you first met.

True, he hasn't taken to attending church or opened the family heirloom Bible (it was brought here all the way from Scotland! I found it shoved behind a row of books when I was dusting the parlor). But truly, truly there is a mutual respect growing between us now. Conor is a good man in so many ways, Nelly. I see that more and more each day, and it fills me with such wonder and thanksgiving. The Lord's hand is in this, and I increasingly grow convinced I was always meant to play a part here.

That doesn't mean, however, that I think the Lord necessarily intends for our relationship to progress past friendship—or at least not until Conor finally reconciles himself with the Lord. I'm content with how things are right now. Indeed, I'm not at all certain I would wish for it to be any different. But I also cannot discount that God may yet have a plan that includes both Conor and me. All that can be done, I believe, is to wait with patient trust and see where God will lead.

I just glanced at the clock, and it's time for Beth's lessons. I'll continue this letter later this evening . . .

Abby continued to marvel over the change in Conor and Beth. A week later, she was still shaking her head as she shared a cup of tea at Ella's late one morning.

"In his own way," she explained, "it's almost as if Conor truly *is* trying to begin anew." Abby stirred a teaspoon of sugar into her tea. "It's almost as if I'm meeting him again for the first time."

Ella passed a plate of pumpkin nutbread slices across the table and smiled. "What do you think of this 'new man'? Is he at all to your liking?"

"Well, of course—" Abby's hand froze in mid air over the fragrant nutbread. "Now, Ella, don't you dare start matchmaking again."

The red-haired woman laughed. "Oh, Abby, Abby. Sometimes you get as rattled as a new mother mare with her first foal. All I wanted to know was what you thought about Conor, and if you finally felt comfortable here at Culdee Creek. He was, wasn't he, the primary sticking point in your decision to stay?"

"I suppose he was." Abby took a sip of her tea, then picked up a slice of nutbread. "I do find his new behavior quite pleasant," she said, finally feeling calmer.

The subject of their conversation stuck his head in the door. "Oh, there you are." Conor whipped off his Stetson and leaned in. "Some of the stall door hinges are just about worried clear through. I need to ride to Grand View to get Simon Nealy, the smithy, to fix them for me. If you want to come along, we might as well shop for supplies, too."

Doing her best to ignore Ella's delighted grin, Abby laid down her nutbread. They *were* getting low on flour and other kitchen staples, and she did want to do a bit of Christmas shopping.

Abby nodded. "I'd love to go. When do you want to leave?"

"Would a half hour be enough time?"

"More than enough." She paused, a sudden thought assailing her. "Should I ask Beth if she'd like to come, too?"

Conor shook his head. "No, not this time. Let's just make it you and me."

Ella choked back a giggle. Abby didn't like the sound of that. Had she been set up, or were Conor's motives innocently separate from Ella's machinations?

Well, Abby decided, there wasn't much to be done for it anyway. She had already accepted.

"Fine." Abby shot Ella a quelling glance. "Just you and me."

Conor shoved his Stetson back on his head and grinned. "See you out front of the house in a half hour then."

With that, he departed as swiftly as he had arrived, leaving the two women to sit there, staring after him. Finally, Ella broke the silence. "I do declare, but the man's acting as chipper as a boy at his last day of school. Wonder what's gotten into him?"

Abby wheeled around in her chair, opened her mouth to deliver another lecture, then thought better of it. What was the use? Conor *was* acting . . . well, almost light-hearted, of late. Besides, the only thing that would put an end to Ella's romantic efforts was when she finally faced the fact that Abby and Conor MacKay were ill suited for each other.

"It's amazing what letting go of a load of anger and resentment can do for a person. It heals so many wounds." Abby took one last swallow of her tea, then set down her cup and rose. "I hate to cut short our little visit, but I need to go and prepare for the trip to Grand View."

Ella made a playful, shooing motion toward the door. "By all means, go and get ready." Then her expression sobered. "You're the balm for his wounds, you know? Conor's beginning to heal."

Though her friend's words sent an unexpected surge of joy through Abby, she quickly squelched the unsettling emotion. "No, Ella," Abby gently corrected her. "I'm

155

not the balm, only the instrument. It's the Lord who heals, and heal He will, if only Conor asks."

§

The ride to Grand View began pleasantly. When he wasn't occupied handling the team of two spirited horses pulling the buckboard, Conor busied himself pointing out the local landmarks. Abby eagerly studied anything he found of interest, but, after a time, they both lapsed into silence. To Abby's surprise, it was a silence that was not at all uncomfortable. It was almost . . . almost as if they were becoming friends.

As if the thought were some interesting pebble she had picked up along the wayside, Abby turned it over and over in her mind until it took on a beauteous shape, and a luster that it had not possessed before. Friends . . . She almost laughed aloud. Who would've thought it?

Abby decided she liked the idea, and liked it very much.

"What are you smiling about?" Conor broke into her reverie. "You look like a contented kitten just finishing her bowl of cream."

"It was nothing." She pretended to find sudden interest in a pair of red-tailed hawks circling an expanse of tall, dried grass. "It's just such a beautiful day for the middle of December." Abby glanced back at him. "Do you think we'll have a white Christmas this year?"

At her abrupt change of topic, Conor's mouth quirked in wry puzzlement. He shrugged. "If this Christmas is like most, I'd say no. Most times, we don't get any real snow until January. Then look out for the next three to four months!"

"Well, perhaps you're right." An errant breeze whipped by, ruffling Abby's thick brown hair and brushing icy fingers across the back of her neck. She shivered, and hunched her shoulders until the breeze died away. "I'm rather partial, though, to a white Christmas."

"Beth likes them, too." He shot her a sidling glance. "She's really taken to you, you know? Says you're teaching her to sew on that machine of yours."

Suddenly unsure of herself, Abby shifted on the buckboard seat more fully to face him. "It's all right, isn't it? My teaching her to sew?"

Conor must have caught the edge in her voice. He laughed. "Of course. I've never seen her so proud of anything as she was of that dress you helped her make. It's the first dress, you know, that she's worn in a long while. I only hope she's taking to her schooling as avidly as she has to that sewing machine."

"Oh, she has," Abby hastened to assure him. "She has a quick wit and prodigious memory."

"Yeah," Conor growled, his mood appearing to shift direction as swiftly as the Front Range weather. "Sometimes, though, I wish her memory wasn't as good as it is." His grip tightened about the reins until his fingers turned knuckle-white. "She still has occasional nightmares about her days at school."

The seconds ticked by. When he said no more, Abby felt the tension tauten her until she was strung as tight as a bow. Yet still she sat there, silent, forcing herself to wait until he was ready to go on.

"You asked me once to tell you more about Beth," Conor finally rasped. "I'd like to tell you now, if you're still of a mind to hear it."

Abby nodded. "Yes," she said softly, "I'm still of a mind to hear it."

He shot her a fleeting glance, then turned his gaze back to the road ahead. "Squirrel Woman–Beth's mother–died of smallpox a little over two years after the birth. Soon after, I hired my first housekeeper. She lasted three years before she quit to marry the local parson.

157

She was decent if a bit stern at times. After that the pickings took a drastic, downhill turn. The women were either lazy slatterns, judgmental old biddies, or husband-hunting opportunists."

He slapped the reins over the horses' backs to urge them to quicken their pace. "Then Maudie came to work for me. She was young, pretty, and a lot smarter than the rest. But she, too, wanted something, and that something turned out to be me. I'll admit I succumbed to her physical charms. Why not? She offered them freely, and I'm still a healthy, virile man. When it became apparent, though, that I'd no intention of wedding her, she devised a scheme to win my heart through my daughter."

"She pretended to care for Beth, didn't she?" Abby offered, guessing where this particular tale was leading.

"Yes." Conor grimaced. "Maudie treated her so sugar sweet, even I began to suspect something. Beth, however, was so starved for a mother's love that she gobbled up all the hugs and syrupy words like a child let loose in a candy shop. By the time I finally had enough of it Beth was attached to Maudie. It nearly broke her heart when I told her I was sending Maudie away.

"Maudie was none too happy with me, either," he continued. "She knew, though, there was one sure way to punish me for rejecting her. She used that knowledge without remorse or hesitation."

"Beth?"

Conor nodded slowly. "On that cold spring day in March when she was to leave Culdee Creek, Maudie waited until I rode out to feed the pastured cattle. Then she sweet-talked the hand who was to drive her back to the Springs into taking her along with Beth to school first. Claimed she wanted a chance for a last good-bye. Maudie made him stop a short ways from the schoolhouse, so she and Beth could walk the last part together."

Abby listened quietly.

"Somehow, Maudie managed to slip around to the back door of the schoolhouse while the children and their teacher, Peter Sullivan, were outside at recess. She stole the big gold pocket watch Sullivan always kept on his desk during the day. Beth entered from the front door to put away her books and lunch pail, before joining the other children outside. She was the one accused of taking the watch, when Sullivan finally discovered it was missing."

"Did Beth see Maudie take the watch?"

"Yes, but I didn't find that out until much later."

"She was protecting Maudie, wasn't she?"

He turned an anguished gaze to Abby, his smoky blue eyes boring into hers. "She loved and trusted Maudie. She was just a little over eight, and didn't understand how deep cruelty could go. But she learned about it that day in spades."

With a flurry of pounding hooves a herd of pronghorn antelope ran pell-mell across the rolling hills before them, momentarily drawing both Conor's and Abby's attention. The sun broke through the thick clouds, gilding both the graceful beasts and winter-browned land in dazzling brightness. And, off in the distance, the ebony behemoth that was the Union Pacific, Denver, and Gulf locomotive whistled stridently, chugging and puffing its way toward Grand View.

For an instant longer, Abby allowed her gaze to linger on the unpretentious yet surprising beauty of this land, then she turned back to Conor. "Go on," she urged.

Conor dragged in a shuddering breath. "First Sullivan made her stand before the class, hoping to shame her into telling him where she'd hid his watch. He called her a bastard, a half-breed little thief! Beth kept insisting that she hadn't taken it, so then he beat her across her knuckles until they bled. When that didn't work, Sullivan locked her in the small, dark storage closet next to the wood stove. He left her there for six hours with the stove burning, until I came to fetch her!"

His shoulders slumped and his voice dropped to a rasping whisper. "By the time I carried her out of the closet, Beth was nearly unconscious from the heat and lack of water. And, when I finally got her home she wouldn't talk. She didn't talk for five months. *Five months!*"

A hard, brutal look glittered in his eyes. "I rode back to the school the next day. Just after the children left, I beat Sullivan to within an inch of his life. Ended up in jail for a few days before my lawyer got me out."

Conor gave a low, guttural laugh. "I didn't care, save that it kept me from Beth. Sullivan deserved it, and more."

Abby didn't know what to say. What words could assuage the horror and grief Conor must have felt in discovering what had happened to his daughter? What comfort could she offer, sensing he might well be carrying a heavy burden of guilt over his part in instigating Maudie's cold-blooded revenge? And what blame could she lay at his feet for his retaliation against such a vicious, unfeeling teacher?

It was wrong to repay violence with violence, but Abby couldn't find it in her heart to condemn him. That judgment must remain with the Lord.

She understood now the reasons for both Conor and Beth's distrust. No wonder her presence in their house had been barely tolerated. No wonder the ensuing housekeepers who came and went after Maudie had not stayed long. The house had all but seethed with pain and anger.

"Beth told me the rest," Abby said. "How you went to the school board and they rebuffed you; how you told them all off before pulling her out of school."

"Yeah." Conor gave a snort of disgust. "The self-righteous fools chose to back Peter Sullivan. It didn't matter to them that he'd humiliated Beth, beaten her, and

160

nearly killed her by locking her in that closet. There was no proof that Beth *hadn't* stolen the watch, and since Maudie was long gone by then . . .

"Took me until Beth finally talked again to be sure myself, though I suspected the truth after hearing that Maudie had gone with her to school that day." He lifted his gaze to the sky, then fleetingly closed his eyes. "So now you know the whole, sordid story." Conor turned to her, a bitter smile on his lips. "Or at least my side of it anyway. I'm sure you've already heard the local version, long before you ever came to Culdee Creek."

"Oh, I got an earful. But I also know how easily prejudices and misinformation can transform events into a faint imitation of what truly occurred."

"So you believe me?"

"Yes, I do."

Conor cocked his head, a half-smile lifting one corner of his mouth. "You're a strange one, you are, Abigail Stanton. But I thank you, nonetheless."

Abby's pulse quickened. In the ravaged depths of his eyes, a strange new emotion, soft and gentling, mingled with a puzzling question. What did that emotion presage? she wondered. And did she dare encourage it?

It didn't matter. Time would reveal all that needed to be revealed. For now Abby was content to await the future, and accept its advent in God's own good time.

What *did* matter was that Conor had given her a gift this day. He had laid bare his soul, finally revealing one of the reasons for his anger and mistrust. In the doing, he had risked all.

The healing . . . the forgiveness . . . had indeed begun.

She reached out, placed her hand over his. "No, Conor MacKay." Abby smiled. "Rather, I thank you."

11

The LORD seeth not as man seeth; for man looketh on the
outward appearance, but the LORD looketh on the heart.
1 Samuel 16:7

Conor drew up before Gates Mercantile and glanced at Abby. "Why don't you go on inside and start your shopping, while I head down to the blacksmith's? I need a haircut, too, so after the barbershop, I'll meet you back here in about a half hour."

Abby nodded. "Sounds fine to me. If I get done early, I'll make a quick trip to the post office to mail a letter to Nelly, then hurry back." She took up her purse and two big straw baskets, gathered her skirts, and climbed down from the buckboard.

With a tip of his hat to her, Conor urged the team onward.

From the boardwalk that fronted the store, she watched him drive off down the rutted, dirt street, then turned and entered the Mercantile. Immediately, myriad odors assailed her. Abby inhaled deeply of the sweet, rich scent of molasses, the aromatic bite of coffee, the tang of vinegar, and the heady fragrance of spice and ripe pears and apples.

In the center of the store, flanked on both sides by two long, wooden counters and tall shelves filled with all sorts of goods, stood a big, pot-bellied stove. Seated around a small table beside its radiant warmth were two elderly gents playing a game of cards. Abby recognized three women from church: Mrs. Nealy, a portly matron with frizzy brown hair, the blacksmith's wife; Mrs. Edgerton, stern-faced and rail thin, the wife of the local butcher; and Mary Sue Edgerton, her pretty, eighteen-year-old daughter. They were standing in front of the dry goods counter, talking with Mr. Gates, the proprietor. The women turned toward her and smiled.

She walked over to them. "Good day and Merry Christmas, ladies," Abby said in greeting, then nodded to Mr. Gates.

Mrs. Nealy eyed Abby with an inquisitive smile. "Merry Christmas to you, Mrs. Stanton. So nice to see you again. What with all the problems at Culdee Creek, it must be such a relief to come to town from time to time."

"I can't say as that I know very many women who don't find shopping a fine way to spend a day," Abby replied cheerily. She'd been warned by Ella about the woman's tendency to gossip and chose to ignore Mrs. Nealy's attempt to elicit information about the MacKays. "Especially with Christmas only a couple of weeks away."

She met Mr. Gates's understanding gaze. "I've got quite a list for you today, when you're finished taking care of these ladies."

"We'll only be a few minutes more, Mrs. Stanton," the gray-haired man said. "I was just finishing up with Mrs. Nealy's baking items."

Mary Sue Edgerton scooted around her mother and took Abby by the arm. "Ella's told me you're quite the seamstress, Mrs. Stanton. Could you advise me on some fabric I've found?" She tugged Abby toward the other counter, where several bolts of colorful ginghams and calicos lay.

Abby paused to set her baskets on the floor at the end of the counter, then focused her attention on the material Mary Sue chose first to unwrap from the bolt.

"I know this isn't appropriate for winter wear"–the young woman ran her hand over the fabric to smooth it out–"but I'm already beginning a few summer frocks for next year. What do you think of this? I want one especially for the annual town dance on May 1st." She cast Abby a sideways glance. "I'm hoping Conor might finally come. Perhaps if you began now to encourage him . . ."

The calico was a subtle print of maroon and blue-edged diamonds on a field of white. It would set off Mary Sue's vibrant blue eyes and lush, wavy, ebony hair to perfection. Abby was tempted to tell her the fabric would not suit.

Then remorse filled her. She had no right to interfere with another woman's marital designs. Mary Sue seemed pleasant enough. Conor MacKay had the right to choose whomever he wished, if and whenever he decided to wed again.

Abby smiled up at Mary Sue. "Of all the fabrics here, this looks the most flattering one for your coloring. The cloth is of a very good quality and will drape well for any pattern. It should make a lovely summer frock."

The younger woman's eyes lit with pleasure. "Oh, I do hope so. I want Conor to notice me for the full grown woman I really am."

"Well, I can't promise I can convince him to come to that dance in May," Abby said with a laugh, "but I'll try. It would be good for him, I think."

Mary Sue nodded vehemently. "I think so, too." She gave Abby's hand a squeeze. "Thank you so much for helping me with this. You're such a dear!"

Mr. Gates had just finished with Mrs. Nealy. Catching Abby's glance, he signaled for her to come over. "If you'll excuse me," Abby murmured. She extracted her hand from Mary Sue's, and headed to the other counter.

"So, what can I do for you today, Mrs. Stanton?"

Mr. Gates graced her with a warm, welcoming grin. He was in his early sixties, of medium height and build, and he wore a pair of spectacles that seemed perpetually smudged and perched on the end of his nose. "Need some flour, do you?" he asked. "And how about salt, baking powder, and sugar?"

"As a matter of fact," Abby agreed with a nod, "those items will do for starters. Make that five pounds of flour, two of sugar, a tin of baking powder, and half a pound of salt. Plus, a jug of molasses, an ounce of cloves, nutmeg, cinnamon, and cardamom, and some candy sprinkles."

"Planning on a mess of Christmas baking, are you?"

"Yes. Yes, I am."

The front door opened. A gust of cold air swirled in, then the door closed. Abby, busy checking items off her list as Mr. Gates filled them, paid the new arrival little heed. The matrons Nealy and Edgerton, however, lost no time in muttering their disapproval from their spot a few feet down from Abby at the counter.

"The nerve of her, to presume to do her shopping at the time of day the rest of us shop," Abby could hear Mrs. Nealy whisper indignantly. "Who does she think she is?"

"Who else?" Mrs. Edgerton snipped back. "She's just like the rest of them, a shameless tramp."

Abby went still, then glanced over her shoulder. There, illuminated in the sharp winter sunlight, stood a young woman of seventeen or eighteen. She was tall and slender, but sweetly curved. Her pale blond hair was piled high on her head, exposing an elegant neck which disappeared in the collar of the ruffled white blouse that peeked from beneath her opened, dark wool

165

coat. Her skin was flawless, her lips full and sensuously molded, her nose delicate and regal.

With downcast eyes, she walked up to the counter beside Abby. Mr. Gates paused in his task of wrapping Abby's various spices in paper cones he had quickly made, and frowned at her.

"You might as well take a seat over there, Hannah." He indicated a chair by the door. "I'm going to be busy a while filling Mrs. Stanton's order."

At the mention of Abby's name, the girl lifted her gaze. It was all Abby could do not to gasp.

In the depths of Hannah's clear, turquoise blue eyes burned the deepest, most soul-searing anguish Abby had ever seen. She could almost feel the girl's hopelessness and despair. Compassion filled her.

Dear Lord, Abby thought. *Dear Lord.*

Then, as quickly as she'd exposed her heart, Hannah shuttered it once more. The girl's head dipped. She gathered her skirts, and wordlessly walked to the chair by the door. She sat, never looking up again.

Suddenly, the stove's heat now seemed stifling. Abby turned back to Mr. Gates. "I need to mail a letter at the post office," she mumbled. "Once you've wrapped all my things, why don't you see to Hannah's needs? I can finish up my order when I return."

Mr. Gates's bushy gray brows lifted in surprise. "Well, I suppose that'd be–"

"I do believe *I* was here, waiting my turn, long before that . . . that *woman* came in." Mary Sue rushed up to the counter on Abby's other side. She clutched the bolt of maroon and blue calico. "I demand you wait on me next, Mr. Gates."

Abby graced Mary Sue with a quiet, considering look, then nodded curtly. "Do as you see fit, Mr. Gates. I'll be back shortly."

Turning on her heel, Abby strode toward the door. Just short of it, she paused to rebutton her coat. As she did, Hannah looked up. Their glances locked, and something fragile passed between them. Something guarded, tentative . . . yet intently seeking.

Abby smiled. "God loves you, Hannah," she said, her voice pitched low so no one else could hear them. "Merry Christmas."

The girl's eyes grew wide, and instantly filled with tears. Abby swallowed hard, not knowing what else to say. Grasping the latch, she twisted it and shoved open the door.

Frigid air rushed in and whirled around her. Abby hurried outside. The door slammed shut behind her. Before she had taken two steps, however, the dark mass of a masculine body loomed before her. With a squawk, Abby plowed right into him.

Strong hands gripped her arms. A smug chuckle rumbled from a big chest.

"Well, well, now. What do we have here?"

The familiar voice, thick with an oily gratification, wrenched Abby from her tormented musings. She jerked her horrified gaze upward. Brody Gerard leered down at her.

"Didn't think I'd have the pleasure of your company again so soon, Mrs. Stanton. Did you come to Grand View alone? Perhaps we have time for another quick, passionate encounter."

Hot blood flooded Abby's face. Anger filled her. "Unhand me this instant," she demanded. "I want nothing to do with you. Do you hear me? Nothing!"

"I'd do what the lady asks, Gerard," came a deep voice behind Brody that vibrated with a quiet fury. "Do it, and do it now."

Conor, Abby thought with a rush of relief. Thank the Lord.

Brody Gerard froze. The smirk vanished from his face. His hands, however, tightened on Abby's arms.

"And what are you going to do about it if I don't, MacKay?" he snarled. "You're not on your ranch now. There'll be no hands to back you."

"I'll take my chances," Conor growled back. "I kicked myself for letting you get off Culdee Creek anyway, without beating the tar out of you. It's right nice of you to hang around Grand View for a spell. Long enough, at least, for me to correct that little oversight."

For the first time, uncertainty flashed across Brody Gerard's face. His grip loosened. Abby twisted free and stepped away.

Ever so slowly, he turned to face Conor. The two men eyed each other for the longest time. Then Gerard laughed, his voice still defiant.

"I got better things to do today than get into a fistfight with you. Especially," he rasped, "over the likes of her. Maybe some other time, MacKay."

Conor stood there. Though his hands hung loose at his sides, his stance was wide, poised for a fight. He nodded slowly. "Some other time, then."

Brody Gerard mottled with rage. He turned and jerked open the door. Sticking in his head, he leaned into the mercantile store. "Hannah, get out here! I ain't standing around all day at your beck and call."

Hannah, who was still sitting beside the door, jumped to her feet and hurried outside. Gerard cast her one sneering look, then grabbed her by the arm and headed back down the boardwalk.

Abby made a move to go after them. Conor gripped her arm and pulled her back.

"Whoa now," he said. "What do you think you're doing? I thought I just heard you telling Gerard you wanted nothing to do with him." He arched a dark brow. "Or did I misunderstand?"

Abby squelched the impulse to kick him in the shins. Snide comment or no, it really wouldn't do to repay his recent rescue with violence.

"I just wanted to stop him from treating Hannah that way," she said. "He has no right–"

"That's where I beg to differ," Conor was quick to interject. "He has every right, I imagine, to treat her any way he likes."

Abby stared up at him, confused. "What do you mean? You defended my honor against him. Why won't you defend Hannah's as well?"

"Why else?" Conor's features hardened into a mask. "Hannah's a prostitute. She deserves whatever she gets. And I'm guessing, from his presence here in Grand View, that Brody Gerard has taken on a new job working for the local madam."

Abby slid the last tray of cookies from the cookstove oven and placed it on a trivet to cool. Then she turned to survey the results of the past several hours' work. Across the big kitchen tabletop, covered with old newspapers, sat five plates of colorfully decorated cookies, a dark, rich fruitcake brimming with nuts and candied fruit, two pumpkin and one dried apple pie.

The kitchen was fragrant with the scent of baked goods. Abby knew the mouthwatering smells must surely be seeping under the parlor's closed door, where Conor and Beth MacKay were engrossed in some secret undertaking. At yet another peel of girlish laughter emanating from the other room, she smiled. It was good to hear Beth so happy. Perhaps it would indeed be a merry Christmas for them all.

Abby glanced at the small, polished oak cabinet clock sitting on the cupboard shelf. Half past nine. It would soon be time to head off to her own bunkhouse and bed. But not before, she quickly reminded herself, setting out the manger scene that she had and used every Christmas Eve since she was a child.

It would be the only holiday decorating she planned to do in her own little dwelling, and only there because such a blatant religious symbol would hardly be permitted in the MacKay household. Sadly, they hadn't even thought to put up a Christmas tree and decorate it. Knowing that, Abby was certain Conor would never tolerate her manger scene.

She sighed. Though much progress had been made in the past weeks, she feared the name of God would never be allowed here. Still, it *was* Christmas. In the morning, Abby intended on giving out the gifts she had brought and made. Surely even Conor would not begrudge her that small token of the holy season.

When the last batch of cookies had cooled, Abby lifted them from the cookie sheet and onto the last empty plate. She decorated the little gingerbread men with the remaining icing, used colored candies for their eyes and mouths, then stepped back to study them with satisfaction. As she did, the parlor door opened, then closed again.

"Abby?"

She turned to find Beth standing there, dressed in a ruffled blue gingham dress, black stockings, and high-topped, buttoned shoes. Her hair was neatly combed, her cheeks flushed, her eyes bright with excitement.

Both delighted and surprised, Abby cocked her head. "Well, don't you look pretty?"

Beth glanced down, suddenly shy. "Do you really think so?"

170

After wiping her hands on her white cotton apron, Abby walked over and crooked the girl beneath her chin. Raising her head, she smiled down at her. "Oh, yes. I do indeed."

"I think you're pretty, too."

"Me?" It was Abby's turn to blush. "Why, thank you, Beth. That's one of the nicest compliments I've ever had."

The girl grabbed her hand. "Come on. I've got something to show you. Something Papa and I did just for you."

Abby arched a brow in surprise. Then, realizing how she must look after hours of baking, she pulled back. "Wait a minute while I take off this apron." She hung her apron on a hook near the sink, swatted at her nose and cheeks in case some flour still lingered there, and gingerly touched her hair to make sure it was reasonably in place.

Beth grinned and held out her hand. "You look fine. Papa likes you just the way you are."

Her words gave Abby a jolt of pleasure. "Thank you, Beth," she murmured, attempting to make it appear as if she were giving the girl yet another lesson. "A lady, however, always tries to comport herself with dignity. And a flour-smudged face and hair askew are hardly the proper impression to leave with anyone."

Beth shrugged, apparently not at all convinced. "Maybe so, but Papa seems to like you just fine with flour on your nose. He says it makes you look"–she struggled momentarily with the correct word–"fetching."

Abby gave an unsteady laugh, took the girl by the hand, and walked with her to the closed parlor door. Beth halted her there.

"Now, close your eyes," she ordered, "and I'll lead you in. Otherwise, it won't be a surprise."

"A surprise?" Obediently, Abby closed her eyes.

"Yeah, and it's a big one, too. The biggest one, I reckon, that we've ever had at Culdee Creek."

Abby heard the door open, then felt another tug on her hand. She allowed herself to be led into the parlor. The scent of pine and beeswax reached her.

"You can open your eyes now."

The unexpected sight that greeted her took her breath away. There, taking up the entire right hand corner near the fireplace, stood a magnificent fir tree. Its lush, gray-green branches were decorated with lighted beeswax candles, rows and rows of strung cranberries, colorful paper ornaments cut in various sizes and shapes, apples, and several oranges studded with cloves. It was the most beautiful Christmas tree Abby had ever seen.

She turned to find Conor and Beth standing there, smiling back at her. Tears filled her eyes. "It's—" Abby struggled to put voice to emotions which had suddenly spiraled out of control. "It's the most wonderful surprise I've ever had. I didn't expect . . ." Her throat went tight, and tears spilled down her cheeks.

Overcome by gratitude and delight, Abby ran to them. She grabbed up first one of Beth's, then Conor's, hands. "Thank you," she whispered. "Now, it truly seems like Christmas."

"Ella said it'd be important to you." High color stained Conor's cheeks, and he gave Abby's hand a quick, awkward squeeze. "Beth wanted you to have some sort of gift for Christmas. She's spent the past few weeks cutting out decorations and stringing cranberries at Ella's."

Abby covered the little girl's hand with her free one, and squatted to meet her beaming gaze. "So this is why you've been running off to Ella's so much of late."

"Well, I sure couldn't make all the decorations here. You'd have found out for sure." Beth looked up at her father. "There's just one thing left to make it a real Christmas tree, Papa."

Conor quirked a dark brow. "And what's that, girl?"

"Ella said we need a manger and the wise men, and Mary and Joseph, and all the shepherds."

Her father frowned. "We don't have any such things, and well you know it."

Beth turned to Abby. "But I bet you do, don't you, Abby. Ella said you told her about your manger scene."

"Well, yes," Abby agreed carefully, shooting Conor an uncertain glance in case he should imagine that she had set this up with Ella. "But I wasn't planning—"

"Can Abby put her manger scene beneath our tree, Papa?" The little girl pulled free of Abby's clasp and grabbed her father by the hand. Jumping up and down, she began to pump his hand in excitement. "Oh, I so want to have a real Christmas tree, and it won't be real unless—"

Conor heaved a great sigh, and rolled his eyes. "Fine, fine. If Abby agrees, you can bring in her manger scene and put it under the tree." He turned to Abby. "But only because it's Christmas, and Beth wants it."

Beth released his hand, and turned to Abby. "Can we go now, and bring back the manger scene? Can we, can we, Abby?"

She held out her hand. "Yes, we most certainly can."

They left the parlor, and strode through the kitchen, where Abby threw on her shawl and insisted that Beth don her jacket. Then, hand in hand once more, they walked out the back door.

With a cry of delight, Abby looked around, then upward. Crystalline flakes danced and swirled in the cold night air. A light dusting of white already coated the ground. And, high above, millions of stars twinkled through a light curtain of falling snow.

"Oh, Beth," Abby exclaimed, her heart near to bursting with happiness, "it's snowing. It's snowing!"

The girl laughed. Then, after a moment's hesitation, she flung her arms about Abby's waist and gave her an

173

exuberant, bone-crushing hug. "Merry Christmas," she cried. "Merry, merry Christmas."

Abby leaned down, enfolded Beth's little body in her own arms, and held her close. Love for the child swelled in her heart. "And merry, merry Christmas to you, too."

❧

The mantle clock was just chiming midnight when Abby crept back into the main house, a basket of gifts over her arm. She had not told Beth about them, wanting them to be a surprise when the little girl awoke later that morning. Ever so carefully, she tiptoed through the kitchen and into the parlor.

Though the candles on the tree had been doused to prevent any possibility of inadvertently causing a fire, the warm red glow from the hearth was sufficient to illuminate the room. For a long moment Abby gazed at the tree. It was indeed beautiful, but the most glorious sight of all would always be the memory of Conor and Beth standing there, their eyes alight with anticipation and a satisfied joy.

The room was warm, cozy, and the fir smelled so heady, so good. Abby knelt before the manger scene placed beneath the tree, and began to pull the cloth wrapped gifts from her basket. There were doll dresses, a pair of knitted mittens, copies of Louisa May Alcott's *Little Women* and *Little Men*. And, though until tonight Abby had wondered how it might be received, a pretty red dress she had made for Beth.

Beside the pile of Beth's gifts Abby laid a package for Conor. It was a fine pair of rich brown calfskin gloves. She had seen how worn his own pair had become, and now that the coldest months of a Colorado winter were fast approaching, she hoped he would be able to put her gift to good use.

There were also gifts for all the hands of colorful new bandanas, and several presents as well for Ella and her family. As Abby finished laying out the last of her gifts, she leaned back to survey the bounty. There was only one thing left to complete the picture, and add the final, finishing touch to this very special Christmas.

Reaching into her basket, Abby withdrew the last, but definitely not the least, of all the items. It was a baby Jesus figurine. She never put it into the tiny manger until the stroke of midnight on Christmas Eve. As she did so now, a bittersweet surge of emotion engulfed her.

Two years ago this very night, a four-and-a-half-year-old Joshua had last laid the Baby Jesus into his little manger. Two years ago. How long it now seemed. Like a lifetime. A vast, yawning eternity of empty, heart-wrenching loneliness. Yet here she knelt again, performing the same ritual in someone else's home, sharing Christmas with people who were not her own family, and in so many ways not like her at all.

Fear and confusion engulfed Abby. Sorrow, so heavy it all but dragged her to the floor, pressed down on her. A sense of disorientation swallowed her.

Oh, Lord, what am I doing here? she silently cried. How has my life come to this that I now find myself all alone, kneeling on Christmas Eve on the floor of some stranger's house? All I want, and oh, how I want it, is to be with my own family on this night of nights.

Clasping her arms tightly to her, Abby began to rock to and fro, fighting against the agonizing welter of emotions that rose within her. Yet still the tears rose, spilled over. Abby sobbed, softly, brokenly.

In the next moment, in a rush of movement, other arms, strong arms, encircled her. She was pulled up hard, tightly, against a masculine chest. Conor, Abby thought through her hazy, pain-wracked blur. *Conor.*

175

He smelled of man, and wool, and leather. He felt warm, solid, comforting. She snuggled closer and sobbed harder. Her hands moved, sliding up past hair-roughened skin within his open shirt, to encircle and clasp behind his neck. Ah, but he felt so good, so very, very good!

"What is it?" The words rumbled in the depths of Conor's chest. "Tell me, Abby. Tell me."

The tenderly couched words plucked at her heart. She yearned to tell him all. Of her loss, her despair, her confusion and need. Of her rage against life, and her anger at God. Somehow she knew he would understand. But the words lodged in her throat, and would not come.

All she could do was sob, her body shaking with its intensity. And all Conor could do was hold her, rocking her gently as if she were a babe in its mother's arms. Rock her, croon nonsensical words, and endlessly, soothingly stroke her hair.

His tenderness stunned Abby. His kindness overwhelmed her. Gratitude, and a hunger so intense it took her breath away, welled up and overflowed within her. She lifted her tear-streaked face, gazed deep into Conor's eyes. There she saw an answering hunger, and an unguarded yearning in him the likes of which she had never known before.

As two long-starved, they came together, their lips meeting and melding. Like two long-starved, they drank of each other, sipping deeply at the wellspring of each other's souls.

At long last, though, they parted. Abby suddenly remembered herself, where she was, and what they were doing. She pushed away, breaking the kiss, and shoved to her feet. Flushed and shamefaced, she couldn't bear to look at him.

"I-I'm so sorry," she stammered, backing away. "I don't know what came–"

"Don't, Abby." Conor stood. "You did nothing wrong. *We* did nothing wrong. It was only a kiss."

Fighting to recapture her shredded composure, Abby clenched shut her eyes. Perhaps it was only a kiss to you, she silently cried, but to me . . .

"You've nothing to be embarrassed about." As if reading her mind, Conor took a step toward her, and reached out to grasp her arms. "I don't think any less of you. I pray you don't think any less of me, either."

Abby backed away. "I don't understand. How could I possibly lay any blame on you? It was I who responded to your innocent overtures, and all but begged you to kiss me."

"And I think you take far too much credit for what happened." He fixed her with an unwavering look. "I hardly pushed you away, did I? But I'll tell you true, Abby. I didn't hold you or kiss you just now in the hopes of taking advantage of you. I swear it."

"Then why did you . . ?" A sudden realization, a wild joy, swamped Abby. On its heels quickly followed the fear. She did not want him to want her. She did not dare let herself want him.

What had been little more than a pleasant stirring of desire was rapidly becoming something far deeper. Something that not only encompassed her heart but reawakened old hopes, dreams, and unfulfilled yearnings.

Yet surely nothing could come of a relationship with Conor. They were too different. He did not know God. Indeed, she was not even certain how Conor felt about the holy bonds of matrimony, or if he would even honor them.

Where could a woman like her fit into his life? And would he be any different, in the end, than had been her father and Thomas? Would he allow her to become the woman, the person, she'd always wished–and now intended–to be?

177

Abby backed farther from him. "I don't want to know why you held and kissed me." She vehemently shook her head. "It doesn't matter anyway."

"Doesn't it, Abby? Doesn't it?"

The truth hovered between them—implacably ruthless, inescapably relentless—and clear as the light of day. But it was also a truth not easily or wisely faced tonight of all nights. With a despairing cry, Abby turned and fled. Fled from Conor, and from her overwhelming feelings.

Yet even as she ran, Abby knew she could not run forever. Her growing desire for Conor MacKay was a force that couldn't long be denied.

12

*Humble yourselves in the sight of the Lord, and he shall
lift you up.*

James 4:10

Conor awoke early the next morning. He
walked to the window just as the sun's
rays peeked over a cloud-shrouded horizon, momentarily gilded the land, then were smothered behind
another turbulent gray cloud. He stood there for a long
while in his frigid bedroom, gazing out the frost-edged
window at the white expanse of rolling hills and snow-
topped, scattered stands of pines. Unbidden, his
thoughts harked back to his midnight encounter with
Abby.

The sound of the back door closing, and footsteps
moving cautiously across the kitchen floor had awoken
him. Though his first impulse had been to grab his Colt
45 revolver and slip downstairs to confront the intruder,
somehow Conor had known it was Abby.

He'd found her in the parlor kneeling before the Christmas tree, sobbing as if her heart would break. In the next
instant Conor was on his own knees beside her, gathering her into his arms. To his profound surprise and pleasure, Abby had instantly snuggled close, clinging to him
as if he were the long lost beacon in her darkness.

She had smelled so good, felt so right in his arms. It was the most natural thing in the world that they should eventually kiss. He had wanted her for a long while now. He had been relieved that she had at last responded to him. It marked the beginning, he had thought, of a new relationship, fraught with mystery and wonder.

With a shuddering sigh, Conor leaned his head against the ice-coated window. He closed his eyes. He had not thought any woman could ever again make him feel so vulnerable, or leave him so confused and yearning. Yet, in the space of a few fevered, chaotic minutes, Abby had done just that.

He straightened and gave a wry laugh. How ironic, after all these years, that he should moon over some woman he might never have. Since Sally and Squirrel Woman, all he'd wanted from any woman was the periodic easing of his body's physical needs. He had given little thought to the haunting, less tangible needs of his heart.

The wisest move, Conor decided, would be to put aside his growing desire for Abigail Stanton. If that required more frequent visits to Sadie Fleming's whorehouse outside Grand View for a time, then so be it. It was far better than making a fool of himself in his own house.

Yet, if the truth were told, only Abby held any appeal. Only Abby plucked at his heart, touched him as no other. Even more confounding, since he had met Abby he no longer cared to use women solely for his own pleasure.

He inhaled a deep breath and turned from the window. Walking back to the chair holding his clothes, Conor slipped on his denims, socks, and boots. What a fine Christmas this had been, he thought, with a wry shake of his head. As a sign of good faith, he had allowed Abby to have a Christmas tree. She, in turn, had gifted him with a mind-numbing load of doubts, fears, and unrequited needs.

Merry Christmas, Conor congratulated himself grimly. Merry Christmas and–

A knock, tentative and timid, sounded at the door. Conor grabbed up his woolen shirt and pulled it on. Then he strode across his room and wrenched open the door.

Beth stood there in a pink and white flannel nightgown, its high neck enclosed by lace and ribbons. At sight of him, her happy expression faded.

"Wh-what's wrong, Papa?" she asked. "I heard you moving about, so I thought it was all right to come visit."

Conor's heart gave a guilty lurch. He forced a smile. "It's nothing, girl. Nothing at all." He began to button the front of his shirt. "What can I do for you at such an early hour?"

His daughter's eyes brightened once more. She brushed a tangled hank of hair from her face. "I went downstairs for a peek at the tree. I saw some presents there. Some presents for you and me!"

"Indeed?" In the intensity of the moment, Conor hadn't noticed much else last night but Abby. Now, though, it all made sense, her presence there so late in the parlor.

Beth's head bobbed in agreement. "We gave Abby a Christmas gift, so she must have given us some, too." She grabbed his hand. "Can we go down and see them, Papa? Can we open them?"

So, Conor thought sourly, Abby had not seen fit to stop with just her rejection of him. She had chosen to twist the knife deeper by being kind and thoughtful, and full of the Christmas spirit. A sudden impulse to take up her gifts and fling them back at her filled him.

But he couldn't, and wouldn't. This was the first time they had celebrated Christmas since Squirrel Woman had died. He had not seen Beth this excited or happy in a long while. His tumultuous feelings for Abby notwithstanding, Conor wasn't about to deny his daughter this fleeting moment of joy.

Unfortunately, if Beth's enthusiasm for this Christmas celebration were any evidence, it would not be the last. Whether intended or not, Abigail Stanton had seen to that, too.

"Yes." Conor nodded, pasting on a happy face as he allowed himself to be tugged from his bedroom. "We can go down and open the gifts."

Five minutes later, as he added fresh logs and tinder to the hearth and stirred the coals to a renewed flame, Beth excitedly sorted presents, delighted to find the majority were for her. She had the good manners, however, to wait until her father finally joined her before tearing into her little pile of gifts.

Conor watched her, unable to long hold back a grin of pleasure. Only when she had finished opening and remarking over all of hers did he at last unwrap his own gift from Abby. The gloves were a surprise. He fingered the fine leather, his emotions mixed. He also, he belatedly realized, must have frowned.

"Why do you look so angry, Papa?" Beth gazed up at him in concern. "Don't you like Abby's present?"

"Yes, I like it very much." He sighed. "It was kind of her to do this for us."

"I didn't know Christmas could be so fun. I always wanted to get gifts like the ones I saw under Aunt Ella and Uncle Devlin's tree each year, but I didn't know how really, really nice it was until we finally had Christmas in our own house. Let's do it again next year. Please, please, Papa?"

Gifts, fun, excitement. They weren't the true reason, Conor knew, for the celebration of this holiday. He could almost hear his mother, her voice soft and dear, speaking to him, reminding him even now of what he had chosen so long ago to forget. Forget the fleeting moments of Christian happiness he had had with his own family, because it hurt too much to remember.

"Be always mindful, Conor, lad," she had instructed him one Christmas when he was nearly the same age as Beth, "of the lowly stable and its precious occupant. And make of your heart the humble, hallowed bed in which to lay the Holy Child."

Something stirred deep within Conor, a movement, a subtle shifting of memories and convictions. He did not know if he could stoop so low again. It was a mighty thing to ask of a proud man. But for a brief moment, for his daughter's sake, Conor would try.

He gestured toward Abby's little wooden manager scene sitting beneath the tree. "Christmas isn't about gifts, girl," he rasped, his voice thick with emotion. "It's about the baby born so long ago to a simple man and woman of Israel. Would you like to hear the story?"

"Yes, Papa." Beth nodded solemnly.

After all these years, Conor wasn't so sure he could trust such a tale to memory. He rose, walked to the big oak cupboard and bookcase. From the top shelf he took down an ancient Bible and began to leaf through the timeworn pages. It had been his father's Bible, passed down from generation to generation of devout Christians, all the way back to his grandfather Sean MacKay, the first MacKay to emigrate from Scotland during the horrible years of the Highland Clearances.

As he turned the pages, searching for the story his mother always read to him on Christmas Eve, a sense of continuity, of union and fellowship with all the MacKays who had come before him washed over Conor. It was a glorious, if humbling experience. The realization made his eyes burn and his throat tighten.

With trembling fingers, Conor finally touched the page wherein began chapter two of St. Luke, the physician. "And it came to pass in those days," he began to read, "that there went out a decree from Caesar Augustus, that all the world should be taxed . . ."

§

All day Conor pursued Abby, searching for an opportune moment to confront her about their midnight kiss. His pursuit, however, proved fruitless until late that evening. After the big Christmas dinner given for the hands and an endless and totally unexpected round of Christmas carols led by the ever ebullient Irishman, Frank Murphy, Abby's frenzied efforts to put the kitchen aright then began. Though he waited patiently through it all, after a time, Conor couldn't help but view Abby's endless dashing about the kitchen as a pretense to avoid him. At long last, with a silent house and Beth put to bed, that patience finally wore thin.

As she stood at the sink washing the last of the dishes, Conor poured them both a mug of coffee. Pausing beside her, he impaled her with a hard-eyed stare. "We need to talk. Come. Sit."

Her hands shook so badly she dropped the dishrag she'd been holding. "I-I can't," Abby stammered, not quite meeting his gaze. "It's late, and I need to finish the dishes."

"And if the rest sit until tomorrow, who's to care?" Conor refused to be deterred. "I'm the only one you really need worry about." He indicated the seat across from him, where he had set her coffee. "Now, sit, will you? And wipe that petrified look off your face. Why now, because of one little kiss, do you act as if I've suddenly become some monster?"

Abby blushed crimson. "I don't think you've become a monster, Conor MacKay. But please, just let it be. I can't deal with this, or you, right now."

184

Anger swelled in Conor. He had been right. She had been avoiding him all day. "How long do you plan to pretend it never happened?" he demanded. "How long will it take before you *are* ready to talk?"

When she refused to answer, he slammed his fist on the table. The coffee mugs trembled, and some of their contents sloshed over the sides. "Blast it, Abby! Don't do this to me." Try as he might, Conor could not control the frustrated rage boiling within him. If he did not take care, there was no telling what this infuriating woman might drive him to.

"If my holding and kissing you revolted you so badly," Conor tried again, attempting to take a less threatening tack, "just say so and be done with it. Tell me I was out of line, that you don't want it to ever happen again. But don't dance around me, pretend I'm not there, all the while hoping and praying that I really *will* go away."

Like a flower wilting on the stem, the fight seemed to drain from her. Abby lowered herself into the chair. She buried her face in her hands.

"I'm sorry," she moaned. "I don't mean to make you feel bad just because you kissed me. It's just . . . just that I'm so confused."

Conor gripped his mug. "Well, I'm confused, too." He stared into the dark depths of his coffee. "I ache to hold you, Abby. I yearn to kiss you again and again. Yet you make me feel to reattempt either would be to cause you dishonor."

He laughed, and the sound was bleak, despairing. "And you think *you're* confused!"

"Please, Conor. I said I didn't wish to talk about this."

"Why?" He jerked his gaze up to meet hers. "Because you might find yourself admitting to some feelings for me? Because you might find yourself in my arms again, kissing me?"

Fire flashed in her eyes. "You'd like that, wouldn't you? You'd like me to throw myself at you like . . . like all the others."

The accusation struck Conor full in the face. Pain twisted in him. So, he thought, she didn't know him that well after all.

"You see me as some depraved monster, don't you, Abby?" he asked softly. "A man who'd stoop so low as to take advantage of a woman in her moment of weakness. A man," he added as a sudden thought struck him, "who, because he's no longer a practicing Christian, can never be worthy of you."

"No, no." Abby moaned. "Please, Conor. Don't drag my religious beliefs into this. It's far more than just that."

"Then tell me what it is, Abby. Help me understand."

She sighed, and closed her eyes. "I . . . can't. It's too personal, and I don't wish to talk about it."

In the void she'd purposely created, fresh questions, myriad scenarios, crowded into Conor's mind. Did the problem lie with her first marriage? Had her husband been cruel to her or forced his lovemaking on her until she'd come to loathe the marriage bed, and anything remotely related to it? Or, was it something more simple and direct, like a continuing fear of him or, even, some quandary over her growing feelings for him?

A wild hope flared. Could it be? Could Abby actually fear her own desires?

The question took Conor aback. He'd known for awhile now that things were changing between them. But never had he imagined a woman like Abby would ever want him.

Relief, then joy filled him. Yet, at the same time, both emotions were tempered by the realization of his profound responsibility in the matter. What Abby might be offering was a precious gift, a fragile flower that could be savored or thoughtlessly, greedily crushed. It all depended on the handling–*his* handling–of her offering.

If he had been a godly man, perhaps he would have known the proper way to approach Abby. But he wasn't God-filled. After all these years, he did not even know how to begin again.

More importantly, he wasn't so sure–even for Abby's sake–that he dared try.

He groaned in exasperation and shoved a hand through his hair. "Why in the blazes do you have to make this so hard? Though I'll admit to wanting you, I don't want you like 'all the others.' If I did, it'd be far easier on the both of us."

She shot him a quizzical look. "You're beginning to confuse me."

"Well, confusion can sometimes be the first step to enlightenment."

"I suppose so." Abby frowned. "If it were just us, this would all be easier, Conor. In time, we could work out our problems like two adults. But it isn't just us."

His heart sank. "Beth."

"Yes." Abby nodded. "Beth. If we allowed . . . allowed *things*"–she bit her lip and blushed again–"to grow warmer between us, and it didn't lead to marriage, well, one way or another, I couldn't stay on."

"So, after just one kiss, we're now speaking of marriage, are we?"

Abby rolled her eyes. Was the man truly as thick-skulled as he seemed to pretend to be? "I'm not saying I'd ever want to marry you, Conor MacKay. But if you haven't surmised it by now, that's the only course any relationship I'd have with a man could eventually take."

"As a matter of fact, I had pretty much surmised that about you, Abby." He took a deep swallow of his coffee. "But I'll tell you true. Marriage is the farthest thing from my mind, too. I am willing to go slowly, though, and see where this leads. That's more than I've been willing to do with anyone else for a long while now."

"That's very flattering." Abby tried to soften her next words with a smile. "But I repeat. While we dance about, testing and toying with the idea of possibly becoming more deeply committed, where does that leave Beth? *We* know it might lead to naught. Will Beth?"

"No, Beth might not understand. And, despite all our efforts to the contrary, she might still get hurt. I don't want that to happen. But there are no guarantees in anything in life." Conor hesitated, then locked glances with hers. "I wouldn't risk hurting my daughter again for just any woman, Abby. But I just might for you."

A sudden light flared in his eyes. "There's more to this than Beth, though, isn't there? If I were a betting man, I'd bet you're just using her to hide behind rather than face your true feelings and risk being hurt again."

For a long while, Abby rolled her mug between her hands, studying the swirling, black depths of her coffee. How could she make him understand, she wondered, when she barely understood herself?

"Perhaps you're right, Conor," she murmured at last. "Maybe that's why it's best you leave this be. Leave it be, and permit us to go on as before."

"And forget about the kiss we shared? Forget about the feelings growing between us?" He exhaled a weary breath. "Blast it, Abby. There you go, running like some spooked mustang."

She looked up at him then, and the expression in her eyes was haunted, anguished. "With the Lord's help, I do the best I can, Conor. I've come a long way in picking up the pieces of my life since Thomas's and Joshua's deaths, in seeing it through here at Culdee Creek as long as I have. Perhaps I still have got a long way to go, but I must do it at my own pace. My pace, Conor. Not yours, or anyone else's."

"I respect that wish, Abby. Truly I do."

"Then why can't you be satisfied with our just being friends? It's all I can deal with right now."

"Friends?" Conor gave a bitter laugh. "If I haven't made it clear enough, let me do so now. I want to be more than friends."

"But not enough to think of taking me to wife."

"That's hardly an appropriate subject at present, and you know it. Besides, marriage is more than *I* can deal with right now."

"Then we're at an impasse," she said softly. "I will not allow us to become more than friends. I won't come to your bed or permit our relationship to take us that far."

At her bluntly spoken words, once again Conor felt his anger rise. Suddenly he felt cast adrift in a sea of bewildering, distasteful choices. Friendship, he sneered to himself. He wasn't so sure he even knew how to be friends with a woman, especially one he desired more and more with each passing day.

Yet here she sat, defying him, as immovable and unyielding as the mountains of the Front Range, as gloriously upright in her convictions. Humbling as it was for him to admit, Conor knew his own back was up against a wall. Abby had left him few options.

He sighed, lowered his head, and massaged his throbbing temples. What was he getting himself into here? First, he had been forced to swallow his pride and apologize for the incident with Brody Gerard. Whether Abby realized it or not, uttering those words of contrition had nearly ripped his guts out. And now he had to be the one to give in, concede defeat. The woman had bested him again!

"Fine. Fine," Conor gritted through clenched teeth. "Though I don't hold out much hope that this friendship idea will work, perhaps it is the best of all evils."

"It is, Conor. For us, *and* Beth."

He all but crushed his mug of coffee between his hands. Summoning his last ounce of willpower, he gave a curt nod of assent. "And Beth, of course," Conor conceded, knowing he had no other choice. Or at least, he amended that quickly, no other choice for now.

Abigail Stanton hadn't won. No, not by a long shot. There were many, many more skirmishes to come–and he was a master strategist in a war she knew very little of.

13

Many waters cannot quench love, neither can the floods drown it.

Song of Solomon 8:7

True to his word, Conor made no further mention of the Christmas Eve kiss. For all apparent purposes, he appeared to have accepted Abby's request that they just be friends. December faded into a typically cold, bitter Colorado January, and Abby began to relax once more in his presence. She buried her own, still confused feelings, pretending, as well as she could, that their passionate encounter had never happened.

Things resumed their usual, comfortable routine. Life seemed safe. Abby began to hope that all could be as before.

One snowy day near the end of January, Ella asked Abby and Beth to go sledding on some hills just north of the ranch. Tired of being cooped up inside, Abby readily agreed. By mid morning, the group was bundled in warm coats, boots, hats, and mittens, and happily dragging sleds behind them as they trekked up the first hill.

"Thank you for inviting us, Ella," Abby exclaimed as she trudged through the knee-deep snow. "I really needed this."

"Yes," her friend admitted, "it does get a bit close indoors after a while. Considering there's at least another three months left of cold and frosty weather, we may just need to make this a regular excursion."

Abby grinned. "Most definitely."

Ella cocked her head. "Do you know how to ice skate? There are several ponds not far away that freeze over very well at this time of year."

"Oh, yes. I love it. I've even been told I'm quite the graceful skater."

"Then you'll have to give me lessons." Ella laughed. "Not with the actual act of skating–I can handle that reasonably well–but with being more graceful. Devlin tells me I look like a lumbering ox on the ice."

"It's funny, isn't it, how a man manages to lose whatever small shred of tact he possesses, once he has taken you to wife." Abby reached the top of the hill. Below them, Beth and little Devlin Jr. had already taken off and were sailing down, their delighted shrieks reaching all the way up to the two women. "My Thomas–the Lord rest his soul–could get quite condescending at times."

"Oh, I think Devlin means his little jibes all in good fun. Or, at least, most of the time." The red-haired woman's smile faded. "He just can't help himself sometimes. It's been a hard year, since Mary was born. Though the episodes are few and far between nowadays, Devlin can still occasionally get into one of his black moods."

Suddenly, her eyes filled with tears. "Oh, Abby," she wept, "I just don't know what to do with him anymore. I love Devlin so, and he loves me, but the d-doctor warned us not t-to–"

The conversation had taken a startling and quite unexpected turn. It was evident that Ella needed to talk. Abby glanced around. Not ten feet away lay several fallen, rotting trees. She gestured to them.

"Why don't we sit over there, and wait for Beth and Devlin Jr. to rejoin us?" Leaving her sled where it lay, Abby took Ella by the arm and gently guided her to the fallen logs.

By the time they had taken their seats, Ella had managed to regain her composure. She quickly swiped away her tears and forced a tremulous smile. "It's really nothing, Abby," she said in an apparent attempt to reassure her. "I just get a bit weepy from time to time. You know how it is, what with all the responsibility of a husband and family."

"Yes, I remember it well." Abby took Ella's hand in hers. "But I get the feeling this is something more than the usual demands and concerns of family life. I don't wish to pry, but"–she flashed another grin–"besides being a graceful skater, I've got a very sympathetic shoulder to cry on."

Ella sighed and looked away. "Doc Childress told me if I got myself in a family way again, I risked dying in the birthing. I bled badly after Mary came. Doc almost couldn't save me. He said it would probably only get worse with each succeeding confinement."

"I'm sorry, Ella." Sympathy filled Abby. "I know how much you love your children."

"Yes, I do." Ella turned back to Abby. "But if two were all the good Lord wished me to have, I could content myself with that. The problem isn't so much with having more babies, but with Devlin, and our religious beliefs. Well," she added sadly, "more with *my* religious beliefs, I guess, than Devlin's. At the very best, he's lukewarm in his devotion to God."

Though the MacKays attended the Episcopal Church, Abby knew they were both Roman Catholics. She also knew that it must be difficult for Ella to share such a highly personal matter. In better society, such things just weren't routinely discussed.

193

"I assume then," she said, addressing the subject with the greatest delicacy, "that female preventatives are out of the question. Is there nothing else you can do to avoid another confinement, save not perform your wifely duties?"

Ella hung her head. "No. Or at least very little else with any real chance of success," she replied in a choked voice. "I fear this will tear our marriage apart."

Just then, Beth and Devlin Jr. topped the hill. Abby smiled and motioned for Beth to go on sledding. The girl hesitated, then turned to her little playmate, set him back on the sled, and climbed on behind him. With another shriek of delight, they set off down the hill.

"If Devlin truly loves you," Abby then said, returning her attention to Ella, "he'll understand. The conjugal act isn't all that necessary anyway, save to procreate children."

Ella's head raised. Surprise lifted her brows. "When a man and a woman are truly in love, Abby, the conjugal act is a very important part of the marriage. Their physical union is a great gift of the Lord's, and one that's deeply valued and enjoyed. Wasn't it that way with you and your Thomas?"

At her friend's sharp scrutiny, Abby felt her cheeks grow warm. In the flicker of an eye, the conversation had taken an unexpected turn. Now she–and her marriage–had become the focus.

"It doesn't matter how things were between Thomas and me. I only wished to offer you comfort, to help put things in their proper perspective."

"And I deeply appreciate your efforts. Truly I do." Ella patted Abby's hand. "I won't pry further into your personal life with your husband." She inhaled another deep breath. "For us–and especially for Devlin–conjugal intimacy is very important. But now that Doc has said this, well, Devlin's even accused me of loving God more than him!"

194

Ella gave an unsteady laugh. "When it comes to the importance of the Lord in my life, he just doesn't understand."

Abby thought of Conor. As difficult as it had been to refuse his offer of a deeper relationship, she had been right to do so. If such problems could arise in a marriage where both spouses were Christians, even if one was lukewarm, how potentially catastrophic might it be when one had completely turned his back on the Lord?

"You must pray unceasingly that Devlin comes to understand." Just as unceasingly, she added silently, as she had begun to pray of late that Conor might return to the Lord. "Perhaps this is a time of testing. If so, both of you will come out of it even stronger Christians and spouses than you were before."

"Devlin has called on the brothel outside Grand View, Abby. At least four or five times since September."

Abby choked back a gasp of dismay. "Oh, Ella. I'm so sorry. So very, very sorry," she finally managed to say.

"Devlin doesn't know that I know, Abby." She turned more fully to face her. "I think he's stopped going there. We were fighting a lot in those days. He'd gotten so upset that he had started drinking sometimes in the evenings after I went to bed." She sighed. "I suppose he imagined it would dull his needs . . ."

Abby couldn't imagine continuing to live with Thomas if she had ever discovered he had been unfaithful. "How can you stand to be in the same room with him now? How can you even bear to look at him, Ella?"

"How?" Ella's eyes filled with tears. "Because I love him, Abby. Love him, and forgive him."

"But is he truly repentant? Can you be certain he isn't still sneaking off to the brothel from time to time?"

"I think Devlin's sorry for what he did. He appears to have accepted my decision to abstain from any further intimacies. We don't fight anymore, he doesn't drink and, once again, he's the loving, attentive man I first married."

"Then why do you think this might tear your marriage apart?" Abby asked, now puzzled. "If Devlin has come to terms with the problem, and you've forgiven him—?"

"He's a healthy, virile man, Abby!" Ella blurted, her voice raw with her grief. "He'll try his best for a while now. But it can't last forever. He's going to get even more frustrated. And to tell you the truth, I don't know how much longer I can last, either. I miss lying close to him at night, being held in his arms. Forgive me if this sounds crude to you, but I miss the touch of his flesh on mine, his tender caresses. And I miss the exquisite union of our hearts and bodies." She moaned piteously. "If only I'd never known!"

If only I'd never known . . .

Ella's words echoed in Abby's mind. She realized that what Ella missed she had never truly known. Never known, and never wished to know . . . until she'd met Conor MacKay.

He drew her in so many ways. Drew her with his darkly handsome countenance, his piercing eyes, his tall, strong body, and his magnetically powerful personality. Yet it was the secret, undiscovered depths of his heart that beckoned to Abby most forcefully of all.

Beneath that aloof and arrogant façade lay an intriguing human being. He was brave and principled in his own way. He was capable of great gentleness and love. He was fair and generous to those who were loyal to him. And he was beginning to show he was capable of seeing her for the woman she was, and even respecting her beliefs and needs.

True, it had been a battle at times to eke out Conor's reluctant demonstrations of respect, and convince him of the need for compromise. But he listened and, even in his

196

worst moments, he heard and understood her. He seemed–save for the continuing thread of bitterness that wound through his life, and his adamant refusal to follow the Lord–everything Abby could wish for in a husband.

Yet, she fiercely reminded herself, she hadn't come to Culdee Creek to find another husband. She had come to find herself. Abby still feared that the two might be mutually incompatible. Indeed, after her early experiences with her father and Thomas, she had a great deal of reason to fear.

Far better to keep to the straight and narrow path she had chosen after her husband and son had died. Far better to look heavenward, and eschew the call of the flesh. In time, with holy discipline and self-sacrifice, she could surely mute this heart-tugging attraction she felt for Conor.

And if she couldn't . . . well, in time her work here would be done.

"I see that I've upset you."

Like a voice calling from the mist, Ella's statement beckoned Abby back. She gave a start, then focused her vision on her friend. "No, you haven't upset me, Ella," Abby said. "Rather, you've given me much food for thought."

"About Conor?"

She hesitated. "Yes, about Conor."

"Why do you fight your attraction to him so? Surely by now you've come to understand him and see him for the good man he really is."

Abby met Ella's questioning, bewildered gaze. "It's not as simple as that."

"Falling in love rarely is a simple thing. There are always two people involved, and those two people bring their past and all their hopes and fears into the relationship."

"That's just the problem." Abby sighed. "Neither Conor nor I are ready. He's already told me marriage is the furthest thing from his mind. And, for my part, I'm not so certain I'll ever again be willing to submit to the domination of a husband."

"Conor's but a wounded animal, circling the idea of ever committing his heart again." Ella smiled. "And you might well change your view of marriage, if you find the right man. Though Conor's strong-willed, I hardly think he's of a mind to dominate a woman. He learned that the hard way, with Sally."

She laughed. "Besides, if I'm not far off the mark, I don't get the impression you'd let a man dominate you, either. You certainly haven't let Conor push you around."

"It's different once you're married. You know as well as I do the Bible teaches that wives should be subject to their husbands."

"It also teaches that a husband should honor his wife and love her as he loves himself," Ella countered quietly. "How can a man truly do those things if he treats his wife like some possession, or even like a child? To my mind, to honor someone is to treat them with the utmost respect." Ella wet her lips then forged on. "He cares for you, you know?"

She looked away. "I don't want to hear that, Ella." Abby's voice dropped to a tortured whisper. "I don't want to know."

"Your denial won't change what is."

"I didn't mean for this to happen!"

"Neither did Conor, I'm sure. But it has. And the question now is: What are you going to do about it?"

Abby shook her head, misery swamping her. "I don't know. He kissed me on Christmas Eve. I've never been so frightened in my whole life as I was afterwards, when I realized what we'd done, and how easily it could've led to . . . to other things."

"A kiss isn't a sin, Abby." Ella scooted close and wrapped her arm about Abby's shoulders. She gave her a quick squeeze.

Abby lifted eyes burning with despair. "I wanted far, far more than a kiss from Conor, Ella. The feel of him pressed close to me, the scent of his skin, his taste . . ." She clutched her arms tightly to her. "I've never felt like I felt with him that night. For a moment in his arms, I forgot about everything else. Even," she said, her breath catching, "even about God."

"Oh, Abby, Abby." Her friend laid her head against hers. "Don't you think it was the Lord who made us that way, when a man and woman come together in love? And doesn't such a love, when sanctified by the holy bonds of matrimony, honor the very God who made them?"

"But, if it had happened that night, it wouldn't have been sanctified by marriage," Abby wailed. "And yet I came so close to not even caring. Oh, Ella, what kind of woman have I become?"

"A woman who has finally awakened to herself, and her true woman's needs?"

Abby flushed. She hadn't meant to imply that Thomas hadn't fulfilled her. To say any more would surely dishonor his memory.

"I tell you true, Ella," she finally forced herself to reply. "I fear those woman's needs. For me, they seem nothing more than an occasion for sin."

The red-haired woman nodded. "They can indeed be. It seems to me, though, that instead of turning from Conor and what you two might share, you need to battle the temptations and not let them overcome you." She arched a brow. "Isn't he worth the risk?"

Abby lowered her head. "I don't know, Ella. Is anyone worth the risk of losing God?"

"No, no one is," she replied. "But is that the choice the Lord is asking of you? Think long and hard on that one, Abby."

With a slow, tender movement of her mouth, Ella returned Abby's wobbly smile. "What matters most, though, I think, is caring about and needing the other person badly enough to risk all. It's finding the courage to follow one's heart. And it's clinging to the faith that love can surmount what has happened before, and surpass what's yet to come."

ॐ

Abby spent a restless night pondering Ella's words, and her friend's heartbreaking revelation of her husband's infidelity. Any woman would've found such a betrayal painful. Knowing how deeply Ella loved Devlin, Abby sensed that this particular breach of trust was especially devastating.

What if she allowed herself to fall in love with Conor with the same intensity of love that Ella felt for her husband? Then what if he decided that he wanted nothing more to do with her? What would she do then? The consequences were too terrible to consider.

Time and again, Conor had proven himself to be a hard man, used to taking what he wanted, yet also equally as willing to deny himself if that served him better. What if he decided it best for him to withhold his love? Even worse, what if he offered her his love, but refused to wed her? And what if, in the end, he was incapable of loving again as Abby wished to be loved?

With a groan of despair, she reared up in bed, pounded her pillow, then flipped over onto her side. Love was too hard, too fraught with dangerous consequences. No wonder her father had decided to make the choice for her. Had he even, in his wisdom, purposely chosen for her a kind but passionless man? In many ways, it now seemed safer than risking one's happiness and independence by chaining one's heart to some hopeless dream.

Yet why, then, did her yearning for Conor grow stronger with each passing day? Why was it becoming increasingly harder to see him, be near him, and not want to fall into his arms? Was it because it really was God's will that she should come to love and wed this man, or simply something baser? Something she must fight against with all her strength?

The battle raged for hours but, at long last, exhaustion claimed Abby. She drifted off to sleep—a sleep rife with dreams of heat and fire, and a terrible punishment.

Flames surged up around her. Smoke engulfed her. She choked, clawing at the air.

Abby awoke with a start to find herself sitting upright in bed. Immediately, the scent of something burning assailed her. She gagged as foul, acrid smoke filled her lungs.

A crackling noise reached her. She noted, for the first time, a faint light permeating the room. She looked upward.

There, above the woodstove, flames licked at the ceiling. The metal stovepipe glowed an eerie red.

With a cry, Abby flung back the covers and leaped from bed. She slammed her feet into her boots, and threw her wool coat over her shoulders. Heedless of the frigid weather and slippery, snow-covered terrain, she ran outside.

The back door of the main house was unlocked. She rushed inside and headed for the stairs leading up to the bedrooms.

"Conor," she screamed, taking the steps two at a time. "Conor, come quick. The bunkhouse is on fire!"

As she reached the top of the stairs, Abby heard a muffled curse, then the sound of bare feet slapping against the floor. Breathing hard, she clutched her coat over her nightgown, slid to a stop outside his bedroom, and waited. A minute later Conor, bleary-eyed and haphazardly dressed, appeared in his doorway.

"What happened?"

"I-I don't know," Abby stammered. "I'm guessing it's a chimney fire. The upper part of the stovepipe looks red hot, and the ceiling and roof above it are in flames."

He shoved a hand through his uncombed hair. "Water will be hard to come by in this freezing weather," he muttered. "We'll have to use snow."

Conor fixed her with a fierce look. "Run to Devlin's house and rouse him. I'll roust out the hands."

The two headed down the stairs, hurried across the kitchen, and parted on their separate missions. By the time all available help had been commandeered, the entire bunkhouse roof was in flames. Smoke billowed from the open door. Ladders were soon placed against the little house, and buckets of snow were hauled up in an attempt to douse the fire.

It did little good. As Abby stood there watching the men fight what was rapidly becoming a losing battle, she suddenly remembered her belongings. Frantic, she ran over to Conor, who was directing the fire fighting efforts.

"My things!" she gasped. "My trunks and sewing machine. Is there any way anything can be saved?"

With a face smudged black from the smoke, Conor turned and looked down at her. "We can try, but I can't promise we'll salvage much. The fire's out of control."

"Wendell, H.C.!" He shouted over the din, signaling the two closest hands. "Over here."

The two men hurried to his side.

"Wet some blankets, cover yourselves, and see what you can save from inside. Try for Abby's sewing machine

202

first, then her trunks. But don't risk your safety. If it looks too bad in there, get out with what you can."

The men nodded. A few minutes later, covered with wet wool blankets, they headed into the bunkhouse. They soon returned with the sewing machine and one trunk. Another trip inside, and they dragged out Abby's other trunk plus an armload of books. This time, though, thick, black smoke followed them. Abby could see the tongues of flame leaping within, devouring everything in their path. The two men bent, coughing and struggling for breath.

Finally, a soot-blackened Wendell staggered over. "That's about all we d-dare bring out, Mr. MacKay," he panted. "What with all the smoke, we could hardly see or breathe that last trip inside."

Abby grasped the ranch hand by the arm. "It's okay, Wendell." She forced a smile. "You've done all you could. There's nothing left in there that's more important than your—"

Her breath caught, then Abby uttered a small cry. "My pictures! Joshua's drawings and lock of hair!" She had lost so much. She could not bear to lose what little she had left.

Without thinking, Abby darted toward the bunkhouse. Conor grabbed her by the arm and jerked her back.

"Where in the blazes do you think you're going?"

Tears streaming down her face, Abby twisted and fought to free herself. "Let me go! My metal box!" she sobbed. "I have to get my metal box!"

Conor pulled Abby to him. "Are you mad? Didn't you just hear Wendell say that was it? It's too dangerous to go back in there, Abby. The roof is going to collapse any second now."

"I don't care! It's all I have left of Joshua and Thomas," she wailed, even as she fought to control the mindless panic rising inside her. "Let me go. Let me go, I say!"

"Ella." Conor motioned to her. "Come here, quick."

Ella hurried over.

Conor shoved Abby into her arms. "Hold onto her, and don't let her go."

"Please, please, Conor," Abby begged, now sobbing hysterically. He didn't understand. No one could understand. "Just let me go in. The box is on the table. I left it there tonight. I'll be in and out in less than a minute. I have to have it, Conor. I just have to."

He stared down at her, his features set in a steely resolve. In the depths of his eyes, however, something wavered, momentarily softened. "No, Abby. I won't let you do it," he said with a quiet conviction. "It's too dangerous."

Conor bent and picked up the scorched blanket Wendell had dropped. "But, if it means so all-fired much to you, I'll go instead."

For a moment frozen in time, their gazes locked. Something precious, poignant, passed between them. Then Conor released her and backed away.

"Hold onto her!" he ordered Ella. Throwing the blanket over his head and shoulders, he turned and, without a backward glance, ran into the flaming bunkhouse.

14

I will bring the blind by a way that they knew not; I will lead them in paths that they have not known.

Isaiah 42:16

Flames shot from the broken windows. A deafening roar filled the air. Clouds of smoke billowed and furled, its wind-borne soot blackening everything in its wake.

Precious seconds, then minutes passed. Still Conor did not come out of the burning bunkhouse.

Terror filled Abby. *Lord! Please, Lord!* she prayed. *Don't let any harm come to him.*

Then, without warning, a fire-eaten roof timber fell, crashing down into the bunkhouse's interior. With a cry, Abby wrenched free of Ella's grip. Her booted feet slipped in the muddy mire. She skidded, lost her balance, and fell to one knee.

Conor. Conor was in there. She *had* to get to Conor.

Behind her, voices lifted. Voices crying out her name. Frantically, Abby shoved to her feet and kept on running. They must not catch her, she thought through her panic-stricken haze. They would hold her back, keep her from Conor.

Then, from out of the conflagration that was now the bunkhouse, a dark figure appeared. Flame-covered, it hurtled itself through the fire, sailed out over the small porch, then plummeted down to the muddy ground.

Conor hit hard, grunting in pain. In his hands, though, he clutched the small metal box. Then, as if it were suddenly too hot to hold, he flung it away, and began rolling wildly in an apparent effort to extinguish his still burning blanket.

Abby was the first to reach him. Heedless of her own safety, she began slapping at the flames. "Conor," she cried, when he tried to roll away. "Lie still! Let me put out the fire!"

A moment later, Devlin and H.C. rushed up to help her.

Devlin pushed her aside. "Let us do it," he ordered gruffly. "We've got gloves on."

Ella joined them, dragging Abby back. "Let the men take care of him, Abby."

Abby stood there, her nightgown wet and mud-soaked to the knees, shivering and sobbing. "It was m-my fault," she wailed as she watched the men fight to smother the flames. Then she could bear to watch no more. She turned and buried her face in Ella's shoulder. "If something should happen to C-Conor I don't kn-know what I'd do. *It was all my f-fault!*"

"Hush, hush," her friend crooned, patting her back. "It's no one's fault. And Conor will be fine, just you wait and see."

With a sickening implosion of falling timbers, the entire roof of the bunkhouse collapsed. Abby wheeled about. Soot mixed with glowing red embers surged upward. Then, like a gentle fall of snow, the flakes of burnt, blackened wood covered them.

Now that it was all but over, the horror of the night rose to consume her. Abby clenched shut her eyes. The loss of her home and belongings. The realization that Conor had nearly died. She swallowed hard against a sudden rush of nausea. She had been so self-serving and stupid in her concern over some possessions, no matter how dear they were to her.

Abby turned. Conor still lay on the muddy ground, Devlin and H.C. kneeling around him. They had turned him over, and were pulling off the remnants of the charred, smoking blanket. She squared her shoulders and rejoined them.

"Conor." She sank to her knees beside him. "Are you all right?" Ever so gingerly, Abby touched him. "I'm so sorry I asked you to go back in there. It was selfish and thoughtless of me. Can you forgive me?"

Without using his hands, he shoved awkwardly to his elbows. His face was black. In the light of lanterns that some of the other hands had quickly brought over, Abby could see myriad scorched patches on his shirt and denims. A freshened pang of guilt assailed her. Impulsively, she reached for his hand.

Conor jerked it away. "Don't touch my hands. The rest of me might be a bit worse for the wear, but I burned my hands." He sucked in a ragged breath as he extended his arm to H.C. to be pulled to his feet. "Your metal box was fire hot. I didn't have time to do anything but grab it and run. As it was, I barely avoided that first timber that crashed down, splitting the table."

Abby climbed to her feet. "Let's get you into the house and better light." She scooped up two handfuls of clean snow and gently applied some to each of Conor's palms. "Please help him," she directed Devlin and H.C. "The sooner I can get a good look at his hands the sooner we can get him treated."

The two men lost no time and began to lead Conor away. He glanced over his shoulder. "Don't forget your metal box," he called to her. "Just be careful. It might still be pretty hot."

207

After what it might have cost Conor, Abby was not so certain she ever wanted to see that box again. Its safe retrieval, however, had been bought at great cost.

She carefully grasped the box with a large piece of Conor's discarded blanket. Then, accompanied by Ella, Abby followed the men into the main house.

Beth was standing at the window. When they entered, the frightened little girl took one look at her father and ran to him.

He put up his hands in a warding motion. "Stay back, girl. I'm hurt pretty bad." He indicated a nearby chair. "Why don't you sit there for right now? Once we get settled, I'm sure Abby will need your help." Conor shot Abby a piercing look. "Won't you, Abby?"

She nodded and smiled reassuringly at Beth. "Help Conor to the table," she then ordered Devlin and H.C. Closing the back door after Ella, Abby began to remove her wool coat when she froze in her tracks. Red-faced, she met her friend's gaze.

Ella smiled in gentle understanding. "Why don't you put that bib apron over your nightdress and start seeing to Conor? I'll be back in a few minutes with some clothes for you."

Abby managed a weak smile. "Thank the Lord there's another woman on this ranch."

Ella gave Abby's hand a quick squeeze. "Hold up. It'll all work out," her friend replied just before she slipped out the door.

Abby turned back to Conor. Besides his hands, his shirt and torso had taken the brunt of the flames. She choked back a freshened swell of tears and forced herself to concentrate on the job at hand. "Get his shirt off," she briskly ordered Devlin, "while I find something to soak his hands in."

Moving to the cookstove, Abby took down the long bib apron that hung nearby, then walked back to the pegs beside the back door, and hung up her coat. After quickly donning the apron, she pulled out the wash basin, filled it with cool water from the pump, and carried it to the table. By then, the two men had managed to get Conor's ruined shirt off.

Abby surveyed his naked torso. As she feared, multiple reddened patches marked his skin, especially over his upper back and chest. There were spots where the flames had even singed away some of his chest hair. Fortunately, none of the burns on his trunk looked severe; they would most likely just blister, peel, and then heal. His hands, however, were another story.

Conor's palms, which had come into prolonged contact with the overheated metal box, were already beginning to swell. The skin was a mottled white and red. "Here." Abby shoved the pan of cool water over to him. "Put your hands in there. It'll ease the pain and, hopefully, slow the damage being done."

He did as told, though the initial contact with the water obviously hurt. He made a sharp, hissing sound through his gritted teeth, and closed his eyes.

Once more, Abby steeled herself to him and his pain. The only thing that mattered now was caring for him as best she could.

While Conor soaked his hands, Abby took down another basin, filled it partially with more, cool pump water, then added some hot water from the big cast iron kettle she always kept simmering on the stove. After placing that on the table, she sent Beth off to gather clean washcloths and old laundered sheets to tear into bandages. In the meanwhile, Abby pulled out the hand soap, a box of cornstarch, and the jar of beef tallow she kept available for cooking.

Finally, Abby paused once more at the table. "You men aren't needed anymore right now," she said finally, glancing from Devlin to H.C. "Is there anything else you

209

need for them to do"—she turned to Conor—"until I call them back to help you up to bed?"

"Just make sure the fire's out, will you?" he rasped. "And then bring in the rest of Abby's things. No sense letting what we did manage to save get ruined, sitting the rest of the night out in the snow."

"You sure you're all right?" Concern roughened Devlin's voice.

"Yeah." Conor nodded. "I'm sure Abby *and* Ella"—he added as she walked back in the kitchen, a basket of clothing tucked over her arm—"can take care of me just fine. Thanks for all your help, both of you."

Devlin motioned for H.C. to join him. As the two men headed back outside, Ella handed the basket to Abby. "Why don't you take a few minutes to clean up and get into some dry clothes. I can get started on Conor while you dress."

Abby took the basket. Then she paused, her gaze once more settling on him. Freshened emotions welled within her. In pain, his hands badly burned, Conor's first thoughts had still been of her. His kindness made her want to weep.

Conor must have noticed the abrupt swing in her emotions. His eyes darkened, warmed with affection. Then he jerked his head in the direction of the stairs.

"Get on with you. I'm not going anywhere." He managed a lopsided grin. "Though I must say you do look fetching enough in that nightgown and apron to follow you upstairs."

She blushed furiously. What an incorrigible man! Even a pair of badly injured hands failed to quench for long the lustful fires that burned within him. Abby couldn't bring herself to chastise him, though. Especially not when his statement far more pleased than scandalized her.

"A gentleman," she replied tartly, softening her words with a smile, "wouldn't have been looking."

"Well, I never claimed to be *that* much of a gentleman."

With his teasing banter, the strain of the past hour momentarily eased. What always, always mattered most in the end, Abby reminded herself, was human life and the precious experience of others. Though she had lost much in losing Thomas and Joshua, she realized now the Lord had gifted her with other, equally precious people. People like Ella, Beth, the ranch hands, and Conor. She had only to open her eyes—and heart—and accept what the Lord had offered.

"No, I suppose you're not much of a gentleman at that," Abby agreed, filled suddenly with a strange but glorious sense of release. "But then, if you were, I also wouldn't find you half as interesting, would I?" She grinned, then, clutching the ends of her apron together, began to back from the kitchen. "And that, I think, would be a great pity."

ð

It was well past dawn the next morning when Abby dragged herself out of bed. Sunbeams streamed through the lace-curtained windows of Evan's old bedroom, puddling in a bright pool of light on the floor. She blinked to clear the haze, fought back a renewed surge of exhaustion, and forced herself to wash and dress.

Luckily, Ella was only a size larger than Abby. With minimal adjustments, she was able to get the blue woolen skirt and green and blue flannel shirt to fit. The woolen chemise, drawers, and petticoat were also comfortably roomy, but Abby did not care. They were clothes, and they were warm. Until she could get to town to buy more fabric and thread, she resolved as she finished buttoning her high-topped shoes, threw aside the buttonhook, and headed for the door, Ella's things would serve quite nicely.

From her open doorway, Abby peeked down the hall. Both Conor and Beth's bedroom doors were still closed. She tiptoed to the stairs. After what they had all been through last night, it was best to let them sleep as long as they wished. Which for Conor, she added wryly, would probably only be as long as the dose of laudanum she had given him last night lasted.

Time enough, though, to put on some water for coffee, check the chickens for eggs, and attempt to milk Ethel. Conor would definitely not be milking the cow for some time to come. And, though she had never milked a cow, it surely could not be all that difficult.

Devlin was just leaving as Abby entered the kitchen. He paused in the back doorway. "I went ahead and saw to Ethel this morning." He indicated the bucket of foaming milk sitting by the door. "I didn't think you'd have much time for it, what with having now to care for Conor along with all your other chores."

Abby smiled. Though she was none too keen about the pain he had caused Ella with his infidelity, Devlin MacKay had always seemed a pretty decent sort. "That was kind of you. The truth is, I don't know how to milk. Could you teach me? You've got enough chores of your own, without adding more."

"Sure, I'll teach you. How about meeting me in the barn at five this evening? Ethel will need to be milked again by then."

She nodded. "Five, then."

The foreman hesitated, then stepped back inside and shut the door. "What do you think about Conor's hands? Will he ever be able to use them again?"

Abby walked to the cookstove, took up the coffeepot, and carried it to the sink. "I don't know," she replied, as she worked the pump and filled the pot with water. "His burns are bad, but at least none of his skin was charred. I'm hoping he didn't burn so deeply that there'll be permanent damage. I'd like to get a doctor out here as soon as we can to look at him, though."

"I was thinking the same thing. Once it warms up a bit this morning, I'll send Wendell to Grand View to fetch Doc Childress."

"Good." Abby placed the coffeepot back on the stove, then squatted to stoke the firebox, and open the dampers to get the fire hot again. "Ella and I did the best we could last night, but I'll feel better when Doc gives us the okay."

Devlin eyed her, then bit his lower lip. "You mustn't blame yourself for what happened to Conor, Abby. He did what he felt had to be done."

She glanced away. "He wouldn't have done it if I hadn't made such a fuss and begged him."

"He knew it was important to you. And whatever's important to you, is important to him."

Abby closed her eyes for an instant, then looked at Devlin. "Thank you for trying to make me feel better."

"It's the truth, Abby. If I'm not too far off the mark, I think you're beginning to realize it, too." He sighed. "Maybe it's not my place to say this, but I think my cousin's falling in love with you."

A strange mix of terror and wild joy filled Abby. She shoved to her feet. "Devlin, don't," she moaned.

Scowling in frustration, he took two steps toward her. "And why not? Conor's been like a brother to me all these years. If you knew what the both of us have been through, growing up . . . Well, never mind. What matters is that I care about him and his happiness."

"That's enough, Devlin."

Almost in unison, their heads swung toward the hallway door. At the sight of Conor standing there, a blanket wrapped about him, his hands swathed in bulky bandages, their eyes widened in surprise.

Devlin reddened. "Conor, I'm sorry, but–"

"What's between Abby and me isn't any of your business, and you know it," Conor growled. "Now, before you sink even deeper into that hole you're digging, why don't you just hightail it out to your chores?"

Devlin grinned sheepishly. "Reckon I'd better." He looked to Abby. "Still game for that milking lesson at five today?"

She nodded. "Sure."

"No more lectures, I promise." Devlin turned and left the kitchen.

Abby readjusted the cookstove dampers now that the fire was going strong, then straightened and walked over to Conor. "You shouldn't have come down without help," she half-scolded him. "You could've fallen."

"I'm not some fool, crippled invalid."

With exaggerated deliberation, she looked him up and down. Above the blanket he managed to barely clutch to him spread an impressive, if reddened, expanse of hair-roughened chest. Below its bottom edge, the elastic knit cuffs of his cotton, long underdrawers peeked out. "Unless I'm missing something," she drawled, lifting her gaze to meet his, "you don't look like you managed to dress yourself. That appears to me like a man who could use some help."

"And I say, instead of berating me for coming downstairs, you should be thanking me for rescuing you from Devlin's meddling. Or would you prefer," he continued with a challenging lift of a brow, "that next time I just leave you to wriggle your way out all on your own?"

Abby couldn't quite meet Conor's piercing stare. "No, no," she muttered. "I appreciate your intervention. But that still doesn't change the fact that you're standing here in basically nothing more than your underwear."

Conor grinned. "And you're not fainting dead away because of it, either. Now, I reckon that's real progress."

"And exactly what progress would *that* be?" Abby asked, cocking her head. Then, thinking better of her question, she hastily waved a dismissing hand at him. "Never mind. I shouldn't have asked."

"Ask away, Abby. You know I'd tell you anything you want to know."

"You need to get upstairs and get dressed." She quietly changed the subject and took hold of his arm. "Come on."

"And how do you suggest I dress myself?" He lifted his bandaged hands.

"I'm not suggesting you dress yourself. Considering your current limitations, I'm just saying I'm the most logical, and easily available person to help you."

For a long moment he didn't respond. "Abby," Conor finally ground out, "I can't ask that of you. Call back Devlin or get one of the hands to come over."

"For heaven's sake, Conor MacKay," Abby exclaimed, leading him toward the stairs. She knew it would be difficult for the both of them, but after what he had done for her last night, she could overlook propriety this once. "It's not like I haven't seen a man in drawers before! Besides, I'm helping you because it's the most practical way to handle the situation, and not for any other reason whatsoever!"

At that, Conor threw back his head and laughed. "My deepest apologies. How could I have possibly misunderstood?"

"It must be the laudanum muddying your mind," she muttered as they climbed the stairs.

"To be sure. Except that it wore off hours ago."

Abby glanced sharply at him. "Are you in pain? We could go back to the kitchen, and I could give you another dose."

"No." Conor shook his head. "I can bear it a while longer. Besides, I don't like how fuzzy-headed it makes me."

Twenty minutes later, Conor was shaved, dressed, and back downstairs, sitting at the kitchen table. Abby shoved a half-filled mug of coffee over to him. "Can you manage it while I cook breakfast, or do you need help?"

Ever so carefully, Conor grasped the mug between his two bandaged hands and brought it to his lips. He took a deep swallow, then set the mug back down, sighing in satisfaction. "Never thought coffee could taste so good."

Abby smiled, then turned back to the bowl of baking powder biscuits she was mixing. "Glad you like it."

Conor didn't say anything and, after a time, Abby glanced up. He was staring at her, a look of undisguised yearning in his eyes. Her heart plummeted to her belly. Her pulse quickened, and her throat went dry.

"Abby, come here."

Panic seized her. She looked away. "In a minute. I've got to get the biscuits in the oven."

Once more, silence settled over the room. Then Conor sighed. "Forget it. I was out of line even to ask."

Abby closed her eyes, struggling mightily against the urge to throw down her spoon and run to him. The last thing she wanted was to hurt Conor, or be the reason for such an edge of defeat in his voice. But she feared . . . she feared . . .

With sharp, jerky motions, Abby ladled the biscuit batter into the baking tin, opened the cookstove oven, and shoved the pan inside. She stood there for what seemed an eternity, before she finally turned back to face Conor. He sat at the table, head down, staring into his coffee.

Abby poured herself a mug. Then, squaring her shoulders, she marched to the table and sat in the chair closest to his. "I'm here now, Conor," she said softly. "What do you want?"

He didn't look up. "Nothing. Forget it."

She laid her hand on his forearm. "Then if you don't want to talk, I will." She swallowed hard, then forged on. "First, I want to thank you from the bottom of my heart for what you did last night. It was the sweetest, most gallant thing any man has ever done for me. I'll never forget it."

Conor continued to avoid her gaze. "You'd lost so much. I couldn't bear to see you lose the pictures of your family, too."

"You sacrificed so much to help me. I'll do what I can to ease the time for you until your hands are healed."

He looked up, a faint smile on his lips. "Like milk Ethel?"

"Yes," Abby agreed with a nod. "And keep up your ledgers if you wish, and shave you, and help you with your clothes, and shovel snow off the porch when it snows, and–"

"Hold up, hold up," Conor said, now chuckling. "I think I get the picture." His smile faded. "I appreciate your offer, Abby, and I may take you up on some of them. But you needn't feel bad because of what happened."

She clasped her hands tightly about her mug. "I should never have asked you to do what you did," she whispered. "You could've been killed."

"While you were upstairs changing last night, Ella told me you were frantic when I didn't come out of the bunkhouse, that you broke away from her, and were running to get to me when I finally came out. Not very many people would've been willing to do that, especially not for me."

"Then they're stupid, blind fools." She choked out the words, her sudden surge of emotions tightening her throat. "You're the bravest, kindest, most wonderful man I've ever known."

"Am I, Abby?" He brushed her cheek with the back of his bandaged hand. "Just not so wonderful that you want more from me than friendship. And not so special that you'll ever wish to kiss me again?"

She took his hand and kissed his fingertips. "What I want, and what I dare risk, are two entirely different things, Conor."

"Abby . . ."

Anguish burned in his eyes and tautened his mouth. His jaw went hard, and a muscle twitched furiously there. Then, in an explosion of frustration, he pounded his fist on the table.

"Blast it!" he cursed, grimacing with the pain the action caused. "I've never wanted a woman like I want you!"

At his words, a strange mixture of misery and desire stabbed through Abby. She buried her face in her hands, facing, at last, what she had fought so long to deny.

Dear Lord, what am I to do? I love him. I love him! But I love You even more, and I fear . . . I fear that my love for him will lead me into sin.

He spoke, after all, only of wanting her, not loving her. What Conor felt was desire . . . lust . . . passion, but not love. He had already told her he did not wish to wed. Yet because she had finally admitted to herself that she loved him, he could now slowly but surely begin to break her heart.

"I'm not as strong as you are, Conor," Abby whispered through the sheltering barrier of her hands. "I don't know how to fight these feelings I'm having. There's even a part of me that doesn't want to fight." She looked up and met his gaze. "But I must, and I will. And you must help me. You must."

His eyes narrowed. He leaned forward, his shoulders hunched, his body gone tense with wariness. "And exactly how, Abby? By denying my desire for you? By

218

pretending that I don't care? How do you expect me to do that?"

"I don't know," she wailed softly. "I've never felt like this before. God forgive me, but I never wanted my husband or felt about him the way I feel about you. These feelings . . . they're all so new, so terrifying, yet so wonderful. But I don't want to sin, Conor."

Abby closed her eyes, suddenly so lost and confused she could barely stand it. "I always wondered what it could be like to desire a man the way he desired me. And now I know, Conor." Her voice broke. "God forgive me, but now I know."

15

Can any hide himself in secret places that I shall not see him? saith the LORD. Do not I fill heaven and earth?
                                                     Jeremiah 23:24

Despair swamped Conor. Abby was asking—no, begging—for his help, and he didn't know how to help her. She asked him to do the impossible, to help her fight what he now realized was a mutual and desperate need for the other. Yet how could he do such a thing, when every fiber of his being—body *and* soul—cried out for her?

"So where does that leave us, Abby?" he forced himself to ask, dreading the answer.

She sighed and shook her head. "I don't know."

"You're going to leave Culdee Creek, aren't you?"

"And leave you like this?" Abby gestured at his hands. "After what you did for me? You know I'd never do such a thing."

"So you'll stay out of pity and guilt," he snarled, an inexplicable anger filling him, "until your debt is repaid. Is that it, Abby?"

"When that debt, as you call it, is repaid, then I'll still stay on because I want to."

"Why?" Conor's voice went raw with his conflicted emotions. "Why would you stay on here, when you just finishing telling me I've become an occasion of sin? Doesn't the Bible warn that if a man takes fire to himself, he risks being burned? Well, let me assure you you're playing with fire here, even if of an entirely different kind."

"For a man who has turned his back on God," Abby observed, "you certainly have an extensive knowledge of His Word."

"Don't try to sidetrack me, Abby. My knowledge of the Bible isn't the issue here, and you know it!"

"Yes," she agreed softly, "I do. So I'll just come out and say it. I've many reasons to stay on here."

He leaned back in his chair. "We've got time. Why don't you tell me what those reasons are?"

Abby sighed. "Well, I first wanted to come here and work for you because I saw this as a haven, a place where no one wanted much from me emotionally, and I could tend to my own needs. The Lord, however, quickly set those misconceptions straight. I was here because *He* wanted me here."

Conor gave a disgusted snort. "There were lost souls here who needed salvation, after all."

She shrugged. "Perhaps. It's certainly what I thought, once I became convinced coming to Culdee Creek was His will." She smiled sadly. "You can't blame Him for wanting all of His children to be saved, can you?"

"If you really want to know the truth," Conor muttered, "I haven't given God or His desires a whole lot of thought for a long while now."

"Yes, I know." Abby took a sip of her coffee before continuing her story. "But then, over time, I began to realize that you and Beth weren't the only ones lost and searching. I was, too, however hard I fought to deny it. Little by little, though, I discovered that, just as you

221

seemed to need me, I needed you and Beth to help me find the way back." She exhaled slowly. "That's why I want to stay on, Conor. Even in the short time we've been together, you've given me so much. You've opened doors to my heart I thought forever closed, and I've grown."

She laid her hand on his arm. "The risk of getting burned by your fire is far outweighed by what I stand to gain. And that is the Lord's greatest gift of all to me. In coming to know you and Beth, I've rediscovered the joy, and challenge, and hunger for life again."

"And here I thought it was my irresistible manliness and impressive land holdings. I don't know whether to be insulted or flattered."

"You could just say thank you, and let it go at that."

Conor rocked forward on his chair until all four legs once more touched the floor. "Yes, I could, but I'm not used to accepting compliments like that anymore."

"Especially from a woman."

"Yes." He nodded. "Especially from a woman."

"There's always a first time for everything." Abby graced him with an arch smile.

He stared out the window. "I knew your coming here was going to set everything on its head. I sensed that from the first moment I met you." Conor turned back to her. "And I almost fired you the day I came to the Springs to bring you back. I was that scared of you, though at the time I didn't know why."

"It's understandable—your fear, I mean—considering the bad experiences you'd had with housekeepers."

"But my fear wasn't that kind of fear." He shook his head. "No, not by a long shot. Then I remembered a favorite saying of my grandfather, Sean MacKay, about fear, and how it can betray you and weaken your judgment. It was like I heard him speaking to me that day when I thought about not bringing you to Culdee Creek.

Speaking to me, warning me not to make the biggest mistake of my life."

"He sounded like a very wise man," Abby said. "Is he the man in the painting over the parlor mantel?"

Conor nodded. "One and the same. He's also the man who led many of the clan MacKay from the Highland village of Culdee in the district of Strathnaver, to this country during the years of the Highland Clearances. Though he never saw Colorado himself, he made my father promise to name any land he ever claimed as his own after their home in Culdee, Scotland."

"Hence the name of this ranch," Abby finished for him. Admiration for Conor's ancestors swelled in her breast. She'd heard of the terrible hardships the Scottish Highlanders had suffered during the Highland Clearance in the late 1700s through to the middle of this century. Thousands of peasants had been forcibly evicted from their ancestral lands to make way for more profitable undertakings such as sheep.

"The Culdees," Conor continued to explain, "were members of an ancient ascetic religious movement in the eighth century Celtic Christian Church. The name comes from the Gaelic word, *Celi De*, and means something like 'friends or family of God.'"

"So," she murmured wonderingly, "you come from a long line of Christians, do you?"

"Roman Catholic Christians, to be exact," he was quick to correct her. "My ancestors were staunch Catholics and Jacobites. They stood with Bonnie Prince Charlie, and suffered greatly when he was defeated at Culloden."

"I've heard about the tragedy of the Scottish people after Culloden. It must have been hard on your family."

"Yes, it was, yet they never lost hope, or dignity, or allowed it to embitter them." Conor took a long draught of his coffee. "None of them turned mean, or sought the destructive solace of the bottle. Not, at least, until they came to America and a generation passed. Not until my pa and his brother, the two youngest sons of Sean MacKay."

She looked at him and said nothing. Suddenly, Conor wanted to tell her all. Only then could he be absolutely certain that she harbored no illusions about him. Only then would he truly know the extent of her commitment to him.

"My pa's name was Robert MacKay, though most folks called him Robbie," Conor resumed his tale. "He, and his younger brother Angus—Devlin's father—were born late in life to Sean MacKay, and his second wife, Rose. My grandfather only lived six years after Angus's birth. My grandmother, burdened with the care and support of two young children, soon remarried. Her new husband, though, was as unlike my grandfather as any man could be.

"He was hard on the two boys. When he'd get liquored up, he'd beat them. Pa ran away from home at fifteen, hitched a ride with some settlers moving out here. Ten years later he bought this land. A few years after that, Angus joined him."

"Their stepfather's cruelty had left a permanent mark on them, though, hadn't it?" Abby asked, her eyes glowing with sympathy and understanding.

Conor hung his head, then nodded. "Of the two, I reckon Pa escaped the worst of the abuse, if Devlin's claims are even half of what really happened. But when I was growing up, you couldn't have convinced me of that. Pa was an embittered, fatalistic man who, after my ma's death, turned increasingly to the bottle. The last four or five years he was alive, we were constantly at each other's throats. Sally and I lived in this house with him, and the ongoing animosity put a considerable strain on our marriage."

"How did your father die?"

"He'd been drinking one night, late in January. We got into another argument about his management of the ranch. One thing led to another and he hit me. If it hadn't been for Sally, I think I'd have killed him. As it was, she clung to me for dear life and screamed at him to get out."

He released a ragged breath. "Reckon Pa wasn't so drunk he didn't realize the danger he was in. He grabbed a fresh bottle of whiskey, mounted up, and rode off into the dark. It was the last time I saw him alive. That night it snowed pretty heavily. A search party found him four days later, frozen to death in a dry creek bed five miles from here."

"I'm so sorry, Conor."

"Yeah, so am I. Sorry I didn't have a better father."

"What about your mother?"

A soft, sad smile touched his lips. "She was an angel from heaven, my ma was. She told me stories, taught me my lessons, and tried to shield me from my father's wrath when he was drinking. Most of the time it worked." His mouth twisted grimly. "Reckon that was the difference between Devlin and me as boys. His ma died bearing him. He never had anyone to stand between him and his father."

"She's the one who taught you your Bible verses, wasn't she?"

"Yeah." He gave a cynical laugh. "For all the good it did me."

"She helped mold you into the man you are today, Conor MacKay," Abby countered with ardent conviction. "That was her greatest victory and finest accomplishment."

He shrugged. "Maybe so. There are times, though, when I wonder if all her efforts weren't in vain."

"They could well be if you let this bitterness toward your father, and mistrust of others, defeat you."

Conor sighed. "I vowed never to let myself become like him. Even after my ma died, I clung to the religious faith she'd instilled in me. Once I wed Sally and Evan was born, I began to hope I'd finally overcome the taint of my pa's blood. Then Sally left. Ran off with her music teacher—a teacher I paid for with the money I scratched out of this ranch in those early years. But I did it all because I loved her, and wanted to give her what she claimed to want more than anything else in the world.

"Even in the face of Sally's betrayal, I clung to the conviction that life was good and ultimately fair. I didn't give up hope, even then. Once I'd heard Sally had died in a Denver boardinghouse fire, I risked falling in love again with Squirrel Woman, the Indian girl I'd hired to care for Evan."

"Yet then she died and left you, too."

Conor shoved awkwardly to his feet, and walked to the back window. "Yeah," he said, his voice gone low and husky, "then she died, and I just couldn't keep up the pretense anymore. I drew into myself, angry at life, and at God. Little by little, my anger and bitterness visited itself even on my children, to the point that Evan finally balked. A year ago, when he turned seventeen, he cleaned out all the cash in my safe. All I got in return was a note assuring me that he'd taken nothing more than his rightful inheritance, and that we were now even."

"Have you had any word from him since then?"

"No." At the admission, anger filled Conor once more. "Can't say as I care if I ever do, either. My own son robbed me. I hate to think what I'd do, if I ever saw him again."

"So now Beth's your one and only chance. The last opportunity you have to redeem yourself, and be the father you've always wanted to be."

Conor turned from the window. "The father I wanted but never knew how to be. If it hadn't been for you, Abby, I might have gone on and ruined my chances with Beth,

226

too. Seems I've learned to be an excellent teacher, when it comes to showing a child how to mistrust, hate, and treat others discourteously. But you opened my eyes, and that was the best thing that could've happened to me."

"It wasn't me, Conor." Abby smiled. "It was the Lord."

A fierce, sweet tenderness welled within him. "All I see is you, Abby, and that's God enough for me."

"Don't say that, Conor. There is only one God, and that's the Lord Jesus Christ."

His gaze caressed Abby's downcast face, savoring her soft skin, the tender curve of her cheek, her full, ripe mouth. Suddenly, Conor was overcome with a need to take her into his arms and kiss her. He walked to the table to stand beside her.

"Abby?"

"Yes?" She lifted her gaze.

"I don't ever want you to leave Culdee Creek."

Her eyes widened, and she swallowed convulsively. "I don't understand."

He inhaled a deep breath. "I guess what I'm saying is that maybe the idea of us getting married isn't quite as far-fetched as I first claimed. Maybe, if you're willing, we could try on the idea for a while and see how it fits." He managed a sheepish grin. "I'm sadly out of practice, but if you can put up with my bumbling efforts at courtship . . ."

Abby went silent, her face pale, her lips parted in surprise. "I-I don't know if that would be wise," she murmured, when she finally found her voice. "As I said before . . . I'm not so certain we're suited."

"Why?" He leaned forward, impaling her with a fierce stare. "Because I'm no longer a good Christian?"

"I won't lie to you, Conor. It is a concern of mine," she admitted. "The Bible warns that we're not to be unequally yoked."

"The Bible also states," Conor countered with a grim smile, "that the husband is sanctified by the wife."

"And is that why you want to wed me, Conor?" Abby asked softly, her gaze never wavering. "Because you wish to return to the Lord and His ways?"

"I'd be lying if I said that, Abby." He walked back to his chair and sat. "But I won't stand in your way or forbid you to speak of Him in my house. I'll wed you in a Christian church before an ordained minister. And if Beth ever expresses interest in learning more of God and the Bible, you may teach her. As for me, though, I don't see any place in my life for religion."

He ran his fingers down her arm, then touched her hand. "I'm not a perfect man, by any stretch of the imagination. I have my faults. But I'm a hard worker; I love my daughter, and I try to treat people fairly. I could give you a good life. I'll treat you with respect."

"What about love, Conor?" she blurted unexpectedly, gazing up at him with tear-bright eyes. "What about love?"

Heat flushed his face. Blood pounded through his head. His throat went dry, yet Conor forced words past anyway, knowing nothing would satisfy Abby but the truth.

"Love's a strong word, and far too freely bandied about for my tastes," he growled, struggling to keep an edge of irritation from his voice. Why was the woman never satisfied? Hadn't he all but proposed to her? "It's also a word I never thought I'd use again in my dealings with women."

She sat there, stiff and unmoving. "Go on," she finally urged. "Tell me more about this proposition of yours, and exactly how you think you're offering me something better than you've offered any other woman."

"Blast it, Abby!" Conor expelled an exasperated breath and then, ever so carefully, took her hand and cradled it in his thickly bandaged one. "I care for you. Care for you deeply. And I don't think there's any doubt in your mind how much I desire you. But love . . ." He sighed and shook his head. "I'll tell you true. I'm afraid—no, terrified—of letting myself love again. To lose someone you love, well, I don't know if I could survive it again."

"Do you think it's any easier for me?" she demanded, her voice gone hoarse and raw. "I've lost loved ones, too, and it nearly tore my heart out. Maybe I didn't love my husband as truly and deeply as a wife should, but my son . . . my darling little Joshua . . . that love was deep and total and eternal. The pain of losing him lives on even now."

Now that she'd begun, the words rushed out like water bursting through a floodgate.

"Yet still, in coming to know you, I've regained the hope that I could love yet again, Conor. I've discovered there's still room in my heart for others, as damaged and battle-scarred as it now may be. You, Conor MacKay, have opened the world to me again. Instead of endlessly worrying if I'd survive another loss, I look to life now with renewed joy."

"Then you're far braver than I am," he ground out, ashamed of his own cowardice. "But then, I've always sensed that about you. Sensed it, and yearned for a little of your courage."

"Ah, Conor, Conor." Her eyes filled with freshened tears. "Of myself, I have no courage. All I have, all that is of any worth in me, comes from the Lord."

"Then don't turn from me, Abby," he pleaded now, clasping her hand between both of his. "You may be the closest I'll ever come to God again in this life."

"Standing close to me won't bring you salvation, Conor. For that, you must walk on past me, and find the Lord in the secret places of your heart."

"And if I can't, Abby?" he asked, fearing the answer even as he asked. "What then? Will you turn from me, refuse to consider the possibility of becoming my wife?"

His words pierced Abby's heart. How could she ever turn her back on this man? He had said he would not stand in her way when it came to worshiping the Lord. He had agreed to wed in a Christian church, and even to allow her to teach Beth about God. But to marry an adamantly steadfast, fallen away Christian . . .

Yet Abby also knew, from so many things Conor had said, that he believed in God. She was well aware of his knowledge and understanding of Scripture. Did that not count for something? Indeed, he was a man who tried, in many ways, even as he tried to deny it, to live according to Christian principles.

But there were so many times when he had not lived very morally too.

Still, there was hope, despite his current claims to the contrary, that Conor might still repent of his sinful past and return to the Lord. He had already changed in the four months she'd been here. Perhaps, instead of agonizing over his potential threat to her soul, she should consider the possibility that marrying him was, and always had been, God's will for the both of them. Might not she be of greatest service as Conor's helpmate and fellow wayfarer on the journey of life?

Now that she finally faced it, the answer seemed so clear, so right and good. Tears filled Abby's eyes, spilled down her cheeks. "No, I won't turn from you." She lifted Conor's fingers to her mouth for a tender kiss. "The Lord knows my heart, as He knows yours, and it's a heart that cries out with love for you.

"It is also," she added, with a shy little smile, "a heart that cannot help but be willing to consider the possibility of becoming your wife."

230

16

The LORD is the strength of my life; of whom shall I be afraid?

Psalm 27:1

For a time, Abby and Conor decided to keep their courtship a secret. Both were too unsure of themselves and each other to risk involving or disappointing those close to them. Both also discovered that they suddenly felt as shy and awkward as a young couple. So, in secret they came to know each other's hearts, and the trust, respect, and love—though they rarely spoke of it in such terms—grew.

The waning months of winter passed. Spring came. Conor's hands healed and he regained their full use. The bunkhouse was rebuilt. And once the essential furniture and a brand-new pot-bellied stove was installed, Abby moved back in.

Culdee Creek fairly buzzed with renewed energy. This welcome surge of vitality, not to mention Conor's growing interest in Abby, according to Ella, was the perfect excuse to convince him to attend the annual May Day dance in Grand View.

One bright, sunny day near the end of April, Abby, as she followed her friend down to the pond, carefully considered the proposal. "It might do him a world of good," she said. "Beth told me once that Conor used to love to dance."

Ella laughed. "Oh, I'll say he did. He was so quick on his feet. He used to twirl Sally around and around until she was breathless and begging him to stop."

"It's been that long since he danced last? Since Sally left?"

"I'm afraid so." As they walked along, Ella reached over and squeezed her hand. "Squirrel Woman was too shy to go to the town dances. She knew she'd never have been welcome at them anyway. Conor knew it, too, so he never asked. Though he didn't give a fig for what others thought of him, he wasn't about to subject her to unkind remarks and community censure."

"She seemed like a good woman," Abby murmured. "Squirrel Woman, I mean."

Ella smiled sadly. "She was beautiful, gentle, and full of a simple, honest love. I think, if she'd lived, she would've finally healed that terrible wound Sally's desertion inflicted on Conor's heart. But the Lord must have had other plans. I'm just glad He finally sent you here."

Abby shot her friend a sharp glance. Had Ella guessed what was going on between her and Conor? A part of her longed to share the precious secret. She certainly hoped to do so soon, but there were still a few issues she and Conor needed to work through first. At the very least, even after all these months, he had yet to come right out and tell her he loved her.

In her heart, though, Abby knew he loved her. She recognized it in the looks he gave her, felt it in his touch, and heard it in his voice. She sensed, though, that he had yet to admit it even to himself, and tried to respect his restraint. It was, however, getting harder and harder to do so.

"It'll be such fun," Ella exclaimed, apparently unaware that Abby's thoughts had been elsewhere. "We can go together, you and I, Conor and Devlin. That emerald green frock you're working on now will be perfect for the dance. You'll be the most beautiful woman there!"

The day of the dance, however, Mary developed a hacking cough and fever. Ella refused to leave her, and Devlin saw no point in going without his wife. So, after saying their regretful farewells, Conor and Abby soon found themselves driving off alone in the buckboard. As the sun set behind them in a glorious explosion of magenta and gold, they headed east toward Grand View.

For a time, they rode along in companionable silence, savoring the cool evening air and gratifying comfort of each other's presence. Finally, though, Conor sighed. "Somehow, ever since you moved back into the new bunkhouse, it just doesn't seem the same. I miss you and our time together in the parlor every evening. It's as if you're now so far away."

"It's for the best, Conor," Abby said. "Until we decide what we want to do about . . ."

"About us?" he supplied gently.

"Well, yes." Her heart rate picked up a notch.

He turned back to the road ahead. In the distance, the lights of Grand View twinkled brightly.

"It's been over three months now, Abby. Since we agreed to consider the possibility of marriage, I mean. Are you any closer to accepting my proposal than you were then?"

"It's not I, I think, who still hesitates," she replied.

Conor frowned. "I don't understand. I just said I proposed, and you still think I hesitate? Come on, Abby. Tell me what the problem is and be done with it."

She rolled her eyes, then sighed in exasperation. Could this man possibly be as thick skulled as he seemed just now to be? "The problem is, Conor MacKay, that *I* have to be the one to tell *you* what it is. The problem is that I have to all but beg you for even a simple admission of love."

"Oh." He drove along, his brow furrowed in thought. "I thought the depth of my feelings for you had become evident," he finally said. "Why else do I spend every free moment I can with you, not to mention all the time I have to be away from you, missing you and counting the minutes and hours until I can be with you again? And if you think my heroic restraint when I hold and kiss you is the mark of a man who doesn't care deeply . . . well, you're sadly mistaken. I lost count weeks ago of all the nights I've gone to bed, and laid in the dark—"

"That's quite enough," Abby hastily cut him off, realizing his frustration mirrored her own. "I think I get the point."

"Do you really, Abby?"

Would Conor never understand? "I just wanted to hear the words," she whispered. "That's all."

He pulled back on the buckboard reins. The horses halted. After winding the reins around the hand brake, Conor turned.

"Then hear them now." He took both of her hands in his. "And never doubt me again. Though I know I've danced about this for a while now, let me assure you once and for all that I love you, Abigail Stanton. Love you with all my heart. Will you marry me?"

Tears misted her vision. *At last.* "Yes." She nodded her joyous assent. "Yes, I'll marry you."

Conor pulled her to him. "Then let's set a date, and make it public. Preferably before I go mad."

"October," she whispered. "A year from the day we first met."

"October?" Conor groaned. "Have a heart, Abby. That's five more months!"

"How about August then? That's only three months away."

"How about June?"

"Next month?" Abby did some quick mental calculations. "No, that won't be enough time. I'd like to invite my parents and brothers to the wedding. They'll need to make arrangements, then travel out here. How about the 4th of July?"

"Fine," he muttered. Releasing her, Conor once more took up the reins and urged the horses onward. "But not a moment longer."

A satisfied grin on her lips, Abby settled back in her seat. "July 4th it is then," she agreed, "and not a moment longer."

ॐ

As Abby stepped from the town hall and closed the door behind her, the sound of laughter and gay fiddle music dimmed to a muted clamor. She inhaled deeply of the crisp, clean night air, grateful for the sudden cessation of noise, cigar smoke, and press of overheated bodies. From the start, the May Day dance had been a joyously carefree social event, though Abby had barely danced with Conor all evening. Mary Sue Edgerton, stunning in her new calico dress, as well as some of the other unmarried Grand View ladies, had quite handily seen to that.

Mary Sue wouldn't be at all happy, once word got out of her and Conor's engagement. Abby only hoped the girl would not long hold a grudge. As unintentional as a romantic relationship with Conor had been, it was now an undeniable fact. It was also a fact that would soon be common knowledge.

She hugged herself close, as much for the warmth as for the sheer happiness she felt. *Abigail MacKay. Mrs.*

235

Conor MacKay. The words, though possessing a foreign sound, were also the most wonderful, soul-satisfying words she had ever heard.

In but two months' time, she would be Conor's wife.

Overhead, the stars glittered like bits of glass strewn across an ebony velvet sky. The dark heavens seemed so close, so encompassing, so benevolent. Just like the loving God who had led her at last from the vale of her sorrow.

She would always miss Joshua and Thomas. There would be times, even in the distant future, when a precious recollection of one or the other would still most likely rise from the depths of her mind to pierce her heart anew. Most especially the memories of her son.

But the Lord called her now to walk on. Not by setting up, at long last, the mission for indigents that Thomas had always dreamed of. She'd stopped fooling herself long ago that that had ever been her true calling. No, rather, Abby felt summoned to serve God in another way, and she now knew what it had always been. Conor . . . Beth . . . Culdee Creek . . . And the Lord saw this, and knew that it was good.

Abby glanced down the long row of false-fronted buildings and boardwalks that lined both sides of Winona Street. Grand View was no Colorado Springs, either in size, wealth, or fine amenities, but the town provided the basics and then some. Abby looked forward, as the summer drew on, to involving herself in some of the more social aspects of the town's Episcopal Church.

Life now seemed ripe with promise. Abby turned to head back inside to the dance. Whatever problems might still lie ahead, she'd not face them now alone, or without–

A cry, faint and frightened, reached her ears. Abby wheeled about and peered up and down the street. In the distance, the mournful howl of a coyote echoed through the surrounding hills. Some horse stabled in the Nealy's livery kicked at his wooden stall. Then, once again, all was silent.

Abby shrugged. "Must be hearing things," she muttered, turning back to the door.

"H-help me!"

A woman with scraggly, pale blond hair hanging in her face and down her back, staggered out from the alley across from the town hall. She wore a shapeless, oversized red dress and black wool coat that she just managed to clutch over her swollen abdomen. As she ran awkwardly toward Abby, bare feet flashed white in the moonlight.

"H-help me!" she panted. "Don't let him . . . take me back!"

Apprehensively, Abby glanced toward the door. Perhaps she should go for Conor. He would know what to do.

With a cry of pain, the woman stumbled and fell. Abby thought no more of going for help. Gathering her skirts, she leaped off the boardwalk and ran to the woman's side.

"Help me," the woman sobbed piteously, shoving to her hands and knees. "I can't go back. They'll take away my baby."

Abby knelt beside her. "Who'll take away your baby?" She laid a comforting hand on the woman's shoulder. "Surely you're mistaken. No one would do such a thing."

"Y-yes, they would."

Turquoise eyes met hers in the moonlight. The sight of a pale, thin, yet hauntingly familiar face plucked at Abby's memory. Where had she seen this woman . . . this girl . . . before?

"Hannah," she breathed in shocked recognition. "Hannah, is that you?"

The girl nodded. "Yes. Please, I—"

"There you are, you little slut!" Brody Gerard stepped from the alley Hannah had just fled. "Get your sorry behind over here. Do it now, before you cause a ruckus that I'll make sure you regret, and regret long and hard."

Frantic hands groped at Abby. Wide, terrified eyes gazed up at her. "Don't let him take me back," she pleaded. "Please. I'll do anything. *Anything!*"

In rising panic, Abby glanced from Hannah to the man now bearing down on them. An impulse to rise and flee filled her. What could she do against a man as big and mean as Brody Gerard anyway? He could knock her flat on her back with one swipe of his hand.

She turned toward the town hall. Bright light from its windows partially illuminated the street where they knelt. The loud strains of fiddle music mixed with laughter, and the pounding of dancing feet on the wooden floors. No one would hear her if she called for help. Whatever she decided, the likelihood was that she would make the decision alone.

As had Hannah, Abby realized with a swift stab of compunction, if in an altogether different sort of way. Alone, betrayed, abused, she fought still to escape the brutal unfairness and exploitation of her life, if only she could. If only someone would just reach out a hand, and help her. If only someone would see her as the child of God that she was, and have the courage to stand up for her.

Stand up for Hannah, and for what was right and fair.

"I won't let him take you back. I promise," Abby said, her mind made up. "But you must help me. Together, we might be able to best him."

Hope flared in Hannah's eyes. She brushed a hank of hair from her face, and nodded. "I'll do anything you want."

238

"For starters, stay there on the ground. It'll be harder for him to drag you off that way," Abby whispered, as Brody Gerard drew up before them.

"Get your hands off her." Gerard's glare sent shivers down Abby's spine. "She's coming back with me."

Abby shoved to her feet. "No, Hannah's not," she said with a quiet but firm emphasis. "She doesn't want to return to that life, and you've no right to take her back to it."

"Who's to stop me?" Brody gave a harsh, disparaging laugh. "You?"

"If that's what it takes, then yes, me. Now, let Hannah be. She's not going with you, and that's that."

Behind Abby, the town hall door opened momentarily then closed again. A wild hope that someone had seen them and gone for help filled her. She squared her shoulders.

Brody grasped Abby's arm, and jerked her hard up against him. "You've always been a bit too uppity for your own good." A mean, leering smile curled his lips. "Maybe it's time I took you down a peg or two."

"Let me go!" She tried to break free. "Take your hands off me!"

Brody pressed her even closer. "Who needs Hannah anyway? She's fat and awkward with that bastard child of hers. Maybe I'll just take you instead."

"Let her go!" Hannah grabbed his leg. "Don't you *dare* hurt her."

"Slut!" Brody sank his fingers into Hannah's hair and wrenched her head back. "Don't you ever tell me what to do." His teeth pulled back from his lips in a malevolent sneer. "Unless you've got a hankering for another beating."

"Well, well." Out of the night a fourth, unexpected, and decidedly male voice intruded. "One woman wasn't enough for you, was it Gerard?"

239

Brody's head whipped around in the direction of the town hall. Abby twisted in his grip, and was just able to catch a glimpse of Conor's backlit form, standing in the bright light of the open doorway. Behind him, men and women crowded, jostling and shoving for a look.

With a foul curse, Brody Gerard shoved Abby away. "I've no beef with her." He motioned toward Abby. "She was interfering with my bringing back a runaway, that's all." None too gently, he pulled Hannah to her feet.

"Was she now?" Conor walked over to them and looked at Abby. "What's going on here?"

"I stepped outside for a breath of air," she hurried to explain. "While I was out here, Hannah came running, begging me to help her. She doesn't want to go back to that vile house where she lives. I told her I'd help her."

His dark brows lifted in surprise. "You told her what? Abby, have you taken leave of your senses?"

His question momentarily took Abby aback. How, indeed, was she to help Hannah? "Well, I suppose . . ." She hesitated, her thoughts racing. "I suppose she could stay with me in the bunkhouse, until I figure out what to do next. She certainly can't go back with the likes of him! After tonight, he'd likely kill her."

"I doubt that," Conor countered with dry sarcasm. "I'd wager she's one of Sadie Fleming's most valuable girls."

"Well, I don't care. She's near to having her baby, and a whorehouse is no place for that!"

Conor's lips tightened. "Well, she's not coming to Culdee Creek. I won't have a woman like that on my ranch."

It was all Abby could do not to remind him he had already had several women like that on his ranch. No purpose would be served, though, standing out here in the street, arguing in front of a now smirking Brody Ge-

240

rard, and what was probably half the town of Grand View. Still, she had given her word to Hannah.

Abby stretched to her full height. "Fine. If Hannah can't come back with us to Culdee Creek, I'll stay here with her."

Conor's mouth dropped. "What? Where do you propose staying? At Sadie Fleming's?"

"No, of course not." Once more, Abby's thoughts raced. She didn't know any of the townspeople well enough to impose on their charity, as if any would've even been willing to take in Hannah anyway. "I'll just get a room at Mrs. Lombardy's rooming house, or stay at the Crown Hotel."

Behind them, feet began to shuffle restlessly. Someone snickered, and a few unintelligible, whispered comments floated through the air. Fury darkened Conor's eyes.

"You know I can't let you stay in town," he finally said, his voice pitched low. "It wouldn't be safe."

"I'd be just as safe as Hannah."

For the first time, Conor's glance swung to the blond woman. He looked at her, his gaze severe, uncompromising, contemptuous. Abby swallowed hard, choking back a cry of protest against his overt display of cruelty.

To her credit, Hannah met his scathing assessment with a calm, steady one of her own. She had nothing to lose, Abby realized. Despite the sad events of her past, this was a woman of merit and grace. In that fleeting moment, Abby's feelings for the girl transformed from those of simple compassion to respect.

"Have it your way," Conor muttered at last. "She can come to Culdee Creek and stay with you in the bunkhouse. But it's only temporary. She doesn't get a free ride, and if I catch her cozying up to any of my men . . ."

"For pity's sake, Conor," Abby exclaimed. "She's almost nine months pregnant!"

241

Apparently Conor chose to ignore that last remark. He turned to Brody. "Let the girl go, Gerard. She's coming with us."

The man eyed Conor with an ill-disguised fury. "You're making a big mistake, MacKay. Your reputation's already shot to blazes in this town."

"Then it won't matter much what else I do, will it?" Conor took a step toward Brody. "Now, do as I say. *Let the girl go.*"

"And if I don't?" Gerard released Hannah. Fists clenched at his sides, he stepped back.

Abby sucked in a frightened breath. She hadn't thought that the two men might come to blows. But now, as she watched Conor ball his fists and assume a fighting stance with shoulders hunched and legs solidly spread, it appeared as if it might just come to that.

"Well,"–Conor gave a nonchalant shrug–"I reckon it's past time you finally got the whipping you deserve. Just never thought I'd be doing it for the sake of some soiled dove."

Brody shot the men beginning to gather around them a nervous, skittering glance. He took another step back, wet his lips, then began to chew at them. "It . . . it wouldn't be a fair fight, MacKay. The rest of these men–"

"Wouldn't interfere," Conor cut him off silkily. "Remember, my reputation's shot to blazes in Grand View. I'm sure they really don't care who beats up who."

"Easy for you to say." Brody kept on backing up until he was free of the loose circle that had formed around them. "Some other time, MacKay."

"Yeah," Conor muttered as he watched Brody Gerard turn and hightail it down another alley. "So you keep saying."

Abby turned and took Hannah by the arm. "I told you I wouldn't let him take you." She smiled down at the girl.

Hannah's eyes filled with tears. "Oh, thank you. Thank you!" Sobbing as if her heart would break, she flung herself into Abby's arms.

As she clasped Hannah to her, Abby's gaze locked with Conor's. She managed a bright if tremulous smile.

He didn't smile back.

17

A time to kill, and a time to heal; a time to break down, and a time to build up.

Ecclesiastes 3:3

By the time they returned to Culdee Creek that night, Hannah was exhausted. She was still sound asleep the next morning when Abby arose. After dressing quietly, Abby tiptoed from the bunkhouse. Before she was halfway to the back door of the main house, however, Devlin MacKay hailed her.

She smiled in greeting. "Good morning, Devlin. How's Mary—"

"Mary's fine," he cut her off tersely. "This isn't about Mary anyway." He scowled. "I heard you brought back one of Sadie Fleming's girls last night."

"Yes," Abby replied slowly, gathering from his tone of voice and dark expression that Devlin was not pleased with the news. "She's pregnant, and no longer wishes to remain in Mrs. Fleming's employ."

"Why, in heaven's name, did you bring her back here? She's a prostitute, Abby. There are young men working on Culdee Creek who'll be susceptible to her advances, and I certainly don't want my children exposed to the likes of her." He paused, his eyes narrowing. "And what about Beth? Did you even stop to think about her?"

Abby had not, she hated to admit. In the heat of the moment last night, all she had thought about was Hannah. She had not thought of the possible impact on anyone else.

"I confess I didn't consider the children." She hung her head in shame. "Perhaps I was wrong. But the fact remains that if the adults on Culdee Creek deal with Hannah in a mature, Christian way, the children–"

Devlin gasped and his face went ashen. "Did you say her name is Hannah?"

Abby stared up at him in surprise. "Yes, I did. She's very pretty, with beautiful light blond hair. She's about eighteen or so."

With a slow, unsteady motion, Devlin shoved his hand through his hair and closed his eyes.

A sick realization filled Abby. There was obviously more than one reason Devlin MacKay didn't want a fallen woman at Culdee Creek, and the worst reason of all had just materialized. Hannah must be the woman Devlin had called on at Sadie Fleming's.

The enormity of what she had done struck Abby with the force of a blow. Ella . . . dear God, what would this do to Ella?

Anger swelled in her. It was all Devlin's fault, and now his sins were coming home to roost. For an instant, she couldn't hide the reproach she knew must be in her eyes.

Then, as quickly as she recognized how revealing such an action must be, Abby averted her gaze. No purpose was served in adding to the problem. What was private between him and his wife should remain that way.

"Though you may think Hannah's coming to Culdee Creek is bad," Abby forced herself to say, "perhaps the Lord's hand is in this. If we can help her turn back to God and the life of a good woman, not only she, but her unborn child might be saved. Isn't that worth the risk, Devlin?"

Furiously, he shook his head. "No. Never." His glance hardened, turned angry. "I want her gone, Abby. Gone today."

She stared up at him for a long moment. "I don't think that's the Christian thing to do," she said finally. "To cast out a woman who has nowhere else to go, a woman ready to birth . . . Well, it wouldn't be right."

"Christian!" Devlin snarled, his hands clenched at his sides. "I'm sick to death of hearing that word! All it has done is make everything worse!"

Compassion filled her. Devlin wasn't a heartless man. He was just lost, and so very, very anguished.

Abby smiled in gentle understanding. "It may seem so right now," she said, "but the Lord's ways aren't always immediately clear to us. Yet, even in our darkness we must try to do good however we can, and trust that God will make it right."

Devlin gave a harsh laugh. "Yeah, you just go ahead and trust, Abby. Me, I don't plan to wait until the Lord gets around to making it right." He turned on his heel and stalked away.

"What are you going to do?" A cold fear clutched at Abby's heart. "Devlin, what are you going to do?"

"For starters," he tossed over his shoulder, "I'm going to have a talk with Conor. After that,"–he shrugged– "who knows?"

"I want to thank you for sharing your bed with me last night, Mrs. Stanton," Hannah murmured shyly, as she helped Abby fold a pile of freshly laundered sheets and lady's undergarments that afternoon. "It was very kind."

Abby glanced up and smiled. "I couldn't have a mother-to-be sleeping on the hard floor, could I? I still remember how uncomfortable it got, that last month before I birthed my son."

Hannah blushed, and hung her head. "Still . . ."

"Still nothing." She replaced the sachet of dried lavender atop the petticoats, then shoved the new dresser drawer closed and walked over to the young woman. Abby took her hand. "Listen to me, Hannah. The past is over. You don't have to speak of it unless *you* need or want to."

The girl looked up, a sad smile on her lips. "Maybe not for you, ma'am, but there are plenty of folk who won't ever let me forget what I did, and was."

Abby gave Hannah's hand a reassuring squeeze. "That may well be. But those folk are either too blinded by their own faults or too overcome with guilt at their part in helping bring you to this state. Yet you must still forgive them. It's the only way to truly gain the Lord's forgiveness. That, of course," Abby added, "and a deep and lasting repentance."

"I don't know much about God, ma'am. Leastwise not of the kind of God like you said loves me, that time we met in Mr. Gates's store." She sighed, and shook her head. "I never knew of God, not those years I took care of my sick mama, or when she died and I was sent to that orphanage. And there certainly didn't seem to be any God looking after me when I finally ran away at fifteen and ended up in a brothel after a man tricked me with promises of food and a warm place to sleep."

As she listened in growing horror, Abby's stomach began to twist into knots. There was no comment she could make, though, to such a tragic story.

"I tried to run away from that brothel," Hannah continued, "but each time the madam's bodyguards would find me and bring me back to a terrible beating. After a while, I gave up trying. Besides, it didn't seem to matter much anymore if there was a God. I figured He didn't care for me anyway, leastwise not after what I'd become." She managed a teary-eyed smile. "But I never forgot your kind words that day. I've clutched them to me ever since.

"It was your words, ma'am"—Hannah touched her belly with something akin to loving reverence—"and the precious baby growing inside me that made me decide to try once more to run away."

Abby's throat went tight. "I'm glad to hear that my words gave you some comfort. I truly meant them."

A warm certitude glowed in the girl's eyes. "I know that, ma'am. I don't know how I knew it, but I did. That's why, when I saw you ride into town last night, I dared come to you. If anybody would've helped me, I knew it would be you."

Guilt pricked at Abby. If only Hannah knew how close she had been to turning her back on her. But she had not, thank the Lord. She had not then, and she would not in the difficult days and weeks ahead. She only hoped Ella would be more tolerant and understanding than her husband.

"I thank you for your faith in me." Abby released her hand and, walking back to the pile of laundry, pulled out her chemises and underdrawers. "Now," she urged as she began to fold the garments, "tell me, when is your baby due?"

"Most any day now, I reckon."

Abby frowned. If that was the case, she had a lot to get prepared, and soon. There were clean rags and extra sheets to gather, some sort of a cradle to fashion if one could not be found on the ranch, and Ella to convince to help her with the delivery until Doc Childress could be fetched. Abby only hoped Devlin would not forbid Ella from any interaction with Hannah.

"We've got our work cut out for us, don't we?" she asked brightly. "Good thing Conor had this rebuilt bunkhouse sectioned off into a main room and two smaller backrooms. We can turn my sewing room into a private room for you and the baby."

Footsteps sounded on the wooden porch. Knuckles rapped on the stout portal. Abby quickly put away the last of her undergarments and hurried to the door.

· Conor stood there, a scowl on his face. "I need to talk with you, Abby. Now, if you please, in the main house."

Of late, Abby observed wryly, there were a passel of menfolk walking around with scowling faces. If she were a betting woman, she'd lay odds it had to do with Hannah. She turned to the younger woman. "I'll be back shortly. Don't wear yourself out now. My new rocker is mighty comfortable on a sore back."

At that moment in the very act of putting her hand to her back, Hannah gave a soft laugh. Abby smiled, then turned, closed the door, and followed Conor through the backyard to the main house. As they walked along, Abby took note of the clear blue sky, full of clouds scudding along in the blustering spring winds, and the bright sunshine. In the windbreak of the house, it felt almost warm.

Patches of bright green grass poked through the winter brown turf. In a long-neglected flowerbed lining the base of the back porch, tiny, grape-like clusters of purple muscari and yellow and white crocuses were just now beginning to bloom. Abby made a mental note to see if she could beg some flower seeds from the ladies of the Episcopal Church the next time she was in town. A pretty, summer flower garden did wonders for the soul.

Conor paused at the back door and held it open. Wordlessly, Abby walked inside. After closing the door behind them, he motioned for her to take a seat at the table.

"Want a cup of coffee?" He walked to the cupboard.

"No, not just yet." Abby began to trace nervous little circles on the checkered tablecloth. Then, catching herself, she clasped her hands firmly before her.

At long last, Conor took a seat across from her. "It's about Hannah," he said without any preliminaries, stirring two spoonfuls of sugar into his coffee. "I know you're not going to like this, Abby, but on further consideration I've decided it isn't wise to allow her to stay."

"Not even until after her baby's born?"

"No." Conor gave a sharp shake of his head. "Not even until then. There's a place in the Springs that might take her–"

Something snapped in Abby. "So, just because Devlin can't live with a physical reminder of his transgressions," she blurted out angrily without thinking, "Hannah has to slink away like some stray dog with its tail tucked between its legs. Yet who is the greater sinner in this? Devlin who broke his holy vows, or Hannah, who was forced into a horrible life against her will?"

The color drained from Conor's face. "You . . . you know about Devlin and Hannah then? How? Ella?"

Dear Lord, what have I done? Abby thought with an anguished surge of remorse. *What have I done?*

"Yes," she forced herself to reply, even as she quailed beneath Conor's now angry, relentless glare. "Ella told me, though of course she doesn't realize that it was specifically Hannah. By his reaction this morning, Devlin gave himself away. All Ella knows is Devlin paid Sadie Fleming's several visits this fall."

"Blast it! Now the fat's really in the fire." Conor groaned and buried his face in his hands.

250

"Not necessarily." Abby's thoughts raced, trying to find a solution to the ever-worsening dilemma. "You don't *have* to tell Devlin I know, and Devlin doesn't *have* to tell Ella about Hannah."

"And what about Hannah? Can we trust her to keep quiet?"

Abby sighed. "I imagine she's not going to do anything to jeopardize her stay here."

His jaw set, his mind apparently made, Conor looked up. "Hannah has to leave, and you know it, Abby. There's just no getting around it."

"So, she's never to have a chance." A deep, despairing sadness flooded Abby. "Is that it, Conor?"

He rolled his eyes, and expelled a frustrated breath. "Why does it have to fall on me and you to give her a chance? Tell me what makes us suddenly the saviors of soiled doves?"

"Because one of those doves begged us to help, that's why." She leaned on the table, her glance imploring. "Don't make me turn her away, Conor. It would break my heart."

"Do you realize you're placing me square in the middle with this, between you and Devlin, and possibly Ella, too? Do you know the trouble that may come from this?"

"I think so." Abby straightened. "At least let Hannah stay until her baby's born and she's recovered from the birth. Give her six months."

Conor grimaced. "*Three* months, and that's tops. I don't want her getting the idea she's got a permanent home here."

Three months wasn't much time but, for now, it was a reasonable compromise. Abby nodded. "Three months. Then we reconsider if she can stay longer or must leave. Deal?"

He cocked a dark brow, then sighed his acquiescence, and defeat. "Deal."

&

Abby waited until the next afternoon for Ella to stop by. When she did not, Abby decided to take the matter in hand. Her excuse for a visit, she decided as she trudged up the hill to Ella's house, would be the announcement of her and Conor's engagement.

She found her friend behind her house, hanging laundry on the clothesline. At her greeting Ella turned, a wooden clothespin in her mouth, a wet nightshirt in her hand.

"Hello," she mumbled without much enthusiasm. "Give me a moment to finish hanging this, will you?"

Abby nodded, and waited patiently until Ella was done hanging the nightshirt. Then she strode over and took up her friend's hands. "I've some wonderful news to tell you."

Ella eyed her warily. "You do?"

"Yes." Abby couldn't hide her grin of delight. "Conor proposed again last night, and I accepted. We're to be married on July 4th."

Ella's eyes grew wide. "I'm so happy for you and Conor. I kept hoping and praying . . ." She paused, cocking her head. "Did you just say Conor proposed *again*?"

Abby blushed. "Yes, I did. The first time was the morning after the bunkhouse burned down. I wouldn't say yes then, but I did agree to a courtship."

"A courtship that obviously was known only to the two of you." Ella didn't look very happy.

"Oh, Ella, don't be mad." Abby squeezed her hand. "We just didn't want to disappoint anyone, in case we discovered we weren't suited. Perhaps it was wrong or selfish, but we meant well."

"I suppose you did." As Ella pulled her hand free, she gave a dismissing wave. "Just like you meant well in bringing that woman to Culdee Creek."

Abby's heart sank. So, her fears about Ella's sudden distancing of herself had not been far off the mark. She motioned to the crude, log bench standing beside the back door. "Why don't we sit for a spell and talk this out? Okay, Ella?"

"Don't see as how it'll make much difference," the red-haired woman muttered, heading toward the bench.

Gathering her skirts, Abby followed her. For a long while, the two women sat there, silently watching the wind-whipped ponderosas covering the hills behind them, and the beautiful, bright blue sky. Finally, Abby couldn't keep quiet a moment longer.

"I gather Devlin told you about Hannah's arrival," she began, choosing her words carefully.

"Yes, he did. He's none too pleased about having a woman like her around the children." Ella's face took on a pinched, distressed look. "He said Conor wasn't much help, though. Seems he promised you three months with this woman or some fool thing like that."

Abby squelched her twinge of irritation at Ella's tactless assessment. She was upset and frightened, fearful of where all this might lead. Perhaps the best course of action was to bring those fears to light and name them.

"Do you think that's Devlin's only reason for not wanting Hannah here, Ella?" she prodded gently.

"You know it isn't."

"What are the others, then?"

"He doesn't want to be reminded of what he did." Ella swiped away a tear. "I'd imagine he's also afraid that this Hannah might recognize him, and let it slip where she's seen him before."

"So he's told you not to come near her, hasn't he?" Abby scooted closer and put her arm about Ella's shoulders. "Perhaps he even imagined that if I discovered you weren't coming to visit because of Hannah, that I might send her away."

"I wouldn't put it past him," her friend said with a sniffle. "Right about now, I'd reckon Devlin's mighty scared."

"But is that what *you* want, Ella?" She began to stroke Ella's arm. "Do you think my bringing Hannah here, because she begged me to help her and had no one else, is reason enough to destroy our friendship?"

"N-no." Ella began to weep. "But Devlin won't understand. He'll be angry."

"His anger is but a mask for his fear." Abby clutched Ella close. "His fear of losing you, if you discover his unfaithfulness."

"But I already know," she wailed. "And I've forgiven him."

"Devlin doesn't know that, Ella." Taking her by the shoulders, Abby gazed into her friend's tear-reddened eyes.

"Should I tell him I know?"

"It might bring about a much needed healing for the both of you."

"Yes," Ella agreed softly. "It just might. Perhaps I've been a mite uncharitable toward my husband, in allowing him to suffer so long over this. Perhaps I enjoyed his guilt and torment, and wasn't all that eager to ease his burden. After all, he hurt me deeply."

"It was a very human reaction, to be hurt and want to hurt in return."

Ella nodded, her gaze thoughtful. "Yes. But it was also as damaging as the unfaithful act that set it all into motion. As Christians, we're not only called to imitate Christ in deed but to react like He would, too."

"Yes, we are. It's not always easy, though, is it?"

"No, it's not." Ella's smile broadened until a look of joyous understanding filled her eyes. "The truth has been there all along, hasn't it, Abby? If only I'd had the courage to face it."

"And now you do."

"Yes," Ella agreed with a nod, "now I do."

May 3, 1896

Dearest Nelly,

So much has happened of late. A young woman named Hannah has come to live with me in the bunkhouse. She's a reformed prostitute and will soon deliver her first child. Though it's not quite the same scale as Thomas's mission for outcasts and indigents, I'd imagine he'll look down kindly on my efforts nonetheless.

I am also beginning to make plans for a July 4th wedding to Conor. Yes, your direst fears have come true. But I love him, Nelly, and he loves me. More than anything I've wanted in a very long time, I want to be a wife to him and a mother to Beth. Please be happy for me, and wish me the best.

Everything is at last falling into place as I feel certain the Lord always intended it to. I think back now to that day you and I first came to Culdee Creek. I recall how angry I became when you accused me of running away and shirking my duty to myself, others, and even to God. Well, perhaps you struck closer to the truth than I cared to admit.

I'm not running away anymore, Nelly. I'm facing life, embracing it willingly, joyously now. I have so very, very much to live for, and so much still left to give. The Lord has opened my eyes, and Conor and Beth have opened my heart.

We plan to wed in Grand View's Episcopal Church. I've sent word to my parents and brothers, inviting them to come. Won't you please consider coming, too? I do so want you and your dear husband to be there with me on the happy day.

Well, I must close for now. Time for Beth's lessons. Did I mention in my last letter that we're now including Scripture in her reading assignments? She tells me she wants to be baptized on our wedding day. I'm praying with all my might that it won't be long now before Conor, too, returns to the Lord.

Fondly,
Abby

Five days later, in the middle of the night, Hannah went into labor. With help from Abby and Ella, she had delivered a healthy baby boy by dawn. After cleaning up mother and son, Abby sent an exhausted Ella on her way. Then, pulling up the rocking chair beside the bed Conor had hastily built for Hannah's room, she sat back to watch.

Jackson Cutler—for Cutler was Hannah's given name—nursed hungrily at his mother's breast. His pink little lips encircled the plump tissue, his cheeks pumping furiously. One tiny fist, perfectly formed, curled about a pale lock of his mother's hair that had tumbled down near his face. His own hair, though, was dark brown, already thick and, now that it was dry, even possessed a hint of a wave.

"So, what do you think of my precious little boy?"

Abby lifted her gaze from the infant to its mother. "He's beautiful, Hannah. Absolutely beautiful."

She smiled in sleepy satisfaction. "Thank you. I think so, too."

"Would you like for me to leave the two of you alone for a while? I don't wish to intrude."

"You're not intruding, ma'am. It makes me feel safe when you're near. I'm certain my little boy will feel the same way about you, when he's old enough to know."

If he's even fortunate to still be here, Abby thought glumly, remembering her bargain with Conor. But Hannah didn't need to know that now. Now was a time of rest and contentment, a time to savor the triumph of accomplishment. She'd come through one of the greatest trials of a woman's life safely and well.

"I'd like very much to share in his care and upbringing," Abby said instead. "He's a very special child."

"Yes." Tenderly, she stroked his cheek. "He is."

Abby closed her eyes against a sudden swell of tears. Babies. Oh, how they now always brought back the bittersweet memories. They were memories, though, no longer as hard to bear.

She wondered if she and Conor would someday have a baby of their own. If they did the child would never fill the aching hole in her heart left by her beloved Joshua. That child, like little Jackson, would just make a new place all its very own.

Slowly, thoughtfully, Abby began to rock. The morning came and went. In time, she slept the deep, restful sleep of the weary but contented. She dreamt of sunshine, flowers, and children playing in the spring grass. Dreamt of her and Conor watching those children, full of love and pride. The dream was like an answer to some prayer.

"Abby! Abby, wake up!"

A hand, shaking her, jerked Abby from her dream. Her eyes snapped open. Ella stood there, a look of grave concern on her face.

"What's wrong?" She bolted upright in her chair. "Is Hannah all right?"

"I'm just fine, ma'am." A sweet voice rose from the bed beside her. "So's Jackson."

"It's not Hannah, Abby." Ella grasped her arm. "It's Conor."

"Conor?" Freshened terror filled her. "What's happened to Conor?"

"Nothing yet," her friend muttered. "But Evan's come home, Abby, and unless I miss my guess, there's a fight brewing."

18

*Rejoice with me; for I have found my sheep which was
lost.*

Luke 15:6

Heart pounding, Conor stormed out of the
house and headed for his son who was,
even then, dismounting from a mangy, brown mule. At
the sound of his footsteps on the front porch, the visitor
paused and looked up. For a long moment, their gazes
met.

A wild mix of emotions stampeded through Conor.
Relief, at seeing Evan alive and well, if now thin to the
point of gauntness and dressed in little more than rags,
warred with anger for the pain and heartache his leaving had caused. The overriding impulse to take his son
in his arms and forgive all, however, was quickly
squelched by the memory of his theft. A theft, Conor
reminded himself bitterly, that had put Culdee Creek
seriously in debt, forcing the sale of over five hundred
prime grazing acres and cutting the ranch's original size
nearly in half.

So, instead of walking down the steps to greet his son,
Conor stood on the porch, his hands gripping the railing.
"Before you get too comfortable there," he growled, pur-
posely leaning on the railing in order to tower over Evan,

"why don't you just state your business, then mount up and ride on out? You're not welcome here anymore."

Anguish flared in the depths of Evan's smoky-blue eyes, then was gone. "I know." He sighed. "I did wrong, Pa, in leaving like I did. I've grown up this past year, though. It's time we talked. Really talked, I mean. Man-to-man."

Conor gave a harsh laugh. "Man-to-man? Does that mean you plan to pay back all the money you stole? A *man* makes good on his debts."

"Yeah, and I would, if I still had any of it." Evan lowered his shaggy head, and began to roll the tattered brim of his sweat-stained, dusty brown hat in his hands. A lock of blue-black hair tumbled down onto his forehead. "I lost most of your money in a gold mine in Irwin. The rest, I reckon," he added with a sheepish grin as he glanced back up at Conor, "went for the liquor and fancy ladies in Irwin's bawdy houses."

No wonder I couldn't find you, Conor thought, holed up in some gold mine all the way down in the Gunnison area. "Well, if your clothes are any indication," he observed with a disgusted snort, "I'd say your dream of striking it rich was far from fulfilled."

"The two miners I grubstaked were liars and cheats. I was a fool to believe their promises."

"Yeah, you sure were."

With great effort, Conor restrained the urge to rush down off the porch and beat the living tar out of Evan. He would have, too, if he had thought it would do any good. But it wouldn't. The sooner Evan was gone from Culdee Creek, the sooner he could forget he even had such a blamed fool son.

Conor motioned toward Evan's mule. "I reckon we've visited long enough. Time you were heading back."

"Pa, I'm sorry. So very, very sorry," Evan cried out. He strode up to the base of the steps, his eyes full of tears.

He lifted his hands in the air. "Please, Pa. Don't send me away. No matter how long it takes, I'll work for you to pay off my debt. You don't have to show me any special favors just 'cause I'm your son. I can live in the bunkhouse with the other hands. Let me make it up to you. Please, Pa!"

At his son's impassioned plea, something snapped in Conor. He'd wanted to keep their meeting civil, if cold, and quickly send Evan on his way. Any other response might have laid bare the depth of his grievous pain—a pain Evan had so callously inflicted when he'd ridden off that day last March. A pain he couldn't bear to endure again. But it apparently wasn't to be. Evan just wouldn't let it be.

With a foul curse, Conor rushed down off the porch. He grabbed his son by the collar of his frayed and threadbare woolen shirt and jerked him up. "There's nothing you can do to make it up to me!" he snarled, his voice gone low and deadly. "*Nothing!* Do you hear me? Get your sorry carcass off my—"

"Conor, don't!"

A voice, belovedly familiar and urgently entreating, pierced the mists of his fury. Still holding Evan in his grip, Conor half-turned. Abby stood there, her face flushed, her chest heaving.

"Please, Conor," she said softly, extending her hand to him. "Don't do this. You'll regret it for the rest of your life."

"I doubt that." Conor released his son and shoved him back. "This low life, no account"—he gestured disgustedly toward his son—"stole from me, then squandered all the money. Now he has the gall to come crawling back."

"And how much better are you?" Evan snapped. His lip curled in disdain as he turned and looked Abby up and down. "You treat women like I treat money. I see you've already traded in Maudie for another one. Can't say as how this one's any better looking, though, than most of the fancy ladies I've had a taste of."

"Insolent pup!" Conor whirled around and struck out, his fist smashing into Evan's face. Like a felled tree, his son toppled backward. He struck the ground hard, blood spurting from his nose and split lip.

With a cry, Abby rushed forward. She knelt beside Evan, pulled out a handkerchief, and applied it to his nose. "Lie still," she ordered when Evan struggled to rise. "Let me staunch the bleeding first."

"I don't need your help," he muttered, even as he allowed her ministrations. "Just get out of my way, and I'll move on. No sense hanging around where I'm not wanted."

Conor moved to stand beside Abby. He grasped her arm and tugged. "He's right. Let him go. He's a thief and liar. I can't stand the sight of him."

To his surprise, Abby twisted free of his hold. Over her shoulder, she shot him an outraged glance. "How dare you speak like that of your own flesh and blood? Are you so free of sin that you can judge him?"

Conor released Abby's arm, and stepped back. "You don't understand, Abby. You can't. You weren't here."

"I understand a lot more than you think." She turned back to minister to Evan. "I understand that your anger right now stems from the pain Evan caused you when he left. I also understand that you're a proud man, and it's hard for you to forgive, much less ask for forgiveness. But you must, Conor. You must!"

Heat flooded his face. Freshened anger filled him. "This isn't the time or place, Abby. He's nothing to you. Get up and let him go."

Evan shoved her hand away. "I told you. I don't need your help. And I certainly don't want his! I'm not staying where I'm not wanted."

She looked from him to Conor. "Well, I see bull-headed pride runs in the family. Guess it shouldn't surprise me." Abby climbed to her feet, and met her fiancé's still scowling gaze. "Don't know as how I'm all that eager to marry into it."

Conor sighed. *Here we go again!* "And what is *that* supposed to mean?"

Abby shrugged. "It's one thing to wed a man who no longer claims to be a practicing Christian. It's quite another to wed one who refuses to act like one."

Evan shoved to his feet. "Well, well," he said with a muffled chuckle, still clutching Abby's bloodstained handkerchief to his nose, "what's this? Has my pa finally decided to take another wife? And a devout one, at that? May the ground open up and swallow me!"

"Don't start, Evan!" Conor shot his son a murderous look, then turned back to Abby and took her by the arms. "What's between Evan and me has nothing to do with you, or how I plan to live my life with you. Don't get into the middle of this, Abby. Let me clean it up right here and now so we can go on with our lives."

"As if nothing has happened?" she swiftly supplied. "As if this rejection of your own son doesn't matter? No." She gave a firm shake of her head. "I can't marry you if you do this, Conor. I just can't."

Utter frustration flooded him. Blast Evan for coming home when he did. A few more months, and it would not have mattered. Leastwise not between him and Abby. But now it did matter, and matter greatly. He'd just have to deal with Evan later. The boy wasn't worth losing Abby over.

"Fine." Conor released her and stepped back. "Evan can stay on a while."

"You need to ask for your father's forgiveness, Evan." Abby turned to the younger man. "And you, Conor," she added, glancing at him as Evan huffed in protest, "need to forgive your son."

Conor's heart sank. He shook his head. "I can't, Abby. Too much has happened. Too much time has passed."

"You know you want to, Conor. Deep down in your heart of hearts, you want your son back."

Her eyes were luminous and loving and knowing. In their depths Conor saw his own secret yearning, a yearning to have his son back. He had lost so much, and he longed to regain it all. A wife and a family that would never truly seem complete without both of his children . . .

"Yes, I suppose I do," he whispered hoarsely. "I suppose I do."

With that admission, Conor offered his hand to his son. "Welcome home, Evan. I've missed you."

Eyes wide, mouth half-open, Evan looked from his father to Abby, then back again to his father. "And I've missed you, Pa." He hesitated, then clasped his father's hand. "I've really, really missed you."

Two weeks later Abby dug happily in the rich, dark earth of her new flower beds along the front porch. Soon the soil would be spaded free of the invasive clumps of grass. Then, after some aged horse manure had been worked in to enrich the plot, she would be ready to plant the flower seeds she had accepted from several of the ladies of the Episcopal Church quilting society she had recently joined.

By late summer hollyhocks, delphiniums, bachelor buttons and daisies would be blooming. And next year she would see about purchasing some rosebushes to flank the walkway up to the front porch. Nothing, absolutely nothing, set off a garden like roses.

She leaned back, brushed an errant strand of hair from her face, and gazed up at the gloriously blue sky. Her whole being sang with happiness. It felt so good to belong somewhere again, to be able to make long-term plans and eagerly anticipate them. It felt good to be needed and to take care of loved ones again. She felt alive, vibrant, and so very full of joy.

The crazy quilt patchwork of her life was finally filling in again, scrap by colorful scrap. Since Evan's return, father and son had made their peace. Slowly but surely, they appeared to be forming a new bond.

Abby smiled to herself. She had never seen Conor so content and at peace with himself, either. But then he had both of his children back at last, and soon he would have a new wife, too.

With renewed vigor, she resumed her digging, working her way around a particularly stubborn patch of grass. The bed was almost ready. After lunch, she would get one of the hands to bring over a couple of wheelbarrow loads of well-aged manure. Then—

The sound of angry male voices floated by her on the breeze. She paused, listening hard. It sounded like Evan, and some other man whose voice she couldn't quite make out. Abby laid aside her spade, and rose.

Gathering her long skirts, she hurried around to the back of the house. There stood Evan, his fists clenched at his side, his body stiff with outrage, facing down Devlin MacKay. Not far away on the small bunkhouse porch stood a pale, teary-eyed Hannah, clutching her infant son.

"You take back what you said to Hannah," Evan was saying, anger roughening his voice. "Family or not, no man talks that way to a lady in my presence and gets away with it!"

Devlin gave a harsh laugh. "And I'd be the first to agree with you, sonny, if there was a lady present. But this woman"—he gestured disparagingly toward Hannah—

"is nothing more than an immoral, self-serving slut. It makes me sick to see her, not two weeks from her childbed, already plying her wiles on the likes of you. Leave her be, Evan. Leave her be."

"You've no call to tell me what to do," Evan snarled. "No more than you've got any right to insult Hannah like you do."

"Blast it all!" Devlin mottled in frustrated rage. "I knew you when you were in diapers and short pants. I care about you. Do you want to ruin everything you're beginning to rebuild with your father? You will, I promise you, if you persist in sniffing around this piece of—"

Evan didn't wait to hear another word. He took a swing at Devlin, and only the quickest of reflexes, as the older man leaped aside, kept fist from making contact with face. In his anger Evan lunged forward, nearly losing his balance before catching himself and wheeling back around. He advanced again on Devlin.

"Stop it!" Abby shoved her way between the two men. "Stop it at once."

Devlin froze. "Get out of the way," he growled. "You brought this on, you know. Now stand aside and deal with the consequences."

"Yeah," Evan cried from behind her. "Get out of the way, Abby. Devlin needs a lesson in manners."

"And you think you're just the man to do it, are you?" Devlin glared at him over Abby's shoulder. "Well, maybe you didn't learn as much as you thought you did this past year."

"Oh, stop it, I say," Abby cried in exasperation. "Both of you are acting like two school boys. And neither of you have thought past the ends of your noses. What about the pain you'll cause Conor, *and* Ella for that matter, if word gets out you two were fighting? I beg of you, don't force them to take sides."

"They'd never have had to take sides to begin with," Devlin muttered, scowling down at her, "if this woman hadn't come to Culdee Creek."

"Why can't you just let it be?" Abby demanded. "Just let it be before you cause her even more pain."

She knew Ella had talked with him, and that he now realized his wife was aware of his infidelity. It didn't appear, however, that she'd also been informed of the intimate connection between Devlin and Hannah. Perhaps *that* was the burr that yet chafed beneath his saddle.

At her words, something flickered in Devlin's eyes. He had guessed, Abby realized, that she spoke now of Ella, rather than of Hannah. His gaze narrowed. His jaw hardened.

"Easy for you to say." His voice went low, husky, and so very anguished. "Easy for you, after you've gone and made everything worse."

Beneath his anger, Devlin's fear was almost a palpable thing. Abby knew he feared losing Ella. He also feared the long-term consequences of his actions with Hannah, that her presence now at Culdee Creek represented.

But he also feared an even deeper abandonment and was consumed with self-loathing—a personal abhorrence that Abby now realized permeated his entire life. Whatever horrors he had endured as a child, it would take more than just Ella's love and understanding to heal.

"There's nothing that can't be set aright with love and forgiveness," Abby whispered, meeting his burning gaze. "Give it to the Lord, Devlin. *Give it to the Lord.*"

He staggered backward, looking as if someone had struck him. Then, with one final searing look, Devlin turned on his heel and stalked away.

"What in the blazes was all that about?" Evan demanded, thoroughly bewildered.

Abby turned. Fleetingly, she locked gazes with Hannah. Though there was no rancor or judgment in her heart

266

against the girl, Abby knew the young woman had guessed the reason for her and Devlin's hushed interchange.

"It's nothing, Evan," Hannah mumbled from the porch, cuddling baby Jackson more tightly to her. "Devlin just doesn't think I am a good influence to have around, what with the children and ranch hands and all."

Evan shot her a shy, admiring look. "But you've given up those fancy lady ways. Devlin needs to take you at your word, like Abby says. You deserve a second chance like anyone else."

"Yes, she does," Abby interjected. "You, though, Evan, need to steer clear of Devlin for the next few days. He'll get over his animosity toward Hannah in time, if you don't fan the flames any further."

"He started it," he grumbled, shuffling his feet and looking down, "when he started talking to Hannah as mean as he did."

"And you came to my aid like a knight in shining armor." Hannah rendered him her brightest smile. "For that, I'm eternally grateful. But Abby's right. I'm used to unkind words. What matters most is that my presence here doesn't cause further problems. That, far more than Devlin's occasional rudeness, could endanger my remaining at Culdee Creek."

Evan's eyes widened. "I reckon I hadn't thought about that. It just goes against my grain, though, to have a man talk disrespectfully to a lady."

"But you will try your best, won't you?" Hannah persisted, her voice softening to dulcet, pleading tones, "Please try not to stir up any more trouble with Devlin."

Few men, Abby realized, watching the pair, could resist Hannah when she turned on the full force of her charm. And Evan was far from mature.

He managed a cocky grin. "For you, ma'am, I'd do anything."

"Well, I don't think Hannah will require quite that much of you, Evan." Abby walked over and took Hannah by the arm. "All she wants is some peace and quiet in which to raise her son. A son," she added, delicately sniffing the air, "who seems in dire need of a changing."

Evan's expression suddenly assumed that darting, eager-to-escape look typical of a man in close vicinity to a baby with a dirty diaper. "Oh, yeah . . . yeah. Reckon I'd better get back to my chores then."

"Reckon you'd better," Abby agreed dryly. She watched him hightail it down to the barn, then turned to Hannah. "Why don't we take care of Jackson," she said, motioning toward the baby, "and then have a cup of tea while we talk?"

"Talk?" Hannah's dark blond brows arched in puzzlement.

"Yes." Abby gave a firm nod of her head. "Talk."

ꝑ

"Have you noticed Evan's decided interest in Hannah of late?" Ella asked three weeks later as she and Abby drove into the outskirts of Grand View. "I hate to stir up a hornet's nest, but I think he's falling for her."

Abby glanced at her friend as she urged the buggy down the dirt street. "So, it's become apparent to you, too." She sighed. "Conor apparently hasn't noticed yet. How about Devlin?"

Ella gave a noncommittal shrug. "Oh, he mutters and grumbles about Evan's attraction to her, but I think he fears an illicit, physical interest rather than any real affection. What do you think Conor will do once he realizes his son is falling in love with a former prostitute?"

"I don't think he'll be pleased," Abby replied after a moment's consideration. "It may be the perfect excuse he's been looking for to run her off."

"And risk running off Evan, too?" The red-haired woman paused to grab at her bonnet as a passing gust of wind threatened to rip it, ties and all, from her head. "If it should come to that, warn Conor to go slowly. His relationship with his son isn't totally mended, and Evan's as fiercely proud and independent a Scotsman as his father."

"So I've noticed." Abby halted the horse before Gate's Mercantile. Jumping down, she tied the buggy reins to the hitching post outside the store, then came around to help Ella. "I just hope we can put Evan and Hannah off, if it comes to that. They're both only eighteen."

Ella chuckled. "Young love is about as hard to control as a herd of cattle in a thunderstorm. Considering what they've been through in their young lives, this almost seems inevitable. They're both good youngsters at heart. And Evan's good looks are enough to melt any girl's resistance, even one as pretty as Hannah."

She pulled the shopping list from her purse. "Now, no more problems," Ella ordered, grinning in mischief to soften her words. "Let's get on with our purchases. We've got so much to buy, and only a few hours to do it."

Abby nodded. "I can't believe it's already time to start on my wedding dress. The time surely has flown."

"You've got just over two weeks until the wedding, Abby. Barely enough time to make you a fitting dress."

"Oh, it doesn't have to be anything elaborate." Abby pushed open the mercantile door and walked inside. "It's not like I'm getting married for the first time, you know."

Ella followed. "Nonetheless, you're marrying one of the wealthiest ranchers in the area. Everyone is sure to turn out for the ceremony and reception at church. Conor will want you to look your best." She took Abby by the arm and pulled her toward the fabric table. Behind them, the front door opened then closed again.

"How about this pale green moiré here?" Ella picked up a bolt of fabric and began to unfurl it. "This color is appropriate for summer, and it would set off your hair and eyes to perfection. We could add a false train that could be removed for later wear, trim the gown with creamy white point Venise lace and matching moiré ribbons, add full sleeves ending in deep elbow frills, then—"

"Ella? Is that y-you?"

At the sound of the unsteady, raspy voice, the slick, shiny fabric dropped from Ella's hands. The color drained from her face, and her mouth, poised in mid-sentence, slowly closed.

"What is it, Ella?" Abby asked.

Instead of replying to Abby's query, the red-haired woman slowly, reluctantly turned. She stared at the rail thin, gaunt-faced woman who had come up to stand behind them.

A vague unease settled over Abby. The woman looked to be in her early forties and was dressed in a plain brown dress. In her hand, she clutched an equally plain, brown carpetbag. Her lackluster, golden blond hair was pinned up haphazardly, and several locks cascaded down her neck. Her skin was sallow, circles smudged beneath her blue eyes. She appeared haggard and ill.

The expression on Ella's face belied the fact that this woman was a stranger. The woman smiled in apparent recognition.

"You act as if you've seen a ghost, Ella. It's really me."

"You .... You're supposed to be dead!" Ella forced the words out. "They told us you'd died."

The woman gave a wry, self-deprecating laugh. "I may be soon. In the meantime, though, I'm still very much alive. Alive enough to come back and try to set things right."

Ella shot Abby an uncertain look. Abby stared back, her brow arched in patient inquiry. When no further explanation was forthcoming, Abby decided to take the initiative.

She stepped forward and extended her hand toward the woman. "My name's Abigail Stanton. I'm Ella's friend and the housekeeper at Culdee Creek Ranch."

For a fleeting instant, Abby could've sworn shock registered in the woman's eyes. Then she managed a tight little smile, and accepted her hand in greeting.

"My name's Sally," the woman said. "Sally MacKay, the wife of Conor MacKay, Culdee Creek's owner."

19

*My thoughts are not your thoughts, neither are your ways
my ways, saith the LORD.*

Isaiah 55:8

With horror and dismay Abby stared at Sally MacKay, Conor's first and only wife. Sally . . . come back from the dead. Sally . . . still legally wed to Conor, for he'd never divorced her, believing she'd died in that boardinghouse fire.

She swallowed hard, fighting the sudden surge of nausea that threatened to overwhelm her. It was over then. All their plans. All her hopes and dreams. She closed her eyes. *Oh, Conor. Conor, my love.*

Sally withdrew her hand. "Is . . . is there something wrong, Abigail? You look as if you might faint any moment."

Ever so reluctantly, Abby opened her eyes.

Ella rushed to her side. Clasping Abby's waist, she offered a quick, supportive hug. "Abby's no more shocked than I am, Sally," the red-haired woman briskly replied. "We all heard the story of your untimely death. And, if you'll excuse my bluntness, your sudden and unannounced appearance after all these years would be enough to unsettle anyone."

"Yes, I suppose it would." Sally paused to glance around the mercantile. "Did Conor come with you? I'd like to explain to him first. After all these years, I owe him that at least."

"You owe him a whole passel more than that!" Ella retorted. "He didn't come with us, though. I suppose you'll be wanting to ride back with us to the ranch?"

"If that would be all right. I just now arrived on the train and had planned on hiring someone to drive me out. But I'd much prefer riding there with you." Sally gestured to her carpetbag. "That's all the belongings I possess, so it shouldn't add too much to any parcels you might have."

Ella glanced at Abby. "Well, we had planned on being in town a while."

"What we had planned," Abby quickly interjected as freshened pain stabbed through her, "isn't important now. What matters, Sally, is getting you back to Culdee Creek."

"How kind of you to say that, Abigail." Sally smiled. "Conor must be very pleased to have such a thoughtful woman as housekeeper." She turned to Ella. "That brings to mind one important question. I assume Conor has long ago remarried. Could you tell me his wife's name, and something about her?"

"Conor hasn't remarried," Ella all but snapped in reply. This time, she didn't even look at Abby.

"Really?" Sally cocked her head.

"Why don't you bring that up with him?" Ella began to pull a still benumbed Abby behind her. "Let's just head on back to Culdee Creek. There's no sense prolonging the suspense of your reunion."

"No, I suppose not," the blond-haired woman replied. She walked to her carpetbag and picked it up. "Lead on, then, if you will."

The ride back to Culdee Creek was one of few words. It was for the best that they didn't say much, Abby decided as they drove along. What with the chaotic way her own emotions were churning, it would not take much of any well-meant but nervous chatter to set her off.

She tried, as best she could to still her wildly racing thoughts, to quiet her heart and mind and place her trust in the Lord, but it was so hard. The woman crammed into the two-person buggy seat on the other side of Ella was a living symbol of all her dashed dreams, flung onto the sharp, brutal rocks of reality.

Why now? Abby asked herself. If Sally had come back just a month later, she and Conor would have been wed. Yet, even as she lifted the anguished question heavenward, Abby knew the answer.

While Sally lived, in the eyes of God, Conor and she were still bound as man and wife. Abby's marriage vows, though made in love and full sincerity, would have been invalid. However unintended, she and Conor would have committed adultery.

God forgive her, but she almost wished that they had.

As they pulled up before the main house, Conor, drying his hands on a dish towel, walked onto the front porch. Abby steeled herself for the confrontation to come.

They climbed down from the buggy and Sally approached him. His puzzled expression turned to one of shocked disbelief. Conor halted at the head of the steps. The dish towel dropped from his hands.

At the sight of his expression, Sally's footsteps faltered. She paused at the foot of the stairs.

His gaze, however, was fixed behind her to Abby, who had remained with Ella at the buggy. As their glances met, a loving entreaty darkened his eyes.

A desire to run to Conor and throw herself into his arms almost overwhelmed her. Run and claim him as hers, no matter the consequences! But she didn't. With the last shred of willpower she possessed, Abby remained at the buggy.

"C-Conor?" Sally finally said, her voice ragged, her tone uncertain. "Conor, I've come home . . . to make amends, to beg your forgiveness."

Conor jerked his gaze from Abby. He glared down at Sally. "You're about thirteen years too late," he stated coldly. "Now, why did you really come back? Did you hear rumors of Culdee Creek's wealth, and think to cash in on it? If so, you're a year too late. Evan managed to cut the worth of this ranch in half when he robbed me and ran away."

"Evan?" Sally's thin face brightened. "Is Evan all right?" Her expression fell. "But you wouldn't know, would you? You just said he ran away."

"Well, he's back now," Conor growled. "Seems like this is a year for the return of all the prodigals in my life, isn't it?"

"He's here? Evan's here?"

A look of annoyance darkened Conor's face. "Didn't I just say that? But no matter. Just as soon as I find a spare hand, I want you off Culdee Creek."

Sally reached out a hand to him. "But Conor, I–"

"I want you gone. Do you hear me?" All the anger and anguish of the past thirteen years welled up to engulf him. "You're nothing to me. Haven't been for years now. And I don't owe you a thing. No court in this land would grant you any claim to this ranch or any of its assets, after what you did."

"I didn't come back for money." She gave a choking laugh. "I've got consumption, Conor. I may not last out the year. I came for your forgiveness, and Evan's, and in the hope that I might spend my last moments on earth making it up to you and our son."

"Get out of here!" Conor made a sharp, stabbing motion out beyond her in the direction of the main gate. "It sickens me even to have to look at you."

"Conor. Please!" Sally sank to her knees and lifted her arms. "Please don't send me away. Let me explain. Give me a chance–"

"Mother?"

Evan and Beth, a basket of wildflowers in her hand, had just walked around the corner of the house. At the sight of Sally on bended knee before his father, the young man paled. He looked to Conor, then back to Sally again.

"Are you my mother?"

With a heart-wrenching cry, Sally shoved awkwardly to her feet. She ran to Evan, and threw her arms about him. "Y-yes," she sobbed. "Yes, I am!"

Conor cursed. "Blast it all, Sally! Don't drag him into this. This is between you and me."

"He's my son, Conor," Sally said, clinging to Evan as if her life depended on it. "At least give me a few moments with him before you send me away. Allow me that much."

Evan, a decidedly uncomfortable expression on his face, looked up from his mother. "What does she mean, Pa? You don't really mean to send her away, do you?"

"She walked out on us thirteen years ago, Evan, and in all that time has never seen fit even to let us know she was still alive. She's nothing to us, Evan. Nothing!"

"For all her failings, she's still your wife, and my mother." Evan dragged in an unsteady breath, and wrapped his arms around Sally. "You could at least let her stay a few days, so we could talk to her."

"If you're so all-fired eager to talk to her," Conor snarled, his frustration growing, "you're free to do so in town. In fact, you're more than welcome to be the one to drive her back to Grand View right now."

"Maybe I'll just do that," Evan countered, a defiant gleam now in his eyes. "And maybe I'll just keep on going after that, too. Any man who'd turn away his own wife–"

"No, no!" Sally jerked free of Evan's clasp. She staggered backward, shaking her head. "I didn't come here to cause division. I just wanted to make peace."

She began to cough, deep, gut-wrenching spasms that shook her whole body. She doubled over, wrapping her arms about her middle, and nearly fell. Evan grabbed her. She fumbled at the pocket of her dress, pulled out a handkerchief, and pressed it to her mouth.

Still the coughing went on, until Conor thought she'd choke to death right there in front of them. Finally the attack abated. Ashen-faced and perspiring, Sally wiped her mouth with her handkerchief, then lowered it from her face. Blood smeared her chin.

The blood caught Evan's attention. He grabbed at Sally's hand and, twisting it, looked down at her handkerchief.

"Blood! She's bleeding, Pa!"

Abby and Ella rushed forward. Sally pulled free of her son's hold. "It's nothing. Nothing new, anyway," she hurried to explain. "It's just the consumption. I cough up a lot of blood at times."

Abby looked to Conor. "You can't send her away like this."

His jaw hardened. "Oh, yes I can. It's not my fault she's sick."

"It's no one's fault, Conor." Abby climbed the steps to confront him. "That doesn't justify sending a sick woman, your wife, away when she's ill."

Frustration filled him anew. Now, above all, must he fight Abby, too? "I don't need to be reminded of what she is to me, Abby." Conor shoved a hand raggedly through his hair. "But having her here"–his voice dropped for her ears only–"threatens everything we've worked so long to build between us."

She gazed up at him. In the luminous depths of her eyes, Conor saw her pain—and regret. The sense of the jaws of a trap closing encompassed Conor. His heart sank. Not now. *Not now!*

"Sending her away won't change the fact that she's still your wife, Conor," Abby whispered.

"Then I'll divorce her," he rasped, refusing to give up, to lose what mattered now more than anything or one had ever before. "Blast it all. I'll divorce her!"

"Take her in." She touched him on the arm. "This isn't the time or place to make such decisions."

Despair settled about him like a dark, heavy shroud. He twisted his arm until his hand clasped her wrist, squeezing it tightly. "Don't close your heart to me, Abby," Conor said, his voice gone raw with entreaty. "We'll work this out in time. I swear it. Just don't turn from me."

Eyes glistening, Abby managed a tremulous little smile. "I'll never close my heart to you, Conor," she said in reply. "No matter what happens, I'll always, always, love you."

༄

"There, now that you're finally all settled in," Abby said as she finished tucking Sally into Evan's upstairs bed, "why don't you take a nice long nap? After your long journey and all the stress and excitement of your return to Culdee Creek, I'd imagine you're exhausted."

Sally, dressed in one of Abby's extra nightgowns, smiled wanly. "I must say I am." She pulled the cotton sheets and blanket up to her chin. "I just feel guilty taking Evan's room from him and causing you all this extra work."

"Evan doesn't mind one wit bunking in with the other hands. In fact, if I miss my guess, he'll actually enjoy his time there, with several men more his own age to talk

278

with." Abby walked to the wardrobe, opened the door, and placed Sally's carpetbag inside. Then she picked up the worn brown dress, petticoats, undergarments, and stockings. "I'll get these washed while you nap and hopefully have them ironed before you awake. It's a nice warm, windy day, so everything should dry pretty quickly."

"You're very kind, Abigail." Sally paused, opened her mouth to speak, then clamped it shut again. "I'm so glad Conor and Evan and"—as if struggling for the name, she faltered briefly—"and little Beth have you to take care of them. How long have you been here?"

"Since last October." At mention of her arrival at Culdee Creek, now eight months past, a pang of sadness struck Abby. So much had happened since then. So many obstacles had been overcome, so many doors opened. Yet now the most formidable obstacle of all loomed before her, and the door of finality and parting threatened to slam shut in her face.

Sally eyed her closely. "Eight months. Not all that long then. Not long at all, to have drawn them so close to you."

Abby clutched the bundle of soiled clothes to her. "We were all lost and hurting in some way or another. It was natural to turn to each other."

"Conor's in love with you, isn't he?"

The question was like a blow to Abby's gut. She had not expected Sally to be so perceptive. Yet, though she would not lie, Abby also did not feel it was her place to inform Sally of her and Conor's relationship, or plans to marry.

"That's a question better asked of your husband," Abby replied instead. "I'll tell you truly, though. Whatever your relationship was or becomes again, I'll not interfere in any way. You're still his wife—both in the eyes of man and God."

Sally's eyes filled with tears. She lowered her gaze to pick at the fine embroidery that hemmed the sheets. "I

279

don't hold out much hope of again becoming Conor's true wife. I've hurt him too deeply for that." She looked up, her eyes glistening. "I came back because I had nowhere else to go. But I also came back because I'm dying, and I want–I *need*–to atone for the pain I've caused both him and my son.

"My greatest fear, though," she added, the tears beginning to fall, "is that I might not have enough time left to win their forgiveness. I need that forgiveness so very, very badly."

Abby's heart filled with compassion. Whatever the woman had been or done, she had suffered and learned, and now sought to make amends. It was her right, at the very least, to try.

"There's one who will surely grant His forgiveness, if only you go to Him with a humble and contrite heart," Abby said. "And His forgiveness is of far greater value than any we mortals could ever give."

Sally smiled through her tears and nodded her head. "I've already returned to the Lord, Abigail. There was a priest–Father Gabriel Maguire–at a mission near Cripple Creek. He took me from the cribs there when I first sickened with the consumption and nursed me back to health. He was so good and kind. After I regained my strength, I begged him to let me stay with him and care for the sick, indigent miners and soiled doves like me. His holy, loving example inspired me to return to the Lord."

She sighed. "I was so happy there, in spite of the consumption that was eating its way through my body, helping Father Gabriel and serving the Lord. In time, though, he convinced me to return to Culdee Creek and seek forgiveness."

I should have known the Lord's hand was in this, Abby thought. God worked in such mysterious and unexpected ways–ways she didn't always understand or anticipate. All she could do was trust and accept that whatever God intended, it was intended for the good of all. Yet still, this time, Abby realized with a troubled foreboding, she feared–oh, how she feared–the price He might ask of her.

"He was a wise man," Abby finally replied. "Nonetheless, I know it must have been hard for you to come back here. You're a very courageous woman."

"I'll let you in on a little secret, Abigail," Sally said with a shaky laugh. "I've been scared witless since the moment I stepped off the train in Grand View. And before that, every time I even contemplated coming back, I shook in my boots."

"Yet still you found the strength to come."

"The Lord gave me the strength," Sally corrected gently. "I couldn't have done it without Him."

"It's not over yet. You've hurt Conor deeply. He's not a man easily given to forgiveness."

Sally nodded her agreement. "I know." She sighed and closed her eyes. "I think I'll take that nap now, Abigail. Suddenly, I'm overcome with a bone deep weariness . . ."

"Yes, sleep, and regain your strength," Abby urged softly. "Time enough to begin anew when you're rested." She turned and walked toward the door.

"Yes, time enough," Sally mumbled drowsily from behind her, "if the Lord is willing."

Abby entered the kitchen with Sally's load of laundry. Conor was waiting for her, a mug of coffee clenched in his hands. Without looking at him, she laid the clothes in the alcove beside the backdoor, then proceeded to fill a large pot of water from the hand pump. She placed the pot on the stove and bent to stoke the fire.

At last, though, her initial preparations completed, she turned and acknowledged Conor's presence. He met her gaze with a steady one of his own.

"So, how's Sally?"

"She's taking a nap. She was exhausted." Abby paused, biting her lower lip. "She's very, very ill, you know, Conor."

"Yeah," he muttered. "So she says."

"I've seen the signs of consumption many times. Sally has a very bad case. She spoke true, when she said she may not last the year."

He looked away. "And what do you want me to do about it? I was forced to cut her out of my heart and life when she left. I won't take her back."

Abby walked to the table, pulled out a chair, and sat. "You can't know that for sure. At least not now, in the first flush of emotion over her return. In time, if she can be healed of her disease, you might find there's still some small spark of affection left for her in your heart."

Conor riveted the full force of his piercing stare on her. "And where would that leave you, Abby? Free of all obligation to me?"

She expelled a frustrated breath and shook her head. "You're quick to attribute unkind, ulterior motives to my concern for Sally."

"Well," he said with a bitter laugh, "your behavior toward a woman who might threaten your future at Culdee Creek, not to mention with me, is unusually kind. Any other woman—especially a woman who claimed to be in love with a man—wouldn't be taking this quite so calmly."

"Is that what you think I'm doing? Taking this calmly?" It was Abby's turn to laugh. "Do you know what I felt when I first learned who Sally was, Conor? I felt as if my heart was being torn from my body. I saw the end to all my hopes and dreams. I was terrified."

"Then you do still love me! Will you stick this out with me, and still be my wife?"

Abby went silent. She could not bear that heartbreaking look of hope burning in Conor's eyes. Love might not be enough this time. Their love for each other could never be sufficient to sever the holy vows he and Sally had made. Their love could never be greater than God's will.

"Though you divorce Sally," she began with quiet emphasis, "you divorce her only in the eyes of the law. In God's eyes you'll still be husband and wife."

Conor slammed his fist on the table. "She broke the vows, not I. Yet you still insist on holding me to them, now, after thirteen years?"

"She's your wife, Conor. Your wife!"

He leaned forward. "Would you have shackled yourself to your husband for the rest of your life, knowing how unfulfilled you were with him? Would you, Abby?"

Though she'd never admitted it to Conor, or anyone else for that matter, as time went on, the consideration of remaining wed to Thomas for the rest of her days had begun to fill her with despair. Yet not once had she ever considered divorcing him. She had given her vow to God, and see it through she would.

"Didn't you make holy vows in a church when you wed Sally?"

Conor scowled. "Yes, I did."

"And didn't you give them in good faith and mean them?"

"Yes. Just as I'll mean them when we wed." He sighed and leaned back in his chair. "If Sally had stayed, I'd have seen them through no matter what. But she left. She broke the vows and, as far as I'm concerned, freed me as well."

A sudden sense of futility swamped Abby. She buried her face in her hands. "I don't know if we'll ever see eye-to-eye on this. One thing I do know." She looked up, her hands falling to rest on the table. "This isn't going to be solved today. You and Sally need time."

"I don't need anything with her," Conor snapped. "She can stay a week or so to regain her strength. She and Evan can visit to their heart's content. But then I want her gone. I want things to go back to the way they were. I want for us to get married like we planned."

It was what Abby wanted, too. But what if it was not what the Lord wanted? What if she had been wrong all along, and He had sent her to Culdee Creek for other reasons? What if He had never meant for her to wed Conor?

She closed her eyes, blotting out the sight of the handsome, tortured features of the man she loved. To give up Conor after she had fought so long and hard. To turn her back and walk away. Surely, surely God didn't mean for her to do that.

And what if He does? a tiny voice whispered. *What will you do then? Whom will you obey—the Lord or your heart?*

At that moment, Abby could not honestly say. Things were not so clear anymore. What she used to accept as truth now made little sense. What had once been guided by faith now seemed fruitless and self-defeating.

And where she had once followed in trust, she now feared to go.

20

I cry in the daytime, but thou hearest not; and in the night season, and am not silent.

Psalm 22:2

"I don't care what you say, Abby. I don't like her!"

At Beth's impassioned words, Abby and Hannah looked up from the butter molds they were packing with granules of freshly churned butter. The two women exchanged concerned glances.

"Do you want me to leave," Hannah asked softly, "and give you some time alone with Beth?"

"No." Abby punctuated the single word with a resolute shake of her head. "You're part of the family now. It's no deep, dark secret how either Conor or Beth feel about Sally."

Indeed, Abby thought, in the past month since Sally's arrival, it seemed as if the battle lines had been drawn. She and Evan against Conor and Beth. She should be thankful, she supposed, that Conor had allowed his wife to stay on past the initial two weeks. It had been especially difficult when Abby had first informed him that the wedding was off. Only her assurance that she still loved him and wanted to marry him had kept Conor from physically removing Sally right then and there from Culdee Creek.

Yet, though Sally seemed to rally with the care and good food, and even had begun to help with the less strenuous household chores, Conor refused to have her at his supper table or even to interact with her. Now his antipathy was rubbing off on Beth.

"Is there something Sally's doing to upset you?" Abby asked the youngster. "If so, I'm sure she doesn't mean it. She's just trying so hard right now to make friends."

"Papa doesn't want to be her friend." Beth twisted her mouth in distaste. "Neither do I."

Abby glanced at Hannah, who smiled in sympathy. "I must commend you on your loyalty to your father," she replied, choosing her words with care. "He's been hurt very badly, and it's hard for him to forgive that. But I truly believe Sally has changed, Beth. That's why she came back. She regrets the pain she caused your father and wants to make amends. That's a very brave and admirable thing, don't you think? To admit you're wrong and seek forgiveness?"

Beth gave a grudging shrug. "I suppose so." She paused. "Still, I don't like her. She's caused problems between you and Papa. I want you for my new mama, and now there might not ever be a wedding." Her eyes filled with tears. "If you can't be my mama, will you promise never to leave us? You can stay on as our house-keeper, can't you?"

At Beth's piteous plea, Abby's heart twisted within her. Sally's return had put a strain on more than just Conor. Abby struggled mightily with the desire to stay and fight for those she loved. And yet, she knew she was no closer to a decision than she had been at the start.

That realization profoundly disturbed her. Abby felt truly abandoned and betrayed by God. It was He who had led her to Culdee Creek. She knew this beyond a shadow of a doubt. He'd also surely led her here for Conor and Beth, and even Hannah.

She also knew the Lord had led her here to help her. Led her here to force her once more to look outward from her own grief, and open her heart to the grief and needs of others. And led her here to a man who—no matter what ultimately happened—Abby knew she would love for the rest of her days.

Yet just when she had finally accepted all that God had offered, He appeared again to be snatching it away. *It is not for you, Beloved,* He seemed to be saying. *Your time here is over, your purpose served.*

In a confusing, anguished welter of emotions, Abby once more heard the words the Lord had placed in her heart that day she had first come to Culdee Creek. Heard and, as she listened, felt the anger, the rebellion, the deep bitterness swell within.

Do you see then, begin to understand why I sent you to them? Do you hear, and know My will at last?

No, Abby thought, I don't. If to know Your will is to turn from the people I need and love, then I don't think I want ever again to know it.

Abby stared down into Beth's questioning, troubled eyes. She knew that the time might indeed come when she must leave. Too much of her self-concept and way of life was tied up in her religious beliefs. Though she might be angry, she couldn't so easily turn her back on God's laws. They had long ago become too much a part of her.

To turn her back on them now, even at such a critical juncture in her life, could well be her final devastation.

"I can't make such a promise, Beth," Abby forced herself to reply. "Though I want to with all my heart, I can't promise that I'll stay on forever as your housekeeper. It's a decision that your father and I must make together."

She almost added "God" into that equation, but she didn't. As painful as it was to consider, much less admit,

Abby didn't know where the Lord figured into any of this anymore.

ℰ

After another sleepless night, Abby rose the next morning, bathed, dressed, then headed to the main house to start breakfast. As she neared the backdoor, Hannah, little Jackson slung in a shawl at her chest, walked up with Evan at her side. In his hand Evan clutched a pail of milk.

Abby glanced from the blushing girl, who shot her a quick, apologetic look, to the beaming face of Conor's son. With relief, she noted that it had evidently been Evan who'd forced his assistance on Hannah. "Helping Hannah with her morning chores, are you?" she asked mildly, glancing at the tall, strapping young man.

"Just carried up the bucket of milk for her, ma'am," Evan hurried to explain. "What with her having the baby along and the long walk up from the barn, I reckoned it was the gentlemanly thing to do."

"I suppose it was," Abby murmured, distracted at that moment by the sight of a frowning Conor glaring at them from an upstairs window. A prickle of premonition coursed down her spine. He was beginning to notice his son's infatuation with Hannah.

She extended her hand toward the bucket of milk. "Here, let me take that. I was just going into the kitchen to start breakfast anyway."

"And I," Hannah quickly added, taking her cue from Abby, "need to nurse Jackson, then give him his bath."

Evan's crestfallen look was almost comical. "Then I reckon I'd best be off to the rest of my chores."

Abby took the bucket then nodded. "I guess you'd better. We're having fried eggs and sausage, if you think you can gather enough eggs in the next fifteen minutes."

His expression brightened. "Sure can, ma'am. Sure can."

The two women watched Evan turn and hurry down to the chicken coop.

"I swear I'm not leading him on," Hannah's soft voice pierced Abby's distracted thoughts.

Abby shot her an arch look. "So, you don't find him at all attractive?"

Hannah blushed. Jackson squirmed against her, and made a sweet, sleepy sound. She patted him gently on the back.

"I didn't say I don't find him attractive," the girl admitted finally. "All the MacKay men are handsome. But I'm not in the market for a husband just yet, and I promised you I wouldn't return to my old ways."

"Promise yourself, Hannah." Abby set down the bucket. "I may not always be here. Your fine resolve should spring from your own heart, and be for yourself."

"So, you *are* serious about leaving, aren't you?"

"It's been on my mind." Abby met her concerned gaze. "But don't worry. If I leave, and Conor doesn't want you here anymore, I'll take you and the baby with me."

"It wasn't me or Jackson I was thinking of." She took Abby's hand. "It was you. You and Mr. MacKay are so in love. And he needs you. He needs you badly."

"Perhaps that's part of the problem," Abby muttered. "Maybe I've been fooling myself all along. Maybe he does it all just to please me, not because his heart is truly changed."

"I wouldn't know." Now it was Hannah's turn to sigh. "I've never had a man in love with me. Leastwise," she added with a sad little smile, "not in love with the real me."

Abby squeezed her hand. "Be patient. You'll find that man someday. I know it." She withdrew her hand. "Enough of worrying over the future. I'll have problems aplenty real soon, if I don't get going on breakfast."

"I'll be over to help just as soon as I nurse Jackson. His bath can wait until later."

"Get on with you." Abby made a shooing motion. "I can manage just fine until you're done."

With a laugh, the girl wheeled about and headed for the bunkhouse. Abby tarried a moment longer, gazing after her, before picking up the pail of milk and walking to the back door. Conor was there to open it for her.

"Here,"–he held out his hand–"give me the milk."

Abby handed over the pail, then followed him into the kitchen. As he strained the milk through the additional, cheesecloth-covered pail, she busied herself getting out the frying pan and other cooking utensils.

"So, how long has this infatuation been going on between Hannah and Evan?" he asked suddenly.

Abby knew better than to pretend ignorance or dissemble with Conor. "For a while now," she admitted. "Hannah swears she's not trying to lead Evan on, though, and just wants to be friends."

Conor shot her a narrow look. "So Evan's the one who's pushing it?"

"It seems so." Abby took out a sharp knife, then walked to the cupboard to take down a large pottery bowl.

He scowled. "Reckon I need to talk with the boy then."

Somehow, Abby didn't think Evan would take such a lecture well, especially from his father. Bowl and knife now in hand, she turned to face him. "Why not just let it be, Conor? If Hannah continues to discourage him, he'll eventually give up."

"And if he doesn't?" An edge of anger now threaded his voice. "What then? And what if that girl isn't telling you the whole truth? I'll tell you straight out, Abby. I won't have any son of mine marrying a woman like her."

His harsh words just now, combined with the strain of the past weeks, was suddenly too much for Abby. "And why not?" she cried, her patience snapping. "We've all sinned, and some stubbornly continue to even when the truth hits them square in the face. At least Hannah is trying to mend her ways."

His jaw clamped shut. Fury flared in his eyes. "And exactly what is that supposed to mean?" he demanded.

She glared back at him, myriad responses—none of them kind or tactful—crowding forward, ready to spring forth from her mouth. Deciding flight was the better part of valor just now, Abby wheeled about. With a disgusted snort, she clasped the bowl and knife tightly to her and headed for the cellar stairs.

Near the remaining slab of last winter's bacon, she found the smoked sausages. Her anger giving her added strength, she quickly hacked off a long string of ten thick, plump links, and placed them in the big bowl. Then Abby turned back to the cellar stairs and promptly slammed into Conor.

He grabbed her arms and grunted as the thick bowl slammed into his belly.

Startled, Abby immediately jumped back. "Conor MacKay, you should know better than to sneak up on a person like that!"

He rubbed his belly. "Never been attacked by a bowl before." He managed a wry grin. "Didn't realize they could be such lethal weapons."

"They're even more dangerous when thrown at someone's head. Which is exactly where this one will land, if you do that again."

Conor's grin widened. "Now that's what I like. A woman with a little sass to her."

"If that's meant to be some sort of backhand apology for your behavior upstairs," Abby snapped, "it's not working."

"Abby, I'm sorry. Let's not fight. I can't take that, on top of everything else going on right now." He moved back toward her. "Come here. Let's make up. It seems like months since I last held and kissed you."

Her love for him burning away the remnants of her anger, she instinctively took a step forward. Then reality hit her again square in the face. For an instant, Abby was torn between the recollection that Conor's wife was only a couple of stories above them and the aching need to be held by him. The long-denied desire, however, finally won out over principles. Setting the knife and bowl of sausages aside, Abby flung herself into Conor's arms.

Their bodies met, their lips touched. They held each other close, hearts beating as one, and kissed as if it was their last. Kissed as if nothing existed but this moment, and this moment must satisfy them for an eternity.

At long last, though, Abby's fevered thoughts cooled enough for her to remember where she was. Shame filled her at her selfish betrayal of Sally. She leaned back, shoving at his chest. "Conor," she said, her voice still so husky with longing that it surprised even her. "Conor, we can't. Sally . . . your wife . . . upstairs."

With a snarl of pent up frustration, Conor released her. "I don't care if Sally's upstairs. We can do what we want. The only people we need to please are ourselves."

"It's not that simple, and you know it." Abby picked up the bowl and pressed it tightly to her, a physical symbol of the barrier she meant to raise once more between them. "Too many people depend on us."

"Blast it, Abby! I'm sick to death of having to pretend to be so morally upright. I'm tired of meeting everyone else's needs, and none of my own." His smoky blue eyes burned with an anguished entreaty. "All I want is you, Abby. That's all."

She shut her eyes, unable to bear the sight of his pain. "That's all I want, too," she whispered. "But you have a wife."

"Yet you won't marry me if I divorce her; you won't be my mistress if I remain wed to her; and if you stay on as just a housekeeper, I think I'll go mad," Conor finished in weary frustration. "So where does that leave us, Abby?"

"Nowhere, I guess." She expelled a long breath. "But you know what's even worse, Conor?"

"No, I *can't* imagine anything worse," he drawled, "but I think you're going to tell me anyway."

"What's worse," Abby said, choosing not to comment on his sarcastic rejoinder, "is your overt, continued cruelty to Sally. You persist in ignoring her, refuse to include her in the family, and she lives in constant fear that you'll turn her out."

"She's tearing our lives apart," he hissed, "and you accuse *me* of being cruel? Rather, you should wonder at my even allowing her to stay as long as I have."

Abby cocked her head. "Why have you allowed her to stay on as long as you have?"

He gave a choked laugh, his expression transforming to one of incredulity. "Why else? For you, and only you, of course. Because I was terrified you'd think I was a heartless beast if I did otherwise, and you'd leave me."

She looked down. The bowl of sausages wavered, then blurred, and Abby realized her eyes had filled with tears. He'd done this for her, she thought, her misery all but drowning her. Had he always done everything out of love for her, and not because he was truly having a conversion of heart? If so, when had she stopped choosing to see it?

"I was afraid of that," Abby whispered finally.

"Afraid of what?" Conor grasped her by the arms. "What?"

"That you did this just to please me, not because you saw the rightness of it, or really wanted to."

"What does it matter why I did it?" He gave her a little shake. "The end result's the same."

Abby lifted tear-filled eyes. "No, it's not, Conor. In your heart you don't want to do it. In a sense you've done it out of fear and coercion. Someday you may resent me for that."

He gave a low, harsh laugh. "I'll risk it. It sure beats losing you."

She stood there, an awful realization beginning to dawn. "No, Conor," she finally said, "it doesn't. Nothing is worth the loss of one's conscience, or the ability to do what is right. And, though I've fought this decision with all my might, railing against God in the bargain, it still doesn't change the reality of our situation."

His grip tightened on her arms. "Abby, whatever you're going to say—"

"I'll say," she cut him off softly. "You should know that by now." Abby closed her eyes. Then, with a despairing sigh, she forced herself to utter some of the most painful words she'd ever spoken. "We can't marry, Conor. Not now. Not under these circumstances. And I can't stay here, either."

"Don't say that, Abby! I don't want you to leave. Just tell me what to do, and I'll do it."

Desperation threaded his voice and shone in his eyes. Abby's heart went out to him. Conor loved her, but he was still so blind. Even his love for her hadn't been enough to open his eyes.

"Tell you what to do," she repeated, smiling sadly. "Tell you to deny your own personhood, Conor? That has never been my intent. It would be as self-serving and destructive as my remaining here while Sally lives. You have to find your own answers to this dilemma, and find some good and honorable ones, too, or nothing else matters. Nothing."

"So, you've made up your mind to leave, and nothing I can say or do will stop you." His hands dropped from her arms. He stepped back, his features hardening, his expression shuttered. "Then go, Abby. Run away. It's what you do best, anyway."

"No, Conor." Abby clasped the bowl to her. "This time I'd be running away if I *did* stay. Yet I still would, if it weren't the worst thing, by far, for the both of us."

⟨⟩

Three days later, beneath a gray, drizzly sky, Frank Murphy and Henry Watson finished loading up the last of Abby's belongings into the buckboard. After covering them with a black tarpaulin, they then drove the big wagon around to the front of the main house.

After the buckboard had pulled away, Abby lingered a few minutes longer, gazing around the bunkhouse that had been her home. Devoid now of all furniture and decoration, the white-washed interior looked empty and bleak. The sound of her footsteps echoed off the barren walls with a hollow, almost mournful lament. She couldn't bear to stay there for long. It was just too sad.

After Conor's hostile comments about Hannah four days ago, she had decided it best to take the girl and her baby with her back to the Springs. Nelly had voiced no reservations over the addition of two women and an infant to her household, and the imposition would, at any rate, be temporary. As soon as Abby could find a teaching position or some other respectable employment, she intended to rent another cottage just for her and Hannah.

Never in her wildest dreams had she imagined the family she would finally build would consist of a reformed prostitute and her child. Abby had thought her family would be the more traditional kind, with a husband and children of her own. But God had other plans, she reminded herself bitterly. Once again, He'd finally taken away what had never really been hers to keep.

She shut the door, opened her big, black cotton umbrella against the gentle rain, and headed around to the front of the main house. The somber little group waiting there filled her with yet another pang. Ella clutched a red-eyed Beth. Evan stood a short ways apart, talking in hushed tones to Hannah, who held baby Jackson. And near the front door, wrapped in a woolen shawl, sat an ashen-faced Sally.

There was no sign of Conor. Somehow, that didn't surprise Abby. She had seen the old mask, the protective barriers, slam back down that morning in the cellar. It was the only way Conor knew to steel himself against the pain. In his mind she had used, then cast him aside like all the rest.

Abby squared her shoulders, pasted on a smile, and climbed the porch steps. Closing her umbrella, she leaned it against the railing and resolutely approached Ella and Beth. As she neared, Beth pulled away and scurried around behind Ella.

For a long moment, neither said anything. Then Abby extended her hand to her friend. "Though we part, I'd like to think we'll always remain friends. We've been through so much—" Her voice broke, and Abby could say no more.

Ella took her hand and gave it a quick squeeze. "I'd like to come and visit you in the Springs, if you think your sister-in-law won't mind one of those awful Mac-Kays"—she punctuated the statement with a teasing grin—"paying you a visit. We could shop a little and talk."

"Nelly won't mind. It's evident from her letters that, over time she's come to forgive Conor his shortcomings."

Abby managed a wobbly smile. "And once I find my own place, you can bring the children and stay a few days. You can come, too, Beth," she added, peering at the girl who still stood behind Ella. "I'd especially like that."

"I don't think Papa would let me come," Beth mumbled, though a sudden light of excitement and renewed joy flickered in her eyes. "He's mad at you right now."

"Yes, I know," Abby agreed, tamping down the freshened swell of pain the girl's reminder had stirred. "But I'm not mad at him, and never will be. And I still love you both."

She squatted and extended her hands to Beth. "Can you not be mad at me, Beth? I couldn't bear it if you were mad at me, too."

The girl eyed her with such obvious doubt and misgiving, that Abby knew a battle of mixed loyalties waged in the child's heart. Finally, though, Beth gave a soft cry and flung herself into Abby's arms. She gathered the girl to her, holding her close.

For a long moment Abby stroked Beth's clean, dark hair, hair neatly braided into two pigtails that fell well past her shoulders now. As if savoring it for all time, Abby noted her bright green hair bows, the pretty green and white gingham dress they'd last made together. She felt the change in Beth's young body, a body growing in height, becoming more slender, and beginning to bud into womanhood.

A bittersweet pang filled Abby. Beth had, at long last, come out of her shell, and now faced life with renewed confidence and joy. She was growing up into a fine young lady and would need a woman to encourage and guide her. As much as Abby wished it, though, that woman could no longer be her.

Over Beth's bent head, Abby's gaze locked with Sally's. Conor's wife stared back at her, her eyes brimming with tears and gratitude. There was one thing more to be done, Abby realized, if both parties were willing.

She leaned back and stared up at Beth. "Could you do me a very, very big favor, sweetheart? I know it might be hard, but you've grown up so much in the months I've been here that I know you'll understand."

Beth studied her warily. "What do you want me to do?"

"Try to be friends with Sally. What with me and Hannah leaving, she's bound to be pretty lonely. And she'll need some help, as weak as she gets sometimes." Abby smiled. "Could you do that for me?"

"Papa won't like it if I do."

"He didn't like a lot of things I did in the beginning, either, but he came around in time. He knew it was for the best, and he'll see your efforts with Sally sooner or later, too, as the right and decent thing to do. Can you trust me in this, Beth, and at least try?"

"I suppose," she agreed grudgingly. "But only for you. I still don't like her."

Abby climbed to her feet. "Give Sally a chance, Beth. You might be pleasantly surprised if you do." She stroked Beth's face, then kissed her.

Next, she made her way to where Sally sat, her frail body bundled against the chill of the day in the thick shawl and warm clothes. The woman looked up as Abby approached. She lifted a skeletal, shaking hand to her.

"Good-bye, Abigail," she whispered. "I'm so sorry to see you go."

Abby knelt beside her chair and took her hand. "And I'm sorry to leave, but it must be done. You're Conor's wife. You two need the time to work through your differences. My presence here is an obstacle to that."

"It's still not fair, Abigail." Sally sighed and looked away. "Not fair to you . . . or Conor."

"It may not seem so now," Abby said, "but in time . . ."

The other woman turned back to her. "Yes, in time, I hope it will be so. It's my dearest wish."

"And mine." Abby rose.

Sally released her hand. "Pray for us, Abigail. We'll need it."

How ironic, Abby thought, that when prayers were needed most of all, there were no prayers left in her, no desire to speak to God. But she kept that secret anguish to herself. Sally carried a heavy enough burden of guilt.

She forced a smile and what seemed, at that moment, an even bigger lie. "I will," Abby choked out the promise. "I will."

21

For a small moment have I forsaken thee; but with great mercies will I gather thee.

Isaiah 54:7

Conor paced the length of his bedroom, his anger and confusion churning chaotically within. Outside, Abby was leaving. Abby . . . the light and joy of his life.

He should have known it would come to this. Only a fool failed to face and accept life's harsh truths. Yet, for a short while again, he'd dared let himself hope and dream. Dared . . . and failed . . . as only the greatest of fools could do.

There was nothing more to be done, though. Now, all that was left him was to pick up the shattered pieces of his heart and go on.

He had no other choice. People depended on him. People like Beth, Evan, and now, it seemed, even Sally.

Conor smiled grimly. One dream, at least, had come true. His family was complete again. His wife and children were all back under one roof. His ranch was safe, as Culdee Creek slowly but surely rose once more from its recent debt. To some people's way of thinking, things were actually looking up.

No, on second thought, he was not as bereft as he had first imagined. All he had lost was a woman. All he had lost was his heart.

ॐ

"Then were there brought unto him little children, that he should put his hands on them and pray; and the disciples rebuked them. But Jesus said, Suffer little children, and forbid them not, to come unto me: for of such is the kingdom of heaven."

From his seat near the open study window, Conor heard the voice of his daughter reading from the Bible out on the front porch. He looked up from his ledger and frowned. He had thought that once Abby was gone the Bible study and readings would end. But now it seemed that Sally had picked up where Abby had left off.

He heard a creak of reed and wood joints as Sally leaned back in the wicker rocker. "That's enough, Beth, dear," she said. "That passage is so rich with meaning I could meditate on it for hours."

"It *is* a pretty story," Beth replied. "It reminds me of when I first met Abby, and what she said to me, the day she first came to Culdee Creek."

"What did she say, dear?" Sally's voice brightened with apparent interest.

"She said that in the eyes of God I'm precious and glorious." As she continued speaking, Beth's voice seemed to soften in fond recollection. "It kind of goes along with this"–Conor imagined her pointing to a verse on the page–"where Jesus says that children are such of the kingdom of heaven. He wouldn't have said that, would He, unless we are precious and glorious to Him?"

"No, He wouldn't," Sally assured her. "Abigail was right."

Another long pause ensued, long enough this time for Conor to rise and quietly look out from behind the heavy drapes. Not more than ten feet away, Beth sat on a stool before Sally, her head lowered, her little shoulders silently shaking. At the sight of his weeping daughter, Conor's gut clenched.

"Why, Beth, dear," Sally cried, struggling to shove herself up in her chair, "whatever is the matter? Was it something I said?"

"No." Beth looked up, her cheeks streaked with tears. "I mean, you didn't say anything to hurt my feelings. I was just thinking about how much I disliked you when you first came. Then, when Abby left because of you . . ."

"And now, Beth?" Sally's hands fisted in the blanket covering her legs. "How do you feel about me now?"

The girl swiped away her tears. "Now, I don't know. Papa's still so sad. But I've tried to be friends with you because Abby asked me to and . . . and I almost think I'm beginning to like you."

Listening to his daughter's halting confession, Conor's fatherly concern transformed into rage. Blast Abby, he thought. Even now, over a month since she had left, her influence over Beth was still strong. He had been right to deny Ella's request to take Beth with her, when she had left for her first trip to the Springs to visit Abby. He had agonized over what was the better recourse–to cut Beth off from Abby completely in order to hasten the healing of that loss, or to allow her to visit from time to time, and gradually wean her away. Now, he was glad that he had decided on the first of the two choices.

"Well, I definitely like you." Sally's voice sounded strangely tight. "And I'm grateful for Abigail's kindness in asking you to be friends with me." She paused. "Why don't we write her a nice thank you letter? I'm sure she'd love to hear from us. We can tell her what we've been doing and all about the ranch."

"Oh, yes, let's do." Beth nodded eagerly. "Maybe we can even dry and press a few flowers from her flowerbeds to send her!"

"Of course. What a w-wonderful–" Suddenly, Sally began to cough. One bout of coughing led to another, until finally her whole body shook and she was gasping for breath.

Beth stood there, staring at her in wide-eyed horror. Then, with a cry, the girl turned and ran into the house.

"Papa! Papa, come quick!"

Conor strode to the study door. She met him there.

"It-it's Sally," Beth screamed in terror. "She's choking, and I-I don't know how to help her."

Conor turned her around and took her by the arm. In the end, there'd be nothing anyone could do to help Sally, but no good was served pointing that out just now. "Come on," he said quietly. "We'll see what we can do."

By the time they reached her, Sally was slumped over and wheezing for air. Conor quickly righted her in her chair. "What do you need?" he asked. "Is there anything I can do?"

Sally, her face ashen and perspiring, her lips blue, gestured weakly toward the glass of water on a nearby table. "W-water," she gasped.

"Beth," he ordered tersely. "Bring the glass of water."

Conor soon had the glass at Sally's lips. She sipped slowly, swallowing carefully. Bit by bit, the fluid seemed to soothe the wracking cough. Her color returned. At long last she handed the glass back to Beth.

"Th-thank you, d-dear." Sally managed a wan smile.

Beth peered down at her, her youthful brow puckered in worry. "Are you all right?"

The blond woman nodded. "Yes." She met Conor's piercing gaze. "If . . . if it w-wouldn't be too much trouble, though, I-I'd like to go upstairs now."

Irritation filled Conor. Though Sally had begun to require increasing assistance negotiating the stairs, in the past month, Evan and Beth had seen to those needs.

Now, though, he was trapped. Evan had volunteered to drive Ella to the Springs, and the hands were busy. Conor knew he could hardly justify calling one of them up to the house for such a trivial thing, especially one he could quickly and easily see to himself.

"Fine," he muttered. "Just put your arms around my neck then, and I'll carry you."

"I couldn't impose," Sally's pallor was now replaced by a rosy blush. "Give me a moment to regain my strength. Then I can lean on Beth."

"After that coughing spell," Conor snapped, his irritation growing, "you'll need a half day or so to recover. Don't argue with me. I've neither the time nor patience."

Sally bit her lip and obediently wrapped her arms about his neck. He stooped, slid one arm beneath her legs, the other behind her back, then straightened. She weighed next to nothing.

Conor swung around and stalked to the front door, Beth following in his wake. Sally said nothing. As they moved through the house, however, she sighed wearily and lowered her head to rest on his shoulder.

At the action, a wild riot of unbidden—and definitely unwanted—emotions assailed Conor. Memories flashed through his mind—memories of another time when he'd carried Sally up to their bedroom. Memories of a beauteous girl, laughing and loving and merry. Memories of her singing and playing the piano for him during the long, dark winter nights.

Startled by his strong recollections, as he reached the stairs and began to climb them, Conor glanced down at Sally. She was not beautiful anymore. Her hair was coarse and lackluster, her skin sallow, her body little more than a rack of bones. Still, he could see signs of the woman she had once been. A feeling akin to pity flared in his breast before he recognized it and fiercely quashed it.

No, never again will I permit such softer emotions for her, Conor angrily reminded himself. Not for one who was long ago the cause of such terrible pain, and the cause of even more now. She deserves this and more.

They reached her room. Conor looked to his daughter. "Open the door and turn down her bed, will you, girl?"

"Of course, Papa."

Wordlessly, he propped his wife against several pillows to help her breathe, and pulled up the blanket to cover her. As he turned to go, however, she touched his arm.

Eyes narrowed, Conor halted. "Yes?"

"Send Beth away," Sally whispered, her eyes dark with entreaty, "but you stay. I want . . . need . . . to talk to you."

"There's nothing I care to say to you—"

"You don't have to say anything," she quickly cut him off. "Just listen. Please."

From the doorway, Beth watched them. Conor knew if he denied Sally just now, Beth might well question the reasons for his refusal. Question them . . . and him.

As he hesitated, snatches of another conversation drifted back to him, taunting Conor with vague recollections of a happier time. An image of Abby, her eyes bright with conviction, gazing up at him from her seat at the kitchen table, slowly filled his mind's eye.

"Beth needs you to set the example of how one should deal with life, Mr. MacKay," he heard Abby telling him once again. *"It is your example that she'll follow the rest of her days . . ."*

Conor expelled a long, frustrated breath. For Beth's sake, and for no other reason, he'd stay and let Sally speak her peace once and for all.

Conor gestured to Beth. "Get on with you, girl. I'll be down shortly."

Something flickered in his daughter's eyes—understanding? approval? Then she wheeled about and left the room. Conor closed the door behind her, pulled over a chair, and set it by the bed. With a weary sigh, he sat.

"Have at it, Sally. What are you so all-fired eager to say?"

"I'd like to talk about forgiveness."

"Well, and isn't that an interesting subject? Are we going to talk about my forgiving you, or you forgiving me?"

She met his mocking glance with a calm, steady one of her own. "I was thinking more of God's forgiveness."

Conor went very still. "What does God have to do with this?" he demanded. "I thought this was between you and me."

"You used to be a godly man, Conor." Sally fingered the edge of the blanket. "If I recall, you were far more devout than me." She looked up. "Was I the cause of your turning from the Lord?"

He had no intention of allowing the conversation to turn to him, and he definitely would not permit Sally to probe into his heart. "What does it matter?" he snarled, glaring at her. "What's done is done."

"No, it's not done." Sally clenched the blanket edge in her hands. "The Lord is ever willing to gather you back to Him, Conor. He's forgiven me, taken me back."

He gave a disparaging laugh. "You go right ahead and think that, Sally. Personally, though, after all the people you've hurt, I seriously doubt God has forgiven you."

"Oh, Conor, don't limit the Lord with your own shallow perceptions of Him. Don't assign Him a level of compassion equal only to yours," she moaned. "God is a God full of compassion, and gracious and longsuffering, and plenteous in mercy and truth."

306

"I didn't agree to stay just to endure your preaching at me, Sally," Conor said through gritted teeth. "If that's all you have to say, it's time I was going."

"No!" she cried, when he made a move to rise. "Please don't leave. I know I'm going about this all wrong, but I just want you to understand why I came back."

"I know why you came back. You had nowhere else to go."

"I came back because it was the right thing to do, Conor." High color flushed her cheeks, and her eyes shone brightly. "I came back not only for me, and my peace of mind, but for you as well. Though you may love another woman now, the wounds I inflicted still fester, eating away at you. I came back because I wanted to heal those wounds and help you be whole again."

Conor leaned forward, his body rigid with barely contained fury. "On the contrary," he drawled silkily. "When you came back you destroyed any hope I had of ever being whole again. You drove away the one woman who could've ever helped me."

"As wonderful as she is, she's never been the one who could heal you. Only God can do that."

Similar words . . . Abby's words . . . plucked at Conor's memory. As if struck, he reared back. *Nothing is worth the loss of one's conscience* . . . he heard her say. *You have to find your own answers* . . .

Had Abby then, seen the same failings in him that Sally now spoke of? Had she known of his fatal flaws, and finally realized she had become more of a hindrance, shielding him from a reality only he could face and change? Yet if Sally had never returned . . . Abby might have never known . . . just as perhaps he might have never known.

You have to find your own answers . . .

A soul-deep anguish flooded him. Dear God, he didn't know how. *He didn't know how!*

Conor buried his face in his hands. "I hate you, Sally," he groaned. "I hate you so much!"

"Why, Conor?" he heard her ask, her voice gentle now. "Tell me why."

Ever so slowly, he lifted his gaze to her and saw such a tender look of love and compassion burning in Sally's eyes that it gave him the courage to tell her. "Because your failings, your despair, your fears, are as much mine as they are yours," Conor said at last, uttering words that he realized were long buried and denied truths. Truths as bitter as gall, as searing as acid, as terrifying as death. "And I can't hide anymore from the image you reflect back to me."

❦

"Abby," Hannah called, as she let the lace curtains fall back in place at the front window, "Ella and Evan are here."

In the act of setting the iron on the cookstove top to cool, Abby glanced up. "What perfect timing," she said with a laugh. "I just finished the last blouse. Can you put these clothes away, Hannah, while I tidy up?"

"Of course." The girl gathered the neatly ironed blouses, skirts, and dresses, and hurried off.

Abby quickly checked the teakettle on the stove. Its watery contents were already simmering and would soon be ready. After removing her apron, folding down her sleeves, and rebuttoning the cuffs, she hurried through the small parlor of the cottage they'd just moved into three weeks ago after a nearly two month stay at Nelly's. She paused at the front door for one final check of her face and hair in the oval, oak-framed mirror before plastering on her most welcoming smile and opening the door.

Ella stood on the stoop, beaming back. Behind her, crisp golden leaves fell from the oak trees, skittering and dancing in the bright October sun. Evan, his arms loaded with packages, halted behind her, peering around Ella for sight of Hannah.

"Welcome, welcome." Abby reached out to grasp her friend's hand. She paused to cock her head. "Hannah will be out in a minute, Evan. She's just putting away some clothes."

Evan's expression of concern faded, to be replaced by a look of relief. "Oh . . . good. I was afraid she was ill or something."

"She's in the best of health," Abby assured him as she led them into the parlor. In the past three months since she had left Culdee Creek, Evan not only always accompanied Ella on her monthly visits, but also managed to find some reason to show up at least every other week on his own.

The young man was definitely infatuated with Hannah. He had come right out and told her as much just two weeks ago. And Hannah, though still wary, was noticeably more animated and happy each time Evan came. They were, Abby feared, truly falling in love.

Just then Hannah appeared from the back bedroom. Evan dumped all his packages on the sofa, and hurried to her. Taking her hand in both of his, he lifted it to his mouth for a long, tender kiss. "I missed you," he whispered, tucking her arm beneath his. "Did you miss me?"

The girl gazed back at him in rapt affection. "Very, very much."

Abby and Ella exchanged wry glances.

"I brought you and Jackson some gifts." Evan gestured to the parcels on the sofa.

"You shouldn't have," Hannah protested, then giggled in girlish delight. "It's wonderful of you, of course, but I know you don't make much—"

"Hush, sweetheart," he silenced her. "I have a roof over my head and three squares a day. If I didn't spend it on you and Jackson, I'd most likely waste it in some saloon. So you see," he added with a roguish grin, "you're keeping me out of harm's way."

Abby chuckled. "Now that's as fine a reason as I've ever heard." She took Ella by the arm and led her into the kitchen.

"Would you like a cup of tea?" Abby took down two porcelain cups and saucers, each decorated with a delicate anemone flower spray, as Ella settled herself in one of the two kitchen table chairs. "I assume our young love birds prefer a bit of privacy in the parlor."

"I'm certain they would," Ella said with a laugh. "And yes, I'd love a cup of tea." She shivered and rubbed her arms briskly. "The weather's taking a turn for the worse, and here it's only mid-October. Where has the summer gone?"

"You mean the second and shortest of our two seasons?" Abby teased, as she set the cups and saucers on the table, then walked back to take up the teakettle from the stove. "We're lucky if we even get four months of summer." She poured boiling water over the tealeaves in the bottom of the matching porcelain teapot–"and we're long overdue for some cold weather."

"I suppose you're right," Ella admitted. "At any rate, it probably won't seem quite so cold for me this winter, what with my husband to cuddle up with, and a new baby growing in my belly to keep me warm."

Abby plopped the teapot down on the table with a thud. "What?" she stammered, not certain she'd heard correctly. "You're not . . ."

Her friend's face split in a wide grin. "Oh, yes, I am. I'm going to have another baby this coming spring."

"But I thought . . ." Abby settled heavily in the other chair and just stared.

Ella shot a quick glance over her shoulder to see if Evan and Hannah could hear. The two were seated on the sofa at the far end of the parlor, hands clasped together, their heads almost touching, talking in whispers.

The red-haired woman turned back to Abby. "I prayed long and hard over it," she explained, "and came to the conclusion that I just had to trust the Lord. That's all any of us can do in the end anyway."

"But Ella," Abby protested, "that doesn't mean you have to risk your life. You already have two children."

"Devlin's my husband, Abby." Her friend's eyes glowed with a loving conviction. "When I made my marriage vows, I cast my lot with him in every way. And Devlin needs me in every way. He'd never have strayed if I hadn't turned him from my bed and heart." She shook her head vehemently. "I'll never, ever do that again."

Abby stared back at Ella, myriad replies springing to mind. To trust, to love so deeply that one was willing to sacrifice all . . .

"I'm not sure I fully understand." Abby took up the teapot and filled both cups with the rich, strong brew. She set the pot down. "But if this is what you want and it makes you happy, then I'm happy for you."

Ella smiled. "You will understand someday. I know it; I feel it in my heart."

"Perhaps." Abby took a sip of tea. "Now," she said when she'd set the cup back down, deciding it was best to change the subject, "tell me of Culdee Creek. How is everyone doing?"

"Well, let me see . . ."

To prolong the suspense, Abby supposed, Ella paused to stir a teaspoonful of sugar into her tea, then taste it before replying. Or perhaps instead, her thoughts swinging in a completely different direction as she noted the pensive look that suddenly darkened Ella's eyes, she was trying to decide how to break some painful news, and stalling for time.

"How's Conor?" Abby asked softly, sensing he was the topic her friend hesitated to broach.

The red-haired woman glanced away. "He's doing ... better. He doesn't act so angry anymore, and that terrible, haunted look in his eyes . . ." Ella met Abby's gaze. "I think he and Sally are beginning to work things out."

Though Abby had left Culdee Creek in the hopes of just such an event occurring in her absence, this particular news was still hard to hear. Sally was Conor's wife. Conor desperately needed to forgive her if he was ever to have any chance of healing. Yet even the most transitory consideration that he might actually come to love Sally again filled Abby with a dreadful, heart-wrenching pain.

One way or another, it seemed, her work at Culdee Creek would then be over. She would no longer be needed.

Abby looked down, fingering the rim of her teacup. "I'm glad to hear that," she finally said. "It's the best ... the best thing that could happen."

"In a sense, I agree. Sally, poor thing, needs Conor's forgiveness. And Conor needs to forgive."

Abby looked up. "Yes."

"But what of you?" Ella reached over and took her hand. "How are *you* doing?"

"I'm doing fine." Abby forced a smile. "I have Hannah and Jackson and a very nice job at Mrs. Water's Millinery Shop."

"Are you attending Sunday worship services?"

Abby looked down at her cup. "Sometimes."

"Oh, Abby," Ella cried, "don't turn from the Lord. Not now, of all times. I know things seem dark and confused, but the Lord has His reasons."

Abby blinked back a hot swell of tears. "I just don't know anymore. I gave my whole heart to Conor. I've never loved a man like I love him. And he needed me. He and Beth." She lifted tear-filled eyes to her friend. "There was no reason for God to take them from me. No reason at all!"

"God always has a reason, Abby. It's just so hard sometimes for us to accept it." She smiled sadly. "Fear gets in the way, doesn't it? Fear of that great unknown, fear that God will require something that we cannot, or don't want, to do. But we *can*, Abby. God never asks anything of us that He doesn't give us sufficient strength to do. And He never, ever asks it unless it's for our greater good."

"I *know* all those things, Ella." She sighed. "I just don't *feel* them in my heart anymore."

"Live them anyway," her friend admonished, a fierce light burning in her eyes. "Faith isn't grounded on emotions. It's grounded on the will. It's grounded in the act of taking up your cross and following the Lord wherever He leads, through good times and bad, through dark days and happy ones.

"We're not tested and tempered in good times, Abby." Ella released her hand and sat back in her chair. "Our true test," she said softly, "lies in the dark night of our despair."

22

Weeping may endure for a night, but joy cometh in the morning.

                                                    Psalm 30:5

Later that night, long after Ella and Evan had headed back to Culdee Creek, long after Hannah and her son were sound asleep in their beds, Abby sat in her bedroom. In the flickering light of her kerosene lamp, she huddled in a worn old wing chair snugged up against the window, and stared, unseeing. Thoughts raced and tumbled in her head.

She had never seen Ella so strong and sure in her convictions as she had seen her today. There was a renewed joy and strength in her friend that Abby envied. Though her words had at times seemed hard and unyielding, Abby sensed, even then, that Ella had spoken for the Lord.

She was blessed to have a friend such as Ella, a woman who possessed the courage to face her own shortcomings and fears, and never let them defeat her. Fear truly did color so many aspects of one's life. But to live in fear was to limit oneself, to blind the eyes, deafen the ears, and fetter the heart.

Sally, too, had overcome her fears. She had returned home after many years to face the righteous wrath and scorn of a husband she had deserted. But Sally knew it was the right and loving thing to do, no matter what the outcome. In the end, it now seemed the victory would be hers.

Next door, baby Jackson stirred, then began to wail softly. With a muted murmur, Hannah rose and padded to his cradle. Then, Abby heard no more.

Even Hannah had found the courage to escape the life she had formerly led. The girl had shared with Abby the numerous times she had attempted to escape and had failed, only to be severely beaten. Yet she had tried again and again, until she had succeeded at last.

Abby smiled. How blessed she was with the examples—and friendships—of so many courageous women. Each one was a shining inspiration to light her way. Yet she would never have met any of them, if she had not followed the Lord's call to Culdee Creek.

Culdee Creek . . .

Abby closed her eyes. She had been so certain the Lord had called her there to the aid of Conor and Beth. She would never have guessed He might have had another motive, a motive that perhaps involved her as much as the two MacKays. She'd never have imagined that her own soul was in as great a peril.

Her faith, from childhood, had come so effortlessly. She had been immersed in it, lived it every waking moment. Her parents had seen to that, the good and pious people that they were. Then Thomas had taken up where her parents had left off, watching over her, continuing to hold her to the same high, if constricted expectations. She had never had to develop or understand her own personal response to God. She had never had to carry her own cross for the Lord, but always, always someone else's.

Always, Abby thought with a wry grimace, until her life and all her former, predetermined beliefs had been devastated. That ordeal had begun with the loss of

Joshua and Thomas. It had been brought to its zenith when she gave up Conor and Beth. Only now could she at last confront what it really meant to love and serve the Lord.

It had never been her place to save Conor and Beth. It had been the Lord's. But her trust in Him had been wanting, though she'd always—and wrongly—imagined it had been her guiding force. Because her trust had been so weak, when the time came for her to leave Culdee Creek Abby had fought God, blamed Him and, like some petulant child, turned from Him.

Yet, like a patient father, a devoted lover, the Lord had led her through all the challenges and difficulties, and waited. Waited for her to end her flight, cease her doubts, open her eyes at last. Waited for her to approach Him as a grown, fearless, confident woman.

Waited . . . and never ever stopped loving her.

Perhaps it was the same with Conor. Perhaps that was why she had to leave him. Only now, deprived of everything that had come to matter to him, could Conor finally find his own way back to God.

Beloved, you understand at last.

With those words, whispered deep in her heart, certitude and a deep, abiding peace filled Abby. She slid from the chair and fell to her knees, her hands clasped before her. She bowed her head. Tears coursed down her cheeks.

"I offer up the sacrifice of the person most dear to my heart, Lord," she prayed, "trusting that Your plan for him, as for myself, will lead us both to You. I thank You also for all that You've given me—good friends, precious insights, and a new freedom like I've never known. A freedom I now offer back to You . . . to do with what You will."

So joy-filled she thought her heart might burst, Abby lifted her gaze heavenward. "It's a good start on a new life, wouldn't You say, Lord?" she asked. "A very good start, indeed."

৾

"Why did you leave us?"

At Conor's softly couched question, the blond-haired woman turned her head on her pillow to look up at him. A smile lifted her lips. "Do you know how long, how ardently I've prayed," she whispered, "for you to ask me that?"

"Well, I'm asking you now," Conor replied huskily. If she only knew how much it cost him to ask . . .

A few months ago such an admission would've filled Conor with rage. He would have never willingly conceded Sally any victory—not after what she had done to him. But it was now the first of November; Sally had been back five months, and she was dying. There wasn't much time left. Before it was too late, Conor needed to know, to understand, and to receive forgiveness as he gave it.

"Yes, you are." For a long moment, it seemed as if Sally's eyes focused on some distant place and time. Then, she sighed.

"I loved you very much once, Conor, but I didn't return to win it back again," she began at last. "I know that kind of love is long over for the both of us. Now we're such different people than we were when we first wed. Also a bit battle-worn and scarred." She managed a sad little smile. "But a lot wiser and stronger now, too.

"We were so young then. I don't think either of us was really ready. I still had so many unfulfilled dreams—my music, a professional singing career. And I think you, so hungry for love and caught up in the romantic illusion of marriage, thought a wife and your own family

317

was the answer to all your pain. Then we had Evan, and your father died, and times got even worse . . ."

The words came hard. At times Sally had to stop and cough. "You had to work so hard, and be away so much, just to save Culdee Creek. I was left home with a demanding baby, and the winter was especially long and bitter that last year. I began to feel as if I was being buried alive. It was then, God forgive me, and I take full responsibility for the decision, Conor, that I began to believe all of Andrew's promises. He filled my head with such wild dreams. I began to imagine we were kindred spirits, and that only he could truly understand and love me as I deserved to be loved."

"You never told me you were so unhappy." Conor clasped his hands between his outspread legs.

"I tried to tell you in little ways, but you were so pre-occupied with the ranch . . ." There was a long pause before Sally continued. "Perhaps I should've tried harder. Perhaps it was just easier to blame it all on you rather than face up to my part, and my responsibilities. Andrew offered such an easy answer, an answer far more attractive than the alternative of being your wife and Evan's mother."

"So you ran off with him, leaving me to face it all alone."

The old pain and bitterness rose in Conor. For an instant, he wanted to get up and leave. But he did not. All these years he had wanted answers, wanted to know what had caused their marriage to fail. Now he would. He would find his own answers, and they would be good and honorable ones.

"Yes, I did," Sally acknowledged his accusation calmly. "Fool that I was, I even thought for a time that I'd found the easy way out of all my problems. That my life would now be as it had always truly been meant to be."

A sad, knowing smile touched her lips. "I couldn't run, though, from my personal demons. I couldn't run from my life's work with the Lord. My singing career did well for a while, but Andrew soon began to squander the money I earned. Then, one night in a boardinghouse in Denver, we got into a terrible fight. Andrew knocked over the lamp in our room. The curtains caught fire, and soon the whole room was ablaze. We managed to escape, but Andrew remembered some money he'd hidden beneath the mattress. He ran back inside for it."

She drew in a long, deep breath and closed her eyes. "By then the whole upstairs was burning. The building was old and tinderbox dry. There was such chaos and confusion in the streets, what with terrified boarders milling about and the fire wagon and all the bystanders that I thought he had come back down and gotten lost in the crowd." Sally opened her eyes. "But if he did, I never saw him again. And I, penniless, with only the clothes on my back, didn't know what to do."

"We heard of the fire and were notified that you'd died in it."

"I didn't do anything to change that idea, either," Sally admitted. "In a sense I *had* died. I couldn't come back to you after what I'd done. And my fine new life had gone up in flames."

"So what did you do?"

"I got a job singing in one of the saloons. There I saw the fancy women making more money than I was. I decided I might as well get paid like them. It was the beginning of my journey into degradation and despair, a journey that didn't end until Father Gabriel rescued me from the cribs of Cripple Creek."

Conor groaned, then flung back his head. "Why didn't you come home, Sally? Sure, I was madder than a hornet, but I still loved you then. I kept hoping against hope you'd come back to me. If only you had come home . . ."

319

"I was afraid, and plumb full of foolish pride, Conor. If I couldn't forgive myself for what I'd done, how could I ever expect you to forgive me?"

Her questions gave him pause. Hadn't he made similar excuses as reasons he could never allow himself to turn back to God? He had always known what such a commitment required, and it terrified him. He would have to open his heart, place his life in Someone else's hands, and trust that it all would not be in vain. Yet how could he?

But how could he not? For a long while now, even before Abby had come into his life, Conor had known that his existence was incomplete, his heart empty. Perhaps it was the reason he had been so leery of taking Abby on as his housekeeper. He had sensed from the start that she would unsettle his life. Fool that he was, he had imagined her only a temporal threat. Then she had blindsided him. He had fallen in love with her and, in the process, had set free all the doubts, fears, and unresolved issues crying out for resolution. At times he'd hated her for it, even as he yearned for the joy that always seemed to dangle just beyond his reach.

Forgiveness . . .

There was so much to forgive, and Sally was only a part of it. The anger, the pain, the sense of betrayal had begun long before she had come into his life. It had started with his father, and with a God who seemed equally as harsh and rigid. His own father could never accept him. How could God?

Yet Abby had loved God, and she'd seen Him as a loving father, a faithful friend. How was it, Conor now wondered, that God could have so many faces? Or were most of those faces put on Him by the misunderstandings and false expectations of his children?

What had Sally said to him, that day he'd carried her upstairs after her coughing fit? *Don't limit the Lord with your own shallow perceptions of Him, or assign Him a level of compassion equal only to yours . . .*

His faith, he realized now, had been colored far more by his father's meager view of God, than by anything else. It had been a faith sown upon stony ground. No wonder the seed scattered there had barely grown, before it was scorched and died. His faith had never been a faith adequate to weather the storms of life, and Conor had finally come to mistrust and despise it.

Then Abby had walked into his life, and all his previously held beliefs had crumbled. Yet even she had warned him. Standing close to her would not bring him to salvation. For that he had to walk on, past her, and find God in his own way.

For that, Conor now knew, he had to remember all the good people in his life. His mother, who spoke of making your heart a hallowed, humble bed for the Holy Child, and not letting pride separate you from God. The courage and goodness of his Scots ancestors, who had braved such terrible hardship to come to a new land, and who had never given up. Squirrel Woman, who had loved with such unconditional generosity, and their daughter, Beth, who thought the sun rose and set on him. And he must even consider Sally, who had come back to share the greatest of gifts—forgiveness.

There was no room left for anger and resentment, Conor realized. There was no time for fear or mistrust. A man of honor could no longer close his eyes, turn away in cowardice, or harbor heart- and soul-rotting grudges. Not if he wished to heal, be whole again, and be worthy of all that was good in his life.

Conor smiled down at his wife. "I'm glad you came back," he tenderly said. "I'm glad you overcame your pride and fear, both for my and for Evan's sake."

Tear glistened in Sally's eyes. "So, beloved, you understand at last."

321

"Yes." He leaned down and took her hand. "I think I finally do."

 c

Three days later, Sally died in her sleep. The funeral services were held one morning two days after. The MacKay family and most of Culdee Creek's ranch hands attended. The Reverend Noah Starr, the Episcopal Church's new assistant pastor, presided over the burial in Grand View's forest cemetery.

It was a cool, crisp, but sunny November day. A brisk wind rustled the branches of the tall, Ponderosa pines. The dried prairie grasses covering the nearby hills waved languorously, glinting pale, flaxen-gold. Black, tuft-eared squirrels scrabbled overhead, and pine needles crackled underfoot.

As was the custom, Sally's grave faced east toward the high plains. The little party of mourners gathered there. The Reverend Starr took out his prayer book and finally, when everyone fell silent, he began to read.

"As a shepherd seeketh out his flock in the day that he is among his sheep that are scattered; so will I seek out my sheep, and will deliver them out of all places where they have been scattered in the cloudy and dark day . . ."

This particular passage from Ezekiel had been one of Sally's favorites. She had had Conor read it to her the night she had died, before he had left her and gone to bed. She had claimed she had liked it because to her it spoke so clearly of God's faithful, persistent love in her life. Listening to it now, Conor thought that it spoke equally as well of his life, too.

"And I will bring them out from the people, and gather them from the countries, and will bring them to their own

322

land, and feed them upon the mountains of Israel by the rivers, and in all the inhabited places of the country.

"I will feed them in a good pasture, and upon the high mountains of Israel shall their fold be: there shall they lie in a good fold, and in a fat pasture shall they feed upon the mountains of Israel . . ."

The Lord had relentlessly pursued them both, Conor mused, and had brought them to the good and fruitful pastures. Yet, though Sally's life was now complete and she had gone on to her eternal rest, there was still much work left for him. Much work . . . in service of the Lord.

"I will seek that which was lost," the Reverend Starr read, his strong, clear voice carrying to the edge of the gathering and beyond, "and bring again that which was driven away, and will bind up that which was broken, and will strengthen that which was sick . . ."

The Lord had done that and more for him, Conor thought. The realization filled him with a deep and quiet joy. It felt good, right, to come home again. Home to the Lord.

The young priest finished the reading, said a few words about Sally, then stepped from the grave. Evan, his eyes red and swollen, took up a handful of dirt and tossed it down onto his mother's coffin. Next came Beth and then Conor. As they backed off and began to walk away, the rest of the mourners took their turn.

It was only then that Beth saw Abby, a slender figure in black standing quietly beside her buggy. Beside her was her sister-in-law, Nelly.

"Papa," the girl cried. "She's come back!" Beth looked up at her father. "Can I go to her, Papa? Can I?"

For a fleeting moment, Conor's grip tightened on his daughter's shoulder. Across the expanse of graveyard separating them, his gaze met Abby's. Something strong and poignant and loving passed between them. His heart gave a great leap of joy.

"Yes, girl,"–Conor released his daughter–"you can go." After a moment he followed her, secure in the knowledge that he finally came to the woman he loved as a whole man with a whole heart.

A man precious and glorious in the sight of the Lord.

Epilogue

February 16, 1897
Hotel Colorado
Glenwood Springs

Dearest Nelly,

Conor and I arrived safely yesterday afternoon, after a glorious trip on the Denver and Rio Grande railroad from Denver through the Rockies to Glenwood Springs. I never would have believed the grandeur of these huge, snow-covered peaks. They certainly put our New England mountains to shame.

The Hotel Colorado, a copy of the Villa Medici in Rome, is indeed as luxurious and extravagant as everyone had said. What a perfect place to spend one's honeymoon! Our suite of rooms is beyond imagining and, like the rest of the hotel, is equipped with those newfangled electric lights. The private bathroom has a marble tub and washstand. There's a twenty-five-foot-high waterfall cascading into a pool in the north court of the lobby. The south court also has a large pool in its center, from which a fountain shoots one hundred feet into the air. The food served in the grand Devereux Dining Room is deliciously sumptuous, and the myriad activities available, even in winter, boggles the mind. We've already tried the hot springs—which Conor and I both adore—and taken a romantic moonlit sleigh ride. I must admit, though, that we've also squandered part of our first day here snug-

*gling in our bed with its gracefully wrought arabesque
tester.*

*Tomorrow, we plan to visit the Yampah Hot Springs
Vapor Caves. These caves are formed by hot mineral
water percolating up through fissures in the rocks, and
supposedly have curative powers for a variety of ailments.
I have to chuckle a little, though. Conor and I have to
bathe separately and wear what amounts to a linen sack
with a drawstring at the neck for swimming.*

*Oh, Nelly, I can't begin to tell you how happy I am!
Each and every day I'm with him, Conor reveals yet
another new and wondrous facet to his personality—and
heart. He's so kind, so tender, so solicitous of my every
need. Yet at the same time, he allows me the freedom to
express my views and listens with great interest and
respect. I—and I'm sure you, too—have to laugh at the dra-
matic change from that first day I met him. Yet his innate
honor and goodness were there all along, buried beneath
his terrible burden of pain, anger, and mistrust.*

*God has been so very good to the both of us. We have
each other, a wonderful family, dear friends, and a beautiful home. Yet, best of all, Conor and I, at long last, share
a deep and abiding religious faith. I have learned so much
in this past year and a half—about myself, others, and
how to come through the greatest tragedy of my life. Even
more importantly, I've learned so much about my relationship with the Lord. I've learned that, though everything is ultimately transient, His love is steadfast and eternal. I've learned to daily cherish His gifts and graces, all
the while remembering that they are His and not mine to
depend upon or cling to. Most of all, my faith and trust
in Him have grown. I place everything in His hands now,
where it was always meant to be. Who else, indeed, can
take better care?*

*Thank you so much, Nelly, for attending our wedding.
That day would never have been as perfect had you not
been there. Conor was happy to have you there as well.
Do I dare hope that you two are finally coming to some
sort of friendship? I pray so.*

326

Well, it's been a long day. A fine, fragrant piñon pine fire is burning in the fireplace, and Conor says it's time for bed. I must admit I think so, too. I'll write more once we return home to Culdee Creek.

Fondly,
Abby

Watch for Book 2 in the Brides of Culdee Creek series

Woman of Grace

by Kathleen Morgan

*The eastern plains outside
Colorado Springs, Colorado
April 1897*

There were days, increasingly now, when the burden of such deep, dark, shameful secrets became too hard to bear. Days that filled Hannah Cutler with such wild hopes for the future that the the old self-serving impulses threatened to fade forever. Days when she was so overwhelmed by the kindness and generosity of others that she thought she might weep with gratitude.

But then there were other days. Days like today, as Devlin MacKay shot her yet another sour look, when Hannah knew those shameful secrets were best kept hidden away. Best kept clasped tightly where no one could threaten the tenuous hold she had on this new, far better life.

Only fools gave others the weapons to destroy them, and Hannah had learned long ago, in many painful, degrading ways, how to survive.

329

She had to admit, though, that she was mighty tired of Devlin's hostility. It had never been his right to pass judgment on Conor's and Abby's decision to allow her to remain at Culdee Creek Ranch. Or to belittle her relationship with Evan either. Indeed, it should hardly be any of his business. But he hadn't seen it that way, and the proud ranch foreman was not the kind of man to easily—or ever—let go of a grudge.

"Come on in," the dark-haired, powerfully built man growled, making an impatient motion for her to enter. "The house is cold enough without you standing there with the door open."

Hannah, a bundle of clean towels and sheets tucked beneath her arm, hurried inside. When no offer of assistance was forthcoming, she turned and shut the door against the blowing snow and howling winds. A dusting of powdery flakes followed in her wake, coating the threshold and floor. With a surreptitious glance at Devlin, who scowled at her even more fiercely, Hannah tried to brush them back toward the doorway with the side of her black, high-buttoned shoe.

"I'm sorry," she said, choking back her irritation at his lack of manners.

Though Hannah wanted to say more, to refute his harsh words and the implied insults behind them, she did not dare. To challenge Devlin would be, as it had always been with other men before him, to risk dire punishment. Though he might not stoop so low as to actually beat her for any implied impertinence, he could do far worse. He could jeopardize her continued stay at Culdee Creek. He could ruin everything.

So with gritted teeth and clamped lips, Hannah kept her glance cast downward and strode across the small kitchen. It didn't matter, at any rate, what he thought of her. She would never have come if it had just been for him. He could have lain here in this house and rotted for all she cared.

No, it wasn't for Devlin that Hannah had dared enter. It was for his wife, Ella, who lay writhing in her childbed, and for Abby. It was for the two women who had first welcomed her to Culdee Creek almost a year ago. Women who had tirelessly championed her when almost no one else would.

As Hannah moved past where Devlin sat, a mug of coffee clenched in his hands, a soft, low moan rose from a bedroom at the end of the short hall. Her footsteps quickened.

"One thing more." Devlin's voice, hard as steel, sliced through the tension-laden air.

She slid to a halt, shoulders rigid, and waited for the blow she knew was about to come.

"Yes, what is it?" Hannah asked softly.

"You can stay because Abby needs your help right now. But just as soon as Doc gets here, I want you out of my house. Women like you aren't fit to be near decent folk or innocent children."

Rage boiled up inside Hannah. How dare he? *How dare he?*

She turned, her gaze meeting his. A look of mutual fear and distrust arced between them. "I'm done with that life, and you know it, Devlin MacKay," she finally spat out.

"Are you?" He gave a harsh bark of derision. "Don't fool yourself. When the going gets rough, women like you always go back to your old ways. After all, it's the only thing you ever learned to do easily and well. Mark my words. You'll go back."

No, I won't, she thought with fierce, fervent determination, even as the old doubts plucked at her anew. I would rather die than go back to that life. I would rather die than prove people like you right. People like you, who have sinned in ways far greater than I ever could.

She almost uttered those very words, almost turned and pointed an accusing finger. But she didn't. Devlin MacKay was too blinded by his own guilt and complicity ever to see the truth. It sat far better with him to lay all the blame on her. In some twisted way, she supposed he also imagined it absolved him. Absolved him, and washed his soul as white as snow.

Or as white as dead men's bones, scattered and forgotten in a desolate, whited sepulchre.

The afternoon burned on. Through the ever-worsening storm, Hannah periodically came and went. Ella's screams grew weaker, her moans lower and farther apart.

The light began to dim, and still Devlin sat hunched over his now cold mug of coffee, staring into its black, murky depths. Bit by agonizing bit, he felt the life, the hope drain from him. Drain away as surely as it seemed to drain away for his beloved wife. His dear, sweet, loving Ella who struggled, even now, to birth their third child.

It seemed like hours since he had sent two of the ranch hands riding out to Grand View to fetch Doc Childress. He knew the men wouldn't fail him. But Devlin was also well aware of the vagaries of spring weather on the high plains. He knew how viciously the winds could blow, how quickly the snow could fall, blanketing the land and swirling so thickly you could barely find your way. Even strong men got lost in blizzards like today's. Even strong men died.

Doc would arrive just as soon as his men could safely get him here. Meanwhile there was nothing to be done but wait. Wait, and endure Ella's gut wrenching cries, knowing there was nothing, absolutely nothing, he could do for her.

Once more the kitchen's back door opened. Devlin looked up. Lamplight spilled into the room, illuminating Hannah's pale, drawn face with red-gold radiance.

No one, he thought bitterly, should be allowed to look like she did. No one deserved, after the life she had lived, to appear so much like an angel with that pale blond hair, big blue-green eyes, and sweet, soft, guileless face.

Those looks were what had gained her sanctuary here at Culdee Creek. That guise of injured innocence had fooled the lot of them. But then none of them knew Hannah Cutler like he did. Few realized the power she held over him.

She could ruin everything.

Devlin eyed her for an instant longer, then turned away. His aversion for her notwithstanding, nothing was served berating the girl each time she entered his house. She was, after all, trying to help Abby with Ella.

At the admission, guilt plucked at him. Here she was, coming and going all day through the raging storm to fetch whatever Abby required, and all he could do was sit glaring and snapping like some wounded, cornered animal.

The comparison struck home. Devlin's mouth twitched sadly. A wounded, cornered animal . . . yes, that was exactly what he had become.

All he seemed to do anymore was lick his wounds in suffering silence, hoping against hope for some miracle to heal him. Sit here in helpless impotence and pray to a God he had long ago turned his back on. A God who had long ago ceased to listen.

Behind him, Hannah closed the door, then headed across the kitchen. The wind momentarily died. In the sudden silence her hard-soled shoes clicked with a staccato rhythm on the wooden floor. Her long skirt made soft, whooshing sounds as it swirled around her legs. As she drew near, the scent of apples and cinnamon filled the air.

"I brought you and Abby some fresh-baked, dried apple pie." She placed a large, covered basket on the table.

Devlin looked up. An infinite number of replies—none of them kind—rose to his lips. He bit them back. Such repeated, intentional cruelty wasn't like him. But then he hadn't been much like himself since Hannah came to Culdee Creek.

"I also brought cold roast beef, potato fritters, and boiled peas. You're probably not very hungry right now," she hastened to add when he sent her a hard, slanting glance, "but it's important both you and Abby keep up your strength. I've already seen to it that your children ate."

His six-year-old son and two-year-old daughter had spent the day at the main house, safely out of the way of the goings on here. Though Devlin couldn't do much for their mother, he at least intended that the children be spared the agony of knowing her pain. At least they would never have to experience the long, torturous hours of wondering, worrying, fearing that she would die.

"Just leave the food, will you?" he growled, swamped yet again by the memory of Ella's labor, laden with its humiliating reminders of his inability to ease her torment. "I'll fetch Abby and see if she's hungry."

He scraped back his chair and stood. "She needs a long overdue break, and I need to be with my wife."

Hannah's turquoise gaze locked with his. "Yes," she whispered. "Yes, you do."

Something flickered in her eyes, something that smacked, to his way of thinking, of kindness, compassion, and even understanding. Fury swelled in him. It was all Devlin could do to swallow a savage curse.

He didn't want anything from the likes of her. It wasn't fair that his good, God-fearing wife suffered so, while a

woman like Hannah had so easily delivered her own
child. But then, when had God ever been fair, or good?

Such fruitless considerations stirred too many painful, chaotic emotions—emotions he could not deal with
tonight of all nights. Before Devlin could say something
that would heap further insult onto those he had already
flung at Hannah Cutler this day, he turned on his heel
and strode away.

Kathleen Morgan is a successful romance writer whose work includes fifteen published novels. She is a member of the Romance Writers of America, and has been a popular conference speaker. Morgan lives with her husband and son near Colorado Springs.

If you would like to be included on a mailing list to notify you of future books in "The Brides of Culdee Creek" series, please write to Kathleen at P.O. Box 62365, Colorado Springs, CO 80962, or e-mail her at kathleen morgan@juno.com. If you wish to receive a newsletter, please enclose a self-addressed, stamped envelope.